PURSUIT of Love

BETHANY ROSA

GALLATIN PUBLISHING

PURSUIT

of

Love

1

BACKFIRE

Eli

June

Eli: My bed is cold without you. Are you missing my sheets?

Cici: Among other things.

Eli: You shouldn't have run away from San Diego, then.

Cici: I didn't run away. A lot of people move for work after graduating college.

Eli: That's what you're telling yourself?

Cici: On that note, goodnight, Eli.

Eli: Night, cutie.

Weeks later

Eli: Did you get silk sheets yet?

Cici: It's freezing in Bozeman. I had to go with flannel.

Eli: That's too bad because mine feel so good right now. There's only one thing that would make them better.

Cici: You can't keep saying things like that.

Eli: Why? It's the truth.

Cici: You're infuriating. Goodnight.

Eli: Sleep well, Cici.

Weeks later

Eli: How's the new job treating you?

Cici: I love it! Everyone here is great. It's such a fun place to work.

Eli: I'm happy for you… Sort of… I'm trying to be anyway.

Cici: Whatever. I bet your bed is already warmed up by now.

Eli: Only when I bring your underwear with me.

Cici: You have my underwear?

Eli: Yeah, but it's time for a replacement pair.

Cici: How about some granny panties?

Eli: As long as you wear them first. Not sure they'll go under a skintight dress, though.

Cici: Who said anything about a dress?

Eli: Sebastian's proposing at the club. You're not showing up in a sack, are you?

Cici: Ugh. I'm so excited! Have you seen the ring?

Eli: Of course. I helped pick it out.

Cici: Send me a picture!

Eli: I'll consider it if you guarantee a replacement pair of sexy panties.

Cici: Meanie. You'll have others for your collection soon.

Eli: None like yours.

Cici: You're terrible. Goodnight.

Eli: Night, cutie.

August

Cici: It's killing me not telling Lily I'm coming. Why do I have to wait?

Eli: Element of surprise. She might wonder why you're visiting so soon. He doesn't want her to have time to overthink it.

Cici: She's not going to say no.

Eli: His anxiety is off the charts. Thank God it's almost over so he'll be normal again.

Cici: I can't imagine normal is much better when it comes to your brother.

Eli: True. So since they'll be fucking like rabbits afterward, what's your plan for the night?

Cici: Staying at my brother's.

Eli: I have a better idea. How about you come to my place and we do the same? It's just one night.

Cici: I've heard that before.

Eli: I'll make it worth your while.

Cici: I know you will. That's not the problem.

Eli: Come on. You'll return home a million miles away the next day. You know what I do to you.

Cici: I'll think about it.

Eli: You better, because I can't stop. In fact, it's the only thing I've thought about since you left.

Cici: …

Eli: Don't tell me you haven't.

Cici: Goodnight, Eli.

Eli: Night. See you in a couple weeks.

My breath stops the minute she steps into the darkened hallway. God, I've missed her. She's positively stunning. The skintight red dress contrasts with her blonde hair to make her stand out like a beacon. I know what she really is, though: a siren with the ability to lure me to my death. The problem is, even knowing what fate awaits me, I'd still walk right toward her with my eyes wide open, if only to spend the last five minutes of my time on earth with her.

As my eyes roam her full length to check out those beautifully toned legs and hips that are begging to be gripped, I can't help the first thing that comes to mind—she's certainly *not* wearing granny panties. It wouldn't surprise me if *no* panties are underneath. My cock hardens at the thought.

"Hey, cutie," I greet loudly over the pumping music. My arms immediately reach out and pull her in, breathing deeply to take in the scent I've been deprived of for too long. The feel of her full breasts against my chest flips the switch from longing to lust. It appears we're both eager to hold each other by how she snuggles into me, pressing her head into my shoulder like it's where she belongs.

If only she felt that way, I wouldn't have had to endure the last three months of pining after the woman who stole my heart and ran a thousand miles away with it. When she told me she was moving after her college graduation, I suggested she stay and give us a chance, but the one time I brought it up, she seemed to pull back, which made no sense considering not only were we on fire in the bedroom, but we clicked in every way possible. Rather than push, I decided to give her space, thinking she just needed to have a taste of independence before getting serious. And I'm still waiting.

Too soon, she extracts herself with a massive smile on her face. "Are you as excited as I am right now?"

Not for the same thing you are.

She claps her hands rapidly, distracting me from the overpowering urge to have my filthy way with her here and now. She better not fool herself into turning down my offer for the night. I've been looking forward to it for weeks. But rather than go down that road immediately, I stay on topic.

"You have no idea. Sebastian's been a little bitch. I'm hoping he settles down after the ring's on her finger. Speaking of, we should get moving."

Grabbing her hand, I guide her further into the shadows and stop, coming face-to-face. My emotions are shouting—lust, desire, want, and way more that need to be kept at bay. Before I give in to the ones she's willing to reciprocate, there's movement drawing our attention to the proposal we've been waiting for.

My brother, Sebastian, has Lily pinned up against the same wall in the exact position he did the night of their first embrace six months prior. I remember hearing all about it while secretly reminiscing about my own sexy tryst with Cici, only to find out later the two women were best friends *and* roommates in their senior year of college. We met each girl separately the night they showed up to the dance club. By the time I'd put two and two together about the women we were seeing, Sebastian was already obsessed and struggling to win Lily over. I didn't want to complicate things, so I never told him that I happened to be screwing her best friend, who incidentally became *my* obsession.

Cici and I stand in silence, watching while it plays out. The minute Sebastian lowers to one knee before Lily, Cici's eyes glisten as she brings her hands to her mouth in anticipation. My face turns up in a smile when I hear Lily's resounding "Yes!" We immediately join the pair, who are still clinging to each other, but as soon as they part, Cici and Lily embrace, jumping up and down, both squealing with excitement. Sebastian and I do the manly bro hug, firmly slapping the other's back.

I'm happy for my twin brother. Settling down wasn't something I expected him to do since playing the field used to be one of our favorite pastimes. We may share the same birthday, but our similarities as fraternal twins are few and far between. He's imposing, broody, and severe, whereas I'm the fun-loving, charismatic one. He resembles the part, too, with dark hair and olive skin, taking after our father. I'm glad I inherited Mother's softer traits, with light brown eyes and hair to match. I'd much rather be described as a golden retriever than a Doberman pinscher.

Cici releases Lily and grabs her left hand. "I'm so excited! Let me see. I've been dying in anticipation."

Lily splays her fingers, revealing the monster rock, which I'm overly familiar with after the lengthy search. Leave it to Sebastian to make sure everyone in the room knows she's taken. He's about as possessive as they come, but Lily seems to love it, making me thankful he found someone to put up with his dominant nature.

"How long have you known? Wait… this wasn't a last-minute trip, was it?" Lily asks Cici suspiciously as Sebastian and I stand to the side.

"Too long—it's been killing me every time we talk. Sebastian didn't want to ruin the surprise and wouldn't let me tell you I was coming. But the look on your face was priceless, so it was worth it. I can't believe you had no idea."

Cici then hugs Sebastian's stiff posture, making me chuckle. "Congratulations. The ring is beautiful. You did well," Cici tells him.

"I'm glad you approve. You made Lily's day by being here. Thank you for helping it come together," Sebastian returns.

With Lily free, I wrap her in my arms and swing her around as she squeals in delight. "Thank God you said yes. Do you realize what I've had to put up with over the past few weeks? It was hell. I'm excited to have you as family, Lily. Congratulations." I set her down next to Sebastian. "All right, lovebirds, let's have a celebratory toast before you two go do your version of celebrating," I say, wiggling my eyebrows.

Cici shoves my shoulder, and Lily ducks her head into Sebastian's chest in embarrassment as we return to the table where the ladies began before Lily set the plan in motion by using the bathroom. A bottle of Dom on ice with four glasses is waiting—a perk of owning the club. It's the fun, albeit tiny, piece of the billion-dollar international holding company my brother and I operate from San Diego. After our father passed away following the death of our mom two years prior, we inherited Dubree Enterprises at the age of twenty-five—almost three years ago now—and have worked our asses off ever since.

Although we bonded over the loss, we handled our grief very differently. Sebastian took control in all areas of life, including putting his heart and soul into the company, while I vowed to live mine to the fullest. Because if you can't control what happens in life, you might as well have fun while living it—which is why chasing thrills has become my favorite pastime. The more adrenaline, the better. Life's too short to waste a single moment, so why not enjoy every aspect before it's too late? Hence, persuading Cici back into my bed tonight.

The ladies discuss wedding plans for the next thirty minutes while Sebastian and I agree with whatever they say. After pouring the last drop of champagne, I address Sebastian. "Why don't you two go ahead, and I'll give Cici a lift to where she's staying. I can tell you're eager to get out of here, and if I see any more PDA, I might lose my dinner." Sebastian and Lily have had their hands all over each other without even realizing it.

Lily says to Cici, "Only if that's okay. But we can take you too. You're going to Jackson's, right?"

"It's more than okay. I second Eli's comment. Being in a car with you guys probably isn't a good idea. Go, I'll catch a ride." They hug and say their goodbyes before my brother and Lily walk away in their newly engaged bliss.

Cici immediately turns to me when they're out of sight. "That was smooth. *To where I'm staying?* So you think I'm a shoo-in, huh?"

"Not at all. I'd take you to Jackson's if that's where you want to go, but is it? Look me in the eye and tell me you haven't missed my cock." I lean in and whisper in her ear, "Come on, Cici, you know what it does to you—what *I* do to you…. The same thing you do to me." I ease back to the overwhelming lust in her eyes. "We create fireworks, babe. You can't deny it."

She's quiet—too quiet.

"Stop overthinking. It's only for one night. You'll be back in Montana tomorrow. Are you afraid it'll be so good that you won't be able to leave again? My sheets will be the deciding factor, of course." I wiggle my eyebrows and smirk, causing her to giggle and let her guard down.

"That's better. Come on, cutie, I'm giving you a ride either way. You can tell me where to take you while we're in the car." I reach for her hand and lead us out back.

She's still not talking. I'm sure she's in her head about whether to come home with me or not. I'll let her stew for a bit longer and take her for a drive. I already know where this night is headed—she'll catch up soon.

"Nice ride," she comments when the lights blink.

"Thanks. It's the fastest on the market, so buckle up, buttercup." I wink, opening the door for her.

My penthouse isn't far from the club, but rather than head straight there, I drive along Sunset Cliffs, where traffic is low this time of night and I can open the accelerator. Cici needs to be shocked out of the conflicting thoughts bouncing around her head. And sure enough, her gaze whips toward me not three seconds after pressing my foot down.

"Eli! You've proven it's fast. Slow down." She panics, gripping the door handle and pushing her foot to the floorboard as if it'll magically apply the brakes.

I laugh, easing off the gas and returning to a normal speed. "Ah, you're back. I thought I'd lost you for a minute."

"My head was stuck in the clouds, reminiscing. I'm trying to absorb being back."

"Did you reminisce about my bed and absorb that you'll be back in it tonight?" I tease while reaching over to squeeze her thigh.

She laughs but doesn't respond other than the telltale clench of her legs from my touch. Instead of asking where she wants to go, I take matters into my own hands and go back downtown to my place. I'll accept her silence as approval since she knows where we're headed. Her acceptance is confirmed when she unbuckles as soon as the car is in Park.

"Wait there," I instruct before hustling over to open the door, reaching for her hand. I'll take any chance I can to touch her.

No words are spoken in the elevator as my imagination goes wild with what tonight has in store and everything I'd like to do to her body. When I unlock the front door, I decide we've been silent long enough.

"I'm sure you thought I only wanted to show off with the detour, but it gave Sebastian and Lily plenty of time to make it inside so we could avoid running into them since they probably lapped the block a few times for a quickie in the car. I'm guessing you didn't tell Lily about us?" I wink at her knowingly and hang her coat on the rack.

Sebastian and I live down the hall from each other, and I figured Cici hadn't told Lily about us, or I would have never heard the end of it. I'm not surprised she didn't tell her, since she was as averse to relationships as I was before meeting her. But something about Cici had me reconsidering my standpoint.

"No. She had a lot on her mind at the time." Cici ducks her head. And because my goal isn't to make her feel bad, I change the subject.

"Can I offer you something to drink?" I ask on my way to the kitchen, trying to keep her engaged.

"Are you stalling, Eli?" she asks coyly, following behind.

"My attempt at politeness, but if you can't handle being this close to my sheets without being in them, go ahead. I'll be right behind you." I'm not letting her take control here.

"You'd like that, wouldn't you—to have me waiting in your bed? Hmm, on second thought, I am thirsty." The words are seductive as she stalks over like a feline on the hunt. My eyes flood with heat as my pants become tighter with each slow step she takes.

"Anything for you, cutie. What are you thirsty for?" I know exactly what she wants, but I'll make her squirm first.

"I'm craving something salty, I think—a little on the thick side. Do you have anything that meets my needs?" She's inches from me, and if my cock were out, it would be up against her. As it stands— pun intended—it's pressing into my jeans hard enough to reveal I'm just as ready for this as she is.

Time to gain the upper hand. "It just so happens I have the perfect con-*cock*-tion. No one's tasted it in quite a while, so I should have plenty. Why don't you make yourself comfortable in the living room, and I'll bring it right out."

Her wheels are spinning as she considers whether to cede control.

"Come on, babe, you don't want your knees to be protesting on this hard tile as I'm fucking that luscious mouth of yours, do you? It won't be gentle. Like I said, it's been a while. Go on. I'll be in shortly." Yep, that did it. A promise of something dirty, and she's putty in my hands. My girl likes it rough.

I smirk, knowing I've won this round.

"Fine, but don't take too long, or I might have to start without you." She turns and stomps around the corner.

"You'll be sorry if you touch that pussy before I do," I yell after her.

I take my time in the kitchen to work up her frustration more than it already is. It's only fair, considering that's been my permanent state since she ran away three months ago. There's no way I would have accepted her being anywhere else tonight. It's all I've thought about after Sebastian suggested flying her down for the proposal. My eagerness at the proposition may have alluded to my hidden obsession with her. He had his suspicions, but I gave him the perfect opportunity to harass it out of me. In truth, there wasn't much to divulge beyond a few hookups for the best sex in history. She's a wildcat in the bedroom, almost as insatiable as me. Then she moved away. End of story. At least, that's what I told Sebastian.

She's probably waited long enough. Rounding the corner to the living room, I open my mouth to say as much but quickly zip it when my eyes land on Cici, curled up on the couch and sleeping like a baby. Well, shit, talk about a fucking backfire. Knowing the tiring day she had flying here before heading straight to dinner with Lily, I shouldn't be surprised. It's also an hour later in Montana, so she's no doubt exhausted, but my cock isn't backing down as easily. That means I'll need to take matters into my own hands.

After gently covering her with a blanket and checking the heat, I go straight to the shower, figuring it's better to handle this now than lie in torment with the object of my desire down the hall. I'm sure being so close to having her again will taunt me all night. No matter how much I've been looking forward to this, it's simply not meant to be. Fuck. I shouldn't be this obsessed after months of separation, but something about Cici won't release its hold on me.

I could say it's our unbelievable chemistry in the bedroom. But that's too easy and doesn't begin to cover it, because it's way more than that for me. I'm the guy who's had his share of one-night stands but never wanted anything serious with a woman. Until Cici, when one night wasn't nearly enough. Hell, no number of nights could satisfy me. Had she not moved away, I would have kept pushing for more despite her resistance. From the beginning, she made it clear she doesn't do relationships, which is funny, considering that's my line. While her fun-loving spontaneity and mad bedroom skills drew me in, she became a welcome challenge, making me want to dive into whatever trouble we could find together.

With the water pouring down my back, my hand grips the raging hard-on I've been sporting all night, and all thoughts make way for the vision of Cici on her knees, sucking me off. Fuck, the woman knows her way around a man's dick, that's for sure. She can take it better than anyone. Eyes closed, I picture her before me, her hot mouth taking me to the back of her throat as I grip harder and pump faster. It takes less than a minute to lose myself, grunting my release onto the shower floor. It's not the first time I've done this with those same visions, but dammit that it could've been the real thing only moments ago.

It serves me right to try and control that woman. I should've let her kneel immediately when she approached me in the kitchen, but I had to go and be chivalrous. That's the fucking problem. I'm not that guy. Hell, I've never thought twice about a woman's comfort if they offer to get me off, but it's different with Cici. She changed me. Made me want things. Made me want to do better. Made me want something beyond temporary.

The question is, why did it have to happen with someone more anti-relationship than me?

Checking on Cici again to see that she hasn't moved and is still out, I head to bed, tossing and turning most of the night. I think I finally doze off for good around four in the morning.

The light from the window causes me to wake, and I glance at the clock to see it's eight already. My stomach twists with dread. Quickly pulling on pants, I rush into the living room, where the blanket I'd covered her with is folded neatly on the back of the couch. Frustrated, I run my hand through my hair and go to the kitchen with one last hope she'll be there. The note on the counter causes the pit in my stomach to bottom out.

> *Eli,*
> *Thank you for the ride last night.*
> *Sorry about falling asleep and not finishing what I suppose we never started. Thanks for the blanket. I grabbed an Uber to meet Jackson for breakfast before flying out. Until next time....*
> *XOXO, Cici*

Well, fuck.

2

SHITUATION

Cici

Nine months later

WHAT THE HELL DID I JUST AGREE TO? I'M SITTING IN MY office at the real estate company I work for, elbows propped up on the desk, head face down in my hands after hanging up the phone with my brother, Jackson. I'm contemplating picking it right back up to change my mind. Dammit. How did I let him talk me into moving back home? Okay, that's an exaggeration. It's only for a couple months, but that doesn't diminish the outrageousness.

Leaving San Diego after graduation wasn't easy, but the need to forge my own path in life was necessary, and I knew I couldn't do that under my parents' watchful eye. The insistent pressure to follow in their footsteps throughout college was miserable, and I hated working for their property management company. Dealing with tenants, doing property inspections—I shiver just thinking about it. My heart wasn't into it, and I knew it wasn't what I wanted for a career.

Bozeman seemed perfect for a fresh start. I'd met a couple of people in the business program at college who were from here and raved about it, saying it was booming. Thank God it worked out. Passing the real estate exam and getting my license turned out to be a breeze with the knowledge I already had from the management side of things.

I hated leaving Lily and my brother. Lily was only slightly easier since she moved in with her boyfriend, Sebastian, after graduation. My brother, however, was more complicated. Putting him in a tight spot with my parents' looming retirement and forcing him to shoulder the responsibility alone wasn't an overnight decision. I'm lucky he understood and supported my choice, even standing up to our parents for me.

If only they had been as understanding. Mom and Dad were disappointed, to say the least. They said I was throwing away a perfect opportunity, disregarding everything they'd done to build a business for their children over the years. It's not that I didn't appreciate it, but whenever we started to talk, I got so frustrated by their guilt-tripping that I lashed out. Then they would counterattack, and so it went until we stopped talking altogether. We haven't spoken since I moved away a year ago.

Jackson took the reins when they retired and exceeded all expectations. He's grown their ownership portfolio by thirty percent and doubled the property management side since taking over. The business is doing way better without me, but my parents are too stubborn to admit it. They also have no clue I'm thriving here because how would they? If only I could rub it in their faces that I'm making good money and enjoy what I do. I'm excellent at real estate—my clients love me, I love them, and I adore helping people find the home of their dreams or at least one they can call their own.

I'm glad Jackson had a chance to witness how happy I am when he visited two months ago. I finally convinced him to look at property in Bozeman. It didn't take long to realize my college friends were right that it was a hot market, and I've been begging Jackson to invest here ever since. We have two buildings under contract from that visit—further reason this decision is stressful. I have five other deals under contract, six houses listed, and ten clients who I'm actively locating property for.

This won't be easy, but I'll make it work because he's been miserable since Mia left him right after their visit. I suspected they were dating the minute he said his temporary assistant would be coming along—the one he was trying to rid himself of weeks earlier, no less. I knew there was more to the story than wanting her here to take notes. And when I saw them together, it was absolutely frickin' adorable. It was good to see my brother happy again after he lost out on my best friend, Lily, to her fiancé, Sebastian.

So here I am, having just agreed to return to San Diego because my brother is desperate to get Mia back. Rather than leaving for family issues as I was previously told, he just explained that she's in the witness protection program for her testimony on a case involving a California crime family. Her dad's testimony would be more substantial, but the FBI can't find him. So Jackson is determined to find Mia's dad and exchange him for Mia since they won't need her at that point. He'd been using private investigators but is taking the search over himself because he hasn't been the same since she left, so he's motivated.

And that's why I went against every grain in my body when I said yes to going home to run the family business while he devotes his time to finding Mia's dad. Truthfully, I would do anything for my brother. We've always had each other's backs. No matter what my issues are, I can do this. Hell, I can do anything I set my mind to. I'll get everything situated in the two weeks I said it would take to go down there—and by down there, I mean to the pits of hell. Hey, did I mention I'm getting a sweet purse out of the deal?

"I can't believe you're leaving me. Who will I hang out with all summer?" Poppy says sullenly while helping me pack for my flight tomorrow.

We met at the office when I moved here a year ago and hit it off immediately, becoming fast friends. We're both fun, single, and out for a good time, all while being badass Realtors. I'm lucky we became such close friends soon after moving here. I'd have been lost without her since I was so used to having Lily by my side. Now, I love my life here. I have my own place, a job that I love, and another best friend.

"It's not all summer. Only a couple of months, if that. God, I couldn't handle any longer. I'm already dreading this as it is."

"Yeah, that sucks about your parents. At least you'll have Lily, though. And I bet the dating pool is way better than here—especially since you've been through the entire singles selection in Bozeman already," she teases as she sits on the bed, folding the clothes I'm throwing from the closet. My suitcase sits open and ready to be filled with enough stuff to last me who knows how long. If only I had an end date to this move.

"Ha. Ha. That's sort of one of the problems. There's this guy I have a history with, and I'm not sure how it'll go. He wanted more before I moved away, and it might be awkward if I dated anyone else. He happens to be Lily's future brother-in-law."

"Oh shit. Eli Dubree? The most eligible bachelor in San Diego now that Sebastian is scooped up? Are you crazy? Why not just tap that while you're home?" Poppy knows about Lily and Sebastian through the stories I've told her, and I'm sure she did her research, but I never mentioned my fling with Eli until now.

"As much as I'd love to—because, let me tell ya, the guy's skills in bed are unique—I don't want to lead him on. That wouldn't be fair."

Oh, who am I kidding? I've missed way more than just his cock. The problem back then was that my feelings had grown deeper, and that scared the bejesus out of me for some reason. It's like my heart was on board, but my head kept putting up roadblocks and giving me reasons to run as fast and as far as I could. To this day, I don't understand why I'm this way. Because it's not just Eli—any man I'm dating will be tossed to the curb at the mention of exclusivity. So, hey, the fact that I was at least exclusive with Eli before I moved was a big deal. But the minute he suggested I stay, my brain went haywire, and it's like I couldn't leave fast enough. So, yes, I know I'm fucked up.

"It wouldn't be leading him on since he knows you're leaving. Isn't that an enter-at-your-own-risk situation? Or did *wanting more* go both ways?" Her eyebrows go up speculatively.

"You know me. Settling down is *not* in my future."

"Boy, do I…. The trail of broken hearts is proof of that. I'm not surprised you have the same thing in San Diego. Maybe he'll be seeing someone, and you'll be free to do what you want."

My gut clenches at the suggestion, which is ludicrous since I've already seen plenty of his exploits over the past year online—not that I'm constantly looking or anything. He's had nothing serious so far and is rarely with the same girl more than once, but the few times he was… it drove me crazy. He continued texting me every now and then after the engagement, but the more time that passed, the more infrequent they became until they tapered off completely.

"He's not. It would be all over the internet if he were," I state with more certainty than I feel.

"Hmmm. I say go for it if the opportunity arises, and I can't imagine it won't. Isn't he your best friend's fiancé's brother? Whoa, that's a mouthful." Poppy wiggles her eyebrows, making us both crack up.

"You should come visit and check out San Diego."

"Yeah, right. I'll be up to my eyeballs in work between your deals and mine."

Since we're in the same office, Poppy will be my boots on the ground while I'm away, showing buyers potential properties and attending closings. "Sorry. At least all my clients know I'll be gone and only available by phone. Plus, I'll watch for new listings that match their profile, so you won't have to worry about that aspect. Thanks for picking up the slack, though. You're a lifesaver. If my brother weren't already in love, I'd repay you by setting you up with him."

"Too bad, 'cause he's a hottie. I'm sad I didn't meet him and Mia when they visited," Poppy says with a pout.

Jackson had to cut their visit short and left the day I planned to introduce them. "Me too. Next time, for sure. Let's just hope he brings her back soon so I can come home. It would be perfect if Grayson was back by then so I'd finally have a chance to meet your brother." Her brother is in the military and hasn't visited the entire year I've lived here. He's fricking hot, and I've been dying to see him in person after being introduced while he and Poppy were on Facetime. He's a little on the stiff side for me, but from what I could tell of his physique… damn.

"His duty ends in December, so he'll be here for Christmas but might not stay if he re-enlists. And anyway, let's not forget about your trail of broken hearts. If we want to be friends for life, you may have to hold back from making moves on my brother. The thought of you and Grayson together is cool but gross at the same time, especially if you guys were just a one-time thing. I don't think family dinners would be very relaxing."

"Yeah, true. Oh well. I'm still excited to meet him, though." She's right about family dinners. Her parents have officially taken me in, and we go to her childhood home every Sunday night, so I'd hate to ruin them. I love it since my parents don't find me worthy enough.

"Hey, I couldn't do this without you. I'm sorry for everything I'm piling on, but I really appreciate it."

"Don't be. You'd do the same for me. I'm more upset at losing my wingwoman than the extra work I'm getting."

I pick up the pillow and hit her with it. "Yeah, right, Ms. Picky. It takes an act of God for you to date."

"Hey, one of us has to have morals. And who would keep all those other guys preoccupied while you steal their friends away?" Poppy laughs.

"Ugh. I'm gonna miss you."

"I'll miss you more."

"You okay with everything?" Jackson asks for the hundredth time this week while he's been catching me up to speed on everything at the office. It's too bad Cindy's still on maternity leave for another six weeks. This would've been way easier with her here.

"Yes, Jackson. I'll be fine. Rebecca's doing well for filling in, plus the staff you have in place are rock stars. You've done well with the restructuring. I'm proud of you, big brother." I give him a pat on the back. We're both in chairs behind his desk so I can see everything he's doing.

"Thanks. It's become a smooth-running machine, but with the deals we have in the works and all the new properties we're managing, someone needs to be here to oversee it all. Rebecca handles herself well, but I'll be glad when Cindy gets back. What a mess." He sighs, looking worn out. I'm sure he's been under a ton of stress preparing for what lies ahead.

"Hey, it'll all work out. Don't worry, I've got this. Plus, you're only a phone call away. Just focus on what you need to do to be happy again. You've been a real Debbie Downer lately."

"Yeah, sorry about that. All right, I don't think there's anything more to go over at this point. Mom and Dad will be back in a week. I'll talk to them more when they're settled, but I left a letter explaining what's happening. When they have service after the cruise, I'll give them a heads-up on their way home. Keep me posted if they get out of hand. They've been mostly hands-off since retiring, besides having me hire Mia, but they shouldn't bother you. I'll step in if I need to, though." He's always ready to step into his role of the stern big brother.

"I appreciate it, but stop worrying. I'm a big girl, Jackson. I can handle them. I've grown up a lot this past year, and I'm not as hung up on the situation as I was before. It's their problem if they can't accept the fact that I'm doing just as well on my own as I would be running this with you, and besides, you're doing an amazing job, and who's to say that would've happened if both of us were at the helm. Maybe they'll come to terms with my decision. Maybe they won't. Either way, I'm done worrying about it, and you should be too." I'm not just trying to make him feel better. I have come a long way. I've mulled over the situation a lot the last two weeks. It sucks being at odds with them, but I've decided it doesn't matter until they accept me for who I am.

The following words prove he's not convinced. "I'm just worried about you is all."

"Well, don't be. I'm happy, and even though I'd rather be home—as in Bozeman—I've loved being back. Lily and I get together almost every night to talk about wedding plans, and it's fun being here to help. Plus, you were right—your condo is way better than mine was when I lived here."

"Well, make yourself at home, but don't get too comfortable, as in no guys. Go to their place instead. Or better yet, don't date while you're here."

"Really? You've had more action in your bedroom than I've had my entire life, I'm sure. But I'll respect your space. It doesn't matter anyway. I'm not planning on dating anyone. What's the point since I'm leaving again? I mean, unless I only want to—"

"Don't finish that sentence," he growls, making me laugh.

"Listen, go do your thing. I'll hold the fort down while you're gone. And Jackson?" He raises his brows in question. "Be safe but hurry up and find this guy," I finish and stand, giving him one last hug, then head home to change for dinner at Lily's.

Jackson's meeting his friends Braden, Sebastian, and Eli tonight before he leaves early tomorrow morning. I'll hang out at Lily's since Sebastian is now weirdly included in that group and won't be home. Not that anything is wrong with Sebastian; he's just not someone you'd picture hanging out with his friends for a night on the town. And he's a major control freak, especially where Lily is concerned. I'll admit, some of it sounds hot, but if a guy tried to control my every move, he'd have another thing coming. But Lily loves it, so that's all that matters.

Eli, on the other hand, barely has a serious bone in his body—probably what makes him so fun to be around. The only similarity between the brothers is that they both look like they just stepped off the runway, albeit from very different fashion shows. Sebastian from Tom Ford, sharp features and crisp suits, and Eli from Ralph Lauren, the preppy boy next door with his sexy floppy brown hair that has you wanting to grab it and pull him closer while he kisses the living daylights out of you.

Then there's Braden, my brother's best friend, the eternal bachelor heartthrob after being jilted by a woman. He's some hotshot attorney and gorgeous enough to be on the cast of *Suits*. In fact, I wanted to date him once upon a time, but then Eli happened, and that was that. It's probably out of the question to have a fling with Braden since they're all buddies now, especially with how Eli and I left things, which couldn't have been more unsettled.

I haven't seen Eli yet—it's only been a week—and I'm nervous, if I'm being honest. This crazy pull between the two of us is always in the background. Although he could be seeing someone right now, most of his exploits are publicized, but I'm sure not everything. The thought of Eli with a girlfriend makes my insides curdle, which is ridiculous since I'm the one who held back. Regardless, it would be hell to watch him with another woman. But I also can't start things up with him again. Poppy may think it's okay, but I disagree. It wouldn't be right to become involved again knowing he wanted more back when we were messing around.

Ugh. Sometimes I wish Lily had known about us. It's not that I intentionally hid it from her at the time, but Lily was experiencing her first relationship then, and I didn't want to steal her thunder by talking about mine. Not that it *was* a relationship. We were simply enjoying each other's company until I moved. What would the point have been to tell her since it wasn't serious? I don't do serious. Still, it would be nice to talk to her about it. But since I can't, I'll at least have to poke around for some information about him tonight. Find out if he's asked about me at all. *Damn, Cici, get a grip. You don't care, remember?* This could be a very long couple of months if I'm already obsessing.

After I change into something comfy but still decent enough to walk through Lily's lobby, I Uber over in case I drink more than I should and knock on her door. Just as I'm about to knock again, I hear running on the other side before it swings open to an out-of-breath Lily.

"What were you doing?" I ask her, laughing.

She leans in to hug me in the foyer. "I'm making you dinner like old times. I was draining the noodles when you knocked, and they can't sit, or they'll stick together, so I had to toss the oil in really quick."

Lily and I go back to ninth grade. We became best friends when she moved to San Diego and started school. And when her dad abandoned her a few months later, she moved in with my family. My parents adored her and agreed to take her in. However, she worked hard to support herself in all ways besides rent. As soon as she graduated with a full-ride scholarship, we shared one of my parents' rental units and spent our college days together until last year, when we both made significant changes in our lives. She moved in with Sebastian, and I fled to Bozeman. I've missed her like crazy since.

"Yay!" I clap my hands rapidly. "Man, I miss those days. Can you believe it's been a year already? How are you and Sebastian? Any doubts, or are you still head over heels in love?"

She answers on our way to the kitchen, "Zero doubts and still head over heels. I'm so in love with him that it scares me sometimes. I've never had anyone care about me as much as he does. He makes me feel cherished. And I don't think I'll ever be bored in the bedroom, that's for sure. He's made me a monster." She growls and we both laugh.

Lily's touch is evident as I walk through their penthouse—a colorful blanket over the couch, framed pictures adorning the surfaces, and a few candles to give it a feminine feel. As expected, a bottle of champagne over ice with two glasses already poured is on top of the kitchen island. She knows me so well.

Sitting on one of the barstools, I hold my glass up, and Lily does the same. "Well, cheers to you, then. You are one lucky girl." We take a sip before she turns back to the stove. "For me? I couldn't handle someone like Sebastian. All possessive and protective like he is. It's just not my thing. I understand his caution, but he's a little extreme."

Ebony, the cat we shared when we lived together, jumps into my lap. After Lily went through what she did with a kidnapping from an overzealous admirer right before graduation, I decided she needed our feline companion more than I did. "Hi, sweetie. I've missed you." I rub her ear and pet her while she purrs as Lily finishes dinner.

"Yeah. He can be a bit much, although I guess I'm used to it by now. I can't imagine how he'll be when we have a baby. He'll—"

"Whoa, hold up. Are you pregnant?"

"No! We've talked about starting a family after the wedding, but I'm still building my career, and he's too busy with the company.

Don't get me wrong, he'd love to have me barefoot and pregnant, but he knows I love working too much, and anyway, with Eli in and out all the time from one adrenaline-seeking adventure to the next, Sebastian's had a lot on his plate."

"What's going on with Eli? I've seen bits and pieces in the gossip section, but nothing out of the ordinary." My interest is piqued. I knew about Eli's thrill-seeking obsession, but not that it was serious.

"I'm not really sure. This past year, he seems to have kicked it up a notch with dangerous activities. It's become an addiction. Skydiving, kitesurfing, rock climbing… you name it, and he's done it or has it on his list. Sebastian's getting worried about him, actually."

"Wow. I knew he had a wild streak, but I didn't realize it was that bad. It's probably just a phase."

"I hope you're right." She shrugs, shaking her head. "So tell me about your day. Are you ready for Jackson to leave, or are you stressed out of your mind?" Darn it. I wanted to ask more about Eli, but I'll have to prod later.

"Probably a little of both. He's driving me nuts worrying so much, but leaving is a big deal for him. He's worked so hard getting the business where he wants it over the past year, and now he's trusting me with the reins. And what he's getting himself into is enough stress alone. Add his concern over leaving me to deal with our parents, and he's like a wire ready to snap. But honestly, Lily, I know I'm capable. I just don't want to screw anything up or let him down. It's a lot to take in." Now that I've said it out loud, I realize how nervous I really am.

"Cici, you are one of the most competent people I know. Not to mention, you understand the business as much as anyone, given the years you worked there in college. You've got this. And I'm here to keep you sane."

"I should be the one keeping you sane through all the wedding planning, not the other way around. But enough with the pity party. I'm so happy I'm here before the wedding. It'll be easier to fulfill my maid of honor duties this way. Speaking of, we need to start thinking about the bachelorette party. Oh, and we should go dress shopping this weekend," I say excitedly.

"Oh my gosh, yes. I'm so glad you're here, Cici. Seriously, we'll be so busy that the time will fly by. You being here was meant to be, I swear." She squeals as she walks over to hug me.

This, right here, outweighs any negatives from any shituation that comes up over the next couple of months.

3

SIDESTEPPING

Eli

"H EY, GUYS," JACKSON GREETS THE THREE OF US. HE'S MEETING me, Sebastian, and Braden for drinks before he ventures out to search for his girlfriend's dad.

"You all set to head out tomorrow?" Braden asks.

"Packed up and ready to go. I've wanted to leave all week, but I had to get Cici up to date first," Jackson replies.

"I can't believe you convinced her to come back. She can't love you that much. What did you bribe her with?" I tease Jackson and laugh, imagining the conversation between the siblings.

"It probably has more to do with how much she and Mia hit it off, but there might be a purse involved. I would've offered more. I'm just glad she agreed to come." Jackson confirms my suspicion of bribery.

"I can't say the same since I've seen Lily less this week than I have all year," Sebastian sullenly pipes in.

"I think that's the only other reason Cici agreed to come. She's excited to be here for the wedding planning. How's it going anyway?" Jackson asks Sebastian.

"I try to stay out of it as much as possible. The wedding planner I hired has saved my sanity. Worth their weight in gold," Sebastian answers, holding his beer up before taking a sip.

"Do you have a time limit you're setting for yourself or a plan for failure?" Braden asks Jackson out of the blue. He's the skeptical one of the bunch and the only one of us with the balls to spring that question on him. I suppose he has more leeway since they're as tight as they are.

"You don't tell someone to plan for failure, dumbass," Sebastian scolds.

Jackson shrugs and answers anyway, "I'll keep searching until I find him. Failure isn't an option."

"Is your sister aware of that? I thought you told her it would be for a couple of months, tops?" Not that I would mind. It would just give me longer to win her over. It's too bad we haven't run into each other yet. I figured I'd see her in passing while she visited Lily, but no such luck yet. Oh well, I've got plenty of time.

"If everything goes my way, it *will* only be a couple months. She'll be fine with Lily here even if it takes longer. I'm sure some shit will come up with my parents when they get back, though. Keep an eye on her for me and let me know how she handles it," Jackson says before taking a swig of beer. I'm planning to have my eyes on Cici more than he knows, that's for sure.

"I'll check on her for you," Braden offers.

Oh, hell no. "Definitely not. Stay focused on your next piece of ass and leave Cici alone. The last thing she needs is a ride on the Braden train," I say pointedly to Braden, then direct my attention to Jackson. "I'll see her more than Braden since she's always with Lily, so I'll watch out for her." It makes sense, but hopefully that didn't just clue everyone in to my ulterior motives.

"She might want me checking in with her since she *was* into me for a while. Right after I broke up with Layla. If I weren't so fucked over the breakup, I probably would've moved in on that." *Fucking Braden.* The problem is, I know that. Cici teased me about going for one guy and ending up with another back when we first met. I like the guy since we've become friends over the last year, but he can keep his paws off my girl.

"Shut the fuck up, Braden. That ship sailed. Leave her alone," I reply, making everyone laugh, and I realize that I may have just shown my hand.

However, Jackson doesn't press the issue and even takes my side. "I second that. Love you, man, but keep your dick away from my sister. I know some of the places it's been. Eli, I'll take your offer if you stay alive long enough in between the crazy shit you do. Tell me if she gets into it with my parents."

He's referring to my hobby of doing anything that gets my adrenaline pumping. Hey, life's too short to miss all the thrills it has to offer.

"I'll second that one," Sebastian adds while giving me a look of reprimand.

Ignoring both, I decide to stick to the subject of Cici and her parents, knowing it'll be tricky for her. "Do they know she's here yet?"

"No, I left a letter on the counter. They'll see it when they get back. They're still on the cruise, but they have a message to call me on their way home so I can at least warn them what they're coming home to," Jackson responds.

"Well, I hope you're more successful than the FBI, not to mention all the PIs you went through, but come on, man, it's a long shot. I don't want you losing your mind if you can't find him. That's all I meant earlier. I realize you feel guilty, but it's not worth throwing your life away." I can't believe Braden is still going down this road. He's fucking oblivious at times.

"Braden, I'm gonna let that slide because you mean well, but she *is* my life. I thought I made that clear. Even if it's not until the end of the trial, I'll get her back, and if her dad is the way to make that happen sooner, then I'll find him," Jackson says before downing the rest of his beer.

"Well then, I hope you succeed sooner than later 'cause I'm gonna miss my best friend. These douchebags aren't as fun." He lifts his glass, and everyone follows suit.

"Good luck, man," I say sincerely.

"Bring him in," Sebastian adds as we clink our glasses in a final toast.

"It's getting late. I should probably go since I've got a meeting first thing in the morning," Cici says, lifting Ebony off her lap and rising.

I'm at Seb and Lily's for dinner and drinks a few weeks later, which has become a frequent occurrence since Cici's been back in town and is constantly doing the same thing. Any chance to be around Cici, and I'll take it. I'm obsessed with everything about her. She's an incredible woman. Strong enough to forge her own path, and resilient enough to step back into the role she left behind only to help her brother, which makes her compassionate to top it off. She's the complete package, and if I have any chance to make this woman mine, I'll need to step up my game.

"I'm heading too. I'll walk you out." *And into my bed.*

Sebastian gives me a knowing smirk. He's pretty much been betting against me from the beginning—not because he doesn't want me to score but because he knows how stubborn she is. And that's putting it mildly.

The girls say their goodbyes, and we walk out the door.

"So how is it being back in the office these days? Do you still feel the same as you did in college?" I ask, not ready to say goodbye.

Cici thinks for a minute before answering, "It makes a big

difference that my parents aren't hovering, involved in the day-to-day. That part I like, but I'm still just not a fan of property management in general. Luckily, it keeps me busy enough that I don't dwell on it, and I know it's only temporary. But I'll be glad to go back to my job for sure."

"Do you want to keep talking with a nightcap at my place?"

"I need to get to bed."

"Well, now that you mention it." Moving in, I push her hair behind her ear and whisper, "I think that's a great idea." She shivers in response with a sharp intake of breath. She wants me as much as I want her. Now if she'd just stop fighting it….

She steps back and pushes the elevator button. "You do this every time, and my answer will always be the same."

"Come on, Cici, we're both up for some fun—why not have it together?"

"I'm leaving now…. Goodnight, Eli."

When I walk into the kitchen, I pull my phone out of my pocket, frustrated with the way things ended yet again.

Eli: How long do you plan to keep avoiding the inevitable?

Cici: What are you talking about?

Eli: You've been back for a month now, and you've been sidestepping me ever since.

Cici: I am not. I'm maintaining healthy boundaries.

Eli: Right. And do you have these boundaries with all men or just me?

Cici: …

Eli: Never mind, don't answer that. Do you truly have no intention of seeing me while you're here?

Cici: I see you almost every night.

Eli: You know damn well what I mean.

Cici: It's not a good idea. I've only got a few more weeks here.

Eli: I've got some great ideas to fill that time.

Cici: I'm sure you do, but no. Goodnight.

Eli: Goodnight, cutie. But this conversation isn't over.

She's fucking killing me. I've spent more time at Sebastian's place these past few weeks than ever before, pining over a woman who's refusing to give in. Sebastian's ready to give me the boot if I don't make a move soon. He says I'm a pushover, but what am I supposed to do? Carry her to my door like a caveman? That's more my brother's style, and although I've been known to dominate, I'm trying to tread lightly with Cici rather than scare her away completely. I'm starting to reevaluate that thought process, however, because patience is getting me nowhere.

"Thanks, Eli. Text me what you find out and tell everyone I said hi," Jackson says over the phone.

"Sounds good. See ya, buddy."

I'm smiling as I end the call. *I'd be happy to check on your sister and find out how she's doing.* This couldn't have been better timing after the way she shut me down three days ago—no time like the present.

Sebastian's office is on the way to the elevator, so I pop my head in as I pass. "Hey man, I'm taking off for a bit."

"If you're lacking work, I could help out with that since I've got plenty." Sebastian is always giving me shit, but hey, I cut him slack for his inferiority complex from being eighteen minutes younger than me.

"Thanks, but no thanks."

"What has you leaving the office midday?" he asks, mildly suspicious and genuinely curious.

"Jackson asked me to check in on Cici. He's worried about her. Said her parents still won't talk to her and are keeping an eye on things through the assistant. I figure I'll swing by and catch her in action… invite her to lunch."

"Stop being a pussy and insist she go with you. How long will you keep this nice-guy shit going before you take what you want? Have you learned nothing from me?"

"How soon you forget that I'm the reason you got anywhere with Lily. I distinctly remember lecturing you on the art of dating, little brother," I jest.

"Well, it's my turn to lecture you now. Stop being a pansy-ass bitch and make your move already."

"Fuck off. Just wait—my slow play will win in the end."

"Yeah, good luck with that. Now get the fuck out so one of us can work."

I flip him the bird and chuckle as I retreat, hearing him scoff behind me. But he has a point. I think it might be time to put a little pressure on the woman.

Stopping at the florist around the corner, I decide to grab a gift for her temporary office. It's the perfect reason to swing in and won't look as suspicious. My mind runs through possible outcomes on the drive over. Will she be happy I'm there or frustrated at the unannounced visit? I'll play it by ear on inviting her to lunch. Who knows? Maybe we won't even need to leave the office for what I have in mind.

I walk in and head back to Cici's currently empty office. The staff up front knows me since I've been here a few times to visit Jackson. He and I met through business a couple years back and became friends. However, I'm unfamiliar with the most recent temporary assistant after Mia left, since his regular one is still on maternity leave.

"Well, hello there. We haven't met, so I'll introduce myself. I'm Eli Dubree, and you are?" I hold my hand out as the lady in question blushes. Yes, I do have that effect on women.

"Oh, hi. I'm… R-Rebecca," she stammers while placing her hand in mine.

I lift it for a kiss, making her cheeks go a deeper shade of pink.

"Pleasure to meet you, Rebecca. I'm here for Cici, but I see she's not in. Will she return soon?" My voice oozes charm.

"Yeah, she just ran for coffee. She shouldn't be much longer. Can *I* help you with anything?" she asks seductively.

"That won't be necessary. I'll just wait in her office. I'd like to surprise her." I make the *sssh* sign with my pointer finger to my lips, leaving no room for argument as I walk into Cici's office. My lips curve upon hearing Rebecca's stuttering acceptance as I shut the door behind me.

I look around a bit before settling into one of the chairs in front of the desk and placing the plant down. If I didn't know Jackson was gone, I'd think he was having an incredibly chaotic day with the files scattered everywhere. He's more of a neat freak from what I've witnessed the few times I've been here. However, the desk is currently cluttered with papers of all sizes, handwritten notes, and files galore. I'm gonna go out on a limb here and say Cici is not the most organized individual.

I hear the door open and turn to the lady in question, who is standing at the doorway, talking to Rebecca with her head turned that direction. I take her in while she's distracted. Her business attire—something I don't witness by the time she makes it to Sebastian and Lily's—is a black pencil skirt and white silk blouse with the sleeves rolled up. Her hair falls in waves over her shoulders while two buttons open to reveal her creamy golden skin with the mounds of her well-endowed cleavage tempting me. I'm dying to get my hands on her again. This will be interesting with no audience and an impossible chance for her to make an abrupt exit, considering this is her office.

She finishes talking and turns around, her eyes going wide. "Oh. Eli, I didn't know you were here." She turns back to Rebecca, and I can only imagine the daggers she's shooting her way while Rebecca relays my request to surprise her. "Ah. Well, surprise accomplished," she states cooly, lips in a thin line while she shuts the door.

I stand before she makes it around the desk and gently grab her arm. "Hey, cutie. Where's my proper hello?" Without giving her a chance to respond, I pull her into me. "That's better," I say, rubbing her back as she takes a deep inhale. It's impossible not to feel the electricity buzzing between us. I find myself nuzzling the side of her head, breathing in her scent, knowing it's more than that for me. There are feelings involved that seem to grow stronger each time we're together.

"Eli, what are you doing?"

"Hugging you. Isn't this how people normally greet one another?"

She retreats and sits behind the desk, ignoring my answer. "So what brings you by?"

"I wanted to stop in, say hi, and bring you a gift for your office, even though it's temporary. I knew Jackson didn't have much in here to lighten the mood." I nod toward the fuchsia-colored orchid between us.

"Thank you, that's really sweet. And it's gorgeous."

"I also thought I'd check in and ask how life is treating you these days," I say casually, unsure if I should bring up lunch or take a sly approach.

"You could have saved yourself the trip and just texted or asked next time I'm at your brother's."

"I could have, but I'm sure you would've said the same as all the other times I tried: you're fine, you're keeping up on everything, you're happy to help your brother out. Or when you answer by text? *Good* is the only response you give. But I want to hear how you really feel." My mouth curves up on one side along with my right eyebrow, insinuating I'm not buying it.

"It is how I really feel." Her annoyance is evident. "And like I said the other night, I have a lot I'm juggling between both jobs, so I don't have much time to chitchat, unfortunately. I'm sorry, Eli," she says, shuffling files around in what appears to be an attempt at making order in the chaos and clearing a small portion of the desk.

"What I see is you trying to avoid answering the question."

She gets a scowl that only makes me want to place a kiss right between her eyes to remove it. "What's the question?"

"How is life treating you, Cici? Are you happy being back home? Or is something… missing?" *As in me…?*

She sighs dramatically. "Yeah, my whole life is missing, since this isn't my home anymore. I'm happy in Bozeman, and I miss it. I love being here with Lily, but it's not where I belong. I have a job, my condo, friends… a whole other life, and it's difficult to be away. I didn't want to come back, and if it weren't for Lily… I'm not sure I would have. Does that answer your question?"

"Thoroughly." After my obvious innuendo, it's apparent she truly has no interest in becoming more. What the fuck was I thinking? "I'm sorry, Cici. It sounds like you made quite the sacrifice. Jackson's lucky to have you. It can't be easy with the rift between you and your parents either." I might as well get to the heart of Jackson's concern so I can let her be. She may still want me as badly as I want her, but that's where it ends—for her anyway.

"It's not the greatest feeling in the world, but I've come to terms with it and don't let them bother me anymore unless Rebecca mentions them. But now that I've asked her not to tell me when they call, it's been better." She must read the skepticism on my face and continues, "Really, I'm fine. I'm glad to spend time with Lily and help with the wedding way more than I could have from home. And besides, it's not forever. The two months I agreed to are already halfway over."

"You realize it might take longer than that to find Mia's dad, right? Or will you tell him he has to quit looking and come home?"

"Okay, Mr. Pessimist. Of course, I wouldn't. I also can't stay forever."

"What's your endgame, then?"

"What does it matter right now? I thought you came to ask how I'm doing, not stress me out more, geez almighty."

I run my hand through my hair, frustrated in so many ways. "I just don't want you to be blindsided if he needs more time. It's not an unlikely scenario."

"Got it. I'll make a mental note." She points to her temple. "Anything else you'd like to know or make sure I'm aware of?" Her anger is bubbling under the surface, and if I push any more, she'll go batshit.

"Sorry, cutie. I didn't mean to come here and cause you grief— just to pay a visit. I care about you. And to be honest… I may have had an ulterior motive. You're here. I'm here. We're fire together, and I'd love nothing more than to rekindle the flame." She opens her mouth to talk, but I stop her. "However, you've made your objections clear, and I'll accept your decision. I'll admit, it won't be easy, but I'll let you be."

"Thank you. And anyway, aren't you too busy running your billion-dollar company to take time wandering over to my neck of the woods? I have a feeling that if I gave in to you, you'd be here more often than not."

"I'm never too busy for you. My job is mostly oversight, and I've got it down to a science. Lucky for me, Sebastian is a workaholic, so he does most of the heavy lifting. I'd feel bad if Lily weren't one floor away from him all day in the marketing department, but we both know he's where he wants to be. I'd have all the time in the world for you, and if I didn't, I'd make time."

"Eli. Stop being so damn perfect. You're making it very hard to resist. Ugh. Listen, I'm leaving soon. We'll both regret it if we cross the line only to say goodbye again. Hey, let's enjoy being friends. You *are* practically my brother-in-law."

I laugh with a shake of my head. "Yeah, no… I will never think of you as my sister-in-law, but nice try."

She laughs. Seeing her smile lightens my mood and brings a semblance of peace that's sure to disappear the minute I leave, but then I have an idea.

"Since we are friends, could you help me out with something next week?" I ask nonchalantly, not wanting to give away how hopeful I am that she'll say yes.

"Depends. What do you need help with?"

"There's a restaurant in our portfolio that's looking to change their menu, and they want us to pop in to taste the new dishes first. I set something up for Monday when they're closed, but Sebastian had a conflict. You could be his stand-in. You'd be doing me a solid—plus, it's your favorite… Italian," I say enticingly.

"Hmm, it's tempting."

"Come on, you'd be helping me out. If I'm the only one to show up, they may not take my word for it. And it would be awkward eating by myself."

"What time on Monday?" she asks, still sounding unsure.

"Since they're closed, anytime. Tell me what works for you, and I'll make it happen."

She checks her schedule before answering, "Okay, fine. I can leave a little early that day. Let me know when, and I'll block it out."

"All right, I'll text you a time and let you get back to work."

"Sounds good. Hey, thank you for the plant."

"You're welcome, cutie. And stop avoiding me now. I'll back off. But know you can call me for anything." I can't resist…. "And I mean *anything*." I wink.

"God, you're such a pervert. Get out of here before I change my mind." She throws a pen at me, laughing.

I catch it, then stand, holding it out for her to take, giving me an opportunity to caress her hand. Walking to the door, I turn to say goodbye. "See ya Monday."

"See you then. Shut the door on your way out."

So much for fucking like rabbits this afternoon. Instead, I have some finagling to do in order to make this restaurant tasting happen. It's good to have friends in a variety of fields, but first, I'll call Jackson on the drive and fill him in on Cici. It's clear he doesn't have to worry about her. She's one tough cookie and determined to come out on top. When she puts her mind to something, she's a force to be reckoned with, that's for damn sure. Her boycott of my bed is a perfect case. But I'll take what I can get at this point.

4

MAN WHORE

Cici

H OLY MOLY. I SLUMP BACK IN MY CHAIR AS SOON AS THE DOOR closes and lay my head back with my eyes closed, trying to calm my pounding heart. How did I manage to make it through that whole conversation and not jump over the desk right into his lap? That man drives me crazy and is undoubtedly the one I can't afford to give in to. Because he's right, dammit, and he darn well knows it. We are explosive together—there's no denying it—but the problem isn't our chemistry in the bedroom; it's our chemistry out of it.

The orchid he brought me is a perfect example. He's kind, thoughtful, too damn perfect, and everything I've avoided in every relationship I've had. The last thing I want is to be attached to someone, to be controlled, to have him try to change me or make me commit. I like my freedom. And dammit, I like running my own life.

If I were to give in to Eli, I'd drown in him and lose myself in the process. And I *will not* end up staying here for a man. If anyone could understand why I moved away, it would be him. We've talked a lot in the past about the pressure I felt from my parents. He understood my position since he himself took over his family's business. The difference was that he wanted to.

Even if I were strong enough to leave after starting something up again, that wouldn't be fair to Eli. He would only end up hurt. But damn, it's getting tiresome to keep up this resistance. So why did I say yes to joining him for a meal? It was a moment of weakness. Let's just hope I don't have another, because I've never in my life wanted someone so badly.

For now? I think it's time for some liquid therapy… right after I call Poppy and spill my guts for some friend therapy.

Poppy picks up on the first ring. "Hey, girl. How's big-city life treating you?"

"Good, bad, and everything in between."

"Oh boy. How about you start with the good?"

"It's fun to be back in the city. The tall buildings, the lights, the people—I've missed it, just not enough to move back."

"And what about Eli? Did you give up and get down yet?" she asks, making me laugh.

"I'm always shocked at your crassness with how conservative you are."

"Just because I'm not banging all the eligible men in Bozeman doesn't mean I don't know how to talk the talk. I happen to like my romance novels just fine. While you're screwing, I'm reading."

"Oh, Poppy, we need to find you a man."

"And give up my vibrator? Nah. I'll pass."

"Who said you have to give up your toys?"

"Every man with small-penis syndrome, which covers about eighty percent."

"And how would you even know that?"

"I read enough of what women are fantasizing about, which

means they're not getting it, so there must not be many well-endowed men in the world."

All I can do is laugh for a minute before responding, "I hate to break it to you, but your theory is flawed. They might not be fantasizing at all since there are *plenty* of big dicks to be had. Which leads us back to you needing a man. Apparently, a well-endowed one."

"With that revelation, I'll be sure to update my dating profile. Now quit stalling and tell me what's going on."

"Honestly, nothing. I'm getting exactly what I wanted, but what I want is denying myself what I fricking want."

"Cici!"

"I made it clear to Eli we're not hooking up… and even though it's for the best, I can't help but mourn the thought of him."

"No doubt. That man is fine, and I bet *he* has a big dick."

"Oh my God, Poppy!"

"He does, doesn't he? Tell me—how long?"

"I'm not answering that," I say while laughing.

"Oh shit, so he's small."

"No. Definitely not," I protest.

She's the one laughing now.

I see what she did. "You are *terrible*."

"But it worked. And I've had you laughing most of the conversation," she says, the smile evident.

"Thank you. You're the best. What's insane is that right after telling him we're only going to be friends, I agreed to go test food with him at this restaurant they're invested in. I'm such an idiot. I just said no to sleeping with him, and now I'm dangling the cookie right in front of me. The problem is, I like being around him too much to resist."

But if I open the door too wide, it's a slippery slope from there. My heart keeps growing each time we're together, while my head tries to wrap it in bungees to stop it. And if Eli starts falling again, we'll both be worse off than before by the time I leave. If only my head weren't at war with my heart when it comes to that man.

"I'm gonna take a stab in the dark and say you like more than just Eli's dick."

I can't help laughing again. "Is that your word of the day or something?"

"How'd you guess?"

"You're insane. Anyway, I've decided I'm putting more distance between us and avoiding him better than I have been if I want any chance of making it through the rest of the time here."

"Could you be overthinking the whole thing? It's not like sleeping with him will change the fact that you live fifteen hundred miles away."

"Not helpful, Poppy."

"Depends on how you look at it, I suppose. I could support you in your decision to remain celibate, or I can encourage you to indulge in some big dick instead."

"I'm hanging up now, you brat. Thanks for listening and making me laugh. I miss you."

"I miss you more. Bye, Cici."

"Bye."

Hanging up the phone, I check for Lily's response about dinner tonight and am relieved to see she's in. Work will keep me busy the rest of the day, and then I'll need something to keep my mind off all this, and wedding talk is the perfect distraction. Thank goodness for Poppy. That was exactly what I needed to unload before seeing Lily and spewing it all to her. It makes no sense to tell her about Eli and me at this point when (a) what happened between us was so long ago and (b) we won't go down that road again.

Rebecca must hear the silence in my office and know I'm off the phone because a light knock sounds before she pops in. "Okay, I have to ask. Who was that guy? Is he your boyfriend?" She's practically swooning.

Oh boy, Eli must've used the Dubree charm when he came to surprise me, and I can't help but smile at the thought.

"That's Eli Dubree, and we're not dating. He's Jackson's friend and Lily's fiancé's brother. He just came to check up on me."

"All right. Is he single, and can you make an introduction?" Rebecca's practically panting as she asks.

I'm not smiling anymore. "He's not really someone you can set up. He's more of a hookup kind of guy."

"I'm way okay with that. He is one fine specimen of a man. I'm sure one time would be worth it."

"Maybe… if you don't mind STDs. He's a man whore, so you might end up with more than you bargained for. Trust me—not worth it. You're too good for him, Rebecca." I'm impressed at how convincing I sound and hope it does the job.

"Shoot. Never mind, then. Darn it. You don't see single men like that every day, that's for sure. Sorry, I'll let you get back to work." She starts for the door but stops abruptly and turns back. "Before I forget to ask, did you want me to come for Cindy's first day back and walk her through everything she's missed? Six months is a long time to be gone. I'd be happy to come in outside of the agency."

Ugh. She really is sweet. Now I feel guilty for scaring her away from Eli. Just because I can't have him doesn't mean he doesn't deserve someone like Rebecca. I'll reconsider fixing her up, but not until I'm gone.

"That's nice of you to offer, but I'll go through things with her and make sure we're on the same page. It would be helpful if you'd type up a list of transactions you've been working on and their status, along with a list of any nuances she should be aware of for the newly acquired properties. Also, could you request a report from HR of all new hires since she's been away and make notes about anyone you deal with regularly? That way, Jackson will be as up to speed as Cindy when he returns next month."

"Good idea. I'll have everything ready by the time I leave on my last day next week. And hey, it's been great working with you. Way to go stepping in when Jackson left. You made the transition seamless. I'll leave a card for Jackson to say goodbye and wish him luck. Also, if you end up with this position open again, I'd be happy to move into a more permanent role."

"I'll pass it on, be sure to put that in your card to Jackson too. Thanks for rolling with the punches, Rebecca. You did great. Best of luck with your next job."

"Thanks, Cici."

She quietly shuts the door, leaving me to chastise myself for being such a bitch about the Eli thing. Thankfully, I only have a few more days of guilt before I'll never see her again. I'm ready to have Cindy back. She's been here for years, and not only is she a rock star at her job, but also understands the family drama. I visited her when I first came back to meet her new baby. She's adorable, the kind of baby to make you want to have one of your own, which Lord knows, I don't. Cindy is a natural mom. Hell, she's been mothering Jackson and me for the past several years, so it's no wonder. I'm sure Jackson will be happy to have her back as well. Rebecca could be a hurtful reminder about the Mia situation. When he showed up one day to find Rebecca sitting where Mia was supposed to be, it didn't make the best first impression—not that Rebecca's to blame, but whatever. All will be right in the world in a few weeks.

Monday couldn't come soon enough with how often it crossed my mind over the weekend. Looking at my clock for the thousandth time, I finally hear Eli's voice outside my door. Thank God, so I can stop obsessing. I've been a bundle of nerves all day in anticipation, which is not normal behavior for helping a *friend*. Stuffing my anxiety down,

I grab my purse and open the door to see Rebecca shamelessly flirting with said friend.

"Hey, thanks for picking me up," I say as I walk right over and give him a hug. *Who am I?*

"Anytime, cutie. You ready?"

"Yep." I beam, then turn to Rebecca. "We'll have to do something special for your last day tomorrow. I'll have Eli help me come up with something. Have a good night!" That may have been a little too overzealous.

"You too," she says with a hint of suspicion in her voice.

Glancing toward Eli on the way out confirms that my odd behavior didn't go unnoticed according to the slight smirk he's sporting. Oh well. Hopefully he doesn't read too much into it.

"I'd like to arrive alive, 'kay?" I say as we near the car.

He laughs, opening the door. "Noted."

We're making small talk on the way when it dawns on me that I have no idea where we're going. It's at that moment that he pulls into the parking garage of a building that houses Dubree Enterprises on the top two floors. "What restaurant is it? It must be close by."

"Depending on your mode of transportation," he says ambiguously.

He leads me into the building and to the elevator, pushing the button for the top floor.

"I had no idea there was a restaurant here, or are they bringing the food to us?"

He gets a mischievous look in his eyes. "There isn't, and they're not." He's being undeniably vague.

I doubt I'll get an answer, but I ask anyway, "Then why are we here?"

"You're about to find out," he says playfully with a wink. And damn him for making my panties melt right then and there.

We pop out of the elevator, only to walk up a flight of stairs and outside a door labeled Rooftop Access to a fricking helicopter in front of us. *What the…?*

I stop dead in my tracks, not willing to go any closer without some answers. "Eli, what's going on?"

"I told you—we're doing a tasting."

"Then why are we getting in a helicopter?"

He smirks. "Well, the restaurant happens to be in Los Angeles."

"Are you kidding me right now?" I screech. "Why wouldn't you tell me that?"

"It was irrelevant."

"I think it's pretty frickin' relevant. How safe is that thing?"

"Safer than a car."

"That's only true if you're driving."

"Harsh." He grabs my hand and tugs me forward. "Come on, cutie, we have someplace to be. And I have the best pilot in San Diego. You're safe."

Reluctantly, I stumble behind and somehow make it into the contraption, wondering why the hell I'm agreeing to this. Note to self: never say yes to Eli without knowing all the facts.

"Here, let me help you," Eli says as he climbs in behind me. Grabbing the shoulder straps on each side of my seat, he helps weave my arms through, then buckles me in. Having him this close is doing bad things to my psyche. My willpower is hanging by a thread.

Taking off scared the crap out of me, so the death grip on Eli's hand didn't even register until after we were in the air. But when I felt his other hand caressing mine, I pulled it back like it was on fire, turning toward the window in embarrassment. The minute I looked out, I was in absolute awe at the city below.

"Eli, this is amazing! It's so different than an airplane. Seeing everything up close through the large windows—it's crazy."

"I'm glad you like it."

"Does it not faze you anymore since you've done it so often?"

"Oh, I'm fazed… just not by the flight."

I shake my head and focus on the outside again instead of the man beside me, because if I look or talk to him anymore, my defenses will keep weakening.

Landing wasn't as nerve-racking as taking off, and once we exited the death trap, there was a black SUV waiting to whisk us away. This lifestyle, it's… wild. I don't know that I have any other word for it than that. Sometimes I forget how much money Eli has, because when we're together, it's simply… us. He's not pretentious; he doesn't flaunt it, do anything over the top, or make me feel like I'm any different than he is. And how *is* that? He grew up obscenely wealthy, so it surprises me that he isn't as pompous as one would expect. Now that I think about it, he doesn't have an ostentatious bone in his body.

We're driven not far to a restaurant downtown, and when we arrive, we're the only people here. At least he was being straight about it being closed for today. I'm still questioning the rest. We're greeted by Chef Antonio, who appears to be more than just an employee when he and Eli embrace as if old friends.

"Cici, I'd like you to meet my good friend Antonio, chef and owner of this fine establishment. He'll be walking us through the menu today. Antonio, this is Cici, another good friend of mine." Eli's fondness for the man is apparent, and Antonio's look of surprise doesn't go unnoticed when Eli introduces me as a "friend."

"It's good to meet you, Antonio."

He reciprocates as I reach out to shake his hand. "You must be something special for Eli to have brought you all this way to meet me."

I'm confused by the statement since I thought we were here by request to run through a tasting, so I give Eli a questioning look, which he, of course, ignores.

Eli looks at Antonio pointedly. "Come on, you know I didn't want to go through the new menu by myself, and I figured Cici here would be less biased, not to mention better company, than you. Don't you think?" he asks Antonio.

Antonio goes from confused to enlightened within two seconds flat, confirming my earlier suspicion. Whether the whole thing was a setup or only part of it, I'm not sure, but something doesn't add up. Rather than ask him right away, I decide to do it later when he's relaxed and might be more forthcoming, because I'm for sure calling him out on this.

We've been here sampling course after course, only small samples of each, dissecting each one and giving our feedback. It's been undeniably fun and beyond filling. My stomach feels as though it's about to burst. They're giving us a slight break before bringing out a dessert sampler, which allows time to chat about something other than food for the first time tonight.

"So how do you like working for the family company of your own free will versus being forced into it?"

"I don't know that I'm here by my own free will." I scrunch my face in consideration.

"You could have said no."

"Really? Could you have turned down Sebastian if he needed you?"

He chuckles and raises his hands in defeat. "Yeah, okay, you win. You were forced. But does it feel different coming from your brother than your parents?"

"Absolutely. But that's my problem, right?"

"Not necessarily. There are a lot of reasons why it might bother you coming from your parents. Maybe it's their tactic. That would be their problem for going about it the wrong way. It could also be that their expectations were way out of line, which would justify your reluctance. You accepted their parameters for helping you financially and decided to go a different way. That doesn't mean they shouldn't be proud of you for the direction you took, so I can see why you're upset about their lack of support, and I don't mean financial."

Could this man be any more intuitive? I feel like he knows me inside and out. I'm so blown away by his wisdom and the understanding to go along with it that I'm at a loss for words. It's a good thing, then, that dessert is served, saving me from the humiliation of asking him to marry me tomorrow. Just kidding. While my heart may have those sentiments, my head is running for the hills.

"Okay, Mr. Know-It-All, tell me how you do it. Your twin brother basically heads the company, and you're there to what—fill space?" Okay, maybe my question came out in defense mode because he hit so close to home on his assessment, but I needed to make up some ground. I take a bite of chocolate mousse to hide the shame, and it's so good, I all but moan in ecstasy.

He laughs, instead of getting defensive as expected. "I'll let you in on a little secret. That's what we like everyone to believe… gives us an edge when I come in to play. Because really? While Sebastian's the instrument, I'm the force behind it, and I don't settle for less than perfectly executed music. We simply use very different strategies to make things happen, and mine aren't so outward." The tone he uses makes his point loud and clear.

"Hmm. I would've never guessed that. You do well at hiding that side of yourself."

"There's nothing to hide. I'm a good guy, making good decisions for good reasons. Just because I know how to get what I want doesn't mean I'm the villain. I rather think it makes me the hero." His smile lights his face, and I can't help but agree with him, knowing he could never be the bad guy.

The next thing I know, his thumb is wiping the corner of my mouth before bringing it to his. His moan of ecstasy matches the one in my head and makes me clench in desire. Yeah, that reaction may be between my legs, but the entire night hits something else entirely.

Basically, he might as well add my heart to his breakfast smoothie tomorrow morning.

"What do you mean you're not ready to come back? I need specifics," I say to Jackson, who's calling from his most recent location in Las Vegas.

"I'm sorry, Cici. I need more time," he pleads.

"How much more?" I ask, trying to keep my frustration in check and refrain from losing my shit on my brother, who probably can't take any more weight on his shoulders. I can picture him running his hand through his hair as he sighs.

"I wish I could answer that. Trust me. I'm just not hitting any solid leads, but I'm feeling hopeful here in Vegas. I think I'm on the right track. It's only a matter of time before someone can point me in the right direction."

"Okay. I have to ask. Are you giving yourself a time limit? Will you come home at some point even if you can't find him?" I'm cringing at having to speak the words. My brother's happiness is on the line—but isn't mine too?

"Do you want me to tell you what you want to hear or the truth?"

"That's what I was afraid of. All right, at least I'm prepared. Will you give me regular updates, then, so I'm somewhat aware of timing and if an end is in sight?" *Because I'm losing hope* are the words I don't add.

"Sorry, Cici. God, I'm so sorry. You really have no idea how much I appreciate you putting your life on hold for mine. Shit, this is all my fault. If only I hadn't let her walk out my door that night, then none of us would be in this situation."

"Hey, don't go down that road. You aren't clairvoyant, so you couldn't have known what would happen. Besides, everything happens for a reason. I'm not sure what it is yet, but trust the process. At least things are going well here. Having Cindy back made all the difference. She's amazing. She handles so much that I have plenty of time to keep my business alive in Bozeman, and with Poppy picking up the slack, it's like I'm not even gone."

"That's great. How about Mom and Dad? Any progress?"

"Negative. And don't expect that to change, although Cindy is pretty determined for us to mend things. I'm not sure what her plan is, but I can tell she's brewing something."

He laughs on the other end, and it's nice to hear. "I'm not surprised. I hope she's got something up her sleeve because it would be a relief to have you all talking again. Holidays would be so much easier."

"Oh, well, in that case… I'll be sure to tuck my tail between my legs so we can all hang out and sing kumbaya," I say petulantly.

"Don't be like that. You know I'm on your side. It would just be great for you all to get along. Anyway, tell me about everyone back home. Anything new?"

"You probably talk to the guys all the time, so I bet you're caught up. But wedding plans are going great. I can't believe it's next month. I'm so excited! You're coming home for that, right?"

"Yeah, but it's at the *end* of the month, so I still have plenty of time. If all goes well, I'll be back before that."

"Ugh, let's not start this topic again. Tell me about your search and what you're doing in Vegas."

We finish our conversation not much later, and after making him promise to be safe and keep me posted, we say goodbye.

I'd better call Poppy and tell her I won't be returning when we thought and maybe not for quite a while. Staring at the orchid, I wonder just how long I'll be here and what it would look like if I stopped avoiding Eli. Am I wasting the opportunity to be with him while I can, or is it smarter to refrain in the long run? I wish the answer was simple, but since it isn't, I'll just keep trudging along.

With one last nervous look in the mirror, I go catch my ride to meet Lily, Sebastian, Braden, and Eli for dinner. One of Lily's other brides-maids, Lucy, who I've met and adore, along with her boyfriend, Justin, who I haven't met, were supposed to join us to plan our prewedding trip to Vegas, but something came up. It's too bad since I was looking forward to the extra buffers between me and Eli.

I've kept my visits to Lily's place to a minimum since the "tast-ing" with Eli three weeks ago. If you can even call it that. It felt more like a date to me. I knew my defenses had been weakening with all the time we'd been spending at his brother and Lily's, becoming more invested in each other's lives each time. Every week we were growing closer and closer, and after that amazing date—I mean, tasting—I almost caved. Especially since I'm celibate and more pent-up than a priest during midnight mass. A vibrator only satisfies to a certain point, and I have frustratingly reached that point.

My nerves are shot as I'm led through the restaurant to our group, who are all here, according to the waiter I'm following. When my eyes land on the table, they zone in on the only free chair—directly next to Eli. My belly flips at the discovery, making my hands go clammy and my heart thump harder. I focus on my smile to mask the un-ease mixed with anticipation at knowing we'll be so close. Lily is di-rectly across from me, with Braden at the head of the table between Sebastian and Eli.

Lily stands to hug me before taking my seat, and when I do, Eli's smell instantly fills my lungs. It's his familiar manly scent, clean and crisp, that makes me want to climb him like a tree. Welcome to the longest night in history.

"May I fill your glass or bring you something else to drink, miss?" the waiter pauses to ask.

A shot of tequila. In fact, make it two.

"Sure, I'll have whatever they're having." Better not out my anxiety by asking for the hard stuff just yet.

"Certainly." He fills my champagne flute. With the pricey stuff, I might add. Only the best for the Dubrees. Have I mentioned yet that they're two of the wealthiest men in California? Their assets are in the billions. Lily did well on try number one. If only we were all so lucky. After her shit childhood, though, she's undoubtedly due.

Once the waiter goes over specials and takes our order, Lily gets right down to business. "So now that we've decided to do the bachelor and bachelorette parties in Las Vegas, let's talk about where we want to stay and what we want to do. It'll be the five of us, Lucy, Justin, and Jackson."

"Well, we'll probably go clubbing. Right? I mean, it's not a bachelorette party without dancing involved," I say.

"Clubbing is a must-do, especially with the connections these two have. But let's not forget, it's not a *bachelor* party without strippers involved. Are you ladies joining us for that, or are we splitting up for the night?" Braden asks Lily and me, only to have Sebastian answer for us.

"We won't be splitting up. I only agreed to this for Jackson and because Justin is coming, which makes it safer having additional security, even though that's not his reason for being there. If you boys insist on a strip club, the ladies are more than welcome to join us, or you can go without me. End of story," Sebastian says, referring to their friend and business associate. Justin owns the security firm the brothers use for their company and personal needs, with which Lily is quite familiar.

"I'm not opposed to a strip club. I think it would be fun. What do you think, Lily?" My question puts her on the spot, making her eyes go wide.

Sebastian intervenes. "You don't have to decide now, sweetheart.

We can talk later, but it's whatever you want." He leans in and kisses her forehead. "Why would I need a stripper in my face when I already have the most beautiful body right here?"

So yeah, he's pretty damn sweet—alpha hole and all.

What the...? A hand suddenly squeezes my upper thigh, dangerously close to the crease between my legs, causing my core to clench in surprise. I quickly school the shock on my face and try to push Eli's hand away to no avail. I ask what hotels they're considering, distracting everyone to prevent them from noticing the battle below. Changing the topic from strip clubs to hotel options was a good idea, as the table resumes discussion. I pretend to listen while casually swiveling my head in Eli's direction, who's carrying on with no hint of his actions below. The conversation eventually moves to dance clubs.

Meanwhile, the hand continues its perusal of my skin as the material of the dress I'm wearing is slowly pushed higher and higher. The next thing I know, my legs are parting involuntarily until his fingers make it to my clit and apply pressure. Eli carries on like nothing is happening under the table as my body does a happy dance from his touch. I grab my champagne for something to do other than pant while silently praying for this to never end.

5

APPETIZER

Eli

THE MINUTE SHE ARRIVED IN A SEXY LITTLE SUNDRESS, I KNEW tonight was when I'd pounce. Granted, I didn't plan on doing anything at dinner, but having her within arm's reach, I couldn't resist, and when her leg brushed up against mine, there was no stopping me. The table couldn't have been a better shield, high enough that no one could tell where my hand was heading. Christ, that soft skin has me hard in seconds. I'm a goner the moment my fingers hit home and feel her clench of desire in response.

The waiter ends my enjoyment by arriving with the appetizers, and I reluctantly pull back. Cici quickly excuses herself to the ladies' room, and the minute she leaves, my decision is made—the only thing I need to eat right now is Cici. Making the same excuse, I slowly extract myself from the table so as not to appear too eager. I arrive just in time, as she's one step out of the bathroom. Not looking, she runs into me, and I grip her upper arms, steadying her.

"*Umph.*" She looks up at me, and when she sees the determination on my face, her eyes go wide.

"You're the only appetizer I want. No arguing, Cici. Unless I hear 'no' uttered from that luscious mouth of yours, you'll come for me like a good girl." Before she has a chance to blink, let alone utter a word, I keep hold of her upper arm and drag her into the men's single bathroom. Thank God it's an elegant restaurant and the bathrooms are cleaner than some people's homes.

With the lock in place, I maul her with her back against the door, causing her purse to drop as she wraps her arms around me. My hands grip each side of her head to keep it in place while my mouth consumes hers. This is no simple kiss but a claim of what's mine. My desperation is apparent in every swipe of my tongue. The relief of having this woman in my arms again causes my heart to thump so fast that I'm anxious, never wanting to let her go.

Unable to resist a second longer, I reach down between her legs and shove her panties aside, finding her dripping. "Holy fuck, Cici. You're soaked. I need to taste you."

Not giving her time to protest, I crouch, rip her panties away with one firm tug, and stuff them in my pocket. Nudging her inner thighs, forcing her legs to spread, I lift her dress to feast on the glorious bare pussy before me—and for tonight, it's all mine. Diving in, I spear her with my tongue, causing her to suck in a lungful of air before releasing a sensual moan. She's delicious. Getting my fill, I slowly lick back up to suck her clit, then flick it a few times and stand. Wrapping my hand around her neck with my thumb at her pulse point, her heart begins to race.

"You're fucking amazing. Even better than I remember. Taste yourself, baby." My mouth takes hers again, and fuck if the moan she gives doesn't turn me on even more as I grind into her.

She parts for air. "Please, Eli."

"Please what, baby?"

Instead of answering, she kisses me again. She's too stubborn to tell me what she wants.

"Tell me what you want, beautiful, or I can't help you," I say while moving my attention to her neck, knowing it drives her wild.

She's making me crazy. I'm squeezing her ass, loving the feel of her plump but firm cheeks, while waiting for the green light to bring my hand around to pleasure her, but she needs to ask for it.

"Come on, Cici," I say into her neck. "Stop being so stubborn and tell me what to do." My hips push forward, my hard-as-fuck cock hitting her clit in the perfect spot, causing her to buck against me. My dick throbs, but it can wait. Pleasing Cici is all that's on my mind, and watching her fall apart is the only thing on the menu.

I hear her sigh the moment she gives up her resolve. "Eli, touch me, please. I want your hand between my legs—your fingers inside me. *Please.*" Yep, she's begging. Right where I want her.

"That's a good girl. All you had to do was ask, baby." I smile into her neck while my hand goes to her soft, slick folds. They find her opening and circle the entrance before thrusting in hard, the way she likes it.

I quickly cut off her scream by clamping my hand tightly over her mouth.

"Shhh. We don't want anyone to know what's happening in here, do we?"

She shakes her head with glazed eyes from her pending climax. She's so close.

"God, woman, what you do to me. I shouldn't let you orgasm as punishment for keeping me away." My hand doesn't stop despite my threat.

She whimpers with need.

"You're lucky I'm desperate to watch. Are you ready to come for me, gorgeous?"

More whimpers.

"Yeah, baby. Let me see you fall apart." I push in further, curling my fingers again and again until her whimpering becomes a muffled scream, her eyes squeezing shut as she shatters. That just won't do.

"Open your eyes, sweetheart. That's it. You're so fucking sexy when you come. I'd die a happy man if I could only watch you fall apart for the rest of my life." I bask in the feel of her orgasm around my fingers until the very last pulse.

My hand lowers from her mouth, and I claim her lips with mine once more, kissing her passionately. I'm lost to this woman. I'm lost to her pleasure. I'm lost to the hold she has on me. I reluctantly pull away from a slight pressure on my chest as she nudges me back.

"Eli, we've been gone too long. We'll get caught." Her body shudders as my hand leaves her tight channel.

"I hate to break it to you, cutie." I rub my nose against hers. "But everyone at that table knows what's happening right now."

"What?" she squeaks, shoving me hard this time.

I don't answer but turn to wash my hands.

"How do you know? No, you're wrong. You go back first and tell them I was on the phone. You overheard me when you came out of the bathroom and stopped to make sure everything was all right. I'll come out in a minute and tell them it was something to do with work. Give me my underwear."

Finished, I turn around and smirk.

"Eli!" She holds her hand out. "Now." She's damn adorable.

Reaching into my pocket, I pull them out and hold her ripped panties up. "I'm fairly certain these won't be staying in place. Tell you what, I'll go ask our server if he happens to have a safety pin or a rubber ba—"

"Go. Just go. I'll be out in a minute." She points to the door aggressively.

I can't help but laugh as I place her tattered panties in my pocket when she opens the door and shoves me out. The lock sounds immediately. Rather than wait for her, I swiftly head back to minimize the awkwardness. If they were clueless before, they won't be now.

For Cici's sake, I'm glad I returned first. There's absolutely no doubt in anyone's mind where I've been and what we've been doing. I'm sure the massive boner I'm sporting on arrival only confirms everyone's suspicion. Sebastian's raised eyebrow and smirk are proof of that.

Braden's the first one to speak up before my ass even hits the chair. "You motherfucker. How long has this been going on?"

Meanwhile, the lightbulb goes on in Lily's head, and the gears start turning, probably replaying any previous encounters, looking for signs.

My gaze is stern. "It doesn't matter. As far as you're all concerned, Cici was on a work call. Leave it at that." I'm not Sebastian scary, but when there's a point to be made, I make it.

Braden just shakes his head in bewilderment, while Sebastian sneers. I catch Lily turning toward him and mouthing the question if he knew, and he shrugs in response. I'm sure that will be a conversation for later. Lily isn't as submissive out of the bedroom as she is in it and definitely won't back down from this. She's perfect for my brother, and I love seeing someone challenge him. I can't be the only one.

Seconds later, Cici struggles to maintain composure as she approaches the table and takes her seat next to me. "I'm so sorry. I got a work call, and it took *waaay* longer than expected." The kick she delivers under the table makes my smirk unavoidable at her innuendo. It's not my fault she took so long to ask for what she wanted.

Lily jumps in to take the heat off Cici. "No worries. We saved you a few different things to try and basically buttoned up the Vegas trip. I'm so excited."

Cici's unresponsive, probably still caught up in what we just did. I imagine Cici will be hearing from Lily by the end of the night, and she'll know our cover's been blown.

"Jackson's looking forward to seeing us. That was a great idea,

Cici. Plus, you can't beat a bachelor party in Sin City," Braden adds, reminding me he talks to Jackson just as much as I do.

Shit. He'll for sure spill to Jackson the first chance he gets. I better come clean with him before Braden does. Not that I think Jackson will have an issue with me and his little sister, especially since I'm positive he already suspected something was up. Seeing Cici freeze in fear at the same realization tells me it's time to change the subject.

"Who wants to have a little fun on this trip? 'Cause I've got three options: a canyon we can rappel into, a racing experience where you drive a car at top speeds around the track, or a ranch outside of the city where we could shoot grenade launchers. Take your pick, but we're doing at least one of them." I point around the table.

"Or Lily and I could go shopping while you men do your macho, manly stuff," Cici suggests. "And I'm sure Lily will be okay for a few hours without you," she teases Sebastian. She's one of only two people I've seen get away with that. And barely.

She's saved from his response with the arrival of our meals.

"My vote's for racing. Give me a fast car with an open road, and I'm all in. Yeah, buddy," Braden says, giving me a high five. I knew he'd be up for something.

Sebastian sighs while shaking his head.

"Dude, I'm going to Vegas for your bachelor party. The least you can do is indulge in something fun for once. We'll be gone for two hours—three, tops. It's my treat," I plead with my brother.

He sighs in defeat. "Fine, I'll do it. But when you say your treat, do you mean you'll put in a full workweek for once?" Sebastian quips—cocky fucker that he is.

"I wouldn't want to take away your reason for griping at me." Besides, he knows I get shit done.

"Oh, trust me, I've got plenty. Another is this addiction of yours to life-threatening activities."

"Just staying young, brother. You should try it sometime. If you keep up this old-man act, you'll become one sooner than later. Lily'll have to trade you in for a younger model." I wink at Lily.

Cici's eyes are bugging out, probably afraid for my life, but this is normal banter for us. Giving each other a hard time is one of our favorite hobbies. My hand reaches Cici's leg, squeezing it in reassurance but maintaining a PG rating this time.

Sebastian doesn't miss a beat, raising one brow while responding, "Says the guy who can't seem to wrangle in a woman."

All right, too far, asshole.

"Boys. We should be celebrating, not fighting. Come on, let's toast to our upcoming trip." Cici jumps in at the perfect time, holding her glass out as the rest of us follow.

Thankfully, the rest of dinner flies by as we enjoy our meals, talking about this and that without bringing up the elephant in the room. I catch glances between Lily and Cici in my peripheral vision, but when I turn, they abruptly stop. Overall, the group did well, feigning ignorance other than that comment from Sebastian, and I'll let it slide since he *is* the reason I made my move.

I finally took my brother's advice after the millionth time to stop pussyfooting around. If she's what I want, then I'm going after her. He was right when he pointed out that I've never backed down from a challenge, so I'm not sure why I was okay accepting failure this time. I'm just glad I ultimately came to my senses because tonight was hot as fuck.

Talk of wrapping up the night begins, and I'm more than happy to help it along. "With everything settled, we can have Lucy start making arrangements tomorrow," I say, trying to close up shop. I'm hoping Cici took an Uber like she usually does so I can take advantage of offering a ride. Since I took the motorcycle tonight, I was careful to consume only one glass of champagne. Plus, when Cici gives in, I want my wits about me.

"Tell me if you need help with something. I don't think I've done enough to earn the title of maid of honor," Cici says to Lily while I pour the last of the champagne into her glass—nothing like a little liquid courage to loosen her inhibitions.

"You're fine. You have so much on your plate as it is. You helped us with the planning and came up with the idea in the first place. That's plenty," Lily placates.

Cici notices the empty bottle before I set it down. "Ooh, that's the end of it. I should probably order an Uber." She reaches for her purse, but when I place my hand over hers to make my suggestion first, her eyes nearly pop out of her head at my outward display of physical touch. She's in denial if she still thinks we're undiscovered.

"Actually, I only had one drink early on, so why don't I give you a ride and save you twenty bucks."

She pulls her hand back like it's on fire, panic written all over her face. "That's silly. We're already downtown. Why drive all the way to Balboa when you don't have to?"

I'm about to reply when Braden beats me to it. "It's on my way. You can hop in my Uber since it's almost here."

The death glare I send his way could melt glaciers.

"Perfect," Cici says quickly before I form a response.

Sebastian and Lily are staying quiet but are obviously confused by Braden's offer based on the glances they're throwing. If Braden thinks he's getting away with this bullshit, he's in for a reality check. He's lucky I've already staked my claim, or he and I would need to have a little talk.

"It just so happens I was planning a night drive anyway, so I insist. No arguing, Cici, you'll come with me." I use the same words from earlier, and they do the trick. She may like her independence, but I know exactly what she wants in the bedroom—and she knows I provide it.

"Fine. Only so you're not butt hurt," she says, trying to play it off.

The table laughs, and Braden snickers my way, knowing he forced my hand. The fucker has it coming.

Outside, Lily and Sebastian climb into their car while Braden gets into his Uber, and the two of us are finally alone. I can tell Cici's uncomfortable and decide to spare her for now as I take her hand, leading her down the street to stop in front of my bike.

"Where's your car?" Cici asks, looking up and down the street.

"Oh, did I not mention I rode my bike tonight?" I ask casually, expecting her reaction.

"Eli. I'm not riding on the back of that. I'm in a dress. Not to mention the last time I was in a car with you, you tried to kill me. This is so much worse," she groans, causing me to laugh.

"Have I told you you're adorable when you argue?" I proceed to place the helmet on her head despite her protest and buckle it below her chin, making sure it's snug, before leaning down to kiss the tip of her nose.

"Let me settle in first and then climb on behind me. I promise I'll drive carefully. Give it a chance—you'll like it." I caress her chin but don't dare lean down to kiss her, or I might not stop.

"Unless I want to wait here for another ten minutes to call an Uber, I have no choice. Just hurry before I change my mind."

Laughing, I swing my leg over and sit patiently while Cici does the same.

"Come on, cutie, don't be shy. Scoot up against me and wrap your arms around my waist. Wouldn't want you falling off the back." The minute she closes the distance, the warmth from her body engulfs me—especially the heat between her legs.

"Good girl." I start the engine and pull onto the road. "Hold on tight, baby."

"Eli, you said you'd go slow," she practically screams, sitting up tall to watch the road.

I chuckle while responding, "I promised to be careful, not slow."

"Eli!"

"I'm kidding. I'm not going fast. It just sounds like it because of the motor. Relax and enjoy the ride. I've got you, baby." My hand covers hers that are clasped tightly against my stomach, squeezing the life out of me. She's so nervous, it makes me smile.

"Both hands on the wheel. Or handlebars… or whatever. Just put them where they go."

I laugh heartily. I've never enjoyed having a woman on the back of my bike so much. And that's saying a lot considering a hand is usually on my crotch when I do. With Cici, all I need is the feel of her body behind me, her arms around my waist, and her chin over my shoulder to make me a happy man. Not that I'd complain if she slipped that hand down. I've got plenty for her to hold on to since I'm perma-hard for this woman. Christ, I've been in a constant state of arousal all evening. I can't get her sweet pussy out of my head. If I don't have more of that tonight, my hand will be working overtime.

"How you doin', cutie?" We're stopped at a light when I check in with her. She's been quiet, which isn't typical for Cici.

"Just saying prayers that we make it alive."

I can't help but laugh again. She amuses me. "Honey, save your prayers for the bedroom. You might need them later. You're safe, baby. Have I made you nervous yet?"

"Are we still talking about the ride? Because—" Right then, the light turns green, and she stops talking as if she needs all her concentration when I accelerate.

Luckily, I don't. "Cici, the only thing you should be nervous about is how many orgasms I'll be giving you tonight. Or whether you'll get one at all. Maybe you should grind on me and get yourself off while you can. Because tonight, baby, I'm in charge."

The words that follow don't match up to the hitch in her breath I felt seconds ago. "Eli, you're not coming in. We can't do this." The sullenness in her voice tells me she doesn't like it any more than I do, but the resolve is there just the same.

I'm not addressing her comments until we're on two feet. Pulling up to the curb minutes later, I hop off first, then lift her from the seat, placing her on the sidewalk. Taking her helmet off, then mine, I stand silently, staring into her beautiful baby blues. She's waiting for me to speak… waiting for my acceptance of her rejection. Fuck that.

I reach up and cup her cheek, rubbing my thumb over her pouty lips before I lean down to kiss her softly. A light brush until I sneak my tongue out for a taste, and then all bets are off as I pull her chin down, forcing her mouth to open for me. Her arms reach around my neck, and the moan she releases makes my cock twitch.

Fighting the urge to go further right here on the sidewalk, I pull back, gripping her head between my palms. "You know you want this as much as I do. Your body's craving what I can give it. Come on, baby, we do so well together. Stop denying it."

She groans, "I'm not. We're great in bed. That's not the problem. I'm only here for a little longer, and we shouldn't go down that road again. You know as well as I do, for some reason, it's not just sex with us. Let's not risk opening that door, Eli. Please… I'm leaving soon."

"Life's too short not to take chances, baby. Didn't anyone tell you to have a little fun before you die?" I ask, quoting lyrics from the song "All I Wanna Do" by Sheryl Crow that coincidently became my life motto.

"Yeah, the man next to me. His name is Eli and he's reckless," she says, playing along.

"Only when it comes to you, Cici." I lean down to kiss her, unable to resist any longer. I'm not sure if this is the start of the evening or the end of it, but if it's the latter, I want to give myself something to take with me.

She lightly pushes my chest and leans back to look up at me. "From what I hear, you're pretty reckless with everything these days. I'm drawing the line on this one. I'm sorry, Eli."

A frustrated sigh escapes unbidden. "You're killing me here. It won't be all those dangerous things I do that'll take me out—it'll be you, leading me to a slow and untimely death."

"So dramatic. I think you'll survive without getting me into bed. You have plenty of others to satisfy that itch."

Is she for real right now? "You're wrong. There's only one, and she's right here."

"Okay, we have to stop. I'm going upstairs now before my resolve crumbles." She steps back and starts walking toward the front door.

"So you're saying there's a chance?" I ask with her back to me as she retreats, adjusting the biggest set of blue balls I've ever had.

"Goodnight, Eli." She laughs, waving as she opens the door to walk inside.

Fuck. This woman. What the hell am I supposed to do with her? She wants this just as badly as I do. Is she right that it's a bad idea to cross this line knowing she'll be gone soon? Hell no. Any amount of time with her is worth a thousand years without. And if I'm lucky, I'll break her walls down eventually.

6

A YOU PROBLEM

Cici

"I'M SO EXCITED WE'RE DOING THIS. I CAN'T WAIT TO SEE Jackson," I say with a huge smile as Lily, Lucy, and I sip our champagne and chat in the Dubrees' private jet on our way to Las Vegas. One of the benefits of marrying a billionaire, I suppose. But now that I've spent so much time with the brothers, it's not something that sticks out when you're with them. Until moments like these, of course. The men are also on board, caught up in their own conversation.

"I know. I still can't believe how long he's been gone. Hopefully he's made some progress. Any word?" Lily asks.

I sigh, hating the answer as much for myself as for Jackson. "No. He feels like he's in the right place, but still no sign of the guy. I'm worried for him. I'm not sure if he'll ever give up. I mean, seriously, he's been searching for almost four months at this point."

Lily gives me a sympathetic look. "That's hard, but it has to be just as challenging for you. What a mess. Have you talked to him about when you want to go home?"

The subtle look from Eli doesn't escape my attention. I'm sure he'd like an answer to that question as well. Not that it matters. I *will* go home at some point. No sense in starting something we can't finish. After that night at the restaurant, I finally confessed to Lily, who told me that Sebastian had known for a while but respected Eli's wishes not to say anything. She wasn't very happy with me or Sebastian for keeping it from her but took all of two seconds to forgive us. I'm not so forgiving, though, and still pissed that we were outed to everyone that night. It could've been avoided if he'd just kept his hands to himself—although it had its upside. I hadn't climaxed like that since… well, since the last time we were together, dammit.

"I can't give him an ultimatum. He's miserable without Mia, and I don't think he'll rest until he fixes the situation. He feels responsible, and I can't be the one to shut him down. Who knows, he said he's getting closer. Fingers crossed." I make the sign and gulp my champagne to swallow down the doubt.

"The guy is well hidden if Justin couldn't find him. I hope for your sake he pops up soon," Lucy adds. Eli referred Justin to Jackson, who hired him to do some research and security detail while he was seeing Mia, knowing she was in trouble. Unfortunately, Mia's situation was dire, and it didn't end well… for any of us.

"Cheers to that." Holding my glass up, Lucy meets me in the middle. I turn my head slightly to Eli's watchful eyes, knowing he doesn't share the sentiment.

Jackson met us in the lobby, and after checking in and dropping our stuff in the rooms, the guys went one way, and we went another. I was worried about being here with Eli and if it would be hard to resist him in this environment. There's something about Vegas and losing your inhibitions, that's for sure. But so far, we haven't had a moment alone or an opportunity for funny business. Hopefully it stays that way.

Seeing my brother again was bittersweet. I've missed him, but the shell of himself he's become is disheartening. It's healthy for Jackson to spend time with his friends and get out of his head for a while. I couldn't imagine being stuck in a continual state of dread like he's been. I'm glad they're doing something exhilarating today and racing cars around a track—anything to free him from the constant pressure he's facing.

In the meantime, the girls and I are shopping. And when I say shopping, I mean hanging out like old times, gossiping, griping, and drinking. I didn't know how much this was needed until now. With Lily and Sebastian joined at the hip, it's a little more difficult these days. Not that I'm complaining—okay, maybe a little—but if Lily's happy, and anyone with half a brain can see that she is, then I'm happy.

"Cici, you and I have something else in common. Did Lily tell you that my parents suck too? Seriously, if my mom were here right now, all she'd be doing is harping on me about my order, so much that I probably would have ordered the salad just to make her stop. What's the deal with yours?" Lucy says in between bites of her fettuccini Alfredo.

Why her mom would be harping is beyond me. I've gotten to know Lucy while I've been back and adore her. She's perfectly suited to be Lily's *backup* BFF, and I've internally given my approval, adding her to our circle. There's only one other friend of Lily's I'm waiting to meet because she's so busy with her kids.

They're not for everyone. Children, I mean. The thing is… okay, I'll admit it: They're not for me. But now that I've thought about it, I'm excited for Lily. I'll be the cool aunt who spoils them and happily sends them home. Only when they're old enough to appreciate me as someone who gives it to 'em straight. Someone who doesn't coddle them or sugarcoat everything. They will love their Aunt Cici, and I will love them right back. A picture forms in my head of us singing at the top of our lungs and dancing on beds like Julia Roberts in whatever movie that was. Then I'll bring them back to their mom and be childless and carefree once more.

"First, your mom is crazy. You *do not* need to watch what you eat. Your figure is phenomenal. But fuck our moms, right? As far as my parents go, they're tough in a disapproving sort of way. They weren't terrible growing up. In fact, they were great, but they became a nightmare when I was old enough to think for myself and they disagreed with those thoughts. They didn't support me so much. Long story short, we haven't spoken in over a year, and it sucks."

"What happened to make you stop talking?" Lucy asks, genuinely interested, while Lily listens to her two besties learn more about each other.

"Well, I didn't enjoy working for my parents during high school, and then in college I realized it wasn't just my parents—it was the business itself. I flat-out don't like property management. When I told them I wanted to do something else, they were mad and felt like I didn't appreciate what they'd worked their whole lives to pass on to us. I tried to convince them I was appreciative, but they didn't view it that way and took my decision to go into real estate as a slight to them. They said that since I didn't want to work in the family business, I didn't deserve any of its benefits and cut me off from their support. Well, joke's on them, because not only am I taking care of myself, but I'm doing something I love."

Lucy holds her glass up, followed by Lily and me, raising ours to meet it. "Cheers," we all say simultaneously before taking another drink of champagne, ending in giggles. This has been the best day ever. The only thing that would make it better is if Poppy were here. Then we could bring all our girlies together. I can't wait to introduce her to everyone; hopefully she visits before I leave.

"Amen, sister. That's exactly how I feel. My parents wanted me to marry someone they 'deemed worthy,' but everyone they deemed worthy was a certifiable asshole who'd either beat their wife or cheat on them. So fuck them. We know what's best for us. We get to choose. We're the only ones who make our life choices. Who's with me?" Lucy's funny and sooo my type of girl. All right, we might be a bit tipsy… or drunk—whatever you want to call it.

"Hear, hear! I'm the only one who gets to tell me what to do!" I clink my glass with Lucy's while Lily cowers next to us. "Come on, Lily. Toast to being a badass bitch," I encourage.

"What if I don't want to be a badass b? I mean, yeah, we're talking about parents here, but I can't relate to that. I've had my taste of independence. Is it bad that I *enjoy* depending on Sebastian now? It's sort of… nice."

Lucy and I look at each other for a second and burst out laughing. Only the two of us would ever understand Lily. We know how Sebastian and Lily work, and it happens to be fricking adorable. I'm not sure how those two found each other, but fate must have stepped in.

"Lily, you're precious, and I fully support your übersubmissive, kinky lifestyle if that's what floats your boat. But if a man tried to control my life, I'd kick him in the nuts right before I kicked him to the curb. That doesn't mean I won't continue indulging in your stories and enjoy living vicariously through you," I tease.

"You wouldn't have to live vicariously through me if you gave in to a certain someone…," she says suggestively.

"Ohhh, that's right," Lucy interjects, having heard some of the details from Lily already. "Why aren't you and Eli a thing yet? Wait. Before you answer that, did Lily tell you I had the hots for him way back when? Like, I couldn't even make eye contact with him, I was so infatuated with the man. Then Justin showed up one day, and I was like, Eli who?" She cracks up. "Okay, now you can answer. What's the deal between you two?"

Lily definitely found an alternate for me since I moved away, which I'm not sad about in the least. I'm happy she has someone to keep her real. That girl, she's too sweet for her own good. With Sebastian and now Lucy, I like knowing she's taken care of.

"Okay, first of all, there won't be *a thing* between me and Eli. And second, what do you mean you had the hots for him? When?" This is news to me. Lily did not tell me this juicy bit of gossip.

"When I was Sebastian's assistant, Eli's desk was down the hall, and every time he walked by, I swear, I'd cream my panties. Sorry, TMI. But that man seriously got my juices flowing. He was sooo off-limits, though. I basically made a fool of myself whenever he was around. But, like I said, that was eons ago. Back to you, when did you two hook up?"

"Which time?" Lily asks sarcastically while laughing. "They go way back. As far back as when Sebastian and I first met."

"Seriously? You and Eli have been seeing each other for that long?" Lucy asks incredulously.

"No. We hooked up back then, and that's it. We are not, nor were we ever, seeing each other." I give Lily a pointed look. "Nothing is happening between us."

"Right. So you haven't done anything since you've been back? And you said it's been four months? How is that possible when your best friend is engaged to his brother?" Lucy isn't letting up.

"I'm not saying it's been easy. I mean, he's sex on a stick. But other than a couple of encounters, we—"

"Whoa, whoa, whoa. Spill, sister. What *encounters*, and why have you not tapped that since you've been back? Especially when you've already tasted the Kool-Aid?" All right, so Lucy has no idea what happened recently. *Love you, Lily.*

"We've kissed, and he's given me an orgasm. That's it. I was this"—my thumb and forefinger go up an inch apart—"close to letting him come to my place and finish the job, but before I made a bad decision, I called it a night." Lucy opens her mouth to speak, but I put a hand up to stop her. "Listen, we have a history, and I'm allergic to commitment. Eli's a relationship kind of guy. It's just not feasible. Not only am I leaving, but he's Sebastian's brother. That would be awkward at future family functions." Okay, that's the lamest excuse I could come up with, but it's worth a shot.

Lucy laughs. "You mean their family of two? And I'm not sure what planet you've been living on, but Eli is not a long-term type of guy. He's a playboy. You might as well have some fun while you're here, especially if he's game," Lucy says.

"Holy shit, you sound like the man himself." I laugh and down my drink, tipping my head back to catch the last drop.

"I agree with Lucy. It hasn't been awkward so far. I don't see why it would be if you both go into it knowingly. What's the problem?" Lily asks.

"The problem is, you guys are familiar with that player side of him, but I've experienced the more serious side, and he'll end up wanting a commitment. I'm not interested." *Or possibly incapable— one of the two.*

"That sounds like a you problem. Eli's a big boy. If he knows you're not the settling type and still wants a little action, then that's his decision, and you should go along for the ride." Man, Lucy's a ballbuster. And since I have no sound argument for that annoyingly rational observation, it's time to change the subject.

"Well, you know what I think? I think we should probably go sleep these drinks off before we doll ourselves up for the big night ahead of us. Who'll be the hottest chicks on the dance floor tonight?" I hold my fist out.

"Us," Lucy says while Lily simultaneously responds, "We will." They bring their fists up to bump with mine.

"Let's do it," I finish off, more than ready to go face-plant into my pillow. Lily and I tend to overindulge in day drinking whenever we do it, which, thank God, isn't very often.

Several hours later, after a nap and one of the best dinners I've ever had, we're in the VIP section at one of the hottest clubs in Vegas thanks to the Dubree brothers' connections. It just so happens to be in our hotel, which is super convenient.

We girls are on the dance floor while Justin is off to the side, keeping a close eye on us. I think he's the unofficial bodyguard for the evening. The rest of the guys are within eyesight, and Sebastian has had his head in Lily's direction most of the night. I've also noticed that Eli's been keeping his eye on me, scowling whenever I'm approached. Not that I've been paying too close attention or anything.

The ladies have been sticking together and only dancing with one another, turning away the men who've tried to make their way in. It's Lily's night, and no one's here for a hookup. Well, I'd certainly be up for it, but not with Eli here. I'm destined for celibacy until I go back home to Bozeman. However, after my talk with Lily and Lucy earlier, I'm reconsidering the Eli situation.

Speaking of, out of the corner of my eye, I see Eli and Jackson walking toward the exit of the club. After telling the girls I'm taking off, I rush to catch up.

"Hey, where are you guys going?" They pause and turn to face me.

"Jackson had a bit much, so I'm helping him to his room," Eli answers with his hand on my brother's arm to steady him.

"S'all good. I can make it," Jackson adds in, clearly drunk as he staggers on his feet.

"Geez, Jackson, drink much?" I go to Jackson's free side and take his other arm. "I can take him up so you can stay with the guys," I say to Eli.

"I'm not leaving you alone to wrangle a 180-pound man of steel to his room. What if he passes out on the way?" Eli asks.

"Then I'll have the staff help. It's fine, I've got him."

"Hey, guyz, I'm right heeere," Jackson splutters.

We both ignore him.

"Cici, quit being stubborn. You can go with me or stay and dance—the choice is yours," Eli states firmly and starts walking again, dragging my brother along, which causes me to follow since I'm holding on to Jackson.

"Argh. You're so infuriating," I say as I trudge along, trying to be helpful and realizing that Eli was right—no way could I have handled Jackson alone.

"Surrry, sis. Didn't mean t'ruin yer night. I haven't drunk in a while." Jackson laughs. "Get it? Drunk in a while, and I'm drunk."

"How are you such a lightweight with all this muscle on you?" I ask as we make our way through the casino toward the elevators.

"He had a lot at dinner and then pounded a couple more here. I think it's been some time since he's let his guard down," Eli answers for him.

"Can't let my guard down. Too important," Jackson mumbles.

"Jackson, I'm sorry. This must suck for you," I say sympathetically. He's really upset. He doesn't typically overindulge.

The minute we enter the elevator, Jackson slumps against the wall and hangs his head. With his eyes closed, he looks like he's passed out standing up.

"You still think you could've handled him yourself?" Eli asks smugly.

"No. You win. Happy now?"

"Not yet, but the night's still young." The sexual tension just engulfed the small space.

"Well, you can go back out and find someone to make you happy after he's settled. We are in Vegas, so I'm sure there're plenty to choose from."

"The only woman I want is right here." His look is smoldering, causing my panties to go up in flames.

Oh God. I really hope Jackson's not listening. "Oh," I whisper right as the elevator opens.

"All right, big guy, time to move," Eli says as he hoists Jackson's arm up and over his shoulder, helping him out of the elevator while Jackson lumbers along. Eli hands me the key he's holding. "Room 3817."

We trudge toward his room, where I swipe the card and hold the door open for them. Eli supports Jackson, going straight to the bed and pulling the covers back before Jackson flops down, mumbling what I think is a thank-you. Seconds later, he's passed out. I go to work on one shoe while Eli gets the other.

"Thanks, and thanks for helping him. Why didn't Braden do it?" I ask without thinking, and I instantly regret it.

Eli quirks a brow. "Would you rather have Braden up here with you?"

"No," I protest adamantly. "It's just that he's Jackson's best friend, and you're here for your brother. He's the more logical choice."

"Well, out of the two of us, I'm the logical one since it was my idea for Jackson to call it a night. Thus, I'm the one who wrangled him out. Plus, Braden's busy trolling, and I figured I'd let him have some fun. You've been away from San Diego a long time, Cici. Our circle has tightened in the last year."

Jackson snores loud enough to wake the neighbors, and we both laugh.

"Come on. Let's let him be," Eli says as he puts his hand on my back and ushers me toward the door.

"Do you think he'll be okay? He won't puke and not wake up or anything, will he?"

"No. He's not that bad. If he pukes, it'll be in the morning when the hangover sets in. He'll be fine."

We step into the hallway and stare at each other in silence. I'm debating what my next move should be. I'm still on the fence about keeping my distance, so I'm not sure whether to walk away and call it a night or seductively ask what his plans are for the rest of the evening. The silence is killing me, so I need to decide.

But when I open my mouth to speak, I don't get the chance.

"Fuck this." Eli's hand appears like lightning, gripping my head to hold me in place while his mouth crashes into mine. It's not sweet, it's not subtle, and it's certainly not slow. He palms my ass and pulls me into his groin, causing both of us to groan in unison from the sensation while devouring each other.

Screw the consequences; this is what I want. "Your room or mine?" I ask between kisses.

Eli jerks his head back in shock, making me smile in response.

"If we go to a room, I'm not letting you leave until I'm done with you. Once the door closes, there's no going back, Cici. You've made me wait too damn long not to have my way with you, and I'll go all night if that's what it takes. Are you ready for that?"

"I'm more than ready. I want it…. I want you."

"Damn, beautiful, it's about fucking time."

7

WHAT HAPPENS IN VEGAS

Eli

KEEP MY ARM AROUND HER AND WALK FORWARD WHILE DIGGING into my pocket for the key. "Lucky for you, we don't have far to go."

"Seriously? You're across the hall from Jackson? That's too close. He'll find out," she whispers as if he might hear.

"Worried you'll be heard across the hallway?"

"Well… yeah. Aren't you?"

Walking her backward into the room, I close the door before answering, "Normally, I would be, especially since I plan to have you screaming all night, but since he'll be dead to the world until morning, I'm not concerned in the slightest. Now, where were we, sexy?" I grip her head and continue where we left off outside before lifting the strap to the small clutch she's wearing and letting it drop to the floor. Now that we're safely behind closed doors, nothing stops me from reaching down to slide the sexy tight dress she's wearing up to her waist.

Watching this girl all night has been killing me. So many times I had to tamp down my possessiveness and stop myself from stomping over to stake my claim. Her sexy body gyrating all night to the beat of the music was more than I could take, and while she was busy dancing, I was envisioning all the filthy things I planned on once she gave in, which was going to be tonight, one way or another.

"Fuck, Cici. No panties?" I grab both globes of her ass and squeeze, loving the feel. Damn, I can't wait to play out all the fantasies I've had for the last few months, and this rear end has starred in quite a few.

"Can't with this dress."

"Guess you just saved yourself a pair, then," I say right before I bring my fingers straight to her core and plunge two in with no pretense.

"Oh God." Her head goes back as she thrusts her hips forward for more. I'll give her exactly what she wants. Fast, thorough, rough, and hard. We were made for each other in the bedroom. Hell, I'm pretty sure we were made for each other out of it, too, but she refuses to entertain the idea, so if this is all I can get for now, then I'll fucking take it.

"Damn, baby, I can't wait to fuck you. You've kept me waiting way too long for this pussy."

"Sorry, so sorry. No more waiting." She's quivering around my fingers already.

I could have her coming in seconds, but I think I'll drag it out. It's almost as much of a disappointment for me to pull my hand away as it is for her, except I know what's coming, so I can take it.

"Eli...," she whines as I pull out.

"Hmmm, I think it's only fair you're left wanting after the past few months I've endured, don't you?"

"Please…. I said I'm sorry."

"You're going to be—I can promise you that." With that, I bend down and sling her over my shoulder with her ass in the air. I can't resist giving it a hard slap on the way to the bed to pull out the first scream of the night. "That's it, baby. Keep them coming. If your voice isn't hoarse by tomorrow, I haven't done my job."

She lets out another small squeal when I toss her onto her back. Every sound from her lips makes my dick pulse with need. It might be time for a quick release before I torture her anymore.

After removing her shoes, I move to my own, then undress fully while she observes, biting her lip. She goes to take her dress off, but that's not happening.

"No, leave it. This is my night. You do what I say when I say it. If you're a good girl, you'll be taken care of. If you're bad, well… we'll see what happens. And since I've been deprived for so long, I need some relief before we go any further."

"It *is* your turn in the grand scheme of things, but I'm sure you haven't bottled it all up for me. It's not like you're a monk or anything."

God, that smart mouth is trouble. Do I expose how deep my obsession goes or play it cool? Fuck it. That hasn't seemed to do anything for me so far, so starting at her ankles, I slowly caress up her legs and pause with my hands on her hips. With my thumbs pressing into the crease between her thighs, I lean forward to look her in the eyes.

"Do you really think I've been able to fuck another pussy while yours has been so close for the last four months?"

Her eyes go wide in shock. "What? You seriously haven't had sex with anyone while I've been home?"

Instead of answering, my hands continue to slide up, taking the dress with me as I go. The minute it slides over her bare breasts, I'm almost diverted from my plan. It takes everything to rein myself in and keep going. But it does make me pause for a detour. Instead of removing the dress entirely, I leave the neck in place, only bringing the bottom up to cover her face and pin her arms straight up with the tightness of the fabric around them.

"Eli, what are you doing? I can barely breathe," she says huskily, blindfolded by the fabric.

"You'll be okay for a minute. Long enough for me to sample these babies before I give *you* a taste of something." That should give her something to chew on for a minute.

My tongue flicks her nipple twice before I take the whole thing in and suck as hard as I can. God, having her in my mouth makes me want to suckle her like a baby while the other breast fits perfectly in my hand. She's so fucking soft and plump, I could stay here all night. Instead, I stay a few more minutes, moving from one breast to the other, massaging, squeezing, sucking, and licking while grinding my dick against her swollen pussy. Cici's telling sounds are what bring me to stop, however, because if I'm not mistaken, she's close to climaxing, and that's not happening yet.

"Dammit, Eli. You can't keep doing this to me." She wiggles, trying to work the dress up. Unfortunately for her, it's tight enough that she won't get anywhere unless I help.

"Oh, I definitely can, and I plan on doing it quite a few more times. Serves you right for what you've put me through."

"How many times do I have to say I'm sorry?"

"As many as it takes until I've forgotten what you're sorry for. You have a long way to go, baby. And right now, you have some making up to do." I sit up and move the dress over her head to uncover her face but leave it around her arms so they remain secure, and luckily, it's tight enough to do the job.

"You ready to use that mouth to *show* me you're sorry instead of telling me?"

The way her eyes glaze over is all the answer I need. I crawl up until my cock nudges her lips, my knees on either side of her face. My hands find hers while supporting my upper body as I look to the glorious sight below me.

"Open up, baby. Prove you're as good at sucking cock as I remember."

She licks her lips and then opens wide as I slowly slide in. *Fuuuck.*

"Lucky for you, this probably won't take long, but I won't go easy on you. I'm teaching this mouth a lesson. Maybe you'll think twice before telling me no next time, huh?" I ask as I retract and push in at a leisurely pace.

She whimpers in response, her hips undulating in desire.

"I bet you wish you had your hands free to touch yourself, don't you? Is your pussy desperate? Good, you need a taste of how my cock's felt ever since you came back. Everything it wanted, within reach, but no satisfaction."

Her eyes squeeze shut at the same time as her legs. This is pure torture for her and fucking paradise for me. I've never experienced anyone close to Cici in the bedroom, and I'm not sure how I've held off this long. But now that I've confirmed my memory wasn't exaggerated, I don't think I'll be refraining from here on out.

"All right, baby, you're too damn sexy to hold back any longer. Take a deep breath." I pull out for a second so she can breathe before sliding back in. A groan escapes from the feel of her slick tongue on my cock.

"Fuck, Cici, your mouth is like heaven. I've missed this." I can't hold myself back from quickening the pace as my pleasure intensifies. My hips start moving naturally, fucking her face as I would her pussy, hitting the back of her throat. "Open that throat for me, baby. Take me in." My grunts match each thrust, and her occasional gag only encourages me more.

"That's it, baby. You take my cock so fucking good." My eyes are locked on my cock sliding in and out.

Knowing I'm close, I pull out to let her breathe. One breath, two, then three before I plunge back in and hold it deep, feeling the sweep of her soft tongue back and forth.

"I'm almost there, fuck. You ready for me?" I pump twice more. "Oh God. I'm coming. Fuuuck… fuck, fuck." My hips buck with each pulse. "That's it, baby, suck it down. Fuck. Yes. Uhhhh." The last pulse shoots down her throat, and I pull out, letting her catch her breath while I catch mine. "Holy mother of God, I haven't orgasmed like that since the last time I came in your mouth. Christ, woman. You've seriously wrecked me." I flop to the side, panting.

"Well, good, because I'm dying over here. Are you going to free my arms now?"

"Negative. Let's go for round two," I say while internally laughing, hopping up to grab a warm washcloth from the bathroom.

"*What?* You're joking."

This time, I chuckle out loud. I certainly wouldn't turn down a repeat performance. However, I'm not a sadist, and her mouth needs a rest—along with some care. "No, but I'm not undoing your arms. I'm not even close to done with you yet." I return and gently clean around her mouth, messy from drool and cum.

As soon as I'm finished, my little spitfire keeps prodding. "What's next on the agenda, then? An orgasm for Cici?"

Throwing the washcloth aside, I lean down and brush her swollen lips with my own, biting the bottom one before retreating, earning a pout when an idea starts to form. "Let's see… you've been close, what, two times? That's not even near what you deserve. Let's make it a game—why don't you keep count?"

"Eliii…."

At that point, I climb between her legs and push them wide, bringing her knees up before diving straight to the feast awaiting. She's sopping wet, making my cock come to life only minutes after release. The thought of penetrating her is almost enough for me to forgo her torment, but not quite. I have free rein since her hands can't reach my head to hold me where she wants, which means her begging is relentless.

I pop my head up. "Cici, the more you ask, the more I'll torture you. Are you ready to take what I give without whining, or do you need some help with that?"

"The only thing you need to help me with is bringing me to climax. Come on, Eli, pleeease?"

"Even though I do love hearing you beg, we'll save that for later. Right now, I want to focus on my treat. So let's take care of the distraction." I grab the neck of the dress to work it back down over her face, but this time, I stop right at her mouth, bunching the fabric between her lips. She's now blindfolded and gagged with her arms secured while the rest of her is gloriously at my mercy. She couldn't have picked a better dress for the occasion. This almost makes the wait worth it.

Cici tries talking to no avail, and her frustration is evident. "Shhh. Be glad you have something to look forward to, Cici. I didn't have the same privilege." She finally quiets.

Instead of returning to dessert, I give the beauties up top some additional love. They're too tempting to do otherwise. I work my tongue around each nipple, flicking them after, then sucking and kneading in turns. Pinching one hard makes her squeal through her gag, and I can't resist checking if her pussy is reacting as well. My hand reaches down and is rewarded by the moisture coating the apex of her thighs. Plunging straight in, her walls flex. She'll be coming within seconds, so after three pumps and a few flicks of my fingers, I retract before her orgasm hits, doing the same thing a few seconds later, only to pull back to her neediest groan yet.

"Since you're otherwise detained, I'll keep count. That's four times you've been brought to the edge. Should we make it an even ten before I let you come? We do have all night." Her muttering of protest makes me chuckle as I head south.

She smells divine—the sweetest brand of pussy I've had. I leave my fingers right where they are to continue teasing while I give attention to her clit. The swollen bud enlarges even more when I suck on it, causing Cici to drive her hips up in earnest. I love having her at my mercy… to touch, play with, and do anything I want. But what I love most is her willingness to let me. Knowing Cici as I do, this isn't just me taking control; this is her allowing me to have it, and frankly, that's what turns me on the most. Shit, it doesn't just turn me on—it makes me feel ten feet tall to be the man capable of taming this fireball, to be the one she deems worthy.

After two more close calls, I slide my hand to her anus and rim the opening. Her cries could be protest or encouragement at this point—I'm not entirely sure. But knowing the result will be positive either way, my objective doesn't change.

"Your ass is mine, baby. It would be part of your punishment tonight, except I happen to know how much you love having my cock here." I circle the opening, making her squirm. "Have you had anyone else in your ass since I trained you to take me?"

When she shakes her head no, the pride that surfaces is overwhelming, and I have the urge to lock this woman away so no one else will have her. For now, though, I'll revel in owning just a piece because all I want to do is sink into the hole that only I've been in.

"Hmm, then I won't stretch you out too much, and we can make that part of your punishment after all."

Spearing her core with my tongue, my middle finger slides in the back door, but when I sense the approaching climax, I freeze.

"That was fast. Somebody misses ass play, huh? We're up to seven, baby. How frustrated are you?" She screams through her gag. "It's only fair you get a taste of your own medicine." I laugh at her angry, garbled words. "I know better than anyone what that's like."

I carefully work up to two fingers in her ass. I'm careful only because I'm worried about sending her over the edge, not hurting her. All talk of punishment aside, my intention isn't to cause her pain, so a little stretching before I do take her here is necessary, especially since it's been more than a year since the last time. Fuck, at this rate, I won't last more than a minute, and I still have two more times to edge her after another close call when I added the second finger.

She's a puddle of frustration. Between the moisture at her core and the sheen covering her body, she's in sweet agony. It's time to sheath myself and take this to the next level. I rise from the bed and find the box of condoms in my bag. I'm always prepared for my wish to come true, and I did have an inkling it might be in Vegas. They don't call it Sin City for nothing. Returning to bed, I raise the dress, finally removing it completely.

"Eli, dammit, I can't take any more. Please let me orgasm." Her hand darts to her pussy.

"Do it, and that's the only one you'll have tonight," I say with authority as I roll the condom on next to her. She stares at me, her hand paused on her clit. She's torn between instant gratification or the result only I can provide.

"You'll regret it. You know it. I know it. Don't waste all that hard work on a quick, paltry release compared to the mind-bending one you're so close to getting. I promise it'll be worth the wait."

She groans in frustration and pulls her hand back.

With the condom on, I crawl back between her legs, hovering on my elbows. "Hi, baby. You having fun yet?"

"You better make it worth it and give me the most incredible orgasm I've ever had in my life after this."

"That's all you want? How about multiple?" I lean down to take her mouth in a sensual kiss this time, reveling in the fact that she's here with me, under me, about to be connected to me and wrapped around my cock. Not able to wait a second longer, I reach down and rub along her slit, coating the tip in her juices before placing the head at her opening.

Fuck. Knowing I'm finally here makes me pause and take in the moment. My head lifts to look her in the eyes as I breach her entrance. She gasps as I slide in excruciatingly slow, savoring the feeling of being right where I belong. The words I want to say are bubbling under the surface, fighting to break free, but that's a bad idea if I want this to happen again. She's not ready. Hell, she may never be ready. So instead of voicing them, I try to convey how I feel with my eyes.

She knows. The fear is written all over her face. The hesitation, the second-guessing… regret. It's palpable, and I can't let her go that far inside her head, or I'll lose her before I even get a chance to keep her. Time to go back to fun Eli, dominant Eli, and pull her out of the spiral she's in before it's too late. When her eyes close to block me out, I retract and slam back in hard, causing them to open wide.

"That's right, baby. Keep your eyes open. Let me see those beautiful blues so I don't lose you. Fuck. You're so sexy," I tell her as I continue pumping in and out. I'm barely hanging on, tempted to finish us off, but I'm damned determined to hit my mark. I reach between us and barely touch her clit when her eyes roll up, forcing me to stop. Perfect timing—a couple more thrusts, and I might've blown my load.

"Only one more, and I'll give you your reward. But first, I need that ass in my face." I pull out and lean back on my heels. "Flip over, baby. On all fours."

She quickly complies, just as eager, if not more so, to have me back inside her.

"Fuck, baby, I've missed this fine ass." I slap it and then part her cheeks. "Fucking beautiful." My thumb pushes on her tight opening, causing her to moan.

"Eli, please stop looking and get busy."

"Sassy little thing. You're like a bitch in heat."

"Dammit, Eli, seriously, yes, I'm—"

I drive into her cunt hard, cutting her off. With powerful thrusts, I fuck her forcefully, almost punishing, taking out my frustration from the last year. Her screams echo in the room, and if I go any longer, the dam I've created is going to burst, and she has one last edging to go.

"Eli, yes, yes. Oh God, please don't stop. I'm right there. Oh fuck, yes, uh… ugh… noooo!" she whines in disappointment, practically in tears at this point. In fact, she might actually be crying. "Eli, please, seriously, I can't do it again. I can't. I need it." She *is* crying. And if I didn't know they'd be tears of joy within two minutes, I'd cradle her in my arms to make it go away. But only one thing can dry those tears.

"Shhh, Cici, it's okay. You did so well. That was your last one. It's time for your reward now. Is your ass ready to take my cock? You ready to come, baby?"

"Yes, please. I need it… so bad, it hurts."

"I know, baby. Let's come together, sweetheart." I slide my dick up and down over her pucker until I push slightly to breach the rim. "Oh fuck, baby. This'll be fast. Your ass is so fucking tight. You're such a good girl saving this hole for me."

Inching my way in to the sound of her moans and pleas is enough to do me in, which is why slow is the name of the game at this point. When I'm to the hilt, I pause a second to steady myself. Her ass is squeezing my cock like a vise, and it's all I can do not to come.

"Oh God, Eli. Please just fuck me. Let me orgasm."

"We're almost there, baby. Can you take me like you used to, huh?" With that, I slowly pull out and slam back in.

Her scream fills the room. "Fuck yes. Again," she demands.

"Hold on tight, baby." And I go for it, fucking her as hard as I can, holding her hips tight as I hammer home again and again. Her ass is taking my punishing thrusts like it was made for my cock. The sounds of my grunts fill the room along with her cries of pleasure. Within seconds, the orgasm rips through her, strangling my cock even more.

"That's it, baby. Now, give me another." Before her first climax is finished, I reach down between her legs and tease her clit, pulling a second, deeper one from her as I finally let go and spill everything I've got. It seems never-ending, even with my release earlier. My relief is exquisite, and after the last pulse, I slowly pull completely out before both of us crash to the bed, breathing heavily.

Pulling the condom off and setting it to the side for now, I roll over to drag Cici up against me. A calmness settles in from having her in my arms. "How do you feel?"

"Satisfied. Very satisfied."

I chuckle. "I'm glad. Me too. Thanks for hanging in with me."

"I knew you'd make it worth it, although I've certainly never had to wait that long. I can't believe you brought me to tears."

"I can't either." I chuckle and kiss the top of her head. "I would never hurt you on purpose. I knew when you reached your limit, and I would've stopped earlier, no matter what number we were at, if it had been sooner. I almost finished in your pussy, but good thing for you, that ass was way too tempting."

"No, it was a good thing for you." She nudges me with her shoulder.

"That it was." I squeeze her tight against me and pass out seconds later.

"Where do you think you're going?" I groggily ask upon opening my eyes to Cici, who is quietly searching for her shoes.

"I'm meeting Jackson for breakfast before we leave, and I can't exactly be walking out of your room at the same time as him. Besides, I need to shower first."

"Fair enough, but were you about to leave without saying good-bye? I thought we were past the awkward next-morning phase."

"You were sleeping, and I didn't want to wake you since we were up late last night. You have a habit of dragging things out these days. Not that I'm complaining. It was amazing, so… well worth it, but you sure do take your time."

"Well, maybe if you'd stop holding out on me, I wouldn't have to." After quickly throwing on a pair of shorts, I go to nuzzle her neck from behind, wrapping my arms around her middle. Fuck, she feels good—so good that I'm sure the tower between my legs doesn't go unnoticed.

"Eli… we shouldn't. Last night was… a moment of weakness. Like they say, 'what happens in Vegas stays in Vegas.' I think it's best to apply that motto here and forget this happened." She tries to pull away, but I hold tight, not ready to let her go.

"Cici, if you think it's possible to forget about last night, you're delusional. And if you can forget that easily, then my skills are lacking these days. Thanks for the heads-up."

"Eli, I'm serious." This time, she successfully extracts herself, going for the shoes she's spotted. "Nothing's changed—I'm still leaving. Let's chalk this up to being in the right place at the right time and move on." With her shoes on, she grabs her clutch and pauses at the door. "Okay?"

"I'll let it go for now, but this isn't over. What time are you meeting Jackson? You need me to stall him a bit so you can get ready?"

"No, I've got enough time. Thanks, though. And seriously, last night was incredible. If only I could clone you and take you back to Bozeman."

"So that I'd be here, jealous of my identical self? No thanks. How about you move back so you can have the original?"

"That's not an option, and you know it. Hey, let's end this on a good note, okay?"

"I think we ended on an excellent note if you ask me."

She gives me a look.

"Okay, okay," I say, putting my hands up. "Enjoy breakfast with your brother, and I'll see you when we head to the airport."

After the door closes, I use the bathroom before finding a shirt, putting on shoes, and crossing the hall to check on Jackson. I want to say goodbye before we take off, and I might not have a chance later since he's spending the morning with Cici.

Two whole minutes and several knocks later, a disheveled

Jackson finally opens the door, smelling like a bottle of booze and looking like hell.

"Holy shit, dude. I was gonna ask how you're feeling, but I guess I don't need to." He groans as I walk past him into the room.

"Fuck, I feel like death, although I probably deserve it after that display. Holy shit, man, why didn't you stop me?" He slumps down on the bed and hunches over with his head in his hands.

"I did. Evidently, not soon enough." Grabbing a water from the minibar, I unscrew the cap and hand it to him along with the pain pills I grabbed from my room.

"Thanks," he says, taking them and gulping down the whole water while I sit on the sofa. "I didn't mean to get that out of hand. It's been too long since I've let loose, and apparently, I've forgotten how to control myself. It was a nice distraction."

"I'm sure you needed it."

"Yeah, just not to that extent. I'm glad you got me to my room. The last thing I remember is making it to the elevator. Shit, I shouldn't have let Cici see me like that."

"Don't beat yourself up over it. You were fine. Just slurring and a bit unsteady on your feet. Nothing major. Cici felt bad more than anything." *Until I took her mind off it.*

"How's she doing anyway? You've been keeping an eye on her?"

I school my features as best I can before answering. She'd annihilate me if he found out about last night. "I've been trying to. She doesn't like being checked up on, that's for sure. Anyway, she's too excited about the wedding next week to dwell on anything else. Are you going to break the news to her that you're not coming?" Jackson and I talk frequently, so I've known for a while now that he wasn't planning on attending. I don't blame him. Seeing two people pledge their love is the last thing he needs while he's distraught, trying to get his girl back.

"Yeah, we're having breakfast. Shit, what time is it?" He grabs his phone and sighs in relief. "Thank God I didn't miss it. I've still got thirty minutes. Anyway, yeah. I'll tell her this morning. She won't be happy, but it is what it is."

"Are you any closer to finding this guy? You've been gone almost four months now. What's your plan? Has Cici said she's okay to stay longer?" Jackson's my friend, and I wanted to check on him and say goodbye, but I'd be lying if I said I didn't have an ulterior motive.

"I was planning to check in with her again at breakfast, but she said she'll stay as long as I need. She'd like answers as well, but I don't have any. All I can do is keep looking and following the scent. And let me tell you, it's faint. Right when I think I'm onto something, the trail dead-ends. The plan is to keep going until he turns up. Could be next week. Could be next month. Could be several. I've got nothing."

I stand and walk over to him as he rises. "I'm sorry, man. I wish I could do more to help."

He puts his hand on my shoulder. "Eli, I wouldn't even be *this* far if it weren't for your poker connections. I appreciate everything you've done. Don't worry, I'm not giving up hope. I'll find him sooner or later."

"You will. It's great to see you, but I don't want to be the reason you're late, so I'll let you be. You look like shit, dude." I lean in to hug him goodbye. "You smell like shit too."

He pushes me, telling me to leave so he can shower.

"Gladly. See you later," I say before walking back to my room.

Well, that answers that. Seems like I'll have Cici for a lot longer by the sound of it.

8

RAIN CHECK

Cici

"**G**OOD MORNING, CINDY. THAT WAS A CLEVER MOVE YOU made," I say as I pause at her desk on my way by this morning. She conveniently left thirty minutes early yesterday after asking my parents to stop by the office at five to sign something for the accountant. The sneaky woman has been trying for months to help mend the relationship between us, playing therapist by bringing the problem up while trying to convince me to talk to them. I'm sure they've experienced the same.

"It was, wasn't it? How did it go?" she asks curiously.

"Better than I would have thought. They were as surprised as I was, but with no one here as a buffer, we had to acknowledge one another."

"Exactly what I was going for. So what happened?"

"We're having dinner this weekend," I say with a smile.

What actually happened is that when I saw them, I realized I've really missed them, and I think they felt the same in return. After the initial shock, my mom came up and hugged me with tears in her eyes, which then caused me to get weepy. My dad was next, and with a lot of I miss yous and regrets, we agreed to have dinner to "get to know one another again." I thought that was fitting since we're both at different places in our lives now. They made sure to tell me there would be no lecturing and they're just genuinely interested in hearing about me. I'm looking forward to it but am keeping my expectations in check from experience.

She immediately lights up. "Wow. That's even better than I expected. Damn, I'm good. It's about time—that only took, what… five months?"

"I guess stubbornness runs in the family. My brother's a prime example of that right now." To my detriment.

At breakfast on our last day in Vegas, he told me he hadn't made considerable headway, but that he wasn't giving up and needed more time. He couldn't say how much more, but I'm under the impression that I'll be here for even longer than anticipated and that I should just come to terms with the fact that there's no end date in sight. This is also why mending fences with my parents is probably a good idea.

"Boy is that the truth. I've never known a more stubborn group of people. I'm happy to hear you've made a step in the right direction."

"All because of you. They told me you've been gushing about how well I've done in Jackson's absence."

"I may have mentioned it once or twice," Cindy says nonchalantly with a shrug.

"Or more like every time you talk to them. You've been plotting this since the day you returned."

"You can thank me later. Remember that they only want the best for you. Sometimes parents get so wrapped up in what they think the right path is, they forget there might be more than one."

Do we all become instantly wise when we have babies? "I'll try to remember that when they start lecturing me about my career choice."

"Something tells me they might not do that. Time heals all wounds, right?"

"I won't hold my breath, but thanks for the vote of confidence. They were a little more receptive, so who knows? Maybe they've come around. Either way, I'll let you know Monday."

"Good luck, Cici. I hope it goes well."

"Me too. Thanks, Cindy," I say, continuing into my office.

I'm hoping it goes smoothly. The last time we had a significant conversation, it ended badly, given we haven't spoken in over a year. Thank God I met Poppy when I moved to Bozeman and we became fast friends. Her family was my surrogate over the holidays and included me as their own. I'm sure they appreciated the distraction since their son couldn't come home last year while on duty overseas.

Speaking of—my phone buzzes almost immediately after sitting down with Poppy's picture lighting up the screen.

She starts talking a mile a minute the instant I answer. "You'll never guess what they said about you in the morning meeting. After asking for the millionth time when you're coming back and getting the same answer as always, Jim said, and I quote, 'It's going to be dark around here until our favorite ball of sunshine returns,' and everyone chimed in or nodded in agreement. I'm not the only one who misses you like crazy," Poppy finishes dramatically.

"Wow, I can't believe they said that. That's so sweet. Tell them I miss everyone and that I'm anxious to be back. I'm seriously considering calling it. It's not like Cindy couldn't handle things without me or Jackson. But it puts him at ease having me here, so I'm not sure what to do," I say, honestly torn between returning to Bozeman or staying longer.

"I'd love to decide for you, but I realize you have a lot to consider. I'm excited to hear how this weekend goes with your parents."

After getting home last night, I texted her about our run-in. "I'm more positive about it after talking to Cindy this morning. It sounds like she's gotten through to them more than I realized."

"I'm glad. It'll be better to put that to bed before you leave anyway. Speaking of putting things to bed, are you and Eli still going strong?"

"We're still friends with benefits, if that's what you mean. Same as before I moved to Bozeman but without having to hide it this time. That's been nice."

After we made it home from Vegas, I avoided him for a week until Lily and Sebastian's wedding, and then there was no getting around the inevitable. Between the rehearsal dinner, walking down the aisle together, and the reception afterward, it was obvious where we were heading. And that we did, straight to his bed the first night, and the second, then the third, and almost every night since. We came to an understanding that we might as well enjoy our chemistry while we could, but with no strings attached. And I've had no regrets, nor does my nether region—we're blissfully content these days.

"I'm sure more things than that have been nice. Is he trying for more or letting it rest for now?" Poppy asks, getting to the heart of the matter.

"It hasn't come up since we aren't seeing other people anyway. But it's not like he doesn't know I'm leaving."

"What he knows and wants could be entirely different things."

"Possibly, but it won't change the outcome."

"Well, at least you're getting all your filthy fantasies fulfilled in the meantime."

I laugh, agreeing wholeheartedly. "Amen, sister. What about you? Are you excited about your date tonight?" Poppy finally agreed to meet a guy she's been chatting with through the app she uses, which doesn't happen very often—as in this is only the third one this year.

"Sort of. I'm more nervous than anything. He could be

completely different in person than by text. I'm not getting my hopes up this time, that's for sure."

"You better go into it with a better attitude than that, or it *will* end up crappy. You bring about what you think about."

Poppy groans. "Yeah, yeah. Your life motto. But I'm picky. I need a guy who rocks my world, someone I'm so attracted to that I don't fix-ate on one or two negative things. This guy already has a yellow card, but I'm hoping he's as hot in person as his picture so I can overlook his unhealthy obsession with *Star Wars*," she grumbles, making me laugh.

"You're hilarious, but I agree with you…. He better be one hell of a hottie to ignore that. Geez, I need to come back so we can com-miserate about the male population over a bottle of wine at least once a week."

"You definitely do."

"Since I'm not there yet, text me ASAP and tell me how it goes," I say sternly.

"I will. Do I even have to ask what your plans are tonight, or do they involve Eli and a certain club he owns?"

"I'm that predictable, huh?"

"I would be, too, if I had access to sex on a stick," she says, mak-ing me cringe at the simplicity of her statement and all it leaves out.

A man who smells like him, touches like him, treats me the way he does, makes me feel treasured, and the scariest of all, causes me to want more than I can handle. That's the problem with the entire situ-ation. It's not just physical. Admitting that to myself is hard enough—there's no way I'd fess up out loud. I'm already aware of how difficult it will be when I leave, and if I validate my feelings by putting words to them, it'll be even worse. So while *I* know it's more than looks and great sex, I'll happily leave everyone else in the dark, wishing I were too.

"You'll find one, I'm sure of it. Keep the faith, and who knows?

Maybe your date tonight will turn out amazing, and it'll be love at first sight."

"Don't hold your breath. I can't be the cause of your early demise."

"If I don't hear from you, I'll assume you ended up at his place."

"Five date minimum, remember," she reminds me.

"Fine, I'll assume he abducted you and call the authorities."

"I'll text you, don't worry, Mom." Her eye roll is evident in her tone.

"You better."

"Good luck with your parents tomorrow. See ya."

"Bye, Poppy."

The rest of the day went smoothly, which I hope is a sign of how well the weekend will go. At least I have nothing to worry about tonight. Since the cat came out of the bag regarding Eli and me, it's become routine for us to meet Lily, Sebastian, Lucy, and Justin at the club on Fridays. We all hang out while the guys keep an eye on things during one of the busiest nights of the week, so it's a win-win. Braden joins us when he doesn't have a date lined up, and this must be one of those occasions, as he's already at our usual table alongside Lucy and her man.

"It's been a while. I was starting to think you were involved and the next time we saw you would be with a girl on your arm. No date tonight?" I ask Braden before saying hi to the others and giving Lucy a quick hug. Taking the seat across from him, I briefly glance around. Lily and Sebastian are on their way, and Eli must be off handling something because he texted earlier to say he was already here.

"No. This case I'm working on is a bitch, and I haven't had time for shit. Figured I'd meet you guys for a couple beers to take the edge off."

The waitress brings me a cosmo, knowing all our drink orders by now. I don't deviate often unless they order champagne for the night.

"That sucks. Though I heard Eli has gotten you out a bit recently."

"Yeah, someone has to keep an eye on that guy, and this one's too smart to do it," he says, pointing to Justin. "Sebastian's too busy, so that leaves moi." He shrugs. "That man is fucking reckless, but he sure comes up with some fun distractions—I'll give him that." Braden toasts the air and takes a swig of his beer.

"So I've heard. Where is he anyway? Have you seen him yet?" I glance around, trying to spot him.

"He was here earlier but got called downstairs. He'll be back soon, I'm sure," Justin says as he scans the club. "Oh, there he is." He points to the first-level bar.

I look behind me in the direction he indicates and watch Eli casually lean against the bar top, conversing with a woman. He's facing my way, and the woman's back is to me. She's a patron, not an employee, as indicated by the drink in her hand and how she's dressed to impress. My hackles rise before I immediately scold myself. I should not be jealous. It's not like we're committed or anything. And with me leaving soon, it makes perfect sense for him to start playing the field.

"You okay?" Braden asks with a chuckle.

When I turn around, I'm met with a knowing smirk, which only irritates me more. "I'm fine. Eli and I aren't serious. He can talk to whoever he wants, whenever he wants."

"The daggers you're shooting say something else entirely. Part of why I'm a shark in the courtroom is because I can read people, and your thoughts are loud and clear, babe."

"Don't 'babe' me, and leave your skills in the courtroom where they belong."

He puts his hands up, palms toward me. "Hey, no need to be defensive. You know… I have other skills I'd be happy to show you while Eli's occupied. You *were* hoping to sample the goods back in the day, if I remember correctly."

"Cut it out, Braden," Lucy scolds him.

He shakes his head and laughs while sipping his beer before we turn to look at the couple in question. My stomach turns sour when Eli throws his head back in laughter at something the woman said to him. When her hand reaches his shoulder as she doubles over, the daggers Braden mentioned sound darn good right now.

"Hey, guys, sorry I'm late. Where's Eli? I thought he was already here," Lily says as she bounces up to the table, hugging Lucy, then me before sitting.

Glad to be distracted from the scene below, I answer as nonchalantly as I can muster while slyly changing the subject, "He's downstairs at the bar. What about Sebastian? Did he go straight to work?" He hangs out with us, but only after he makes the rounds. They say things run smoother when the owners are present, so they make it known when they're here. However, the only person I see Eli making it known to is the bimbo at the bar.

Cici, stop it. She's not a bimbo, just a normal girl looking for a hookup.

"He did, but it won't take long." Lily peers over the railing and makes a face when her gaze lands on Eli. "Oh, who's he talking to?" So much for avoiding that one.

"Not sure, but I should go and find out. He might need a hand." Braden smirks. "Want to join me?" he offers to Justin, who declines, before walking off to join Eli.

"Who is she?" Lucy asks.

"She hasn't turned around for a good look, but I doubt I'd know her anyway. It's probably just another admirer trying to make a move. No big deal." I'm glad Lily's on the side of the table away from the banister to keep my head in the opposite direction from staring.

Lily, however, has a direct line of sight and keeps her eyes trained on them. "Wait, she just turned to look at Braden, and I swear that's Rebecca." I give her a blank look. "The girl from your office who filled in for Cindy when Mia left?"

"Seriously?" I swivel around quickly, and sure enough, it is her. She's angled so she can talk to both men. "Oh my God, you're right."

Did she know he was the owner here? I remember our conversation like it was yesterday. She asked if she could go for him, but I scared her away. All she'd have to do is a Google search to find out this was his club. Would she have done that, or am I overthinking it?

"He met her once in your office, didn't he? I bet they're just saying hi. He wouldn't be picking up a woman when you're together," Lily says confidently.

Poor Justin silently sips his beer, stuck at the table with three women.

"We aren't together. We're just having fun while I'm here. It's nothing. He's free to do what he wants."

Both Lily and Lucy give me looks that says I'm full of shit, and the way Justin raises his brows says he agrees, not to mention the cough he lets out that distinctly resembles the word *bullshit*. He's quieter than the rest of us, but when he does engage, he's funny.

"I mean it. It's no big deal. And anyway, she's sweet. She'd be perfect for Eli… someone he could be with." The minute the words are out, I'm sick. I need to leave stat before my lunch ends up on the table. "Ugh. I need to use the bathroom. Could you watch my drink and purse for a minute?" I'm out of my seat before finishing the question and leave the second they agree.

Racing into the single stall, I lean against the door while clutching my stomach, trying for slow, deep breaths. What the hell is happening? I'm not the jealous type. Hell, you'd have to be monogamous for that to happen, and I've never been. And we certainly aren't, so why am I acting like this? I feel so stupid. I'm the one who won't commit, so it shouldn't bother me that he's talking to another woman. A woman who would welcome a relationship with Eli. A woman who could love him freely, the way he deserves to be loved. Oh God, could I…?

I can't even finish the question in my own mind as my breathing turns erratic and tears threaten my eyes. I've got to be hormonal or something. This is not normal behavior. Whatever it is, I better work on pulling myself together. If I'm gone too long, Lily might think something's wrong. She probably already does since she knows me so well. I'm sure I'm not fooling her. According to Braden and Justin, I'm not fooling anyone. Still, it doesn't matter. I'm leaving. We aren't a thing. My feelings, or whatever is going on, do… not… matter. We should stop messing around before this gets more convoluted than it already is.

Yes. That's exactly what needs to happen. I look in the mirror, silently lecturing myself. We need to stop sleeping together and move on. He can see whomever he wants, and I'll return to Bozeman and get on with my life. Decision made, I stand tall, square my shoulders, and take another deep breath before walking out.

Eli leans on the opposite wall outside the door, his legs and arms casually crossed. He comes forward and pulls me into a hug. "Hey, cutie. Lily told me you were here, so I thought I'd steal a moment alone. Come on." He walks me around the corner, past the roped barrier for personnel only, and into one of the offices lining the hallway.

Gripping my head, he tilts it and brushes his lips against mine. "I've been dying to have you in my arms since you left this morning." He deepens the kiss, and I'm putty in his hands, forgetting about the pep talk from seconds ago.

A minute later, he leans back and stares at me while caressing my face. "You helped me through my day today, so thank you. All I had to do was think of you. And of this—" He kisses me passionately. "—and this—" He reaches under my dress and prods my opening while rubbing his palm on my clit. "—and whatever stress I was feeling vanished."

I moan into his kiss as he continues touching me.

"I'll thank you properly at home," he whispers in my ear.

How can he say something so meaningful, then lewd from one sentence to the next, and act like it's nothing? Does he realize the effect his words have on me? What he's doing to my mental state? He must not have a clue. It's now or never.

"Eli, I think we need to slow down," I say, pushing his hand away.

"Okay, baby. I can wait 'til later," he says huskily, breathing against my neck and giving me chills.

"No, I mean about seeing each other. We should take it easy."

His head jerks back in shock. "Where did that come from?"

"We're spending too much time together, and it's not fair to you. I'm leaving soon. You should be dating and finding someone you can have a real relationship with, not just a temporary fuck buddy."

His features turn angry. "You and I both know that's not what you are, Cici. Call it whatever you need to make yourself feel better, but I'm dating you. We may have an expiration, but that doesn't mean we can't enjoy the time we *do* have together. I'm not ancient, and I'm not settling down anytime soon. This is what I want for now."

"That's the thing. It shouldn't have to be *for now*. There are plenty of women like Rebecca who could make you happy, and you're wasting your time on me."

"Is that what this is about? Rebecca? Cici, she saw me while I was talking with the bar manager and remembered me from your office. She reintroduced herself is all."

I bet she did.

"And actually, she asked about you, and I told her we've been seeing each other." He brushes the hair from my face and gives me a peck on the lips.

"That's the problem. We aren't, though. We're just passing time. I'm holding you back from meeting a nice woman like her. Someone you can have more with."

"Cici, we are not just passing time—we're enjoying the time we have. Why would I want any other woman when there's an amazing one right here?"

I growl in frustration. "You're not listening to me. That's the whole point. I shouldn't be here and won't be for much longer. It'll only be harder when it's time for me to leave if we keep this up."

"Cici, when my parents died, it taught me not to let life pass by and enjoy everything it has to offer before it's too late. Right now? I'm enjoying you before it's too damn late, and I'm sure as hell not seeing anyone else while we're together. Trust me, I know what's coming. You have no intention to stay. I'm not ignorant of the situation, but I'm also not giving you up until I have to. Soak that in, baby, because you're mine, and I'm yours until the time comes to let you go."

"But—"

"Cici, there's nothing more to say, and I don't want to hear another word about slowing down. You're coming to my place tonight so I can remind you that's *not* what you want." He kisses me once more, this time with force, gripping my neck firmly and claiming my mouth like it's his right. My knees go weak, and I whimper at the loss when he breaks our connection. "More of that later. We better go back before they send a search party." He winks before dragging me away.

I'm no match for this man. He's won another round.

"Cici, we're really glad you came over for dinner tonight. I only wish we hadn't waited so long. It's wonderful to have you home." My mom hugs me as our time comes to an end.

The beginning of the night wasn't as awkward as it could have been thanks to Cindy's staged run-in the other day at the office. I'm glad they put their opinions aside and asked about my life in Bozeman. They were genuinely interested in what I was doing and, thankfully, seemed to have no bitterness. They even commented how they'd like to have me back permanently. They never apologized for their behavior, though, and that bothers me. There's something else that's eating at me, too, but I haven't put my finger on it yet. All in all, the night was a success, and I'm relieved we're talking again.

"Thanks, Mom. It's nice to *be* home. I'm glad we cleared the air."

Then my dad takes a turn to squeeze me goodbye. "We love you, sweetheart. I might have an idea where your stubbornness comes from." We both chuckle.

"Yeah, that's what Cindy said. I love you guys."

"You'll be here next week for dinner?" my mom asks once more on my way out the door. We've decided to do this weekly until I leave.

"Yep. Let me know if you want me to bring anything. Goodnight," I say as I fly out the door and shut it behind me. I'm anxious to get to Eli's, which has become the norm these days. Tonight, he's waiting to hear how it went, and I'm looking forward to his take on things.

Eli listens as I recount the details of our reconciliation while we sit in the living room and share a bottle of wine. I've been here so much recently, it's starting to feel like home, which is very dangerous.

"They said they were proud of me for stepping in and handling things so well. That's great and all, but I want them to be proud of *my* accomplishments, not only what they deem worthy," I explain, getting closer to what annoyed me about the whole thing.

"It's a promising start after a huge rift like that. I'm sure it won't go away overnight," Eli states calmly.

"You're right. But it's hard to let go of the resentment I've been carrying for so long."

"Letting go and forgiveness are two different things. To forgive them doesn't mean you have to let it go, but it could help you move on. Forgiving someone is difficult, but the more you practice, the easier it becomes. And remember, it's probably just as hard for them to acknowledge the very things they've been against for so long. I imagine with time, you'll both learn to move past it."

"You sure it was an MBA you got, not a psychology degree?"

He chuckles. "I'm sure, but I'd probably be a decent counselor after seeing one for the last three years. One of my dad's stipulations in the will was weekly sessions to inherit."

"That's a great idea."

"He knew we'd need it after what he planned. He thought of everything before he pulled the trigger—I'll give him that. And honestly, I'm thankful for the requirement. It didn't only help with the grief Sebastian and I went through, but in other unexpected ways. He and I understand each other better, and surprisingly, it's been great for business. It helps me to understand where others are coming from and how to communicate with different personality types, which comes in handy during negotiations." He winks.

I've simply been staring, mesmerized. He has confidence in his words and wisdom in his voice that go beyond his age. I suppose that can happen when the responsibility of a billion-dollar company lands on your shoulders right after college. Losing both parents within such a short time must have been devastating. One from a brain aneurysm, and what most don't know is that the other was intentional two years later—from heartbreak.

"What?" he asks. I must have been silent too long as I pondered how to word my next question.

"Were you angry at your dad for what he did? Or are you still?" If he can let go of that, then there's got to be hope for me.

He takes a sip of wine, and I can see the gears spinning while he formulates his answer.

"I was initially. I mean, there we were, recently home from getting our MBA, thinking we would play a bit while learning the ropes, and then bam, suddenly we're in charge. We were both angry at first, but Sebastian's anger turned into a sense of abandonment, which made him never want to love anyone he could lose, whereas mine turned more into curiosity. What would it be like to care about someone so wholeheartedly that you felt you couldn't live without them? Plenty of people find love a second time, and I was pissed that he didn't even try. But then I considered how he must've felt about my mom to have taken such drastic measures, and....." He hangs his head and shakes it. "While I try my best to understand, I'm not sure I fully do, which leaves room for bitterness, I suppose."

"So do you believe there's more than one true love out there, then?"

He blows the air out of his lungs and raises his brows. "That's a heavy question." Turning to stare into the room, he contemplates before shrugging one shoulder. "How about I'll answer that when I'm eighty and have experienced one or the other. Rain check?"

I laugh. "I'll hold you to it."

"What about you? Any theories on love?" he asks, taking me off guard. I didn't expect the tables to turn.

"Oh boy. Huh… I'm not sure I can answer that. I'll take a rain check as well."

"Have you been in love?"

"Definitely not. I've never had sex with anyone for this long, for crying out loud."

"Has it always been just sex for you? Is that all *this* is?" he asks calmly.

Oh shit, this is uncharted territory—time for a break.

"Shoot. I need to check on Poppy and then use the bathroom. Do you mind if I do that real quick?"

He chuckles knowingly, resigning. "Not at all. Go do that, and I'll bring the wine to the bedroom and meet you when you're finished."

"Thanks," I say, kissing him quickly before retreating down the hall with my tail between my legs.

"Hey, girl, how did your date go?" I ask when she picks up.

"Why are you talking so quietly?"

"I'm at Eli's."

"Then why the heck are you calling me? Don't you have better things to do?"

"Ugh. Yes, but we were talking, and things took a serious turn, so I fled. Now tell me about your night."

"Girl, you are crazy pants."

"Yeah, yeah, tell me something I don't know. I'm assuming it didn't go well since you're not already gushing about it?"

"Meh. It was so-so. He was cute, but not enough to get over his *Star Wars* obsession, which he talked about one too many times. He wants our second date to be the first movie since I told him I hadn't seen it."

"Ooooh, a Netflix and chill night. Sounds like he wants in your pants. Did he kiss you goodnight?"

"I awkwardly dodged him, and we hugged. I might go on one more date, but not for movie night. You, however, need to get your chill on instead of talking to me. Let's chat more tomorrow when you can fill me in on this serious talk you ran from. Have fun, bye!"

"Okay, fine, bye."

Luckily for me, the only thing on Eli's mind when I entered the bedroom was one thing, and one thing only. Crisis averted.

9

BOMB DROP

"**S**ERIOUSLY, ELI, YOU NEED TO SLOW DOWN."

Sebastian isn't the only one using those words, and quite frankly, I'm sick of hearing them.

"I'm fine. It was a close call is all," I argue from the hospital bed I'm stuck in until they release me.

"A close call this time, but what about the next time when it's more than that? What will you be saying then? Nothing, because you'll be six feet under, just like Mom and Dad. This recklessness has to stop. You could've died today. On your birthday, no less. *Our* birthday."

"It's a simple concussion—nothing to get bent out of shape over. I'm the one with the headache to go with it." It's not my fault another car clipped mine and caused it to spiral out of control before slamming against the curbing. The sucker should have known better than to try and pass at the time, but that's a newbie for you. Racing cars is my new favorite pastime after our Las Vegas trip. I've become pretty good and am quite the contender in the local circuit.

"You're not listening to me," Sebastian growls in frustration.

"I've heard that before." My brother and Cici are sounding eerily similar these days.

"This isn't a joke, Eli. My concern doesn't only apply to what happened today. It's about your entire life, for Christ's sake. You need to make better choices going forward. You have no concern for anyone but yourself. Do you think I want to be the last Dubree standing?"

Well, shit. He makes a fine point when he puts it that way. But people race cars every day. It's not like I'm free diving with great whites. However, it's on my list.

"Your silence speaks volumes. I can't stand by and watch you carelessly live your life. It's time for you to grow up and behave like a responsible adult." He runs his hand through his hair and paces back and forth.

"Sebastian, I'm fine. Really. And I'm sorry about ruining dinner plans tonight."

"Dinner is not the issue." He turns and heads for the door, pausing at the threshold. "Don't forget about our meeting with the trust attorney tomorrow. I'll have Darryl drive us over. Be ready to leave by ten." He walks out without another word. He'll get over it when he realizes he's upset over nothing.

My head thumps back against the pillow, making me wince. They need to give me something more potent for this headache. In the meantime, I close my eyes while waiting for Cici.

Something soft touches my hand, gently waking me. Cici's beside the bed, holding my hand.

"Happy birthday," she says shyly.

I chuckle. "Thanks." I bring her hand up to kiss it. "And thank you for coming."

She squeezes my hand. "I don't need your thanks. I'm here because I care about you. That was scary."

"It made for quite the birthday. I won't forget this one anytime soon." I smile.

"This is serious, Eli. Please stop racing." Is Sebastian putting her up to this, or could it be that she cares about me more than she'll let on?

I take in a big breath before sighing loudly. "It's exhilarating. And I'm fine, so why would I stop doing something I love?"

"Sometimes you have to give up what you love to protect yourself. I love dessert, but I don't eat it. Cocaine addicts love cocaine, but it'll kill them. And in your case, you'd be giving up racing to keep yourself alive and ease your brother's fears. He was a wreck when he called me. You're the only family he has left—he doesn't want to lose you."

"Who's the counselor now, huh?"

"Come on, Eli. Think about it."

"What do I get in return?"

"A longer life."

Not the answer I was looking for.

My stomach growls loudly, making us both laugh and thankfully changing the topic. "I'm starving. How about we blow this popsicle stand and grab a bite to eat? What do you say?"

"I say we wait until you're released and make sure it's okay with the doctor."

"They'll release me and probably make it mandatory for someone to check on me every two hours. And you know, it's still my birthday, so can I choose how you do that?" I ask with my best puppy dog eyes, causing her to laugh.

It looks like it'll be a great birthday after all.

"Can you repeat that, please?" I ask as calmly as possible, trying to keep my cool.

William, our family attorney, doesn't hesitate. "To retain your shares of the company and the trust, you'll need to be in a valid marriage by the time you turn thirty," he says formally from behind his desk. We've been here for an hour reviewing assets, and only minutes ago, he dropped this bomb. The first time he said it, I thought I misunderstood something. Because what the actual fuck?

"Why the fuck wasn't I made aware of this until now?" My temperature is rising, and staying calm is no longer an option. So much for my headache going away, even though Cici did her best to distract me from it last night. Too bad it isn't my birthday every day.

My brother and I showed up this morning to what I thought was a routine review of our family trust. I couldn't have been more wrong. Suddenly, I'm told I have a year to marry or lose all claim to my inheritance and company shares. Is this even legal?

"Your dad stipulated that neither of you be told until a marriage occurred or one year before your thirtieth birthday if no marriage was in place—whichever came first. With Sebastian's wedding commencing only two months before your twenty-ninth birthday, I decided to tell you simultaneously."

"Sebastian, we have to find a way out of this. Do something to stop this nonsense. Anything…," I plead to my brother, who's been reviewing this section of the will since it was handed to him minutes ago.

"It's not contestable. The directive is as black and white as it gets. Somehow, I made the deadline without knowing it. And honestly, Eli." He shrugs. "Maybe marriage would be good for you." *He actually fucking shrugged.*

"Glad to know my brother has my back," I scoff.

"Let's not start on who has whose back. We still haven't discussed your extracurricular activities. You sure as hell don't have my back by risking your life on a weekly basis. You need to stop racing."

"No. Bullshit. You don't get to tell me what to do. The only person who apparently gets that privilege is already dead, so fuck off."

William clears his throat. "Gentlemen, let's get back on track, shall we? How about I go over the particulars? First, you must be married by your thirtieth birthday, so one year from yesterday. It cannot be a marriage of convenience, and to discourage that, he's required a six-month engagement period. Your father wanted you both to be in a genuine union of love—his words specifically. Once the marriage is executed, you'll have a two-year probationary period to validate the authenticity of the union. If the marriage dissolves wherein, additional requirements are mandated to retain the trust moving forward. However, upon your two-year anniversary, the stipulation is deemed satisfied, and no further action is required. Thus, the trust will proceed as usual. Any questions?"

Where do I fucking start?

"Did you find any loopholes?"

No pause before William replies, "No."

"Why would he wait twelve months before the deadline to tell us? Had I known, I could have made different decisions or taken dating more seriously."

Sebastian scoffs next to me, but I ignore him. I have more significant problems than my brother's judgement.

William rests his elbows on the desk and steeples his fingers. "That's precisely the reason for his directive. He didn't want it hanging over your head the past few years. He wanted you free to find love in your own time without this influencing your feelings, possibly resulting in a forced-marriage situation."

"Seriously?" I throw my hands up in the air. "Then why make it a stipulation in the first place? Because that's exactly what this is."

"Eli, it might be difficult to process, but try to remember your dad's state of mind at the time. He was devastated at losing the love of his life and deeply wished for both of you to experience the same profound love in your lives. He felt six months would be adequate to find someone who sparked that feeling enough to pursue a serious path toward marriage if you hadn't already."

"So I have six months to search for some woman I want to propose to, and then hope like hell she says yes, or I'm screwed?"

"Essentially, yes. I'd recommend considering anyone you've had a connection with as well as looking into some of the higher-end matchmaking services. They vet their clients well, and I'm sure the long-established ones have developed outstanding algorithms with high success rates."

"Sounds romantic. Exactly what my dad was hoping for, huh?"

I sit in silence for a moment, mulling over the situation. Sebastian and William continue conversing, but I drown them out as my mind spins with possibilities. Start with anyone I've had a connection with? How about the *only* person I've had a connection with? The woman I'd happily kneel for today. And probably the only one who would refuse. What the hell? How am I supposed to find someone else to marry when the only one I want is out of reach?

"Eli!" Sebastian shouts, interrupting my thoughts.

"What?" I snap back, sounding like a petulant child and feeling like one under current circumstances.

"You haven't even been listening. Do you have any other questions before we leave?" Sebastian barks.

Yeah. How do I escape this? Or....

"What if I don't? Who's to say Sebastian doesn't make me partner once I'm cut off and hand me half the trust anyway?"

Sebastian winces, telling me he already knows the answer.

"The will contains a clause prohibiting transfers from any trust, family account, or company shares to any party not meeting the guidelines outlined in the will. If breached, the entire trust can be revoked. He created an ironclad set of guidelines to ensure you followed through with his request."

"This is complete bullshit!"

"Listen, take a few days to wrap your head around this, and reach out with any questions that come to mind. Sorry to be the bearer of bad news." William stands and walks around the desk. "I suppose wishing you luck is in order." He shakes my hand, then Sebastian's. "One year is longer than it sounds. You might be surprised once your mind is open to the idea."

I'm shaking my head, speechless on the way out. *Fucking A.* What the hell just happened? I must be in an episode of *The Twilight Zone.* Or did I hit my head harder than I thought yesterday, and this is all a dream? Definitely a bad dream. Is it even possible to find a woman in that amount of time? Do I say *fuck it* and just give everything up? Or since I have the money now… I could pay someone to marry me. Or I could take my money and run.

"What are you thinking?" Sebastian breaks the silence after we settle in, and Darryl closes the door to the town car.

"Too many things to run through." I sigh. "How the fuck can I get married in a year?"

"Did anyone come to mind by chance?" The innuendo is obvious.

"Don't play coy. Just spit it out."

"You and Cici seem to be cozy these days. Is she a possibility?"

"If she were, I wouldn't be so frantic at the moment. Cici has made it very clear what I am to her and that she has no plans to stay in San Diego. Otherwise, I'd ask her tomorrow."

"What if you explain the situation and convince her?"

"You think that's how I want my marriage to start? I don't want Cici marrying me out of pity. The only way I want Cici is of her own free will. She needs to choose me because she *wants* me, not to help me. Plus, we'd never survive a marriage that started that way. She'd resent me for forcing her into something she wasn't ready for. Her will runs too deep. Just look how far she moved away to escape her parents' plans for her."

"Have you talked to her about a relationship that goes beyond sex? You could at least try before you give up entirely. Weren't you the one who told me to pull my head out of my ass when I wouldn't tell Lily how I felt about her? Now, here you are doing the same thing. It seems you need to take your own advice."

"My, how the tables have turned. I can't believe you're lecturing me on love."

"I didn't mention love. But now that *you* have, is that what it is for you?"

"It's… complicated. She has an aversion to relationships or some shit. I've already had to convince her to keep seeing me twice. Plus, she wants to go back to Bozeman."

"You still didn't answer my question. Do you love her?"

More than anything. I wouldn't think twice about spending the rest of my life with her. She's the last thing I think about before falling asleep and the first thought I wake up to. She grounds me in a way no one has before and inspires me to be a better man. I'd move mountains simply to hear her laugh. The thought of her leaving makes me want to hold on tighter, beg her to stay, and do everything I can to keep her.

"Yes." And I'm pretty sure I've been in love with her longer than I ever realized.

"Then it might be time to have a serious talk. At least tell her how you feel, even if you don't go into the trust issue. She should realize what she's walking away from. Don't you think?"

"I'm not sure what to think at the moment. I wasn't planning on having to marry someone in the next year. I thought I'd have more time to mourn the loss of her and lick my wounds. I also thought I'd have another chance with her, even after she leaves, but if I lay myself on the line and she rejects me for good, then that's it. Game over. I'm not ready to close the door yet."

"What other choice is there? If you let her go without even trying, you'll never be able to move on. Who knows, maybe she'll surprise you. And if not, at least you'll have tried and can gain closure."

We're approaching the office, so it's time to wrap this up. I look at Sebastian and see genuine sympathy. It gives me little comfort, but I'm appreciative nonetheless. "Yeah, you might be right. I'll figure it out. In the meantime, I'd appreciate it if you'd leave this between us. Lily couldn't keep this from Cici, and it's unfair to ask that of her, so I'd like you not to share this with your wife. I realize that's a big ask, but it doesn't do her any good to know and no harm to not."

"We don't keep secrets from each other, but in this case, I agree. I won't say anything if you back me up, verifying that it was only because of your insistence when the time comes. She won't be happy with me, but it's the least I can do, considering you're in this position and I'm not. I'm grateful for that. I'd have ended up paying someone to fake it for two years."

That may be what I end up doing.

Days later, my week turns for the worse, going from terrible to downright dreadful. Jackson called today to say he finally found Mia's dad and would be back tomorrow if everything goes as planned. I'm the shittiest friend in the world to be upset over his success. I should be thankful that it took him seven months to do it, but I think that still makes me an ass. Regardless, that means the deadline is up to win Cici's heart, and it's now or never to make my move. It's time to tell her I love her, and simple words won't be enough to prove how serious I am, so I'm taking the next step tonight, before Jackson returns.

After driving to jewelry stores the rest of the day, making it through dinner was trickier than expected, knowing what I'm about to do. We're seated in the restaurant's upstairs private dining room at an intimate round table with our backs to the room so we can face the city and bay views out the large corner windows. The atmosphere is perfect for the evening, and the staff were given instructions not to disturb us after the dinner plates are cleared, which happens to be now. I can tell Cici's becoming suspicious, which is confirmed by her following words.

"What's up with you? You're off somehow."

"I'm disappointed that it's our last night together since your brother's coming home." It's true, but not the reason for my strange behavior.

"I'm sure we'll be able to sneak around a bit."

"I don't want to be sneaking around."

Her disappointment shows even before she responds, "Oh. Okay."

I reach for her hand to caress it, looking into her eyes. "Cici, you and I have been seeing each other for months now. Only our closest friends and family know about us, and you consistently remind me of our expiration date. But I'd like to ask you to imagine a different possibility. One where you don't leave. One where we have forever." Her eyes go wide. "I'd like you to consider a future here… with me. Because I honestly can't imagine a life without you in it. I love you, Cici. I've loved you for what feels like forever, and I want nothing more than to have you beside me fifty years from now so I can answer your question—because I want to believe in only one true love."

While her eyes glisten, I kneel on the floor and take her hand, pulling the ring from my pocket. She covers her mouth and shakes her head, but I power through, not caring that her answer probably won't be what I want. And even though she may be ready to say no right this second, I'm not going down without a fight. I have a plan.

"Cici, those aren't just fancy words. I'm serious about you… about us. Not only am I asking you to stay… to make my life complete and keep me grounded. I'm asking you, Cecelia Soloman, to marry me. I want you to spend not only tonight but every night for the rest of your life with me." She starts to open her mouth, but I quickly keep going. "I'm also insisting you not give me your answer yet. Take time to think about it. Talk it over, make your lists, dig deep into your heart until New Year's Eve. I'll wait until then, and I'll accept whatever it is, but only if you promise you'll seriously consider it. If you do that for me, in return, I promise to either love you for the rest of our lives or let you go once and for all. Will you at least *consider* saying yes to marrying me?"

She nods as the tears flow.

I wipe under her eyes and then rise to meet her lips, kissing her softly, pouring as much love as I can into it. Putting my heart on the line tonight was scary, and I've done some insane shit, so that's saying a lot. It made it easier not to receive an answer. That may have been a cop-out to prolong what I fear is the eventual outcome, or it could end up paying off, and she'll come to her senses. The only thing I know for sure is that I can't force this stubborn woman to marry me, but I can do my damnedest to sway her.

Reluctantly, I pull back and hand her the ring, which she tries to deny.

"Take it, Cici. I want you to hold on to it. It's yours until the answer is no."

She takes it in defeat. "Eli, why are you making me wait to give you an answer? Things'll be awkward until then."

I return to my seat before responding, "Only if you let it. I plan on behaving exactly as we have been, starting now." I pull her into my lap, facing outward.

She squeals, "What are you doing?"

I don't want her overthinking and interfering with our possible last night together, so the next part of the evening starts now.

"Put the ring next to your purse, sweetheart." She does as I say before I pull her back against me and swivel my chair to face the closest window. I spread my legs, opening hers that are draped over mine, and I tilt her head to the side, swiping the hair from her neck. My lips work their magic there while my hands cup and massage her breasts.

"We can't do this here. They might come in."

"Our backs are to them. They'll only be able to hear your pleasure, not witness it. Too bad for them." She has no idea they won't return until I call for them. I think I'll keep it that way.

She moans, and goose bumps break out on her skin.

"You like the sound of that, baby? You better be loud and give them something to get off to later," I whisper in her ear, and she shivers.

She's writhing on my lap, grinding her ass into my shaft, while I continue devouring her neck and palming her breasts.

"Eli."

"Yeah, baby? You ready to put on a show?" My hand snakes down the front and rubs between her legs.

She moans loudly.

"Such a dirty girl. Let them hear how badly you need it."

Her body stretches, begging for more. I reach inside her panties to find her wet slit swollen in desire. I rim her opening a few times before sliding in. My other hand grips her neck.

"Oh God, Eli, please. Yes, more."

"Louder, baby. They want to hear you beg as much as I do. How bad do you want it? Should we show them?" Her core tightens at those last words, confirming my decision to give her an imaginary audience. My girl likes a little kink, but I've never thought of this before. *Damn.*

"I need it, Eli. Please give it to me."

"Good girl. You beg so well."

I nip at her neck and then suck while my fingers curl up inside her, flicking her G-spot until she comes undone seconds later, contracting as she climaxes. Her moans become louder as she shudders through her release and goes limp in my arms with a contented sigh.

"How was that?" I ask while nuzzling her neck.

"Do you really need to ask? I think the orgasm speaks for itself." She smiles lazily and turns her head to kiss me.

I bring my hand up and shove my fingers in her mouth. "Clean them off, baby." But within five seconds I'm too turned on and replace them with my mouth for a taste. We moan in unison, and before I know it, she's turned around and straddling me, opening my pants to free my aching cock. Reaching into my pocket, I pull out a condom, quickly sheathing myself, shoving her panties to the side, and pulling her down in one swift move. She squeezes her core, and the feel of her tight channel around my dick makes me throw my head back and savor the moment.

"Fuck, baby. You're so hot. Ride me."

I pull down her dress, exposing her tits, and suck one into my mouth, flicking the nipple before biting it. She's bouncing up and down, squeezing my cock, but I want more. Wrapping my arms around her waist, I stand up and press her back against the glass in front of us as she grips me with her legs.

"You ready to be fucked hard, baby?"

"God yes." This woman is insatiable.

"All right, baby, I've got you." She loosens her grip on my neck and leans back against the window as I jerk my hips, pummeling her into the glass as hard as I can.

"Fuck. Feels so good." I continue pumping in and out, panting as her cries of pleasure fill the room, and then I remember where we are.

"They're going to come in any minute. Watch me fuck you like an animal with your tits hanging out. Is that okay, baby? Can they watch?"

Her eyes squeeze shut. "Oh God, Eli. I'm gonna come."

"Good girl, come for them. Let them see you fall apart." And she does, bringing me right over the edge with her.

"FUCK, GODDAMMIT…," I groan, then give one final thrust and go still while my cock pulses out its release before slumping into Cici.

"Fuck, woman. You undo me."

"Ummm. We just had sex in the middle of a restaurant. I'm pretty sure the feeling is mutual."

I lean my upper body back and look at her. "Did you like it? The thought of them walking in?" I want her to admit it.

"I guess I did. It was hot. But if they had come in, I think I would have freaked out and had you stop, so thank God they didn't."

I kiss her nose and say with a smirk, "They were told not to come back after dinner. But it was fun making you think otherwise."

"You brat." She shoves my chest, but we're still connected.

I slowly retract and set her gently on the ground, steadying her while she regains her balance. "That was a perfect start to the evening, that's for sure. I didn't plan on fucking you here, but you were too sexy to resist."

"A perfect start? What are we doing now?" she asks as she puts herself together while I take care of the condom, discreetly tying it up and placing it in my pocket until we get home.

"Now that your brother's coming home, I'm not letting our last overnight go to waste. We won't be sleeping—I can tell you that much. The rest is up for negotiation."

"Is that so?" She returns to the table and pauses, staring at the ring beside her purse. "Eli—"

"Don't, Cici. Put it somewhere safe for now. You have until New Year's. Let it go and enjoy our time tonight. Besides, you won't be able to think of anything other than what I'm doing to you later, I promise. Now, come on, I'm already impatient for round two," I say, wrapping my arm around her waist to lead her from the room. With the bill settled up front, nothing is left to do but bring my woman home and keep reminding her why she belongs with me.

If this is my last chance, I'll need to make it count. The worst part is knowing I won't have another year to hold out hope for her to return like the last time she left. I've known Cici was special since the first night we were together, almost two years ago now. I'd never met anyone else like her. I also knew she had similar feelings toward relationships that I did at the time—no strings attached.

It didn't save me from falling for her, but it did stop me from pressuring for more, knowing it would only push her away. I decided to cherish whatever time we had, and when I let her go the first time, I expected she'd eventually mend things with her parents and return home. Luckily for me, Jackson coerced her into it, giving me this second chance to win her over while ending up madly in love with her. I've done everything I can to show my feelings without smothering her until playing my final hand and laying it out. If she doesn't say yes to marrying me, I'll let her go for good this time—I'll have to. And as much as I've tried, I'm finding it damn hard to prepare myself for that outcome.

"So what's your plan now that I'm back? Are you sticking around for a while or heading back to Bozeman soon?" Jackson asks his sister as we're seated around the table at their parents' house for Christmas dinner. The Solomans were nice enough to include us since Lily's practically family and Sebastian and I don't have any.

Jackson ended up being too late for Mia. By the time they released her from the program, she was already dating someone and decided to stay where she was. So I'm not the only one going through hell today. I don't wish the feelings of loss on anyone, but it helps to have someone to commiserate with, even if he doesn't know I am.

"Are you trying to get rid of me already?" Cici deflects.

"No, but I feel bad for keeping you here so long. I figured you'd be ready to go home." Jackson leaves no room to avoid the question.

Cici's eyes travel from her parents to me.

"I'm not sure I'm ready per se, but I have to return at some point since all my stuff is there, and I still have my condo. Even though I'm subleasing, I renewed my lease for another year four months ago, plus I want to show off my new purse at the office. I'll be the envy of everyone." She puckers and kisses in her brother's direction.

Perhaps I should sweeten my marriage proposal with a Louis

Vuitton per day since she seems to like them so much. I've never understood the fascination, but if that's what it takes....

"You can do real estate anywhere, honey. San Diego is an excellent market, and you know so many people here," her mom chimes in.

That she's suggesting Cici do something other than their family business shows how far they've come. I hoped their renewed relationship might sway Cici in my favor, but her independent streak is embedded into her core. My hope has been slowly diminishing throughout the week, my anxiety slowly taking over.

"I'm just not sure what I want to do." She looks at me once again, and I can see her indecision. How can this be so difficult for her? I've laid myself out and shown her everything she could have by marrying me, but I'm still unsure where her head is. Damn the stubborn woman.

Jackson gets a phone call and leaves the room abruptly. I'm about to follow and walk off my frustration when Lily continues the conversation. "Well, luckily you don't have to decide this minute since you're staying through New Year's, right?" This keeps me waiting in my seat for the answer and saves me from an embarrassingly abrupt departure.

"True. And who knows, maybe I'll return to Bozeman only to change my mind." She shrugs. Is this her way of delivering her answer? If so, I don't accept it. She can tell me straight to my face if she's turning me down. And although I hope that's not the case, if it is, there's no going back... for either of us.

10

HEAD VERSUS HEART

Cici

'M A NERVOUS WRECK. WHY DID HE MAKE ME SIT ON THIS UNTIL today? A rhetorical question since I know the answer. He's aware of my irrational aversion to relationships. I'm not sure why I'm like this. It's not like some major trauma steered me from commitment or anything. I've talked to Poppy and Lily practically every day, and I think they're just as flabbergasted as I am.

Even in the eleventh hour, I'm counting on my leading ladies to keep me sane and my feet on the ground. Dialing Poppy, I bite my nail and bounce my leg, waiting for her to pick up.

"Did you change your mind?" she asks immediately.

"No," I groan. "I don't know."

"Cici, I thought we went over this. If your mind is made up, it's made up. If you're confident it's for the right reasons, then accept it and stop questioning yourself. Or if you are having doubts, you could always ask for more time?"

"I'm not having doubts." *Am I?* "He's amazing… and sweet…

and caring…. and so fricking gorgeous. Not to mention everything I've ever wanted in bed. Oh, and did I mention wealthy? And to top it off, he's funny *and fun*. Who says no to that?"

She's quiet on the other end, letting me process my words and probably wondering how to talk me down from my crazy.

"Not only that, but I don't have a valid reason to say no—except that I'm insane, and that's not good enough. What am I doing, Poppy?"

"I think you're letting your fear get the best of you and panicking over the fact that you love him."

"I doooo…." The sob breaks free, and it goes downhill from there.

This whole week has been one giant sniffle fest. Between the sinus infection I got the day after Christmas and the constant crying, I look like Rudolph the Red-Nosed Reindeer. Luckily, the antibiotics have kicked in, and that part is somewhat better… but the crying, not so much.

Poppy talks me through this round of tears. "Cici, you've got this. You only need to say the words. It's that simple. Stop worrying. And remember, you'll be here tomorrow no matter what, and I'll hold your hand through all the second-guessing you'll inevitably be doing." She listens to me sniffle a few more times before asking, "Will you be okay?"

"Yes…. I don't know…. No. I mean, yes, I will be. I'll pull it together soon. It'll take a while to make myself look decent for the party tonight, so I need to get my shit together anyway."

"Damn right you do. You've gotta be smokin' hot. It'll help with the nerves and give you a confidence boost. You've got this, girl. I have faith in you."

"Thanks, Poppy. Thank you for talking me down from the ledge again. You're right. I've got this. I'm good now," I say, trying to convince myself more than reassure her. "God, I can't wait to see you."

"Me neither. I'll pick you up, and you can tell me all about it on the way home."

"Okay, see you tomorrow. Bye."

"Bye, Cici. And no more doubting yourself."

She hangs up before I can respond.

Easy for her to say. I'm an absolute fucking mess of emotions. But as of now, I have three hours to be ready, and it'll take a miracle to hide these puffy eyes and red nose. Thankfully, there's no more time to deliberate, so I crank my favorite hits station and jam out while I prepare for the most important night of my life.

"Wow, this is amazing," I say while looking around the circus-like enclosed tent that's set up on the lawn at the luxury resort's New Year's Eve celebration. I've never seen anything like it. It's almost enough to take my mind off the ring safely tucked inside my clutch. The lights hanging from the top are shaped like candles and flicker at different lengths across the canopy. There must be hundreds.

"It is. It's so glamorous, I feel like a celebrity," Lily says.

I huff. "You sort of are."

She laughs. "Only in certain circles, thank God. Maybe Sebastian and I should have had our wedding here." We both look around in awe. She may be somewhat of a celebrity since she's been with Sebastian, but she'll always be the same Lily. She doesn't let their money go to her head, and I don't think she ever will. She's too down-to-earth for that, having come from nothing the way she did.

"What are you talking about? Your wedding was out of this world."

"Speaking of weddings, are you ready for tonight?" she asks with concern. "Any change of heart?"

"The head and heart are two different things. Nothing has changed."

"Well, I'm here if you have a freak-out moment before then."

"Thanks." I squeeze her in a one-arm hug. "Hopefully I can keep it together for a few hours. Let's make it go fast by dancing the night away."

"What are we waiting for?" Eli asks, walking up behind us and hearing the last bit. Sebastian is with him, and they hand each of us a glass of bubbly. "Cheers to the evening ahead."

We all raise our glasses and take a sip. "Have you ladies found our table yet?" Sebastian asks.

"No, we didn't make it very far. We were too distracted by the opulence. It's beautiful, don't you think?" I ask them while I stare at Eli. He looks so fricking handsome tonight. His tailor-made suit fits him exquisitely and makes him look like a million bucks—probably not far from the price. His usually floppy brown hair is styled more conservatively with gel, and his five-o'clock shadow is shaved to perfection, giving him the perfect amount of sex appeal. He's utterly delicious.

"I think the most beautiful sight here is right next to me," Eli whispers in my ear, making me shiver. *Funny that we were thinking the same thing.*

"Let's go set our stuff down and mingle," Lily suggests. "When are Jackson and Mia getting here? I'm excited to meet her," she says, never having had the chance before Mia left.

"Any minute, I'm sure. They should have been here by now." I shrug, unconcerned.

Jackson got a call on Christmas from Mia's best friend, who told him it had been a misunderstanding and that Mia never moved on. She's been a permanent fixture since she arrived the next day, and I've spent more time with her this week. She's beautiful inside and out and so perfect for him. I couldn't be happier for Jackson; seeing him back to his usual self is such a relief. If only everyone could have a happy ending like theirs.

After dancing the night away, the final countdown is seconds away, and there are fresh glasses of champagne being passed out. The butterflies in my stomach begin fluttering like crazy. The evening so far has gone perfectly. Between the dancing, great food, and conversation—mostly Mia filling everyone in on her story—I haven't had a moment to worry about what comes next. But now that it's approaching, my nerves are skyrocketing. Thankfully, I was too preoccupied all night to overindulge in alcohol and make it worse.

"*Ten… nine… eight… seven…,*" we all shout. There are smiles all around, and couples paired up and ready to kiss their loved ones.

"*Six… five… four… three….*" Eli and I turn to face each other for the last moments before new beginnings.

"*Two… one…* HAPPY NEW YEAR!" The room goes up in cheer while we continue to stare.

My eyes water as I slowly move my head from side to side and open my mouth to tell him, but he brings his pointer finger to my lips. He takes my glass, placing it on the table next to his, before grabbing my head and kissing me like it's the last time he ever will. The room vanishes, the shouting around us goes silent, and all I'm aware of is the man showing me how deeply he loves me in a single kiss. With one final soft touch of his lips, he pulls back and brushes the tears from my eyes, mouthing the words *I know*, and my heart sinks.

"Happy New Year!" Lily grabs me and hugs me excitedly. I wish I could join in her enthusiasm, but I only manage to hug her back. "Everything will work out," she whispers in my ear before I'm released and passed to the next person.

By the time I'm through with everyone, I'm too dazed to cry as I stoically reach for my champagne to numb the pain, but Eli has other ideas. "I have a room for the night. Come with me so we can talk."

"Do I have to?" Talking about it won't make it better.

"No. You don't have to do anything you don't want to. But I'm asking you to, for me," he pleads. And I can't say no. So I nod, seeing instant relief stretch across his features.

We say goodbye to everyone, ignoring Lily's concern and

Jackson's gaze that asks what the hell is going on without words. Sebastian squeezes Eli's shoulder in encouragement, and it's enough to make me want to run away and hide. But it's too late.

Eli places his hand on my back, holding my clutch in the other. "This way," he says, directing me from the room.

The silence that follows as we walk the grounds is agonizing. His hand remains the entire time, rubbing my back soothingly. When we reach the door to a villa, my legs are ready to give out. After twisting the lock behind us, he takes my hand and leads me to the couch, where we sit facing each other. I open my purse and remove the ring, dreading this moment but knowing my answer needs to be said out loud.

Taking a deep breath, I begin, "Eli, I'm sorry for the way I am. It's irrational and makes no sense, but something's holding me back. It'll probably turn out to be the biggest regret of my life, but I can't marry you." I hold the ring out, and he takes it with a resounding sigh.

"I knew this was coming, but a small part of me still hoped you'd change your mind." He smiles as he puts it in his pocket. "Your head won over your heart. It's not the answer I was looking for, but thank you for placating me by thinking about it. I promise I'll hold up my end of the bargain and let you go."

"Eli, you're amazing. You deserve someone with no reservations who can give you everything in return. I wish I could be that person. For what it's worth, this was the most difficult decision I've ever made."

"And I'm sorry I forced you to make it. I knew better, but I couldn't give you up without a fight." He pushes a strand of hair behind my ear and reaches behind my neck. "Or let you leave without knowing I love you." I'm pulled toward him, and he meets me in the middle. We're inches apart. "Let me make love to you one last time before you're gone." He closes the distance, and our mouths dance lightly. It feels hesitant at first. It's a sensual kiss, teasing, touching, and parting, our breaths mingling in between.

The firm grip on the back of my neck indicates he's holding back, taking his time to savor it all. His tongue reaches out, barely grazing my lips. The minute I feel it, my mouth opens naturally, asking for more, but he draws back slightly.

"Say yes, Cici. Allow me to love you before we say goodbye."

I nod, barely able to speak with how choked up I am. "Okay."

Instead of ravaging me as I expect, he continues in the same manner as before. It's so intimate that pangs of sadness keep pelting my chest. It's like my heart is cracking with each touch, and I'm not sure if I can make it through this without it breaking completely. I'm distracted from changing my mind as Eli guides me to stand and deepens the kiss. It's still soft but so much more at the same time. Our tongues explore, and our hands start traveling, naturally going to disrobe the other. His fingers graze down my back to find the zipper before carefully working it down.

As he works on that, I'm fumbling with buttons, removing his suit jacket before finally sliding his dress shirt down, feeling every solid muscle as I go. One hand continues to grip the back of my head while his other takes its time sneaking under my dress to squeeze and massage my ass until he lowers the top, giving the same attention to my breasts. It feels incredible, and any thoughts of stopping are miles away by now.

I'm working at his pants when his lips leave my mouth to trail down my neck, giving me goose bumps and causing my core to tighten in anticipation. When he finds the sweet spot below my ear, I give up what I'm doing and reach up to rub my hands along his firm chest. He continues to suck and lick downward, grabbing my backside once more to pull me against him. I'm weak in the knees and don't think I'll be able to stay standing much longer as my desire ramps up. I throw my head back and moan his name as his mouth reaches my breast and pulls the nipple in. His arm around my waist is the only thing keeping me upright.

"We should… move this… to the bed," I suggest, barely able to form a sentence I'm so deluged with lust.

"I couldn't agree more." He moves back, to my body's disappointment, and pushes the dress over my hips, letting it pool on the ground. "In case I forgot to tell you, you were absolutely stunning this evening."

"You may have said it a time or two." Or three or four.… I lost count at some point.

"Not enough, then," he says, then kisses me before leading me to the bed. "And now, you're even more stunning. I prefer this look on you," he teases, gently pushing me back. "Go ahead and lie back. I need my fill." I do as requested, watching him slowly peruse my body from head to toe, where my shoes still adorn my feet.

He pulls down the zipper that I never got to and lowers his pants, leaving his boxers on. He kicks off his shoes and socks and tosses them aside.

"Now that that's taken care of, I'll take care of you."

Leaning down to lift my foot, he slowly removes my heel and massages my arch, making me purr in contentment. My eyes close as he continues to work up and down my foot. Suddenly, his tongue licks up the bottom, making me squirm and lift my head.

"Eli, you can't do that."

"Shhh. I want to. Close your eyes, Cici. Just feel."

I huff and lay my head back down, closing my eyes again. Since it's his last night, I'll be quiet and let him do what he wants, but what if my feet stink? *Ugh.* This is crazy. *Oh God*, he's sucking my big toe, and *holy shit*… could I orgasm from this? My pelvis clenches at the sensation. How is my foot affecting me *there*? A moan escapes.

His mouth leaves, granting me a moment to catch my breath. "See what happens when you let yourself go?"

He keeps massaging, working his way up my calf with kisses peppered in, and continues up my thigh. He's getting dangerously close to the place that's yearning for him, and each time his hand almost touches it, I clench involuntarily. My pussy is begging to be filled. And if he doesn't do it soon, I'll be forced to use my words.

"Your body is a work of art. Whatever you're doing at the gym, it's worth it. Fuck, Cici. I should have been doing this nightly for the past few months if only to sear into my memory every square inch of you."

How can he be so sweet when I just refused to marry him? I should be lavishing him with attention, not the other way around.

I lift onto my elbows and look at him. "Eli, I think—"

"Cici, I'm not finished with you, and if you interrupt me again, I'll have to start over."

"But I don't deserve this. You do."

"I hate to pull this card, but you already turned me down once tonight. Are you denying me this as well?"

"Eli!"

He was smirking, so I knew he was just being cheeky, but that was a harsh reality to be reminded of.

"Listen, Cici, I want to touch every inch of you for as long as it takes to savor every part of your body. Just enjoy it, baby. Relax, close your eyes, and take what I give you, which I hope is so much pleasure that you'll never forget tonight. Now go on, lie back."

I huff again and flop down, hearing him chuckle at my petulance. I feel guilty that he's being so damn sweet. I'm stuck in my head for a minute until his mouth starts sucking on my other foot, wrapping around my big toe. I must've zoned out when he moved to my other one, but *oh... God...* I swear I'm going insane. How in the world does this turn me on so fricking much? I'm writhing in need the harder he sucks and swirls his tongue around. "Eli, oh God." My pussy is pulsing.

"You wouldn't happen to like your toes sucked on, would you, baby?" He chuckles, knowing damn well the answer based on my reaction.

He continues up the same way as the other side, ending with my legs stretched out wide. He teases me again, barely missing my core as he massages my thigh, driving my desire for more. He has nowhere else to go, and I think I'll finally get what I want when he moves to my damn hand.

I'd be super irritated if it didn't feel so fricking good. He grazes my breast as he gets higher on my arm, and I'm excited for him to go in that direction, hungry for more, but I should have known better. Instead, he moves to my other hand and repeats the sequence.

"Do you know how fucking sexy you are? This body… Christ. My cock is so hard for you, baby."

He makes it to the top and straddles me, working my shoulders for a minute before finally lowering his hands and getting to my breasts. *Ahhh.* This will do for now, especially the part where he's grinding his dick against my clit. My pelvis is matching his thrust for thrust, and all I want is him inside of me.

"Oh God, Eli. Please. This is torture. In the best way of course," I quickly add on.

"Patience is a virtue, Cici. Didn't the God you keep calling out to teach you that?" I can hear the smile in his voice.

"He also gave me humility, and I'm humbly asking you to move on." At that, he laughs heartily and bends down to kiss me, pinning my hands above my head.

"I love it when you're feisty. Makes me want to tie you up and fuck it out of you."

"Yes, please. Just do it quickly so we can get to the good part."

"If you're smart, you'll leave your hands right here, and I'll get to something good next. I haven't made it to every inch of you yet, but I'm close. Deal?"

"Fine, but I'm reneging if it takes too long."

"I better keep going, then." He devours my mouth while grinding on me, ratcheting my desire right back to where it was moments ago.

"You feel that, Cici? It's all for you, baby."

As I'm about to start begging, he moves down my body and

starts peppering my stomach with featherlight kisses, then licking my belly button, trailing his tongue lower. He slides my panties off as he descends further, and at the first flick of my clit, I almost lose it. But he doesn't continue. Instead, he climbs off the bed, taking my panties with him and removing his boxers. Returning, he spreads my legs further and lowers his head. His tongue slowly glides from bottom to top two times, then begins to lick, kiss, and suck in earnest, making me moan and chant his name, chasing my release.

But he stops and wipes his mouth, rising to bring his head level with mine, kissing me softly.

"Part of tonight was to give you all my love before you leave. And part of it was to make this so damn memorable, I'd be able to hang on to you for as long as possible. I love you, Cici. And I'm about to ask for something I'd never ask of anyone else. You're on the pill, and we've been exclusive for months. No condom, baby, skin to skin—share this with me. One last memory that I'll cherish forever. Will you let me make love to you with no barrier between us?"

Neither of us has ever had sex without a condom before. We've talked about it, and he knows this is a big ask. Hell, this is a big decision. It's more than unprotected sex; it's intimate… special. It's between two people in love. He loves me—I know that. And while I love him, he *doesn't* know that. Could this be how I show him without saying the words? Will he understand what it means? He might not… but I will. Maybe this would help me be at peace with my decision. And if not, at least I'll have shown him how I feel in this way.

"Yes," I say through the tears threatening to break free.

He sighs in relief and smiles. "Thank you. You're giving me a gift I'll never forget." He leans in with a kiss that shows just how grateful he is.

Reaching down, he grabs his length, rubbing it up and down my slit. "Oh fuck. You have no idea how incredible this feels. You're so slick, and feeling you with no condom between us is like heaven."

He lines up and slowly presses forward, groaning as he slides all the way until our bodies are flush, then pauses.

"If I thought that was incredible, it's nothing compared to being inside you. Fuck, Cici, this is the best thing ever. It's like I'm home. Tell me you feel it."

"Yes. It's…." He starts moving, and I lose the ability to speak. "Aaaah." *It feels right.*

"Thank you for this." He kisses me and begins to rock his hips back and forth.

I'm truly wrecked. The experience is surreal, and I'm glad it's Eli I'm sharing this first with.

He continues in and out slowly while we stare into each other's eyes, cherishing the moment.

"Damn, Cici. I never want this to be over. I can't give you up."

"Eli, don't say that."

"I'm sorry. You're right. Fuck, I'm sorry." He pauses and buries his head between my neck and shoulder. "Just give me a second."

The tears are about to fall, and I have to climb out of this sinkhole we fell into.

"Eli, I need you to fuck me hard. Please. That's what I want to remember. Fuck me, Eli."

He doesn't move for a few more seconds and then lifts his head to meet my gaze.

"That's what you want?"

I nod and see his resolve set in.

"Your body's begging to be fucked the way only I know how, isn't it, baby?" He smirks. This is where we work. This is what he gives me that I'll never find with anyone else. And it's what I want to take with me.

"Yes, please."

"Anything for you, Cici. Anything." He grabs the front of my neck and squeezes as his hips pull back, pausing. He stares straight into my soul before slamming into me at full force. "Is that what you want, Cici? A good, hard pounding to remember me by?" he asks as he continues relentlessly.

I nod in response since I can't speak with his hand around my throat. This is what I need.

"My girl likes to be used, doesn't she? Wants to be fucked so damn hard."

He grunts in exertion with every thrust.

I'm close.

"That's it, baby. Take my cock."

He pistons two more times before my core tightens and clenches in orgasmic bliss.

"Fuck, yeah. I feel you, baby. You ready for me to come inside this pussy? I'm gonna fill you so full, it'll be dripping for days." He squeezes my neck tighter, cutting my air supply.

"I'm—fuck! I'm coming. Fuck! Fuck! Fuck!" He releases my neck, causing me to suck in a breath at the same time he hammers home his climax, and suddenly I'm coming with him as my second orgasm hits me within seconds.

I'm screaming in ecstasy as he continues.

"Yeah, baby, filling you with my cum. Fuck. I want every last drop coating this pussy." He thrusts a few more times and stills deep inside for the last two pulses.

He came in me. There's cum inside of me for the first time ever. I have all of him, and it's… intense. I didn't expect to be so moved, but tears begin to fall out of nowhere.

"Cici, baby, what's wrong? Oh fuck, did I hurt you this time?" Eli asks in a panic.

"No. I'm… sorry. I… don't know… what's wrong," I manage to sputter while crying.

He starts to pull out, but I shout, "No! Stop!" causing him to freeze.

What is happening to me? I can't stand to let him go. I don't want a single drop to escape, and it's the most irrational thought I've ever had.

"Cici, what's going on?"

"I don't knooow," I wail. That's it; I've gone mad.

"Cici, everything will be okay, I promise. I love you so much. I'll make sure everything works out. Please don't cry, baby. Talk to me." He's not sure what to do, and I can't help him because I have no idea what the deal is.

"I'm sorry." I hiccup and breathe, trying to stop this madness.

"Don't be. You don't need to apologize for showing emotion, sweetheart. I just wish I knew what to say or do. How about this? Come here." He moves his arm under me and holds tight as he rolls over, careful to keep us connected, with me on top. "Lie down. Just relax."

His hand caresses my hair as my head rests on his chest. I can hear his heartbeat as his lungs expand and deflate, lifting my head with each breath—it's calming. Slowly, the fog lifts and reality sets in. That was a major freak-out for an absurd reason. What the hell? I'm glad he changed positions so my head can stay down a little longer to avoid looking at him. I'm embarrassed and not sure where to go from here.

He's still inside of me. What am I going to do after behaving like a lunatic? It's not like I can admit why. I don't know what got into me, but I couldn't stop the tidal wave of emotion. It took control, and I was powerless to stop it. I'm chalking it up to a moment of temporary insanity.

Eli's voice cuts into my thoughts. "Are you feeling better?"

"Yeah. I'm okay now."

"I'm glad. Did I do something to upset you?"

"No. I think it's a combination of things. Everything from the last few months caught up to me at once. Sorry you had to bear witness."

"I'm not. I'm only sorry I added to your pain. Why don't you close your eyes, let it all go, and we can deal with everything tomorrow." He continues caressing my head while rubbing soothing circles on my back.

Closing my eyes sounds good. I yawn and follow his suggestion. "Thank you, Eli."

He kisses the top of my head. "No. Thank you, Cici."

11

PHYSICAL THERAPY

Eli

S HE'S GONE. I FEEL IT IMMEDIATELY. STILL, MY STOMACH DROPS when my eyes land on the empty space beside me, then the ring on the nightstand, which is sitting on top of another… fucking… note.

Eli,

I'm sorry for finishing what should never have started in the first place.

Please don't hate me. You are such an amazing human and deserve better than someone who can't give you more.

Don't give up on finding love a second time. Then you'll have your answer.

Cici

Was there anything I could've done? Something more I should've said? Had I told her the truth, would she have said yes? Probably, but at what cost? It had to be her decision and her decision alone. Anything else would've been a thorn in our marriage. Fuck. I roll over onto my back, resting my arm over my head, not ready to face the day. Happy fucking New Year.

I have less than six months to find a woman, propose, and marry her. I have no idea what world I'm living in where marriage can still be forced upon someone in this day and age. Fuck my life.

Other than Cici, I can't think of a single woman I would ever consider spending two years with. Yeah, I've had some great sex, but the women themselves, fuck no. And that leaves me two options: leave it to fate or contact a professional matchmaking service. Neither sounds appealing.

That I'm even thinking about this the day after the only woman I've ever wanted in life left me is a testament to how fucked up I am. The problem is, it's all I can think about since discovering three weeks ago that I needed a wife, and now my one hope is gone. She flies out early this afternoon, so technically I could try one last time, but it would be a wasted effort. Her mind is made up for some illogical reason, and there's nothing I can do to change it. That leaves me at square one, and a sudden desire to get fucked up.

Sadly, it's nine in the morning, and drinking is not on the agenda this early, so I need an alternative for now—a brutal workout should do it. Before that, though, I need to get my sorry ass out of this room.

When I arrive home, the first thing I do is change after walking through my door, then head straight next door to Sebastian's and my private gym between our penthouse condos. After entering my code to unlock the door, the sound of the treadmill fills the room. Of course, Sebastian is here.

In no mood to talk, I grab a towel and head straight to the bike, ignoring him completely. Setting the machine to the highest level, I close my eyes and hunch over, pushing my legs as hard as possible, getting into a zone.

Sebastian's voice breaks my trance. "Dude, take it easy. You're gonna wreck yourself."

I lift my head and realize an hour has passed already. I'm dripping with sweat, creating a large puddle under the machine. I sit up to wipe my head while slowing down the pedals. "I'm fine. A little cardio never killed anyone."

"Not so sure about that, especially at the pace you were going. Come do a few reps and tell me what happened. I figured you two leaving together was a good sign, but clearly not since you're killing yourself on the bike," Sebastian points out during a set of curls.

"Nothing to tell. She was gone when I woke up this morning and is flying home today."

"I'm sorry, man. I still think you should have told her what was going on."

I shake my head. "So she'd marry me out of pity? No thanks," I scoff. "Look, it's not like I couldn't see this coming from a mile away. That I was delusional enough to think she'd change her mind is on me. It's time for plan B. I'll contact an agency this week to start searching for someone else."

I have no choice.

"Christ, Eli. Give yourself some time to recover instead of jumping right in."

"Time is a luxury I don't have. You know that as well as I do."

Two weeks later, after a rough day in the office, I pull the note from my pocket that I've memorized by now. It never fails to calm me down. Fuck, I really need to get a grip. Maybe it's time for a night out like old times. Might as well begin my own hunt for a wife and have some fun while I'm at it. After texting Braden and Jackson, even though Jackson still won't leave Mia's side, I head into Sebastian's office just down from mine.

"Hey, I'm headed to the club tonight. Since the agency hasn't found any suitable candidates, I figure I'll start searching for Mrs. Dubree myself."

"You sure that's the best place to do it?" The doubt is loud and clear.

"Don't see why not. You can join us if you want. See the pro back in action."

"I would, just to make sure you don't do anything stupid, but Lily and I have plans. You've been off the market for a while now… sure you remember what you're doing?"

"Dude, I don't have to do anything. The ladies come to me," I say, wiggling my brows.

Sebastian smiles and shakes his head. "Listen, I know how it feels to be rejected. It's okay to lie low for a bit. But whatever you do, don't forget I'm around if you want to talk."

"Thanks, but I'm fine. The quicker I move on, the better. Otherwise, I'm just prolonging the inevitable. Have fun with Lily tonight." I turn around to leave.

"Yeah, you too," he says on my way out.

I'm planning to.

Here's the thing… if you fall off your bike, you've got to hop right back on before it's too late and fear creeps in to immobilize you. That's what I need to do, go out with guns blazing, so this shit doesn't bring me down. I don't have time for wallowing. I don't have time for regrets. And I certainly don't have time to waste. It's a new year, a new day, and soon, whether I want one or not, a new woman. I might as well jump right in since waiting won't change a damn thing.

When I return to my office, a text from Braden confirming tonight and a missed call from Jackson are waiting.

Jackson picks up on the first ring. "Hey, man, I have to pass tonight. I'm not ready to leave Mia after getting her back."

"Yeah, I figured. Not sure I would either."

"Also, you haven't brought it up, so I haven't either, but I'm sorry about Cici. I always suspected, but seeing you at New Year's confirmed it. She told me the bare minimum after I mentioned kicking your ass for hurting her, but it sounds like the opposite is true. I don't have all the details, nor do I want them, but I feel bad for not warning you in advance. She's not the relationship type, which frankly, I didn't think you were either, but she takes shit next level. She never had a boyfriend in high school—not one—and it was the same in college. Not sure why, but it's definitely a thing with her."

"I'm aware. I picked up on it before she left but thought it was circumstantial with her relocation back then. Don't worry, she made it loud and clear this time around." It is nice to hear it confirmed from someone who's known her their whole life. At least I know it was a lost cause and not something I failed at.

"I'm sorry it didn't work out. For the record, I would have approved. I'd offer to kick her ass for you, but (a) she's my sister and (b) you're a big boy, which I'm assuming is why you're headed out tonight. Liquid therapy?"

"You got it. And possibly some physical therapy, too, because why the fuck not?" If I think it enough, maybe I can fool myself into wanting it.

"Whatever you need to do, man."

"Thanks. Enjoy your woman. We'll have to plan a night out with all of us soon. I'll have Braden for a date."

"Not likely. That guy always has a different woman on his arm. You better snag one before he runs through them all."

"Fuck, no kidding. Better make haste. See ya, buddy."

Contrary to my big talk, it's not likely I'll be jumping in the sack right away, but who's to say I can't take my mind off things with a willing woman on her knees? Hell, we've got plenty of those at the club. That's why it was a weekly ritual for us back in the day. Then Mia came along, followed by Cici, so Braden had his pick of the crop. Well, I'm back. Time to prove I've still got what it takes and give him a run for his money. Because fuck it, if I'm getting engaged soon, I might as well go balls to the wall until then.

"You sure you're ready for that, dude?" Braden asks when I tell him my idea for a little friendly competition. I'm unsure if it's because it's so soon after Cici or because I've been out of the game for so long, and I don't ask, since it would emphasize the doubts already in existence. The more I suggest it, however, the more I'm convinced it's the way to go. The two old-fashioneds I had before switching to beer could very well be aiding that thought process.

So my answer comes out confident. "More than ready."

"That's the attitude. Like they say, no better way to get over someone than under someone else."

"Cheers to that." I raise my bottle in salute, then swig it down.

Damn straight. My decision is cemented, and it's time to act before I waver for the millionth time. Maybe incentivizing it will give me the encouragement I need.

"How about a little wager? First one with a woman on her knees gets first dibs on Mia's maid of honor," I suggest.

He laughs. "Dude, you know her best friend is gay, right?" He shrugs nonchalantly. "I'm game, though."

"Shit. First dibs on *all* the women at the wedding, then. And win or lose, we'll at least enjoy the fruits of our labor."

"It won't be *our* labor that'll be working our cocks, unless you're already giving up."

"Shut up, man. Let's go."

"Game on. May the best man come quickly." He winks as we clink our beers and finish them off to seal the deal before walking away in separate directions.

I'm headed downstairs, while Braden stays in the VIP section. It's not rocket science to assume there are more options in the pits of hell than the upper crust, where women are generally looking for something in return. Bellying up to the bar, I order another drink while greeting the bartender on duty and asking about the night. Sounds like it's a little slow after New Year's, but only slightly, considering it's still a weekend.

Drink in hand, I turn around, examining my options. Two groups of ladies stand out immediately, and I zone in to scrutinize each one. The younger ones could be trouble, making me wonder if we're doing a good enough job checking for fakes—something I'll need to investigate.

The other table has potential. Middle-aged, martinis in hand, and dressed slutty enough to imply they're looking for attention. I'm about to make my way over when a woman sneaks beside me, regardless of the lack of space, and uses half my body as the bar itself to lean over, essentially pinning me in place. The first thing I notice is the ass that belongs to said body before slowly eyeing my way up the slim figure beside me. I finally make it to her face, and she's smirking at my blatant perusal when I go wide-eyed with recognition.

"Hey, Eli," Rebecca shouts in greeting, throwing her arms around me like we're old friends, leaving me no choice but to reciprocate.

"Rebecca, good to see you." We pull apart, and I turn sideways to give her space, but she doesn't take it.

"You too. Are you here with Cici?"

It's the absolute last question I want to hear but understandable since the last time we ran into each other, I told Rebecca we were dating. I remember Cici's jealousy at the time and my reassurance in return. I'd had to convince her that I didn't need a woman like Rebecca when I already had the woman I wanted. And now she's fucking gone. Looks like I need Rebecca after all.

"No. She's back in Bozeman. We were temporary. Unfortunately, all good things come to an end." I down my drink and place the empty glass on the bar.

"Really. That's too bad. You're not seeing anyone, then?"

Do I take advantage of the situation and make a pass since she's obviously fishing, or do I spare her and keep looking for a one-off? I'm not sure I can take advantage of someone I've already met, especially since she has a connection to Cici—probably not the best play.

"Rebecca, you seem like a nice girl. Way too nice for what I'm looking for tonight, so I'll save you the trouble and walk away. Enjoy your evening." I take one step before her hand is on my arm.

"Wait." She tugs my arm. "What is it you're looking for? I might be able to help you find it."

This is interesting. As a wingman or a participant?

Might as well shock the shit out of her and give one last out. "I need a hot little number on her knees with my cock between her lips until she swallows every last drop. And it's tied to a bet I'd like to win in the next five minutes, so if that's something you'd like to assist me with, by all means…. Otherwise, I'll be on my way since I'm pressed for time." I raise my arm to look at my watch, exaggerating the motion. I'd rather her back off knowing what frame of mind I'm in rather than feign flattery and fuck her over. By her stunned expression, my crudeness did the trick.

Once again, I move to leave, only to be pulled back. "I'm game…." She pauses, but now I'm the one who's speechless, unable to form a response before she continues. "On one condition."

Ah… she's looking for some two-way action. Plenty of women here would gladly perform with no expectations, and I'm certainly not in the frame of mind to please anyone else but myself tonight.

"Sorry, babe. I'm not in the reciprocating mood, and I'm betting there's a willing party here tonight who's okay with that." I gesture toward the dance floor.

"You haven't even heard my condition yet. Aren't you curious?" she asks seductively.

"Curiosity killed the cat."

She pouts, her lips giving me pause while I envision them on my cock. "But if the cat was happy and *well satisfied*, wasn't it worth it?"

My cock wakes up at the picture in my mind, giving her another few seconds. "I'm listening."

"Dinner. I help win your bet, and you take me to dinner next week."

What the fuck? My head jerks in surprise. "You're offering to suck me off for a meal?"

She shrugs. "A date. I've been into you since the day you came into the office, and I'm a sexual woman. Time is ticking, though, so if you want to win, you better decide fast." She smiles and taps her wrist, pulling the same move I made moments ago.

"Fuck." I run my hand through my hair, perplexed. Is this for real? It's like I'm in another dimension where being an ass is apparently the way to go. Is that where I went wrong with Cici? I was too… nice? I drop my head and shake it, removing all thoughts of her, especially at a time like this. Looking back up at the woman who's here, I know what I need to do.

"This way." I grab her hand and pull, not gently but in agitation. Because I am… agitated. I got played. But fuck it, I'm still a male who thinks with my dick, and right now, it wants those pouty lips to make everything better.

I lead her to a back office and lock the door behind us, undoing my pants the minute we're alone. When she doesn't make a move, I get frustrated. "Did you forget our deal?" I ask pointedly as I quickly text Braden that I won before pocketing my phone.

When I look up, she's standing before me with her arms crossed and lips pursed.

"You change your mind?" I ask in annoyance.

"You didn't agree to my terms."

"I thought it was obvious, given our current situation. You, down there." I point to the floor. "Mouth here." I push my pants down enough to pull my cock out and stroke it. "Then I take you to dinner, *not* a date. Depending on your performance, maybe I'll throw in cocktails. For now, I've got something you can drink right here." I smirk.

Her mouth drops open.

"That's a good start, but down here, babe. It's not gonna suck itself." I jut my hips out, grab my dick, and shake it. Crude seems to be working, so I might as well keep it up. This is definitely entertaining. "Come on, I don't have all night."

She huffs but lowers to the ground. I've been doing this all wrong, apparently.

My hand lands on her head and pushes it back slightly. "Open up. Show me what you've got."

Her lips part, and I guide myself in while holding her head. Fuuuck. I don't care who you are—nothing like sticking your dick into a warm, wet mouth no matter who it belongs to. My head lifts to the heavens, eyes closed, savoring the feel.

I release my hold, and she pulls back, gasping for air, but returns after catching her breath and starts licking the tip. I decide to let her do her thing for a minute.

Her tongue continues to explore. "Attagirl. Get me all slicked up."

Once she's thoroughly licked me up and down, she saturates her lips and slides slowly down my length, sucking me as she retracts, extracting a deep groan out of me. "Again," I tell her, ready for more.

She doesn't disappoint. Her rhythm gradually increases, and her tongue…. Fuck, it never stops. This might be one of the most talented mouths I've had the privilege of sticking my cock into. I wonder if she can take me down her throat. I'm on the lengthy side, and only one woman has been able to take all of it, but I quickly shut that thought down.

I need to focus on *this* mouth and what *it* can do since it's the only one here right now.

"Can you handle more of me?" She takes me deeper in response.

"Let me help you with that." I grab her hair and thrust forward, reaching the back, then retracting to do it again, going further each time, seeing how much she can take.

"Yeah, you've got this. Fuck." Once it's proved she's capable, I unleash myself and let go, fucking her mouth with vigor. Her tongue continues to dance around my cock, and when she reaches up to grab my balls, I come unhinged. My release is the only thing on my mind as my thrusts turn frantic and I chant in pleasure.

"Oh fuck... you ready for it? I'm gonna come down this fucking throat, and you're gonna swallow every... last... drop." I give one final push and unload. "Fuck. Oh Fuck. Yeah, that's it. Take it all. Fuck, fuck, fuuuck." I push harder and feel her throat squeeze my dick as she devours everything I give her. Holding still, I shout until the last pulse drains me.

I stagger back, panting, practically doubled over from pleasure. That is not what I expected. "Fucking hell, woman."

"I guess that means dinner *and* cocktails."

12

ALONE

Cici

"Y OU'LL WARN ME BEFORE YOU START TRYING TO MAKE ME AN auntie, right?" I ask Lily over the speaker while I fix my dinner. Apparently, Sebastian's getting antsy about popping out some babies.

"You'll be the first call I make. I'm still not sure it's good timing, though. I want to start trying, but I want to be a stay-at-home mom, and my job is going so well."

"Loving your job is great, but Lily, you don't have to work. Sebastian has more money than God. You could always have kids and pick up your career when they're older. It's better to be young parents, I think. Then you're more active and done early enough to enjoy the rest of your life." Wow, listen to me—the voice of reason. Weird, considering I'm not even a kid person.

"Yeah. That makes sense. I wonder if I should get my IUD out and surprise him for Valentine's Day next week."

"That would be so sweet. You should totally do it."

"Oh my gosh, he'd be so excited." I can hear her smile through the phone. "He's been asking me for months, but I think he finally gave up the other day when I told him he was stressing me out. He literally won't have a clue. Eeek! Consider yourself officially warned. I'm having a baby."

I laugh. "I hate to break it to you, but you have to make one first."

"Hello? That's the best part."

I laugh but ignore the comment, being severely deprived in that department. "I can't believe I found out before Sebastian. You just made my day." I clap my hands in excitement.

"You're so funny. Speaking of making babies, regarding the making part, are you back in the saddle yet?" The question isn't new, but I figured she was tired of asking and hearing the same answer because it's been a while—apparently not. At least I had a short reprieve.

She's been concerned since New Year's. When she called the next night after getting an earful from Sebastian about his brother's mood, she listened to my sobbing for an hour until Poppy came back over after bringing me home from the airport earlier and relieved her.

Okay, so counseling was a brilliant idea, which I started the week I returned. Not that I'm any different than I was a month ago, but I'm more optimistic about overcoming my irrational issue with relationships. Apparently, I have a disorder called gamophobia—an actual fear of commitment. My counselor picked up on it right away from hearing me speak about leaving San Diego and the family business along with my experience with Eli and past dating habits. We've been delving into it since.

I've considered dating again, but Eli takes up too much space in my brain to spend time with anyone else. I'm working up to it, but until then, I should probably make up something so she'll stop worrying and asking every time we talk. Though knowing my luck, it would probably backfire and make things worse. It's always better to stick to the truth.

"I'm getting closer. A guy from the office has been asking me out, and I'm considering it." It's not a lie. A newer agent *has* been asking, and I *did* consider it… for all of two seconds before I said no.

"That's good. You should, even if it's not someone you'd normally go out with. At least get your feet wet." I can hear the relief in her voice.

I'm terrible for embellishing. Liars never prosper. Or is it cheaters? Oh, fuck, neither come out ahead in the end.

"I'm swamped right now. It's ski season, so a ton of buyers are coming to town."

"Yeah, yeah, and then it'll be spring and then summer, and you'll always be too busy. Just go on a coffee date at least. Pleeaase? For me?"

Shit. She's pulling the big guns out now. When did she learn to use my tactics and turn them around on me? But maybe she's right to start small. A harmless café for an hour to get the ball rolling.

"Fine. I'll do coffee." My eyes roll even though she can't see.

"Yay! That's all you need. One test run to prove you've still got it. I can't wait to tell Mia I talked you into it."

"You guys should not be discussing my love life. Jackson doesn't need to hear that."

"He doesn't, don't worry. Oh, but listen to this, Mia said Jackson's been hinting at marriage again. I think she'll say yes this time." My brother asked Mia to marry him the minute she came home, but she said no, that she wanted to live together for a while first. Hearing they might get engaged is like a punch to the gut. Not that I wouldn't be happy for them, but at the same time, it's a stark reminder of what I gave up and so far out of my reach.

"Wow. Jackson hasn't said anything. I hate not being in the know."

"Move back, then. We miss you."

"I miss you too. Come visit me this summer," I say, ignoring her suggestion and offering one of my own.

"We should. Let me talk to Sebastian about it and check when we could come."

"You've got my hopes up now, so you have to. Tell me as soon as you talk to him. But I'll let you go so I can call Jackson. He better spill."

"Cici, you can't tell him I said anything," she says frantically.

"I won't. Promise. Call me when you decide on a date to visit. Love you."

"Love you more. Bye."

My mind is spinning as I dial Jackson. If that brat was planning to propose and not tell me, he's in for it. But how do I draw it out of him without giving up my intel?

"Hey, Cici. What's up?" Jackson answers.

After a few minutes of work talk and chitchat about the parents, I find a perfect spot to lead into it. "How is having Mia's mom so close? Is it weird?"

"Not at all. She's a sweetheart. We honestly don't run into her all that often, being on different floors. But we do have frequent dinners together."

"Sweet. How about Mia? Everything good? Is living together all you hoped it would be?" He told me she was at her mom's, which means he can talk freely.

"I love it. We wouldn't have moved this fast if she hadn't been gone all that time, but now that we have, I couldn't imagine it any other way. It's crazy."

"I'm happy for you. I guess when you know, you know, right?" Could that be any more leading or what? I'm not liable for my actions if he doesn't say anything soon.

Lucky for me, he takes the bait. "No doubt, which is why I'm asking her to marry me. I'm planning something big."

"Wow. That's great. You mean you won't throw it out in bed one night?" I love giving him shit about the first time he asked her.

He laughs. "Not this time. It'll be something memorable, I promise. You're the first person I've told, and I'm keeping it under wraps so she has less chance to catch wind of it. I want you to be a part of it. Will you come back for a weekend to be here when I do it?"

Oh shit.

"Jackson, I'm up to my eyeballs with work. I've got clients looking for property and quite a few under contract. I don't think I can make it anytime soon." While none of that was a lie, it's not the entire reason I'd like to avoid it.

"That's okay. Tell me when you can, and I'll set a date. Like I said, it'll take a while to figure out, and I really want you to be included, so can you make it happen?"

"Uhhhh, let me look at my calendar." I pull it up to look how far I'm booked out and what closings are coming up. "I don't think I can come until the first week in April." I feel bad it's so far out, but at the same time, just thinking about going back makes me sick to my stomach, but maybe by then I'll have a different mindset.

Eli and I haven't spoken or exchanged a single text since I left. A clean break was probably best for both of us, but leaving the way I did still haunts me. I snuck out like a coward before he woke up and never said goodbye besides the note I left. The last night we spent together was so emotional and life-altering that I couldn't bring myself to face him before walking away. Part of it was embarrassment at my reaction at the end of the night, which took me by surprise, and part of it was the impact that final moment had on me. I wish there was a quick fix to my issue with commitment, but no such luck. And until I work it out with my counselor, I'm conflicted by my decision.

"First week in April it is. No rush, but tell me when you book your ticket. And thank you, Cici. You keep pulling through for me. One of these days I need to return the favor. We've never talked about you and Eli, but I'm here if you need me."

"We didn't and we won't. I'm not interfering in your friendship. Besides, there's nothing to talk about. We had some fun. That's all."

"Then you're right, we won't talk about it, because the only thing

I have to say to that is that you're full of shit. But if you ever decide to have a real conversation, call me. Just remember, I'm your brother and I've got your back no matter what. Got it?"

"Okay. Thanks, Jackson. I love you."

"Love you too. Bye."

As much as I enjoy a good gossip sesh, I have no more brain-power for one, so Poppy will have to wait until tomorrow. After sending a quick text, I run upstairs to draw a bath before locking the front door and fixing a cup of tea to end the night. As I sink into the steaming hot water scented with my favorite lavender salts, my body instantly relaxes. Absorbing the silence of my life, I stare at the orchid, brought with me from San Diego, that sits on my bathroom counter. One tear falls, followed by another, then another, until they begin to spill in earnest. Soon, my body is shaking as tears turn to sobs.

With the regret, the frustration, the loneliness, the confusion, and the utter sadness that's taken over my life, I'm constantly crying—something I never used to do. It would take a miracle for me to shed a tear, and even then, it was short-lived. Now, I cry at the drop of a hat. Sad movies, not so sad movies, fucking commercials even. I'm a fricking wreck, and I'm over it. My body is tired from all this emotional baggage, I can tell. I've been having a hard time getting up in the morning, which is yet another abnormal behavior I've seemed to develop since I've been back.

Am I depressed? Heartbroken? Homesick? All the above? I'd love a magic solution, but without one, I'm stuffing my face with food, working myself to the bone to stay busy, trying to ignore the fact that I'm miserable. If it weren't for Poppy and her parents, I'd have thrown in the towel by now, but they've helped keep my head above water and even made things seem normal during my time with them. Although my parents and I reconciled and we talk every now and then, our relationship hasn't gotten to the point where I'd feel comfortable discussing my problems. I have hope that we'll reach that stage someday.

My counselor has been a saving grace these days. She eases so much of my worry that I can't imagine how bad I'd be without her. The best thing was hearing that I'm not crazy and finally understanding why I couldn't say yes to Eli. I still can't believe it's an actual disorder. Having a name for it was a relief for sure, but it didn't make the hurt go away. That's a slow process… but it is getting better.

Until tonight anyway. Thankfully, we're meeting on Monday because I need a major intervention. First, hearing Lily is starting a family—wow. She's married to the love of her life and trying for a baby. That's huge. Then Jackson and his upcoming proposal to Mia. The two most important people in my life are settling down in their happily ever afters when it seems like I'll never get mine. There's nothing worse than feeling like a failure.

"I'm going to be alone forever," I complain to Poppy at happy hour a week later.

"Hey, you're preaching to the choir here, sister," she says with raised brows.

"True, but you didn't fuck up and say no to the one man you should be with. You just haven't found the right guy yet. You will, though."

"You will too. There's not just one for everyone. Otherwise, how would people divorce and find another?"

"Because they screwed up and settled the first time?"

"Who knows, but I'm glad you at least gave it a shot with someone else. It wasn't miserable, was it?"

She's asking about the coffee date I finally went on today. My counselor agreed with Lily and Poppy that I should go. One hour is not a commitment, nor is it cheating on a nonexistent boyfriend.

"No, it was nice. Matt's a great guy, and we have a lot in common.

We'll probably be friends, but I shouldn't have gone on a date with someone from the office. That might have been an oversight on my part. After telling him we won't be anything more than friends, it felt weird."

"Was he upset or put out when you said that?"

"No. He understood. It's just me, I'm sure."

"Anyway, I'm glad you went, if only to prove that the world won't end if you go out with someone." She laughs, making me smile, and my shoulders relax at the simple statement of truth. "Do you know how many guys are dying to come over and talk to us right now?" Her eyes wander the bar. "If we skim the room and make eye contact with one of them, I bet they'd be here in a heartbeat. Should we try it?" she asks conspiratorially.

"I think one date was enough for today. You're pushing it now."

"Please, Cici. For me? You're not the only sad single woman at this table. Let's get someone to buy us a drink. The first to succeed brings coffees and bagel sandwiches to the office tomorrow, just like old times." She stares at me while I consider. "Come on, Cici. Your wheels are spinning. You know you can't resist a competition." We laugh, knowing she's got me.

"Fine. They have to buy a drink, though, not just talk to us. That's my half of the bar." I point behind her. "And you take the other." My thumb goes back. "That way we're not swiveling around and making it obvious. Deal?"

We clink glasses while she says, "Deal."

I can't believe I let her talk me into this. I'd forgotten about our little game until now. Except before, I was always the one who initiated it, and she would resist. This proves what a good friend she is to deliberately go out of her comfort zone for my benefit. I hate everyone being so concerned about me. I wish I could travel back eleven months and not go back to San Diego. Crap. No, I don't. I would never want to erase the time with Eli, but I'd like to alter our ending.

Poppy snaps her fingers in front of my face, bringing me to the present. "Hey, snap out of it. Focus on the task at hand. I'm winning fair and square, not because you're in la-la land."

I laugh. "Nice try. I'm an expert at this, remember?"

"You *were* an expert. And I've been training while you were gone, so be prepared to lose," she says without a doubt.

I reach my hand over and place it on top of hers. "Hey, I hope you realize how much I appreciate you. Thank you for this."

"That's what friends are for," she says sweetly before snapping her hand back. "But you'll make all these men think *we're* together if you keep this up, and then we'll both be empty-handed." I roll my eyes. "Now, get your head in the game. The clock starts now."

I laugh as I answer, "Fine. I've already got my sights on someone anyway."

"You think I don't?"

We go back and forth like this, giving updates as we casually look around, scoping out our options. It's the after-work crowd downtown, and we're at a popular bar for networking, so it shouldn't be difficult. We didn't specify if it had to be someone coming over to hit on us or wanting to talk shop. They only had to buy a drink, which business associates tend to do anyway.

I'm busy studying the crowd when I make eye contact with a guy in his early thirties sitting by himself at the bar. I don't recognize him, but something in his gaze grabs me. He's good-looking, well-dressed, and alone. I can't see his ring finger from here, but that doesn't mean anything if you know the sleazy things people do when they're out. You can't trust the evidence these days. I'm about to give him an indication that I'm interested, but instead, I freeze and can't bring myself to do it.

Thank God, I'm saved, with no time to analyze the moment and go to war with myself.

"And we have a winner," Poppy whispers proudly right before a guy comes around from behind me to introduce himself.

She's excited, I can tell, and my heart lightens at seeing her shine. I'm glad she won because when we used to do this, it was always me who brought the men over. Maybe she has been practicing. Or maybe she's trying to break me out of my shell. Either way, I'm happy for her and want her to enjoy her moment. I bow out, declining the drink he offers.

"I'm going to head out. I have a few things to prepare for tomorrow." Poppy's look assures me she knows I'm full of shit. "Here, take my seat," I say to…. Fuck, I already forgot his name.

"I'll see you in the morning." I hug Poppy goodbye and add, "With coffee and breakfast."

She laughs. "You better not forget. See you tomorrow."

"Have fun!" I wave and go on my not-so-merry way.

13

MAN UP

Eli

"WILL THIS EVER BE MORE FOR YOU?" REBECCA POUTS FROM the hotel room bed as I put my clothes on after our most recent hookup.

I sigh in frustration, sick of this topic. She's getting increasingly forward, which means she's impatient and possibly fed up with our arrangement. But if this keeps happening, she's not the only one who'll be fed up.

"My answer won't change no matter how many times you ask. This is working, so why screw with it? Plus, I've got some personal issues to handle, and I can't do more than this."

"Do your issues have anything to do with Cici?"

I freeze at that, then try for casual as I turn to face her. "Why would you ask that?"

"I'm not stupid, Eli. I knew from the very first night you were fucked over her, but I figured you'd eventually move on. You haven't, have you?"

"Regardless of whether I have or not, there's more to it. If that were my only problem, I'd have it made, but I've got bigger fish to fry." I run my hand through my hair and stalk toward the door, grabbing my jacket on the way. "Look, Rebecca, this arrangement is all that works for me. And if you're only here because you're holding out for more, we should probably stop now because that won't happen."

Fuck, fuck, fuck. I slam the door too hard on my way out, making me feel like an even bigger dick. It's no secret I've been using Rebecca, but to practically spell it out like I did makes me sound like a complete ass, which I undoubtedly am. She's convenient. And a damn good lay, honestly. But that's all she is. Someone to fill my needs while I mourn Cici and search for a wife. Dammit all to hell.

The minute I park in the underground garage for my building, I bang my hands on the steering wheel and flop back into my seat, resting my head and closing my eyes. Can't anything in life just be simple? I'm not sure how long I've been sitting here until a knock on the window jolts me.

"Come on, let's grab a drink," Sebastian says when I open the door.

We walk wordlessly out of the parking garage and around the corner to a small pub we frequented before women invaded our lives. After ordering a couple of beers at the bar, we grab a table in the corner. I chug half mine in one go.

"That bad, huh?" Sebastian comments.

"That bad."

"Aren't you still fucking that Rebecca chick? You might need to call her for an extra round this week."

I don't answer and chug the rest of my beer instead.

"Wait, today's your regular day, isn't it? Is that what this is about? You end up falling for her?"

"Fuck off. She fell for me. I should have cut things off when I sensed she wanted more. Hell, I should do it now, but it's so damn convenient. Someone to fuck with no feelings or attachment. Then she had to ruin it by asking for more. Shit. I need another beer. I'll be right back."

Sebastian was ready when I returned less than a minute later, firing off his screwed-up suggestion.

"Ask her to marry you. Kill two birds with one stone." The look on his face tells me he's dead serious and thinks it's the most brilliant idea in the world.

"Hell no. I'd never do that to Cici. It's bad enough I have to marry someone to begin with, but there's no way in hell I'd do it with a woman she knows. I feel bad enough for fucking her."

It's something that's bothered me from day one with Rebecca, but Christ, she made me an offer I couldn't refuse, and after that first blow job, it was impossible to say no. I took her to dinner, intending to tell her it would be the last, but before I had a chance, she surprised me by suggesting a purely sexual arrangement. No dating, no friendship, no relationship—just meeting once a week at a location of my choosing to fuck. Who in their right mind would say no to that? Did I mention I wasn't necessarily in my right mind?

We sealed the deal at a hotel down the street after dinner. I set expectations up front and left immediately after, continuing to do so every time since. She's hot, I'll give her that, with great tits, curves, and that goddamn mouth of hers. There was no way my dick was backing out.

About a month into it, she started tossing subtle hints at wanting more, but I'm a master of evasion. It's only in the last few weeks that she's become more pointed with her comments, and then today that damn question. Why couldn't she leave things how they were, goddammit? And to bring Cici into it, fuck that.

"She's not coming back, Eli. You can't live your life for someone who doesn't love you. I've tried to be patient and let you do your thing, but I can't stand by and let you piss away your inheritance because you're in love with a woman who doesn't reciprocate."

"That's classic coming from the man who recently married the woman he loves and is about to start a family. You couldn't even begin to understand what I'm going through. It's not only that she's gone, but I'm being forced to move on like she never mattered. Do you understand what that'll look like? Like my feelings weren't real. Hell, it'll look like I never loved her at all, and that's the last message I want to send. No matter what happens, I don't want to hurt Cici or cause her to doubt what we had. Getting married, period, will do plenty of damage as it is."

"I'm sorry, man. It's fucked up, and if I could make it go away, I would in a heartbeat. But that's impossible, so somebody needs to be strong and push you in the right direction. You might be angry with me, but I refuse to let you fail. I want you by my side, running our family legacy together. If I have to force your hand, then I will. The clock is ticking, Eli, and you're getting engaged in three months whether you like it or not, so think about if it would be better to be with someone new or someone you're already compatible with for the next two years."

"I'll consider it, but I'm not doing it any earlier than necessary. Justin is running his search for candidates, and the paperwork is in progress with our new attorney, so it won't take long once a choice is made. That means no one is needed until May to have enough time to get all our ducks in a row before a public engagement."

Once the matchmaking service didn't work out, Sebastian and I agreed that an arranged marriage made the most sense. Justin, our friend and owner of the security and PI firm we use, is the only other person who knows the truth and found a lawyer to create the NDA and contract while being discreet. He's also using his intel to locate suitable women through dating apps and running background checks to procure a list of candidates. I'll set up dates to meet the women, weed them out, and rank the rest, then have individual meetings starting with number one to explain the proposition. If they say no, I'll move down the line until someone accepts. And if that isn't the most romantic proposal ever, I don't know what is. What a fucking joke.

Here's the deal, though, I refuse to pretend for two years only to break someone's heart in the end. Even if I did find a woman I was attracted to and interested in, I'd want to be honest about why I was moving so fast. And the only way to do that is to disclose the entire situation with an ironclad NDA and prenup. At that point, why worry about finding one I like? I might as well find someone with no baggage, little family, and low expectations. Whoever ends up marrying me will come out wealthy when the marriage is dissolved—the least I can do for taking two years of their life and an incentive to stick it out and keep their mouth shut in the process.

"Have it your way, then. I'll follow up with Justin to see where he is on the list. In the meantime, think about what I said. Rebecca may not be a bad idea since, according to you, Cici will be hurt no matter what. Remember, she made her choice, and it wasn't you."

"Way to hit me where it hurts, bro. Since you care and are only trying to help, I'll let it slide, but you don't understand. Cici loves me, I'm sure of it, and even though she walked away, I refuse to hurt her any more than I have to."

The skepticism is pouring out of him. That's okay. I don't need his validation. It doesn't make a difference anyway. I'm still in the same fucked-up situation regardless.

"I'll take your word for it. Doesn't change the fact that she's gone. The bottom line is, I'm not letting you squander your birthright. Get the list, vet the women, and make a decision. If you screw this up, you're not only fucking up your life but mine along with it. You're fifty percent of this company. Now man up."

"I'm proposing to Mia next week, and I want you both to be a part of it," Jackson says to Braden and me after work one day.

"Dude, congratulations!" Braden high-fives him.

"That's great, man." I mimic Braden, though not as enthusiastically, since marriage is a sore subject for me these days.

"So what's the plan?" Braden asks.

Jackson goes into the details, but somewhere along the line, my mind takes a nosedive while thinking back to my proposal from months ago and how different things would look right now if it had a better outcome. Instead, I've got a standing appointment to fuck once a week and multiple dates scheduled to meet the women Justin vetted to become my wife.

While ruminating, a name from the conversation catches my attention.

"Sorry, what was that?" I look up from my beer, not knowing who said what, only hearing that Cici was mentioned.

"Cici's flying in for it. Are you okay to be around her?" Jackson asks.

Oh, for the love of God. "That's great. Yeah, why wouldn't I be?"

"Do you want an answer to that, or was it rhetorical?" Braden asks with an eyebrow raised in speculation.

"It's fine. We had our fun three months ago. We've moved on by now."

Jackson scoffs, "That's the biggest load of crap I've heard in a while. You have *not* moved on."

Fuck. I quickly think of something to say that'll prove otherwise, considering I'm getting engaged soon, and go with the first thing that comes to mind. "I have." I point to Braden. "Remember our bet after New Year's? I've been seeing that girl since then."

"Dude, seriously? All I heard was that she gave you a damn good BJ," Braden says, still doubting my story.

"What can I say—it had me at hello." *What the fuck am I doing?*

"You're shitting me. You've been seeing this chick for that long and haven't mentioned her? I call bullshit. Jackson, what do you think?" Braden turns his direction, waiting for his reply.

Staying silent, Jackson stares me down, probably torn between wanting to punch my lights out for moving on so quickly after his sister or being relieved that I'm not still stuck on her. I'm unsure which side will prevail, so I brace for impact.

"Come on, Jackson, I smell a liar. Help me out here," Braden encourages.

"I'm not sure what to believe since this is the first I've heard of her, not to mention you're still moping around like your dog died. It's okay if you're still hung up on Cici. You don't need to make shit up. It's not like I'd say anything and make my sister feel worse than she already does. So fess up. Are you seeing this chick or not?"

Goddammit. I don't know which direction to go. I'm supposed to be pulling off a fake engagement soon, yet that won't work if they think I'm still in love with Cici, and they won't believe otherwise unless I give them a reason to. I'm fucked no matter what I do. How did I end up here again? Oh yeah, Cici's coming to visit. Shit. I'm pissed that I'll be committed to someone else when she's here, but I've backed myself against a wall.

"Yes, I am. I kept it on the down-low because we hooked up so quickly. I didn't want anyone assuming it was a rebound. She's been patient with me and knew I was dealing with some shit. Also... you know her and so does Cici, so it was complicated."

"What the fuck? Who the hell is it?" Jackson goes from composed to furious in two seconds flat.

Braden's watching, waiting for the fallout. Yep, I'm fucked.

Here comes the icing on the motherfucking cake. "It's Rebecca, the temporary assistant who stepped in when Mia left."

"You have got to be fucking kidding me. Why would you do that, man? Of all the women in this godforsaken city, you went and chose one that would piss her off. Was that your goal—to get even for turning your sorry ass down?"

"Okay, whoa. Calm down, buddy. I was there that night, and it was a chance encounter. Eli didn't plan anything other than to drown his sorrows. Right?" Braden turns to me.

However, I'm not ready to speak and let my anger take over. To hear someone accuse me of intentionally hurting Cici isn't something I'll sit quiet for. The worst part is knowing how wrong this situation is. I'm a fucking asshole for it, but that's nothing compared to what's coming. I'll inevitably look like a prick in the end, but I won't let him accuse me of hurting her on purpose.

"Let's get one thing straight: I would never intentionally hurt Cici. Rebecca approached me that night and offered to help me win a bet that Braden and I made. It was just sex at first, but eventually it became something more. I wasn't looking, nor did I want a relationship, but she was persistent and worked her way in. It just happened, man. I'm sorry." I run my hand through my hair, wanting to punch a hole in something.

I'm frustrated at not only the entire shit show that's become my life, but more importantly, the realization that I just sealed my fate. There's no way I can pull off an engagement with someone else at this point. It seems like Rebecca is about to have her dream come true after all.

14

OH BABY

Cici

JACKSON WAVES WHEN I STEP OUT OF THE SECURED AREA AND wraps me in an enormous hug while spinning me around the second I reach him. I'm struggling to keep the tears at bay as the familiar tightness in my chest tells me they're just under the surface. Knowing I was coming, I've been even more emotional over the last few days.

I school my features as he sets me down and pulls back. "You happy to see me?" I ask with a smirk.

"I'm so glad you're here. It means a lot. Thanks for coming through."

"Quit thanking me already. I wouldn't miss it for the world. Do you think she knows anything?"

"It doesn't seem like it. You'll have to tell me what you think after you talk to her." He takes the handle of my bag, and we make small talk on the way to the car.

"Are you nervous at all?" I ask as he pulls out of the airport parking garage.

"No, just impatient to put a ring on her finger. I've wanted to make it official since the day she came back. I won't be settled until then."

"And you think she's ready this time? It's only been three months."

"Yeah, well, it was a year in the making, so she better be. But yeah, my instincts tell me she'll say yes."

"Phew, 'cause I'd hate to come all this way and have her turn you down again. I'd make you reimburse me for my ticket." I punch his shoulder.

"Don't worry, it won't be for nothing." He pauses, looking distressed.

"What's that look for?"

"There's something I want to tell you before you hear it elsewhere."

"Is Mia pregnant?" I ask excitedly.

"What? No. It's about Eli."

"Oh geez, what about him?" I'm playing it cool, but my insides immediately clench. Do I want to hear what he's about to tell me? Or should I avoid this talk altogether? "Actually, never mind. Stop right there. Eli doesn't concern me, so whatever it is, keep it to yourself. I'm here for you and Mia, and that's all. I won't even be seeing him while I'm here."

"Actually, that's not true. I wanted all of you to be included, so Braden and Eli will be there too."

Oh, for fuck's sake. "Well, thank goodness we're all adults. It's fine, Jackson. That's all you were worried about?" I ask. I'm a little offended he thinks I'm that sensitive, but with my emotions these days, I suppose he's on point.

"Not exactly. Look, I'm just gonna come out and say it whether you want me to or not. He's dating someone you know, and I'd rather you hear it from me than be taken by surprise, okay?"

"Okay…." Shit. I knew him seeing someone was a possibility, but fuck if it doesn't sting to know for sure.

"He's seeing Rebecca from the office."

Did I just get punched in the gut?

I nod once. "All right." That's all I can say without flying off the handle because the shit that's spewing in my head is anything but calm. I fricking *knew* she'd pounce the minute I left. It wasn't a coincidence when she was at the bar the first time he ran into her. I'm sure she staged it. I wonder how long it took to worm her way into his bed.

"How long have they been dating?"

He sighs, which tells me I won't like the answer. Maybe it was a bad idea to ask. "Never mind, don't tell me. It doesn't matter. We weren't in a relationship, Jackson. Hell, he could've started dating her the same day I left, and he would've had every right, so let's leave it at that. And honestly, I'm not surprised. She had her eye on him from the start. Great. Good for them. They're perfect for each other, and I hope they're happy. Well, I hope Eli's happy anyway." *And I should shut up now.*

Jackson shakes his head in disbelief but doesn't comment.

Luckily, he leaves me alone the rest of the drive. I'm only here for two nights anyway. Between dinner with Jackson and Mia tonight, tomorrow's proposal, and Lily's place, all before flying out Monday, I'll be fine. A couple days from now, I'll pretend I was never here. The prospect of seeing Eli tomorrow freaks me out a little, I won't lie. Pretending in front of Jackson is one thing, but being faced with the man himself is an entirely different scenario—one I'm not prepared for.

Visiting with Mia and Jackson the rest of the day was relaxing. However, going to bed last night wasn't. I lay awake for most of it, tossing and turning, wondering how this afternoon would go and what it'd be like to see Eli. When I finally fell asleep, it was early in the morning and fitful at best. Looking in the bathroom mirror upon waking, I almost lost it with how horrid I looked.

"I'm freaking out right now," I say quietly into the phone. I'm in the guest room getting ready to go while on a three-way call with Lily and Poppy. If anyone can talk me through this, they can.

"You should pretend you're seeing someone too," Poppy suggests.

"Oooh, I like that. It would definitely make it easier," I agree.

"Cici, you don't have a lying bone in your body," Lily points out.

Damn. She's right—frustratingly so. Not that lying is a good trait, but it sure would come in handy today.

"What if he brings *her*?" I ask.

Poppy gasps. "He wouldn't."

"He better not or I'll murder him," Lily agrees.

"Lily! He's your brother-in-law. You can't say things like that."

"Well, you're my sister, so I can."

"I fucking love you guys."

"You'll do great. Just remember how far you've come. And whatever you do, don't ask him how he's doing," Poppy instructs.

"Why?"

"Because it's a no-win question. He either says something like 'he's hanging in there,' which will make you feel bad, or he'll say he's great and make you feel even worse."

"You're right. Anything else?"

"You have everything you need, Cici. You've got this. Plus, you'll be home tomorrow, and everything will go back to normal."

"Okay, this is good. And exactly what I needed. Thanks, guys."

"Stay strong. And remember you're coming here afterward so you can relax. Aaah! I can't wait to see you."

"Oh my gosh. Me too. All right, I better get out of here and tell Jackson I'm ready to go. Wish me luck." My final words are whispered as I hang up and prepare for what lies ahead.

After being wound up all day, my body sags in relief when I knock on Lily's door.

She throws it open, and I practically fall into her arms, letting everything pour out.

"Oh, sweetie," she croons while rubbing my back.

It seems like a full five minutes have passed by the time I peel myself away.

"Hi," I say, then start laughing, causing her to do the same, and before we know it, we're both doubled over, wiping tears away, while standing in the entry.

"Well, on that note, I'll leave you ladies to it," Sebastian says, coming up behind Lily and kissing her neck, then stepping to the side with his arm wrapped around her waist. "Hi, Cici. I'm glad you're here. Lily's been impatiently waiting all day." He smiles fondly and kisses the top of her head. "I'm heading out so you two can catch up. Call me if you need anything, sweetheart."

He kisses her goodbye and walks out, leaving us alone. It didn't go unnoticed that he didn't mention where he was going, which means he's probably going to Eli's or at least meeting up with him somewhere.

I groan, imagining what he thinks of me. "How much does he know?"

"They're brothers *and* best friends. He knows everything. Come on, let's pour some wine, get comfortable, and then we'll talk."

When we've settled on the couch with glasses in hand and Ebony purring on my lap, I jump right in, asking the question that's been weighing on my mind since yesterday.

"Why didn't you tell me that Eli was dating Rebecca?"

She instantly looks remorseful and shakes her head. "Well, I was hoping to hear about Jackson's proposal, but I do owe you an explanation first. I found out about them last week, and at that point, I thought it would be better not to say anything until after your visit. I'm assuming Jackson told you?"

"It was practically the first thing he said when I got here. But after today, you were probably right, because all I did was picture him and Rebecca together the entire time we were there."

"Well, I hope that's not all you did. Tell me about the proposal. I heard of the plan through Eli, but how did it go?"

"Oh my gosh. It was so sweet but definitely over the top. Her smile could be seen from a mile away, though, so he did well. When she said yes, the relief on Jackson's face was hilarious. They're really cute together."

"I'm so happy for them. Did they set a date?"

"The end of August, so I guess I'll be back in five months. You're not getting out of your visit, though. I'm still counting down the days."

"We're coming, don't worry."

Suddenly, my emotions hit me once again, and I'm tearing up at the thought of Lily coming to visit. "I can't wait." I take a deep breath and sniffle, trying to keep from really losing it.

"I'm sorry I haven't come sooner." She leans over and wraps me in a hug.

"I'm sorry, this is silly. I'm constantly crying these days." Ebony, smooshed between us, wiggles out and jumps down. "Ice cream always helps. Do you have any cookie dough?"

She pulls away with a funny look. "I thought you hated cookie dough?"

I smirk. "Right? It's crazy, but it popped into my head one night when I was crying, and now I'm addicted. I keep three in the freezer at all times because I'll start to panic if there's only one." I start laughing but stop when I notice Lily is staring at me strangely.

"What?" I prompt.

She wants to say something but hesitates.

"Are you trying to figure out how to tell me to slow down on the ice cream? Don't worry. I'm well aware I've gained some weight. Eating must be a coping mechanism because I can't seem to stop. I was hoping after a few more counseling sessions I'd be in a better place, but with yesterday's news, I'm not sure about that. So don't be surprised if I'm twenty pounds heavier by July."

She's still silent, studying me.

"Lily! Just spit it out."

"Could you be pregnant?"

What? The? Fuck?

My body jerks back. "NO! I'm on the pill and have been forever. Geez, am I really that overweight?" I look down at my body. "Okay, so I need to cut back."

"Cici, I'm serious." She puts her wine down, raising an arm with a closed fist in front of her so she can lift one finger with each of her statements. "You've been an emotional wreck." The first finger goes up. "You're eating things you never used to." The second. "Eating more frequently." Third. "You *have* gained weight." Fourth. She shakes her head before continuing, "And no, it's not over the top, so don't go there. Lastly, you've been complaining about being tired lately." Her fifth and final finger goes up.

"That's only because I've been sleeping so terribly and crying so much. It's amazing how much that takes out of you."

Both her hands flail up in exasperation. "Exactly! All signs of pregnancy."

"Or… they're signs of depression, which I'm working on," I insist.

She ignores me. "Have you been with anyone since Eli? Would it be his?"

"It doesn't matter because I'm not pregnant."

She looks at me pointedly and crosses her arms indignantly. "Answer the question."

I sit back and cross *my* arms in a huff. "No, I haven't been with anybody else. How could I when there's barely a moment he's not on my mind?"

"So you could be carrying Eli's baby?"

"I'm. NOT. Pregnant."

"Then prove it by taking a test. I'll call to have one delivered right now."

"Seriously? No. I don't need to. You're being crazy." I grab my empty glass and march to the kitchen with Lily tight on my heels.

I lift the bottle of wine and freeze, staring down at the empty glass. If I was pregnant, I shouldn't be drinking, right?

"Cici?" Lily stands on the other side of the island, watching me.

I look up. "Order the test."

Thirty minutes later, I'm pacing in her massive bathroom while Lily stares down, waiting for lines to appear.

"They said it takes three minutes, and it's been less than one," I say as she stares down.

"Then if they're already showing results, that means they must be accurate, right?"

"What?" I run over to look and immediately grab the counter for support—three blatantly positive tests lie before me. My hand instinctively goes to my stomach.

"Oh my God," I whisper. "Oh my God. No. This can't be real. I'm on the pill. I can't be pregnant… they have to be wrong." I turn to the side and lift my shirt, looking in the mirror. My hand rubs the recently acquired pooch on my stomach that I assumed was from overeating and late-night ice cream binges. Now that I'm touching it, I notice that it's not squishy like fat would be but firm. Am I pregnant? Do I have a baby growing inside of me?

My face crumples, and I crash to my knees. Lily instantly sinks down and gathers me in her arms, rocking me back and forth while I cry.

"Shhh. It'll be okay." She continues murmuring soothing words while I let it sink in when something she says gives me pause. "Eli will take care of you."

I jerk away, frantic. "No! We can't tell him."

"What? Why? You have to. It's his baby too."

"Lily, please. I'm not ready. He's moved on finally, and I already fucked him over once. I can't do it again."

"He won't think of it like that. It's his responsibility just as much as yours. He needs to know, Cici."

"Not yet. I'm not even sure how this happened. I'm seriously on the pill. I don't understand. I need to see a doctor." I look up with pleading eyes. "Will you go with me tomorrow? I don't fly out until late. Maybe my regular doctor will schedule me on short notice since it's sort of an emergency, right?"

"I'm definitely going with you. And if yours isn't available, I'll call mine. Sebastian helped me find a new one, and with our last name, she'll take you right away." I nod, too numb to speak. "Stay here tonight, and we'll call first thing in the morning? I'll take the day off."

Stay here. Day off. Sebastian. Doctor.

"Lily, you can't tell Sebastian! He'll tell Eli."

"I can't lie to my husband."

"I'm not asking you to lie. I'm simply asking you not to tell him. This is my pregnancy, so it's up to me who knows, and I don't want Eli to find out yet. Please, Lily, you have to keep this a secret."

"You're going to have to tell him eventually. And what about my driver and security? They tell Sebastian everywhere I go."

"Then I'll have to go alone. It's fine. I'd rather that than either of them finding out. Please, Lily?"

"Ugh, fine—for now."

"For now."

The next day, Lily's doctor sweeps into the room while looking at the file in her hands. My doctor couldn't fit me in, so Lily called in a favor to hers. Being a Dubree certainly has its perks.

Holy shit, my child will be a Dubree.

"Blood work confirms you're pregnant, and based on your hormone levels and the information you provided, you're due September 23. Everything looks great. Labs were normal and right in line for thirteen weeks."

I nod silently. Thirteen weeks. Over three months pregnant. The safe zone. I'm having a baby.

Looking down and shaking my head, I mutter quietly, "I don't understand how this happened." Looking up in embarrassment, I smile. "I mean, obviously I do. It's just that I'm still hung up on the fact that I was on the pill."

"You mentioned that, and while there is a small percentage of failure with any form of birth control, I took the liberty of viewing your medical records, and they show you were prescribed an antibiotic in late December. Do you remember that?"

"Yes."

"Did your doctor explain that those particular antibiotics can interfere with the effectiveness of birth control and tell you to use additional protection until a week after finishing the dose?"

"No."

"If you engaged in unprotected intercourse during any of those three weeks, I would say that's your answer."

15

MOVING FORWARD

Eli

SEBASTIAN IS ONCE AGAIN LECTURING ME ON OUR WAY HOME from drinks with the guys. We've revived our weekly nights out now that Jackson is finally comfortable leaving Mia for a few hours. I'm sure the ring on her finger is a big part of it. It's been three weeks since he proposed, and I still can't get Cici out of my head. She barely looked at me that day and, other than a polite hello, wouldn't talk to me at all. It makes sense now that Jackson confessed tonight to telling her about Rebecca and me. I suppose she would've found out eventually, but it pisses me off that I couldn't explain. This whole charade is pissing me off.

Which is undoubtedly why I'm stalling from making my offer to Rebecca. I'm stuck in a holding pattern, but each evening that Jackson and Braden give me shit about the girlfriend they've never met, the severity of the situation increases.

"You either need to have the conversation with Rebecca or find someone else within a week, pretend to fall instantly in love, and announce an engagement. You're the one who inadvertently put your-self in this position when you ran your mouth to the guys. You're only making it worse by stalling." I may be eighteen minutes older, but Sebastian has always taken the big-brother role. The last round went for five minutes before allowing me a word in, so while I'm not happy with the statement he just made, at least he didn't take forever to say it.

"Thanks for reminding me, and again, easy for you to say." Sebastian lifts his hands in frustration as I shake my head, turning to stare out the window. The worst part is that he's right, which aggra-vates me more. "I'll admit having Cici here set me back, but yeah, it's time to move forward. I'll talk to Rebecca this week and get it done."

He blows the air from his lungs. "Thank fuck. Now let's discuss your death wish with this hobby of yours."

Another thing he's been on my ass about. I turn back pointedly. "How about we don't, and you lay off, considering I'm dealing with shit and it's the only thing keeping me sane."

I went behind the wheel again the day after the proposal, when Cici left San Diego for the third and final time. It's the only thing that completely takes my mind off this crap. At least temporarily. It was agonizing not to tell Cici how much I've missed her. I couldn't tell her how often she's on my mind or that my love hasn't faded. With an engagement around the corner, my lips were sealed shut, and the guilt has wrecked me since.

Sebastian and Braden did their best to distract me that night, but the next day was hell. The only thing I could think of to ease my grief was to distract myself on the racetrack. With the time that had passed since the accident, getting in the driver's seat had my adrenaline pumping the way it did when I'd first started. It was exhilarating and exactly what I needed. And with the shitstorm my life has become, I don't plan on stopping anytime soon.

"I'll let you off the hook for now… if you follow through with Rebecca. You may think I'm being cold, but you can thank me later when you're not sleeping on my couch because you can't afford a place to stay."

"That's a bit of an exaggeration, don't you think? I'd still have the penthouse along with the money I already have. We both know I wouldn't be poor. The worst thing is that I'd have to leave the company."

"I'd say the few zeros you'd be knocked down wouldn't be conducive to the lifestyle you're accustomed to. I guarantee you that racing would not be in your budget. And like I said, I want you by my side in *our* company."

"Our company my ass. Sounds like it's still Dad's if you look at what's happening. Do we have anything else to worry about? Provisions regarding children to be aware of? Wouldn't that be the icing on the cake?"

"I've already checked, and we're in the clear. I've made it crystal clear to our attorney that if there are any more surprises, we'll replace him faster than he can finish the meeting. He's assured me this is the final condition and that the trust will transfer completely upon satisfaction of our two-year probationary periods."

"Thank God for that. I'll have the paperwork finished and add her name to the contract first thing tomorrow. You realize she might not accept?"

"Which is why you need to approach it sooner rather than later, so you can go to plan B if she doesn't. Do you think you'll attempt an actual relationship with her at all?"

"No. Though two years is a long time, so who the fuck knows. But it's not part of the deal, and I'll be making that clear. She's been driving me insane, hounding me for more, and I'd hate to give her false hope. If a ring on her finger isn't enough for now, she's shit out of luck."

"Remember, you need her to say yes, so perhaps try to sugarcoat it a little. And look at the positive—you're already fucking her."

"Sebastian Dubree pointing out the positive. Never thought I'd see the day."

Four days later, I texted Rebecca to meet me in the bar before heading to the room for our weekly fuck session. I'm already regretting this and haven't even made the pitch yet. All day, the doubts kept swirling, threatening to cause me to bow out and find another solution. The problem is, there are none. Sebastian is right—Rebecca will be better than some stranger in my home for two years.

Tucked into the corner, I see her before she finds me. She's dressed to impress and has an excitement about her. It's not hard to speculate what she's expecting, and I can only imagine what her reaction will be when she discovers it couldn't be further from the truth. But that won't stop me from making my intention clear from the beginning.

She lights up when she sees me, a smile overtaking her face. A shadow of guilt peeks out before scurrying behind the clouds where it belongs. There's no room for it here.

"This was a surprise." She sits across from me in the dark, secluded booth in the back of the bar. It'll suffice to provide privacy for the conversation that's about to take place, and I've taken liberties to ensure no one else will be seated near us.

"I imagine it was. As will the reason for my request." I should get a little alcohol in her first to soften the blow, but that could also backfire. Best not to muddle things.

She eyes the files on the table, raising her eyebrows in speculation. "Are we having a business meeting?" she asks teasingly.

"Of sorts. What would you like to drink?" I ask as the waiter approaches behind her. I'm facing the room to make sure no one sneaks up while discussing sensitive information.

She gives her order, and we make small talk while waiting. We've occasionally discussed her personal life before or after our nights of debauchery. Mine, however, I've avoided at all costs, making sure she knew where we stood. Tonight… that all flies out the window.

"Are you familiar with the term NDA, or nondisclosure agreement?" I jump right in as the waiter retreats from delivering her drink.

Her brows narrow in confusion. "Yes, I know what it is. Why?"

"In order to proceed, you'll need to sign one regarding everything discussed tonight." I remove the top two pages from the file and place it before her. "And just so you're clear, if you violate it in any way, you will regret it. I can't begin to stress the amount of trouble it'll cause you if anything you're about to hear is leaked. The repercussions will be dire."

Her confusion turns to shock with the harshness of my words, but I won't sugarcoat it… regardless of Sebastian's advice.

"It's up to you, but if you refuse, this will be our last night together."

And from shock… to horror. Her acceptance won't come as a surprise.

"Why?" she asks suspiciously.

"Sign the NDA and I'll explain."

"I wouldn't tell anyone what you said in confidence anyway. I've hardly talked about you in the first place." She blushes at the comment, giving me a good idea of what she *has* talked about. "Isn't this a little much?"

"It might appear that way, but you'll understand if we continue. Feel free to read it over." I gesture to the ironclad document that needs her signature.

"*If* we continue? Like I said, I wouldn't say anything regardless, so I'm only signing this to satisfy your paranoia."

Without another word, she takes the pen and scrawls her name at the bottom.

"So what's the big secret?" Her words are sarcastic.

With the document completed and safely tucked away, I'm still not entirely convinced. "I mean it, Rebecca. If you breathe a word of what I'm about to say, you'll regret it for years to come. Understood?"

"For Christ's sake, yes. I signed the damn thing, didn't I? What the hell, Eli? Just spit it out already."

I run my hand through my hair and sigh. I've been dreading this moment all week, and now that it's here, I feel no more prepared than weeks ago.

Out of ways to stall, I recite the basics of the trust.

Taking a sip of my drink and bracing myself for the next part, she chimes in, "Holy shit. Did we warp back in time?"

I laugh, which is not something I expected to happen tonight. Suddenly, I realize it's not Rebecca I'm angry with—she's innocent in this. Her only offense is wanting more from someone unwilling to give it. The realization, however, doesn't change the fact that I need her to understand what I'm offering and what I'm not.

"My thoughts exactly. Apparently, these things are still allowed in the twenty-first century."

"So now what?"

"Now, I find a wife." I sip my drink, allowing a few seconds to brace myself. "That's where you come in."

She jerks back in surprise. "Is this your way of asking me to marry you?" The hope in her eyes belies the irritation she portrays.

This is where it's crucial not to glaze over the truth and risk hurting her feelings later. Scorned women tend to make stupid decisions, and there can be no fuckups, or this will all be for nothing.

"No, this isn't a proposal. I'm merely proposing a contract. I need to be married, on paper only, for a term of two years. Then a divorce will take place, and my *ex*-wife will walk away a wealthier woman than she was."

"So you *are* asking me to marry you. I hate to be Captain Obvious, but if we're married on paper and you pay me for a divorce"—she leans in and whispers the rest—"then I'll be your wife."

"That's true, which is why transparency is important here. This is simply a means to an end for me. We'll need to live together and appear enamored in the public eye, but that's where similarities to a real marriage end. The only other thing resembling marriage will be when we fuck. However, it won't be in my bed. We'll have separate rooms."

"You make it sound so enticing." The sarcasm is dripping.

"If it sounds like I'm being a dick, then I am. I won't have you enter this arrangement with unrealistic expectations. If you're clear about where I stand and still interested in hearing the details, then I'll proceed. Otherwise, we can say goodbye and go our separate ways. It's your call, and I completely understand if it's the latter. I realize asking for two years of your life isn't fair, but it will be financially beneficial."

She sits back against the booth and turns her head to the side, breaking eye contact. I signal the waiter for another round and tip back the rest of my glass.

"I don't want to be your whore. What if I don't want to sleep with you?"

"Then don't. But it'll be a long two years of celibacy." I smirk.

She rolls her eyes and crosses her arms.

"Look, I'm not paying you to fuck me—you're already doing that for free." She gasps at the insult, but I continue, ignoring the offense, "Think of it as payment to live with me instead. Whatever makes you sleep at night." Better she knows my aloof attitude won't change with the new arrangement. I've given no indication of our relationship being anything more than sex, and it won't be any different if we proceed.

"What about seeing other people discreetly? There are plenty of open marriages out there."

"Not this one. I'm not willing to have the whole thing blow up in my face if it's discovered or have you suddenly find someone you want a real relationship with and call for a divorce early. There are stipulations in the contract to discourage it, but I'm not taking chances. Are you ready to hear the terms of the contract, then? It might shed some light on that not being an option."

"Can I still say no after having the full picture?"

"You can say no anytime before signing the marriage certificate. Although, you'd be screwing me over in the process if you wait that long since I'd be out of time to find an alternative." Maybe I should keep searching and have a backup prepared to go, but I'd only be adding risk at that point with more people knowing the situation, which is a bad idea. That means I may need to soften up a little since all my eggs are in one basket.

"I'm not out to screw you over, Eli."

I tip my head in acceptance, hearing her sincerity. However, I know what she *is* out for, making me sigh at this no-win situation for either of us.

"I might as well hear the rest of the details," she says with a sigh.

I slide the bottom file over. "This is your copy to take home and review, but I'll hit the bullet points. You should have an attorney review it on your behalf. I'll pay the bill. However, I'd like to approve of your selection first—some I wouldn't trust to keep the information confidential. You ready?"

"How long will I have to decide?"

"The engagement would go public next month, and the documents need to be signed before that. So I'd say you have a week, giving us two weeks to finalize the paperwork with any adjustments before making it official."

"What adjustments? I thought it was done."

"Rebecca, this is your contract as well. If there are things you want added or changed, we'll negotiate…. That's how business works." And that's all this is.

"Okay then, fire away."

"The conditions of the trust require me to be married for a minimum of two years after an engagement period of six months. If, for any reason, the marriage is terminated before that, an investigation into the validity of the union will take place. I'd like to avoid that at all costs. As already stated, you'll live with me, have a separate room, and, other than not dating anyone else, carry on with your normal life. You'll accompany me to events on occasion to maintain appearances. I'll provide you with a ring, ensure you have everything you need financially, and make provisions for clothing and accessories typical of being the wife of a billionaire."

She smiles slyly. "Your proposal is sounding better and better."

"Well then, you'll appreciate the final payment of two million dollars as a settlement in our future divorce. One million for each year of marriage."

"Holy shit. Where do I sign?" she asks, making me laugh in response.

Perhaps the alcohol is setting in, or perhaps I'm warming up to her. "Don't let the prospect of money make you overlook the negative aspects."

"Remind me what those were…."

I find myself chuckling again. "There's a firm prenup with no possibility of additional alimony, but I'd say the biggest drawback is being stuck in a dead-end situation for two years. This won't be a traditional relationship. My stance won't change on that."

"We'll see." She winks.

"Rebecca, if you have any delusion of becoming something more, I'd rather you decline the offer now."

She rolls her eyes. "Relax, I'm only teasing."

"I hope that's true. Otherwise, you're setting yourself up for disappointment."

"Got it."

"I can't stress it enough—this is nothing more than a business arrangement."

"Aye, aye, Captain." She salutes. "I'll take it home to review. Now that that's out of the way, are you ready to head up to the room?"

"I think I'll call it a night. You have a lot to think about, and there's no better time than while it's fresh in your mind." The last thing on my mind is sex. It sickens me to have done this at all, and fucking her right now isn't an option. I highly doubt I'd be able to get it up.

"Don't you want to remind me what else I'll be getting in the deal?" she asks seductively.

"You've had plenty of reminders. Give me your answer next week, and we'll talk about resuming our weekly *meetings*."

She chuckles. "Oh, really? You're holding sex over my head to convince me?"

"The money was meant to convince you, but if my skills in the bedroom are the deciding factor, my ego thanks you." I smirk. "The truth is, if you decide not to do this, I'll need to find someone else, so our arrangement will end anyway."

"All right, all right. Next week. I'll reach out if I'm ready before then."

"Take your time. This isn't a decision you should make overnight, and you need to go into it with your eyes wide open, so review every line of the contract before you commit. Text me if you have questions," I say, laying enough cash on the table for a quick retreat, more than ready to get the hell out of here.

Seeing Rebecca out, the first thing I do after starting my car is dial up Sebastian.

He answers the phone with no pretenses. "Did you do it?"

"Yeah, it's in her hands now."

"What're you thinking? Will she go for it?"

"There's no doubt in my mind."

"I guess congratulations are in order." I can hear his smirk.

"Fuck off," I say, ending the call.

16

REALITY

Cici

'M STANDING AT THE COPIER WAITING FOR PAPERS TO COME OUT when Matt walks up to chat. Since telling him I didn't want to be romantic, we've become good friends and often socialize in and out of the office. It's common for the three of us to be together these days rather than just Poppy and me. However, I've not revealed my pregnancy, hiding behind baggy clothes and empire-waist dresses. I've still only told Lily and Poppy. I'm too afraid to tell my parents for fear of more disappointment, and I'm not sure what will happen when Jackson finds out. I don't want to burden him with the secret, nor do I want to ruin their friendship if he takes it badly or puts the blame solely on Eli. I'm the only one who deserves that since the antibiotic issue was my fault. Technically, though, I could pass the mistake off on the doctor who prescribed them.

The thing is, I don't think of it as a mistake—it suddenly feels like a miracle. I'm not sure when it switched, but I'm fully committed to being a mom, even looking forward to it. I'm taking the role very seriously. No longer concerned about my mental health now that I understand why I've been so crazy, I've been much happier. And realizing there's something so important and dependent on me has made me determined to do everything right. I have a lot of time to make up for since I didn't find out I was pregnant for three months, so I've become obsessed with reading up on what I should do to ensure my baby's health. It's given me something to focus on rather than Eli and has worked like a charm. Eli who?

While Matt and I are talking, the copy machine suddenly goes haywire, and papers start shooting out. I rush toward the end of the machine, reaching frantically to catch the flying papers, when a sharp pain in my abdomen brings me to my knees, and I clutch my stomach in agony.

Matt crouches beside me. "Cici, what's wrong?" he asks frantically.

"I don't know. Shit. Can you find Poppy?" I croak out through the pain.

He doesn't move. "Do you need a doctor? Should I call 911?"

I shake my head fiercely. "No. Just get Poppy. Please," I plead.

"All right, I'll be right back," he says, racing from the room.

It still feels like a knife is stabbing me as I rock back and forth. *Please, please, please let my baby be okay,* I plead to God. Less than a minute passes before Poppy is next to me, frantic.

"Cici, what's happening?"

"I'm not sure, but something's wrong. It felt like something tore when I reached for the papers. I'm freaking out." I look over with tears about to fall.

"Don't panic. I'm sure everything's fine. I'll drive you in, and we'll call on the way." She stands and asks Matt, who's completely lost, "Will you help me get her to the car?"

"Yeah, absolutely." He lowers. "Can you stand, or do you want me to carry you?"

I groan at the thought of Matt carrying me out of the office for everyone to gawk at. "Help me up first."

He maneuvers under my arm and lifts slightly, only to hear me gasp halfway up. Mortification it is. "Never mind. Can you carry me?"

"Of course. I'll be as gentle as possible, okay?" he assures before grabbing under my knees and hefting me into his arms. My body being folded seems to keep the pain at bay.

"Thank you, this is better," I say to ease his obvious distress.

"Matt, I need to grab our purses. I'll hurry and meet you at my car." She starts to leave, but Matt's voice stops her in her tracks.

"Poppy, wait. I'll drive so you can sit in the back with Cici."

She looks at me in question, knowing he'll find out about the baby if he drives us. But right now, I don't care. I'd rather have her beside me like he suggested, and it was bound to come out soon anyway. I nod.

"Okay. I'll be right there," she says before rushing out.

We field questions the whole way until he's opening the door to his truck and sliding me into the back seat. I'm doing okay as long as I stay hunched and minimize my movement, other than my mind running through all the possibilities of what could be happening—none of them good. Seconds later, Poppy climbs in, and Matt pulls out of the parking lot.

I curl into Poppy. "I'm scared. What if—"

"Sssh. Think positive. Let's not jump to conclusions. How about we call your doctor and tell her we're on our way?" She squeezes me and rubs my arm, holding me against her. They answer quickly, and I listen as she tells the office what's happening. After a few times back and forth, she hangs up.

"Okay, they said L&D will admit you, and Dr. Bell will meet us. Try to stay calm. It's better for. . . ." She pauses, looking stricken as she glances toward the front seat.

"The baby?" Matt finishes her sentence, continuing, "I know what L&D is. Labor and delivery?"

We make eye contact in the rearview mirror, but I can't tell where his thoughts are.

"Yeah," I admit.

He sighs. "Was that the reason for your friends-only spiel?"

"No, I had no idea I was pregnant then," I say and shrug. "But I suppose in a way, since the dad was the reason."

He looks concerned. "Should you be calling him?"

"He doesn't know," Poppy intervenes. She's still unhappy that I haven't told Eli.

Matt immediately appears angry. "How far along are you?" The accusation is loud and clear.

"Don't judge me," I snap. "It's complicated."

He immediately backtracks. "I'm sorry. I don't mean to. It's just that I'd be pissed if a woman kept that from me."

"I will tell him. It just hasn't been the right time. Plus, I've been coming to terms with it myself. I'm five months."

He blows out a breath. "Wow. I can't believe you've been able to hide it. And everything is good? Well, until this?"

His concern is sweet, and it's obvious he cares, which sends me into another fit of tears. "It's been perfect until now. What if…?" I sniffle, unable to say the words.

"Ssssh. Everything's okay. Look, we're almost there," Poppy coos next to me. "Don't cry, sweetie. Stay strong for the baby."

I'm frantically wiping my tears away as we pull into the parking lot when the car jostles over a bump, making me hiss from another jolt of pain.

"Shoot, I'm sorry. I was trying to hurry," Matt apologizes.

Poppy pats his shoulder. "It's okay, Matt. Thank you for taking us. Pull up in front of emergency, and we'll go to labor and delivery from there."

He gently swings the car in, slowly coming to a stop, careful not to shake me any more.

"Should I get a wheelchair?" Poppy stands at the open door with Matt walking up behind her.

Matt nods. "Go ahead. I'll lift her in."

"I can probably just walk."

"No," they both say in unison. It breaks the tension and causes us all to chuckle before Poppy heads inside to grab a chair.

Matt steps up to the seat and moves my hair behind my ear. "Hey. I'm sorry if I was harsh earlier. That wasn't fair. I'm here for you if you need more people in your corner. I want to help if I can. I care about you… in a friendly way." He winks, pulling another smile from me.

"Thanks, Matt. I could use the support. You're only the third person to find out, so I'll take you up on that. A guy's perspective would be nice."

"You got it. Head on in with Poppy, and I'll park the car. I'll be right behind you," he says as he reaches to lift me into the chair Poppy parked behind him.

It's still uncomfortable, and now that we're here, I'm freaking out again. Am I being punished for not telling Eli? Is this what a miscarriage feels like? I thought I was past that point, but I guess it can happen at any time. Please, please don't let that be what's happening. Starting two months ago when I discovered a tiny life growing inside me, I've wanted this baby more than I've wanted anything in my life. Now, I'll do anything to protect it.

After being checked in and settled into a room, Poppy and Matt sit beside the bed while Dr. Bell prepares to do an ultrasound. The nurse said the baby's heartbeat is strong, thank God. It allowed for some relief, but I won't be at ease until I'm assured that everything is okay.

We had to tell the staff that Matt was the father so they'd let him in the room, and it added another layer of guilt over keeping this from

Eli. I've decided to call him tonight if everything turns out okay. Matt's opinion is another reason for my decision because deep down I know he's right—Eli deserves the truth.

This is my first ultrasound so far. I had one scheduled for Monday that I probably won't need now. I'm still saying my prayers as Dr. Bell spreads warm goop all over my lower belly.

"All right, Cici, tell me how you've been feeling until this afternoon." She starts moving a wand-type thing with a smooth, flat bottom over my stomach to spread the gel.

"Normal. Nothing out of the ordinary."

"And what happened today?"

I told her everything from the copy room incident until we arrived at the hospital.

"How is your pain level now?" She moves the wand around, and the screen changes as she does, but I can't make out a darn thing. She pauses, punching in numbers, repeating the pattern a few times, still not saying anything to ease my fear.

"It's been better since I've been here, but I haven't tried to stand yet, and that's when it really hurts. Straightening is the worst."

Dr. Bell smiles. "Well, I can assure you the baby is doing great. The heartbeat is strong, and everything is as it should be. Your placenta looks normal, and here—" She rubs the wand over a particular spot and finagles it for a few seconds before an unmistakable shape shows on the screen. "—is your baby."

Poppy squeezes my hand as I wipe the tears away to see better. That's my baby. Oh my God, I'm going to be a mother. It's really happening, and an incredible feeling of joy washes over me. If only Eli were here to share this moment.

"Here you can see the heartbeat." She wiggles the wand and points to a tiny, fast flutter on the screen.

I'm in awe—we all are.

"Wow. That's so cool. You're having a baby," Poppy squeals and pumps my hand up and down.

"See? I wasn't making it up," I say sarcastically, and she rolls her eyes, smiling.

"Do you want to find out if it's a boy or girl, or do you want to be surprised?" Dr. Bell asks.

I turn to Poppy and Matt. "I… I feel like I should wait… to share that part." They understand what I'm referring to, but I can't be specific since Matt is supposed to be the father. How they're seated certainly doesn't back that up, though, so I imagine the doctor has an inkling.

"What do you guys think?" I ask them.

Matt nods in agreement while Poppy answers, "Maybe I should be told, and we can do a fun reveal when you're ready. They're super popular these days, and Lily could do it with me. Please?"

I look at Dr. Bell for thoughts.

"How about I put it in an envelope so you have it if you change your mind or want someone else to take a peek?" She winks. "I'll also print some pictures of the baby. How does that sound?"

"That's a great idea. Let's do it. So if everything looks good, what did happen today?"

Finishing the exam, we learned that I experienced something called round ligament pain, which is common in pregnancy and can be more painful in some cases. She shared some tips to minimize occurrences and things I can do to help when it happens. The relief I feel walking out of the hospital is indescribable. I'm still sore when we leave, but nothing compared to on the way in. The only thing bringing me pain currently is the absence of Eli and the fact that I'm doing this without him. Matt helped me realize today how unfair I'm being, and with my decision made, I'm eager to call and share the news.

After assuring Matt I could drive, he brought us back to the office to get our cars. It's a relief not to keep this a secret anymore. Part of me was worried about what people would think, but Matt's support has me hopeful that others might be more accepting as well. What other people think shouldn't matter, but I'm only human, so it does.

When I got home, I made myself something to eat while working up the nerve to call Eli. I'm finishing up in the kitchen when my cell rings. Glancing at the screen to Eli's name has my heart pounding immediately. Did someone tell him about the baby? Who would have done that? Matt couldn't have, but would he have convinced Poppy to do it? I told them I planned to do it tonight, but maybe they didn't believe me. I'm in full panic mode and barely answer in time.

"Hello?"

"Hi, Cici. How are you?"

Does he mean how am I after today, or how am I in general?

"I'm good. Why?" I ask suspiciously.

"Because I haven't talked to you in a while, and that's usually how you start a conversation?"

I laugh nervously. "Yeah, right. Sorry. How have you been?" *Should I tell him about the baby now?*

"Good, I guess. That's sort of why I'm calling. I need to tell you something before you find out elsewhere."

"Okay... what's that?"

"Well, your brother or Lily might have told you, but I've been seeing Rebecca—the girl who used to work in your office. I met her that day I came in and again at the bar the night you were there. Well... she started frequenting the club, and one thing led to another."

"Yeah, I know. And you don't have to explain," I sigh. "Your private life is none of my business." Not sure why he feels compelled to share, but I really don't want to hear more.

"Maybe not, but I still need this off my chest if you'll listen."

"Well, hurry up because I have something to get off mine too." *And it's more important than whatever this crap is.*

"I'm doing something tomorrow, and I want you to hear it from me before anyone else. More importantly, please believe me when I say that it doesn't diminish anything we had together."

"Eli, you're talking in riddles. What's going on?"

He groans in response before pulling the rug out from under my feet.

"I'm getting engaged… to Rebecca."

What. The. Fuck? My knees buckle, and I sink to the floor.

Seconds pass. "Cici? Are you still there?"

He's getting engaged. He loves Rebecca. He's starting a life with another woman. He's starting a family—oh God, he certainly doesn't need another one. I'd only be creating problems if I told him now. *Fuck!*

"Please say something," he pleads.

Taking a deep breath and pasting a smile on my face to hide my true emotions, I finally speak. "That's great, Eli. I'm happy for you. The call wasn't necessary, but since you did, tell Rebecca I said congratulations."

"Don't do that, Cici. Don't make light of this."

"What do you want me to do?"

"Fuck." He groans in agony before continuing, "I just want you to know that you still mean something to me."

"Well, I suggest you let that go since you *are* asking another woman to marry you tomorrow. Congratulations, Eli, and don't bother calling again."

I hang up and lie on the floor while my body trembles with sobs.

I'm not sure how much time passes until my phone starts ringing and Lily's face lights up the screen.

"Hello?" My voice comes out hoarse from crying.

She picks up on it immediately. "Cici, are you okay?"

Not at all. I shake my head as I choke on the next sob, trying to form words to no avail.

"Cici, what is it? Did something happen to the baby?"

"No," I answer quickly. "The baby's perfect…. I saw it today…. Got pictures… and everything." My words come out between gulps of air.

"What? Why didn't you text me and send me a picture?"

"I was planning on it. Right after calling Eli to tell him about the baby… but he called me first."

There's a long pause while I sniffle some more.

"Oh, sweetie. He told you, didn't he? Sebastian just filled me in, which is why I was calling. I can't believe they kept it quiet until the day before. Wait! So did you tell him about the baby?"

"Noooo," I wail. "I freaked out after he said he was getting engaged, so all that came out was congratulations and not to call me again. Lily, I can't. It's too complicated now."

"Cici, you have to tell him—now more than ever."

"Why? What good would it do? I'm fine on my own, and it would only hurt him at this point."

"That's not true. I know you're still working on your commitment issue, and you may not be ready yet, but don't you think it's time to give a relationship with Eli a try? He loves you, Cici. You can't let him marry her."

"Lily, stop it. He's moved on. He loves Rebecca now, and it wouldn't be fair to come between them. It's too late for us."

"I don't believe that. I'm not accepting this Rebecca woman."

"You can't do that. She'll be your sister-in-law." Holy shit, saying that hits me harder than expected, and more tears silently fall. I don't want to lose it again, so I need her to let this go.

Lily groans, "I don't care. I don't like her."

"You don't know her. She's not bad. Just give her a chance." This. Is. Killing. Me.

Thank God she changes the subject. "Tell me more about the baby. I thought your ultrasound was next week."

Relieved for the distraction, I gladly dive into the events of today, filling her in on my scare and how mind-blowing it was to see the baby for the first time.

"I wish you were pregnant," I whine when I'm done.

"Trust me, we're trying. Who knew my husband would have a breeding kink, but holy hell is it hot. I wouldn't be surprised if I already have a bun in the oven, but I'm okay if not because, man, it's fun making one." She giggles.

My eyes roll. "Ha. Don't worry, with Sebastian, it'll go from a breeding kink to a pregnancy kink. I doubt he'll ever not find something to obsess about. I still can't believe how far you've come, from the shy virgin to surpassing *my* sex life, which is now over for the foreseeable future."

"It wouldn't have to be if you'd listen to me and—"

"Enough. Unless I want to show up to Jackson's wedding at the end of August and shock the shit out of everyone, I'll have to fess up soon. Just give me a few weeks to process that my baby's dad is marrying someone else. Plus, I'm still considering telling people I had a one-night stand with a tourist right when I got back and have no idea who the father is. It would be easier that way—for everyone."

"I'm not letting you do that. You know I love you and I'm usually on your side, but not this time, Cici. Not only does Eli deserve the truth, but it's killing me to keep this from Sebastian about his brother."

I want to be mad at her, but I can't be because she's right. "I'm sorry. It's just that I feel like such a bitch being *that* woman, interfering with a perfectly happy couple and causing problems," I groan.

"Well, buck up, buttercup, because you're all adults. You can't hide it forever, and Eli's not stupid—I bet he'd put two and two to-gether—so the sooner you do it, the better. Whatever happens, hap-pens, and I'll be by your side no matter what."

"Ugh. Okay, give me some time to formulate a plan, and I'll make the call, I promise."

Shit, why did I add that when I haven't one hundred percent decided? The problem is, it sounds like Lily has for me, and really… I have no choice when it comes down to it because she's right. Eli would figure it out in the end.

17

THE TRUTH

Eli

Fuck. *Fuck. Fuck.* Did I make that call to make *myself* feel better or Cici, for fuck's sake? Because, based on her reaction, it had the opposite effect as intended. Or maybe I'm reading her wrong and she doesn't give a shit what I'm doing anymore. Would she care that I'm still in love with her? That she's the last thing on my mind before I fall asleep each night and the first thought I wake up to? I wonder what her reaction would be if I told her that to this day, I still close my eyes and imagine it's her each time I fuck Rebecca.

It's too bad I'll never find out since saying those things wouldn't at all support the validity of my engagement. And while I'd like nothing more than for Cici to know this is only a sham, not only is it not an option, but I might as well stop now and give up if I'm going to blow it before I've even pulled the trigger. I swear I'll have no hair by the time this is over considering how often I run my hands through it, and pulling on it out of frustration.

The only thing keeping me sane these days is getting back into the racing circuit. Sebastian has laid off since he knows I've been hanging on by a thread. Other than the occasional look of disappointment, he hasn't said anything. However, he's not so silent about my impending engagement and is constantly keeping tabs on the progress with Rebecca.

We've finally worked out all the kinks with the prenup. She didn't ask for more than I offered but wanted to clarify contingencies for things such as work, a monthly spending budget and, God forbid, accidental pregnancy. After that topic, I decided I'll be buying new condoms every day and having her pay a visit to *my* doctor, whom I can trust for birth control. There's no way I'd allow myself to be tied to the woman for the rest of my life, and thankfully, he didn't stipulate children.

The appointment is tomorrow afternoon for the final review of the prenup and to sign the agreement regarding the terms of our private arrangement before the formal marriage takes place in December. Later in the evening, we'll make an official statement to the media at the engagement party, removing me from California's most eligible bachelor list, which I've crowned since the day Sebastian got hitched.

The party will function as part of the ruse to make our marriage appear realistic. We invited our closest friends, a few of her family members, and Dubree Enterprise's top business associates to an exclusive event with a surprise announcement for everyone in attendance. That way, it couldn't be leaked beforehand. Only two things were left to consider: living arrangements and a damn ring.

Though most couples cohabitate before the wedding these days, we won't be, and if any of the press or guests ask why, we've prepared an answer: we're keeping things traditional since we have the rest of our lives to live together. Even though it's nobody's fucking business, the media doesn't see it that way—nor does the public, for that matter.

Sebastian had to remind me about the ring, which I'll pick up tomorrow. It's a simple solitaire. Nothing fancy, nothing over the top, nothing special, and nothing like the one I spent days debating on for Cici. That particular piece of jewelry is still tucked away in hopes of a miracle that one day we'll find our way back to each other. After she hung up on me tonight, that hope has shrunk considerably. Add in my commitment for the next two and a half years, and I may as well give up any last shreds, with nothing but memories to hold on to.

Those memories tend to consume my thoughts at night, causing me to toss and turn most evenings, occasionally dreaming of Cici and I together, happy and in love. Sometimes they're sexy, sometimes not, but the best ones are with our future family when I catch a glimpse of what our life would've been like. The mornings after are bittersweet, however. Having her in my dreams is better than nothing, but waking up to reality always wrecks me.

Luckily, this night leaves me in peace with no visions to wake up to. I have enough on my plate without the remnants of a dream to haunt me all day. I'll need to be on my A game to pull off our first public outing as an engaged couple. I'm sure it'll be fine, especially with Sebastian by my side, schooling me to behave correctly, meaning touching and swooning over Rebecca throughout the night. I'm already cringing at the act I'll be putting on and counting the hours until it's over—before it's even begun.

"Are you ready for today?" Sebastian asks as the gym door closes, and I head to the bike.

"Does it matter?" I respond dryly, hopping on.

"I'm not your enemy here, Eli. If you think I enjoy seeing you like this, you're wrong. I don't like that Dad did this any more than you do."

"I know, I'm sorry. I shouldn't take it out on you, but since you're the only one who knows the truth, you're also the only one who gets my shit. Thanks for taking it as well as you have. To answer your question, though—yeah, I'm ready. As ready as I can be with a hundred-pound weight on my chest." I drop my head and shake it.

"Well then, getting today out of the way might lessen that weight a little. With all the paperwork completed and the announcement handled, you can relax until the wedding. That should make the next six months easier to stomach."

"You'd think that, but once it's official, it would look odd if we were never spotted together. Our friends and her family will get suspicious, and I don't need questions being asked or the tabloids running with rumors. I'm not worried about our friends, but I'm certain her family would disapprove of our arrangement."

Sebastian scoffs, "Who wouldn't approve of a one-million-dollar annual salary along with more fringe benefits than any other job in the world?"

"Not the point and you know it. Besides, whether they're okay with it or not, I'm fucked if word gets back to any of our trust advisors. I'd rather this not all be for nothing in the end."

"Then bring her to corporate events and fundraisers, have your picture in the columns now and then. Doesn't mean you need to be together all the damn time. Continue your weekly hookups with her and call it good. But you *will* be living with the woman, so it might be smart to spend more time with her first." He puts the weight down he was lifting and turns, giving me his full attention. "And speaking of spending time with her, if you don't want Lily in on the secret, which I'm still not comfortable with, then you need to have her over so she can get to know her. I told her about the engagement last night, so we'll need to schedule something soon."

"Fucking great." That's the last thing I want to do. "I'll need a break after our performance tonight, so tell her we're both busy and set up brunch at your place in three weeks. Talk about fucking awkward. How did Lily react anyway?"

"Surprised, of course, and fairly pissed about it. I knew she'd be mildly upset since Cici is her best friend, but she reacted harsher than expected. Who knows, she might not take to her, and Rebecca won't need to be around much." He shrugs and resumes lifting.

"Then let's see how tonight goes, and if we can skip the brunch."

"Fat chance of that—don't get your hopes up."

I should just let all hope go at this point....

The signing went smoothly this afternoon. It lasted long enough to review the documents, sign along the dotted line, and make it official. We parted ways so we could prepare for the evening and pack overnight bags. We're staying at the hotel where the party is being hosted to fit the narrative of a couple in love and excited to celebrate. What a fucking joke. However, I'll probably be ready to blow off steam by the end of this anyway.

The car I hired until tomorrow parks alongside the curb in front of Rebecca's house. Unlike my brother, who enjoys being chauffeured everywhere, I prefer to drive myself. Though tonight, I thought it best to play it up for the paparazzi and give them what's expected. There's also a part of me that doesn't want to share my personal pleasures with Rebecca. Those are reserved for special people in my life, and she doesn't qualify.

This happens to be the first time I've seen where she lives since we've always met on location. It's not terrible, but it's also not great, so I can understand why she pushed so hard for us to move in together before the wedding. It was one of my sticking points during our talks that I didn't budge on in order to support the boundaries of this arrangement. I won't dangle any carrots for her to grab onto.

Sustaining the precedent I've set, I type a quick text telling her to come on out. Fuck. I'm aware that I'm being a complete asshole, but it's one of the few things justifying this whole situation to myself. I can't give her the best of me—it doesn't feel right. She may not be the one to blame and doesn't deserve this treatment, but if I behave any other way, then I'll sacrifice my last ounce of self-preservation. There's only one person the real me is reserved for, and since my last shred of hope refuses to snap, Rebecca gets what I'm willing to give her.

The front door opens, and Rebecca emerges looking at ease for the engagement party. She resembles the right amount of sexy and class in a tight green dress that stops just above her knees with a modest neckline. It's sleeveless and showcases her attractive shoulders.

The driver rushes to take her bag before opening the back door.

I smile as she settles in. "You look lovely." I'm not a jerk all of the time.

"Back at you. Thanks for the ride," she says demurely.

"It's the least I could do for our big night." I wink. "Speaking of which…." I reach into my pocket and pull out a box, handing it to her. "It would look odd if my fiancée didn't have a ring, so I picked this up today." I'd asked her size this morning, so I'm sure this isn't a surprise, but she looks excited nonetheless.

Opening the box, her hand flies to her mouth as if it's the most beautiful thing in the world. "Oh my gosh, Eli, it's gorgeous."

"I'm glad you like it since you'll be wearing it for the next couple of years." It's not anything extraordinary for my level of wealth, but I do have standards to live up to and reasoned a three-carat solitaire would suffice.

"I love it. Thank you. Really, it's… perfect." She stares in awe until I suddenly do something unexpected.

"Here, let me help." I take the box and remove the ring, reaching for her left hand to slide it onto her finger until it stops. She takes over, pushing it the rest of the way, then holds it out to admire it.

"Wow. This is really happening," she says in wonder.

We ride in silence for a while as she stares at her ring.

It's important we arrive in good spirits, so I go with a peace offering. "I'm sorry this isn't quite how you pictured things between us. Even though I'm not interested in more than our arrangement, I'm grateful to spend the next couple of years with someone who's not a stranger. There may not be love, but I'd like to be friends."

She beams at my words, then adds, "Friends with benefits."

I chuckle. "Yes… that."

"And since we're staying overnight, we'll be able to take advantage of those benefits again, right?" Her voice becomes seductive as her hand slides up my thigh toward my crotch.

"No reason not to," I respond as her hand tightens around the unavoidable bulge in my pants—sex is sex, and he's eager at the prospect. However, I can't be altering the rules on day one and allowing anything out of the bedroom. Grabbing her wrist, I remove it from my crotch and place it back into her lap.

"But let's wait until later. We have a show to put on first. Are you ready?" I gesture behind her toward the sidewalk we're pulling up to with a jerk of my head. Various reporters are already loitering along the front of the building, anticipating our arrival.

We alerted the media about the party so they could take pictures and ask questions all at once, hopefully getting it over with and avoiding any gossip or speculation. Rebecca and I devised a plausible story of our courtship that isn't too far from the truth. No one needs to know that every "date" consisted of meeting in a hotel room for sex. In all honesty, the amount of talking we've done over the last few months was minimal. In fact, we knew very little about each other before last week when we decided to do a crash course on our lives.

We needed enough familiarity with each other to at least make it through tonight with all eyes scrutinizing our previously unknown relationship. To most, it will be a surprise to say the least. Our story is that we wanted time outside the public eye to date and enjoy our time together, so we decided to keep it under the radar until necessary. And here we are.

"I am," she says assuredly.

My eyebrows go up in skepticism, and she laughs.

"Come on, this'll be fun. Think of it as an acting gig with some improv. And the good news? We both have rewards to look forward to." She seductively tilts her brows.

"Is that so? Well, in that case, let's put on our best show." I wink.

This banter between us is new and not altogether unpleasant. Could this not be as terrible as I've been making it out to be? Tonight won't only be eye-opening for our guests but for me as well with a fresh new look at the situation. God knows I could use one.

My door opens, and I smile at Rebecca before exiting. "All right, let's do this," I say before instructing her to wait for me to come around.

The reporters are already shouting questions as I walk to the door, but I ignore them as I reach for her hand. As she steps out for our grand entrance, a knot forms in my stomach at the camera clicks behind me, knowing these will be the pictures Cici wakes up to. And just like that, my mood sours, and I'm right back to square one with a scowl replacing the smile from moments ago.

As planned, we pose for pictures, make a statement, and answer questions from the media, all while holding hands and embracing as any enamored couple would. During which, I constantly remind myself that it's necessary and try not to think of a certain someone's reaction upon seeing the ensuing stories in tomorrow's tabloids. Who knows? Maybe she'll be relieved that she's finally free. *What the fuck? Why the hell am I still hung up on a woman who wants nothing to do with me?*

Did I do the right thing by calling her last night or set myself back at this point? How will I make it through the next two years if I can't manage to handle one damn night? Time to pull my head out of my ass and do what it takes to pull this off, which might be drinking copious amounts of alcohol.

"That went well, don't you think?" Rebecca pulls me from my thoughts as we break free from the paparazzi and enter the lobby.

"It did. Now comes the real test, though. We'll see how good we are when people who know us scrutinize our answers," I say as I intentionally retract my hand from hers to push the elevator button. Could I have used my other hand? Yes. But the desire to free myself had reached the breaking point.

She remains unfazed. "We've got this. Remember, it's mostly all true with slight embellishments here and there. Piece of cake, right?"

I smile curtly. "Right." Easy for her to say since she's playing to her desires. It's an entirely different story when it's the last thing you want.

What I do want at the moment is a drink.

Somehow, we manage to move through the night without stumbling over our answers while convincing everyone we're besotted and eager to start our lives together. I was worried about meeting her parents, but it seems that if your daughter is marrying someone with gobs of money, the rest doesn't matter so much. And if the apple doesn't fall far from the tree, it would confirm my early suspicion regarding Rebecca and reminds me of a reason I wasn't interested in the first place.

As the night progresses, so does my intoxication level. The consensus is that I'm overjoyed to be declaring our relationship. I'm not one who typically copes through alcohol, but that's precisely what I'm doing. One more squeeze, hand hold, or kiss along with someone telling us how perfect we are together, and I'm going to lose my shit. While Rebecca brightens as we go, my mood darkens with each person we convince.

Our friends and acquaintances were cordial enough and seemed genuinely happy—all but two, that is. Jackson and Lily have been less than friendly and aren't doing well to hide their disdain for Rebecca or possibly just not trying. I *almost* stepped in to defend her until a glimpse of her true colors prevented me from speaking up.

In an unmistakable jab to Rebecca, Lily says, "It's too bad Cici couldn't make it. I'm sure she would've loved to congratulate you in person rather than over the phone last night with Eli."

Oh fuck. Why does the truth sometimes do more damage than good?

Being called out is like a punch to the gut. Looking at Rebecca, shock covers her face for half a second before a brief flash of anger crosses her features. I'm about to intervene and explain the call when she beats me to the punch.

"She would have had to receive an invite, and Eli and I decided it was best to give her the news over the phone since it would've been uncomfortable to celebrate with one of our exes in attendance," Rebecca finishes with a smile, oozing contempt as she wraps her arm around mine and leans close.

Fuck. She's a better actress than I've given her credit for to pull that out of the hat. The revelation gives me pause and makes me want to play back the last couple weeks to see if I missed something along the way that I should be concerned about. Just because we signed the terms of the agreement doesn't mean we're bound to go through with it.

There are consequences in place for not following through on my part—compensation to Rebecca if I call things off. Alternatively, there's a bonus to Rebecca for not backing out. Unfortunately, there's no way to hold her feet to the fire, so we created an incentive to deter her from changing her mind before the wedding.

Besides Rebecca's acting skills, this conversation makes two things abundantly clear: Lily knows way more than I thought, and Cici will undoubtedly hear about anything that happens moving forward. The fact that Lily already heard about my conversation last night speaks volumes. Did Lily call Cici, or the other way around? Does Lily know Cici's true feelings about me? About what's happening?

My eyes find Sebastian's, who stands beside Lily with his arm protectively around her waist. He shrugs as if he, too, has no idea what to make of it. Jackson and Mia are the third couple in our circle, and like Lily, Jackson makes no effort to mask his disapproval.

"Well, you might want to get used to it. Cici is more than just an ex—she's family—and she may not be here now, but there'll be plenty of times in the future when she will be," Jackson says reproachfully, silencing everyone.

The waiter approaches, offering champagne, and after handing one to Rebecca, I greedily take two for myself. Gulping one down in the few seconds it takes for everyone else to partake, I set the empty back on the tray and grab another.

"Cheers." I hold one up to a circle of wide eyes as they meet my glass with their own. "To family," I say and down the next one in three seconds flat, leaving one more to go. "Now, let's get this party started, shall we?"

The rest of the evening is a blur as we mingle with the crowd, repeating our story enough that it's forever ingrained in my brain. I've become quiet, letting Rebecca do the talking, trying to contain my irritation at the injustice of it all. Meanwhile, I'm drinking enough champagne for both of us. When the last guest finally leaves, I'm more than ready to call it a night.

"Two bedrooms?" Rebecca asks as she takes in the room we entered moments ago.

An open door on each side of the main sitting area reveals king-size beds beyond. I couldn't rent two separate rooms and risk having that on record, but this will do.

"I thought I made my stance on sharing a bed clear." I'm curt as I busy myself with inspecting the minibar for a drink.

"Right…. You sure you need another drink?"

Yes… yes, I do.

Picking a bottle, I pour it into a glass of ice and turn around with a smirk. "The wedding's in six months—no need to start nagging yet. Unless you're worried I won't be able to perform." The funny thing is that it's certainly possible. I don't remember the last time I was this drunk—the night certainly took a toll on my sanity.

"Oh, I could work around that. How about you let me do the heavy lifting tonight? Since we're celebrating our engagement, we could always start with a repeat of our first encounter. Would you like that?"

Without waiting for an answer, she slowly walks toward me, her hips swaying from side to side with every step she takes. Her hands reach back to lower the zipper of her dress before it falls to the floor as she stops before me and lowers to her knees.

There's no doubt that Rebecca is sexy. She looked great in the dress and even better out of it. Any man would be thrilled to have this woman offering herself up. But this man wants what he can't have, and that's certainly not the woman in this room. Does that mean I'll turn down what she's offering? Fuck no.

"I'd say that's a good start."

By the time we make it to the bedroom, I'm inebriated to the point of incoherency. In a way, it's what I was going for, but it's undoubtedly not my best moment. Somehow, I end up in bed, on my back, being ridden like a horse with my eyes closed. And you can imagine where my mind is.

It's the best feeling I've had in months. Cici on top of me, taking what she wants, giving us both the pleasure we need. I'm high in the moment, feeling her on top of me, her pussy squeezing my cock just the way I remember. It's so intense, I want it to last forever, but the image in my mind of her bouncing up and down, the body I've missed so much on display before me…. It's too much for me to take, and I explode.

"Oh fuck, fuck, fuck. Goddammit. Yes. Fuck, I love you, Cici!" My final words as the last pulse fades and the lights go out.

18

MISERABLE

Cici

KNEW WHAT I WAS WAKING UP TO THIS MORNING, SO OF COURSE, it was the first thing I Googled after reaching for my phone. My immediate reaction was absolute devastation for the first ten minutes of internet stalking. But then I started fixating on the fact that there's something off about their pictures. They don't look right, and not just the fact that they shouldn't be together, but more than that. I just can't quite put my finger on it.

When they all blur together, I have to quit looking and go to the kitchen for a cup of tea. Bringing it back to bed with me, I dial Lily, who answers on the first ring.

"Good morning, sunshine. I've seen as much as I can online. How was it?" I ask, getting straight to the point.

"It was interesting. I tried to give her a chance… for a second. But it turns out I definitely don't like her. We're supposed to have brunch in a couple weeks over here to 'get to know each other.' Honestly, I think it's a waste of time. I know everything I need to. There's something off about her."

"Lily, you're only saying that because you wanted him to be with me. You can't blame that on her."

"I can do anything I want. Besides, it's not just that. You should have seen her last night, parading around like she was the prize to be had. It was disgusting if you ask me. And then, when I said that I wished you were there instead of Eli telling you over the phone, you should have seen the look on her face."

"*You said what?* Why would you do that?"

"Why else? I wanted to see her reaction, and boy, it did not disappoint. Her talons came right out. She tried to hide it, but I saw her initial shock when I outed him. But then she let her bitch show and made some crap up about both of them deciding it would be best if you weren't there. I call bullshit. And the look on Eli's face only confirmed it."

"Lily…," I admonish.

"Oh, and you should have seen Jackson after that. He was worse than me. Told her that you were family and that she better get used to having you around." Lily laughs at the memory. "I'm not the only one who doesn't approve."

My head looks up to the sky as I groan, "You guys shouldn't be acting like that. This was my decision, not Eli's. You can't blame her. Now I feel bad for both of them."

"Well, don't. What you need to do is figure out how to spill the news, and you need to do it soon. Don't let them get too far into this before you blow it up."

"LILY! I'm not blowing anything up. Even if I do tell him, it's only to let him know that he's having a child, not for him to be with me."

"You mean *when* you tell him, not *if*. I mean it, Cici, I'm not keeping this secret forever. I'll give you two more weeks, and that's it."

"It's my choice, Lily, since it's my baby."

"That's crap. It's my niece or nephew, and they deserve to have a father." She pauses and sighs dramatically. "Also, I'd really like my baby to grow up knowing they have a cousin."

"Wait, what?"

"I'm pregnant, Cici. I just found out. We're having babies together!"

"Oh my God! I'm so excited!"

"Me too. So you'll tell him, right?"

"I will. I just need to figure out how. But I'm so happy for you, Lily!"

"I'm happy for us."

It's been a week since the engagement party, and I have one more before Lily puts her foot down. Until then, I need to figure out what to say and how to say it. I've somewhat relaxed and restricted myself to only looking at their pictures once a day. Okay—maybe twice. But today doesn't count.

I'm considering it research to help prepare for breaking the news. Poppy is on her way, and she better be here soon because my mind is going crazy with possibilities. I've gone back and forth about what to tell him. It's terrible that I've let it go this far without confessing. Even my counselor has been encouraging me to do it.

When I first found out, I was in shock, of course, but then I almost felt like a hypocrite committing to a child after telling him I couldn't commit to marriage. How was it so easy for me to admit my love for our baby, but could never own up to my love for him? I always knew I loved Eli, but my damn phobia issue wouldn't allow me to give in to it. Now I'm worried he'll be so angry about my deception that he'll reject anything I say. Not to mention, he's fricking engaged to another woman. I've only made it worse by waiting, but fear is a powerful thing.

Thank God for the sound of the doorbell, immediately followed by the door opening to reveal my redheaded spitfire of a friend. I need her spunk right now to pull me out of my spiraling thoughts and set me back on track.

"Why are you sitting in the dark?" she asks when her eyes land on my form in the middle of the couch.

I look around, taking in the room. "I didn't realize it was dark yet. I've been staring at the computer for the last hour, waiting for you."

She flips the lights on and cocks her head. "Dare I ask what you've been staring at, or do I even need to?"

"No. You don't. And I'm only looking because I knew what we were doing tonight. I thought it would help set the tone."

"Sure, you did." She plops down next to me. "Let me see while you pour me some wine and refill your tea."

I hand her the computer and go to the kitchen, pulling a bottle of white from the fridge before heating my water. I'm filling her glass when I hear the printer going. Two seconds later, Poppy scurries past the kitchen and into the office, coming back with a piece of paper in her hand.

"What did you print?" I ask as she fishes around the junk drawer and extracts a pair of scissors.

"I decided we need a prop for you to talk to, so… I printed one of the pictures where they're not plastered together to cut them apart." She holds up the half with Eli on it, then hands me the other and says, "Here, you can do the honor of ripping this one to shreds."

"Poppy, I don't hate Rebecca. It's not her fault I am the way I am."

"It's her fault you haven't told him, though. Come on, it's part of the process."

My head drops and I shake it. "This feels wrong."

"Admit it, you're sort of excited. Go on, do it," she encourages.

Holding it up, I look at the picture while Poppy takes over making my tea. It's weird seeing Rebecca on her own. She's happy, but there's something else, too, that I can't quite put my finger on. Poppy's right—I do want to tear it to pieces. She may not be at fault, but a part of me blames her for seeking him out. I know she did, especially after that conversation in the office way back when. To go after him when she knew we dated is what I'm angriest over. On the other hand, Eli deserves to be happy, though I hate that it's with someone I know.

With one last sigh, I hold the paper up and rip her in two, then stack the halves to do it again and again and again until the pieces are so small that I can't anymore. A huge smile breaks out. Poppy and I look at each other and immediately start cracking up.

"That was fun," she says when we calm down. "Cheers."

We clink glasses and sip.

"Now take this one, look him in the eyes, and tell him what you want to say." She hands me the picture of Eli, and I stare at it.

It strikes me immediately. Something's missing. Eli doesn't look happy at all. He seems downright miserable. What the hell? It's so obvious now that they're not next to each other. Her happiness must have drowned his misery out. I suppose they could have had a spat right before arriving, but something tells me that's not the case with Rebecca's unmistakable joy.

"This is all I needed. I'm ready," I state matter-of-factly.

"Good. Let's hear it, then."

"No. I mean, I'm ready to tell him. In person. To his face."

"Wellll, okay then. Do you want to FaceTime him?"

"No, I want to go there and talk to him. I need to make sure he's happy. He doesn't look like it in this picture. Can you tell?" I hold it up for her.

"I mean, I don't know him, but now that you point it out, I'd say he's not the most jovial guy I've ever seen. Is he usually? Or is this his general demeanor?" Poppy asks while studying it.

"He's usually happy-go-lucky—this is definitely not his normal MO. What if there's more to the story? What if Rebecca's holding something over his head, forcing him to marry her? What if *she's* pregnant? What if he's being trapped?" I practically yell the last part.

"Whoa, Cici. Slow down a minute and climb out of the rabbit hole you just fell into. They may have had a spat or something. I'm certainly not team Rebecca, but I'd hate for you to get your hopes up over one picture. And why are you suddenly starting to sound like you want them not to be together? You still love him, don't you?"

"I never said I loved him."

"You didn't have to."

I inhale deeply as the tears start to form, and the truth I've been denying far too long starts tumbling out. "Yes, dammit. I still love him. And now that it's too late, I'd die for a chance to be with him. It's almost like as soon as it wasn't an option, that's when I decided I was ready. I'm such a cliché, only wanting what I can't have." I chuckle through my tears and shake my head.

"Or perhaps you just needed the option taken away to realize what you wanted. I'm worried about you, though. I don't want you to set yourself up for disappointment."

"Trust me, I'm not. And my goal isn't to get him back. I'm just hoping that if I tell him in person, he won't completely hate me for keeping it from him for so long. Plus, this way, I can tell my parents and brother while I'm there."

"I'm pretty sure they'll notice something before the words make it out of your mouth." Poppy gestures to my belly. "Are you sure you don't want to give them a heads-up or something so they don't have a heart attack right when they open the door?"

"Nah. It'll be fun to see the looks on their faces." I laugh, imagining their reaction.

"That's crazy. I can't imagine not telling my family I was pregnant for six months."

"I've had you, Matt, and Lily, so I didn't need to. Speaking of Lily, I better tell her I'm coming. I'll book a ticket for the week after next, even though it's past my deadline. I'm sure she'll just be relieved that I'm doing it."

"Well, now that that's decided, we better work out what you'll say. Come on, bring him with you and let's go practice."

Only a few more days until I go home to drop the bombshell on everyone's lap. I'm starting to get cold feet and seriously contemplating doing it by phone. If Lily and Poppy weren't holding me accountable, I'd probably have already cancelled. On the phone today, after being filled in on their brunch this morning, which unsurprisingly didn't end well, I'd simply made a single comment about not coming this week, and she was having none of it.

So I took advantage of my lazy day and packed a small suitcase for the trip. Other than that, I've been relaxing since it's Sunday and I'll have enough excitement in my life after everyone knows about the baby.

The pregnancy has been going well, but I think the stress of what I'm about to do has been disrupting my sleep, and I've been more tired than usual, which is adding to my anxiety. And because of that, I'm in the kitchen again, snacking like I've been doing all day.

I'm surfing the web while munching and looking for something to make for dinner tonight when my phone lights up with a call from Lily.

"Hey, Lils," I say after bringing it to my ear.

Not even a second passes before her words come out frantic. "Eli got in an accident racing today. He's in the hospital."

"What? Is he okay?" My hand flies to my chest as my heart starts beating a thousand miles a minute.

"Not really…. He's in a coma. They don't know when he'll wake up."

"But he will, right? Wake up?"

"They can't say for sure."

"No." I'm shaking my head while tears stream down as I quietly weep. "No, Lily. He has to be okay. He's going to be a father."

Her words are gentle. "I know you'll be here Wednesday, but I thought you might want to come now."

"Oh my God, I can't even think straight. Of course I do. I'll come tonight if I can. I'll call right now to switch my ticket. I'll keep you posted. Call if anything changes."

"I will. Talk soon."

I hang up, feeling like my world just caved in.

19

IT TAKES TWO

Eli
Earlier that day

REBECCA STILL HASN'T SEEN MY HOME—THE PLACE SHE'LL be moving into in under six months. There's been no reason to have her over since we've been hooking up at various hotels, and any meetings we've had regarding the trust paperwork were at the attorney's office.

Now she's on her way for today's brunch with Sebastian and Lily, and I'm wondering if I should offer to show her around or just say fuck it and meet her in the lobby. I'm not sure if I'm ready to share my private space with her yet, which is a joke considering I'll be married to the woman soon.

It's been two weeks since our engagement party, and we haven't seen each other since. After breaking a hard-and-fast rule of mine and waking up in the same bed the following day, I needed a breather. It was surprising, and not in a good way. I'd gotten so piss drunk the night before that I must have passed out right after we fucked. When my eyes peeled open and I saw her lying next to me, my stomach recoiled at the image, immediately feeling like I'd cheated on Cici.

Which is absolutely fucking crazy to still be thinking. In my mind, meeting with Rebecca only long enough to screw has kept it from resembling something more, something that would replace what Cici and I had, which I refuse to do. I can't anyway, because after all this time, she still owns every piece of real estate in my heart.

We planned today so Lily and Rebecca could get to know each other better, but after seeing their interaction at the engagement party, I imagine it will be a waste of time. Lily seems to want nothing to do with her and appears to blame Rebecca for me and Cici not being together. But Cici made her decision clear before anything happened. Maybe not long before; however, no amount of time would have changed the outcome.

Today should be interesting. And since we have plenty of drama in store, when the text comes in that she's arrived, I decide to delay the inevitable and save showing her around for another time.

When I greet her in the lobby, she's too eager, which worries me that she's already reading too much into this, thinking it means more than simply playing the part. So I take the opportunity to remind her on the way up.

"You realize Lily doesn't know about our situation, right? That's why we're doing brunch. To keep the ruse of being a real couple?" I ask, raising a brow.

"Yeah, but why are you not telling her? I mean, she is family."

Hmmm. I can't exactly say it's because I don't want her to tell Cici. "Because we don't want to burden her with keeping a secret. It's hard enough for those of us involved."

"Technically, it involves her, too, if you ask me. Wouldn't it be a lot easier to have her in on it?"

She's not wrong. "It would, and we may tell her eventually. For now, just play your part. And it would help if you two got along."

"That's not only up to me. Not sure what her problem is, but it seems like it has something to do with Cici, don't you think?" she asks, digging for information.

I shrug. "We dated and she's her best friend. She probably would've liked to see it work out between us."

"Is that what you wanted?"

The elevator doors open, saving me from the truth or the lie I would have told.

"It doesn't matter. Come on, let's see if you can make a friend."

Sebastian must have spoken with Lily about being cordial because the morning went smoother than anticipated. Whatever the case, I'm relieved when we start winding down and wrapping up the meal. It means I'm closer to getting out of here and moving on with my day. I've been itching to get my newest car in on the action, and I have a race this afternoon. I've gone a few laps to test how she handles, but I'm anxious to get her out there and see the results. I still have a few hours to be at the track, but I'm more than ready to leave.

"Well, this has been fun, but I need to head out soon," I say, looking down at my watch as if I'm pressed for time.

Lily chooses this moment to let her claws come out as she turns to Sebastian. "Oh shoot, I almost forgot to tell you. Cici's coming in this week for a visit." Then she directs her attention to Rebecca and me as my head snaps up. "Maybe we should all plan dinner one night while she's here. She's staying with us, so it would be easy to figure something out." The sly smile and mischief in her eyes contradict her blasé tone.

My heart immediately starts thumping at the prospect of seeing Cici, and when I turn to Rebecca to gauge her reaction, I immediately regret it, as she looks at me with scorn. What the hell is her problem?

I'm about to say something, but Sebastian prevents a confrontation by stepping in to save the day. He leans in to kiss Lily on the forehead. "I'm glad to hear that. It makes me feel better about the week ahead. Eli and I have a new merger we're working on. We have a few dinners scheduled and late nights at the office, so unfortunately, we won't be available. But that'll give you plenty of time to catch up." He winks at her. "And now I won't make you go with me to all those boring business dinners." He leans in and nuzzles her ear. "Unfortunately for me, they'll be even more dreadful without you to keep me company. You'll have to make it up to me."

I clear my throat and stand up. "Well, on that note, we should let you enjoy the rest of your weekend."

Rebecca follows my lead and stands, trailing me to the door. She stops and turns before we make it. "Thanks for having us over. I'm glad we had a chance to visit. We'll have to do it more often. Tell Cici I said hi and that I can't wait to see her at the wedding since she is practically family." She smiles wryly.

Well shit.

I can practically see the claws come out as Lily answers, "I'll do that. Hey, Eli, if Sebastian works you too hard this week, you can always stop by for a cocktail on your way in. Cici and I will be up gabbing every night anyway." She beams at me.

The war is on between these two if it wasn't already.

"I'll keep that in mind. Thanks, Lily," I call out as I practically shove Rebecca out the door.

The minute we're in the hallway all hell breaks loose. Damn Lily for throwing the first swing.

"What the hell was that about? Is there something I should know? You told me we couldn't be with anyone else, but is that what Cici is? Your whore on the side?"

"Don't fucking call her that again. Is that clear?" At her silence,

I continue, "Because if anyone deserves that title, it would be the one who's getting paid to fuck me."

The slap across my face jolts me from my rage. "Fuck." I give my head a shake. "I shouldn't have said that."

"No, you shouldn't have." Her voice comes out choked as tears start to fall. Fucking hell. I can't have this discussion in the hallway and risk Lily coming out to see what's happening.

Making a split-second decision, I lightly grab her arm and lead her toward my door at the end of the corridor. "Come on."

As soon as I shut the door, she starts sobbing. I run my hand through my hair in frustration—so much for not bringing her inside.

I instinctively rub her back in comfort as I usher her to the couch in the living room. Sitting across from her, I take a deep breath to prepare my next words. It's a challenge to approach this empathetically when I'm so pissed, but I'm also at a point where I can't risk the fallout.

Finally, I bite the bullet and proceed. "That was wrong of me to say, especially when you're doing me a favor. Forgive me for speaking out of turn."

She sighs, looking straight at me. "Is something going on between you and Cici? I deserve the truth."

"You do, and nothing is happening between us," I answer truthfully.

"But you wish there were," she states rather than asks as if she already knows. "Are you still in love with her?"

What the hell? Where is this all coming from?

"Does it matter?"

"It does. Especially now," she says cryptically, and I don't like the sound of it.

I lean back. "What is that supposed to mean?"

Her eyes begin to glass over, and the words out of her mouth knock the wind right out of me.

"I think I'm pregnant." Her hands fidget in her lap as she drops her head in shame.

"Goddammit, Rebecca!" She flinches. "Who's the father, since it can't be me?" It comes out aggressive because I'm off-the-charts livid. *How could she fuck this up already?*

"Seriously? Who else could it be?" she asks in a tone that implies I'm an idiot.

"You tell me, since there's no way it's mine," I throw back at her.

Her arms cross over her chest in defiance. "Really? In case you forgot, it only takes once."

"When was that, then? Because I've never *not* wrapped it."

Rebecca cocks her head smugly and smirks, bringing my anger to new heights. "You must've forgotten the last time we did it, then."

My retort comes to a screeching halt as I immediately replay the events on the night of our engagement party from the moment we arrived at the room until the next morning. I tried remembering exactly what took place, and despite my best effort, most of it's blank.

"What did you do?" I ask accusingly.

"What did *I* do?" she shrieks. "In case you've forgotten how it works—since it's been so long—it takes two."

"Yeah? Well, I apparently wasn't coherent, so what happened exactly?"

She snorts at the question. "You want a play-by-play?"

Her bullshit is not needed right now. "I want to know how my cum ended up in your fucking pussy?"

"We were in the heat of the moment, and it just happened." She shrugs like it's no big deal, adding fuel to the fire.

Unable to remain seated in such close proximity, I stand. My hand runs through my hair, pulling on it as I pace the living room.

"That doesn't just fucking happen. Did I reach for a condom or mention it first?"

"After sucking you off, one thing led to another, and I ended up riding you. We didn't take a break in between. You weren't the only one drinking. I may not have been as hammered as *you* were, but I wasn't in my right mind either. That night was hard on both of us," she rebukes.

"Right. So you basically took advantage of the fact that I was drunk off my ass and knocked yourself up. Wait a minute—" I stop in my tracks and face her. "—I thought you were on birth control."

"I am…. Well, I was. I mean, I am. I'm just terrible at taking it, and I didn't think about telling you before I got back on track because we always use condoms."

"Except that *one* time, and you didn't think to warn me. What makes you think you're pregnant? It's only been two weeks. Are you just assuming?" I'm completely perplexed.

"I took a home test—they can detect it within a few days."

"You're not supposed to drink when you're pregnant, but you had mimosas today." My skepticism is palpable, but why would she lie about it? Something isn't adding up.

"I didn't want to raise suspicion, and I figured a couple early on wouldn't hurt." She shrugs again, and I'm in no way convinced.

"There's no way I'm taking the word of a drugstore test. I'll schedule you with our family doctor tomorrow, and if you are pregnant, I'll want a paternity test."

"Seriously? You're the only person I've been with."

"Then it shouldn't be a problem, right?" I ask matter-of-factly.

"It's not. I just wasn't expecting to be accused of lying." Rebecca turns her head away, pouting.

"You could've been screwing ten other guys for all I know, and before two weeks ago, that was your prerogative. I'd like to believe you, but even you can admit that we haven't established any sort of trust between us yet, so I'll be verifying if the child is mine or not."

"Fine, but I have a doctor. I'll make an appointment."

"No, it's not up for discussion. This is sensitive information I can't afford to end up in the tabloids. You'll go to my doctor."

"I'm not comfortable seeing someone I'm not familiar with. I don't want some random stranger in my space." She waves her hand around her lower half. "And besides, all doctors are bound to privacy. It'll be fine."

"Did you miss the part where it wasn't a request? I'll drag you there myself if I have to." My patience is waning.

"And if I am pregnant, what then?"

I'm not even sure what she means by that, but I've reached my limit for today.

"One thing at a time. We'll have that discussion after it's confirmed. I have somewhere to be, so I'll walk you out."

I wait one minute after the door shuts, when I know she's cleared the elevator, until I lose it.

"FUUUUUCK! Fuck. Fuck. Fuck." My hand slams down on the countertop before I lean over, resting my head in my hands and praying to God she's not pregnant, that whatever test she took was wrong. And fuck if that makes me a terrible person for wishing a child who could be mine not to exist, but goddammit, I don't want a child with Rebecca. I wouldn't even marry the woman if I had another choice.

What the fuck am I doing? Is this even worth it anymore? My mind is reeling, going in circles with different possibilities. What if she's not and I have to worry about this exact situation for the next two years? What if she sleeps around and ends up pregnant? There are provisions in the will that cover different scenarios, but fuck if I have to worry about this shit the whole time. I'll certainly be getting her an implant for birth control starting tomorrow if it turns out the test was false. Then I'll be backing that up with a supply of condoms that I'll keep behind lock and key.

Although I'm royally fucked if I'm too late for all of that. Could my life get any more out of control than it already has? What the hell am I being punished for? *Goddammit.* Slamming my fist on the counter again, I flee to the garage in a rage, knowing there's no better way to work it out than by replacing it with the adrenaline of the race. Shooting a quick text to Sebastian to explain Rebecca's scheme and that we'll resolve it tomorrow, I power down my phone. This shit will be waiting for me in the morning, and I'll handle it then.

20

CHANGE OF HEART

Cici

CRAP. I DIDN'T THINK THIS THROUGH. THE SECOND I STEP outside the airport, it dawns on me that Jackson has no idea I'm pregnant, and there's no hiding it at this point. In my defense, it was one of the longest nights of my life, wondering if I would be too late when I couldn't get a flight to San Diego yesterday. I ended up booking the earliest one for this morning and was significantly sleep-deprived when texting my brother during the layover. Although under duress, I should've figured something else out, because I have enough to deal with as it is. Uber came to mind, but I didn't want my bag at the hospital, and there's no way I would've stopped to drop it off first. Lily is with Sebastian, watching over Eli and sending updates, so she wasn't an option either.

Poor Sebastian. Eli isn't only his twin brother but all the family he has left. Thank God he has Lily, but I imagine he's going through hell. So far, Eli is still unconscious with no prognosis as to when he'll wake. I'm sure I'll find out more soon, but all I care about now is seeing for myself that he's alive and breathing.

When I spot Jackson's car, I take a deep breath and prepare myself for the onslaught of questions. It's my fault I'm in this predicament, and in hindsight, keeping this from my family may not have been the wisest idea I've had. Oh well, it's happening whether I'm ready or not.

Jackson gets out as I approach the car idling at the curb. His smile is tentative when he sees me—he's happy I'm here but not under these conditions. While he doesn't know the full extent of why I flew hundreds of miles to be here, he was aware of my complicated relationship with Eli and my feelings for him, whether I admitted it or not. But he's about to find out how much more complex it is. As I close in, he holds his arms out for a hug but steps back in shock when I reach him.

"What the hell, Cici?"

I balance the orchid I brought with me on my bag, and I hold my arms out wide. "Surprise!" I say with a nervous smile.

"Surprise? Are you shitting me right now? You're way fucking pregnant. How far are you?"

"Six months?" I squeak out reluctantly and cringe preemptively at the reaction I'm expecting.

His eyes close as he runs his hand through his hair, and then they open with an understanding accompanied by pity. "Shit." His head drops and shakes side to side a couple times before lifting. "Eli?"

All I can do is nod as the tears pool and gently flow over.

"Fuck. Come here." He wraps me in his arms and holds me while I sob.

"I'm sorry." *Hiccup.* "I didn't—" *Hiccup.* "—find out—" *Hiccup.* "—right away." *Hiccup.*

He continues to rub my back and sighs loudly. "Yeah, well,

I'm assuming you knew before now. Why didn't you say anything? Dammit, Cici."

The comfort from his hand rubbing my back is calming, but I stay snuggled up, not ready to face him yet. "I wasn't sure what to say. *Surprise! I got knocked up by accident, and I'm having a baby?*"

"That motherfucker's letting you do this alone? I'm gonna kill him if he didn't already do it himself."

At that, I pull back in shock. "Jackson, don't say that." New tears start falling. "He can't die. He doesn't know." I shake my head. "He has no idea he's going to be a dad, and it's all my fault he's in the hospital. If I'd told him sooner, he wouldn't have been racing and fighting for his life right now."

He crushes me back into him. "Shhh. It's nobody's fault, Cici. Accidents happen, and he may still have been racing even if he knew. You can't blame yourself."

Taking a deep breath, I step back. "Let's go. I need to see him. We can talk more on the way."

He nods and loads my bag into the trunk, asking, "What's with the orchid? Isn't that the same one you took to Bozeman with you?"

"Yeah. I don't know. It's special. And I thought it would be good to put in Eli's room."

He shrugs. "Hm. Okay. Well, let's get going, then."

Right before he pulls away from the curb, I place my hand over his on the gear shift and look him in the eyes. "Jackson, I'm sorry I didn't tell you sooner."

He chuckles. "I love you, Cici, but you're not getting off the hook that easy. Nice try, though. Let's get you to the hospital."

On the way there, he peppers me with questions on how the pregnancy has gone and why I didn't tell Eli. He updates me on his life with Mia, then fills me in on Eli's engagement party. The most surprising part is how Eli has been acting since telling them about Rebecca. Both Braden and my brother agree that he doesn't seem to portray the besotted fiancé he should, and instead, has been more moody than usual.

That lines up with what I detected in the photos that night with Poppy but still makes no sense. Why would he be unhappy unless there's more to the story than meets the eye? Am I right about Rebecca holding something over his head?

Jackson takes a call from Mia, which gives me time to think, and the more I do, the more certain I am that something doesn't add up. Between what Lily has told me, the pictures, and now this, I'm not leaving until I figure out what the deal is.

My stomach dips as we walk into the hospital entrance. I'm relieved to see Lily waiting right inside the doors. According to her response moments ago when I texted that we were pulling in, his condition hasn't changed.

"Wow, look at you," she says, holding her arms out for a hug as she stares down at my belly.

I chuckle at first but burst into tears again when we embrace—fricking story of my life for the past six months.

She rubs my back. "Oh, sweetie. It'll be okay. Everything will work out. Don't you always say everything happens for a reason?" She pushes my shoulders away and holds on to me with a stern expression. "You need to believe that now more than ever."

"I'm trying, but it's hard. All I can think is that it's my fault he's here for not telling him." My hands fly up in frustration.

"No. Stop it. You can't live by what-ifs."

"That's basically what I told her," Jackson says from beside us, making me roll my eyes.

"Can I see him?" I can't imagine coming all this way and not being allowed in the room, and I didn't even consider the possibility until now. I'm not his wife, a family member, or his fiancée. Does the child I'm carrying count? I'm relieved I don't have to pull that card when she answers.

"You can, but I should warn you… Rebecca's there, right at his bedside. Your secret will be out the minute she sees you."

Jackson snorts. "You got that right."

I backhand him in the arm. "Shut up." Turning back to Lily, I say, "How did Sebastian handle the news?"

She asked me last night if letting him in on my secret was okay since she knew I'd be here today. She didn't want to spring it on him and add to the stress he's already under. She also wanted to be the one to tell him and explain why she didn't say anything, which I totally understand.

She winces. "Weird is the only word I have for it. But thankfully, he's not mad at me for keeping it from him… *or mad at you*," she tacks on when my head drops in shame. "Don't worry, I'll explain later. Come on, though, let's get you in there."

"What do I tell Rebecca when she sees I'm pregnant?" I ask as we weave through the hospital. Thank goodness she met us at the entrance because I never would have found my way.

"That it's Eli's and she should bow out now."

Jackson belts out a laugh next to me.

"Lily, I'm serious, what do I say?"

"I *was* being serious. But if you're not ready for that, then don't say anything at all. What's she gonna do—ask who the father is? No one does that."

"Okay, you're right. I won't say anything. She's probably too distraught to care anyway."

"Right…," Lily says sarcastically as she rolls her eyes, which makes me wonder if she's genuinely getting bad vibes from Rebecca or if her animosity is only because she's in the way of Eli and me being together—something that isn't even on the table.

We come to a door, and she stops, turning to me. "Are you ready?"

Not in the slightest.

I nod.

She looks to Jackson. "Do you mind waiting outside? I don't think they want too many people in the room at once. Actually, Sebastian needs a break—would it be okay if I ask him to go with you to grab coffee or something?"

"Sure. I'll be right here. Send him out." He smiles and leans his back against the wall.

The door opens into a bright room, the sun shining through the large window. The first thing I notice is Sebastian sitting on a love seat against the wall, and then the beeping from a machine in the background. I'm afraid to look toward the bed. I haven't asked specifics and have no idea if he has a tube down his throat or is breathing on his own. I don't know if he's bruised or bloody or what the hell to expect, and now I'm kicking myself for not thinking of these things earlier. Suddenly the urgency to see him is overshadowed by the *fear* of seeing him.

So as a stall tactic, I walk straight toward Sebastian, who's now standing, and hug him.

"I'm so sorry, Sebastian. He'll be okay." *He has to be.*

Both are sentiments one is supposed to say but have more meaning for me than anyone knows.

"He will. He has more to live for than just me now." His arms tighten for a millisecond at the last statement before releasing me. I'm sure he's referring to what Lily told him last night, but Rebecca probably assumes he's talking about her.

She's facing away from the door and hasn't seen me yet, so there's no way she'll make the connection. Stepping back, Sebastian glances at my stomach before quickly returning his gaze upward. His suffering is written in his features, and once again, the guilt creeps in, knowing I possibly could've prevented this from happening.

Unable to hold back any longer, I turn around to take in the scene. Rebecca sits in a chair next to the bed, blocking Eli's face.

His listless body under the covers is all that's in view. She's angled away, so she won't set eyes on me unless she turns her head or I walk around for my first glimpse of Eli, which I'm still gathering the courage to do.

Before I take the first step, Lily cuts in. "Sebastian, Jackson is waiting for you in the hallway. He's hoping you'll go grab coffee and fill him in on everything. Would you mind?" she asks innocently, then addresses Rebecca. "And Rebecca, since Cici is here to watch Eli for a bit, would you mind going with me for something to drink or eat? We could all use a short break, don't you think?"

Sebastian knows precisely what she's doing, so he agrees immediately, while Rebecca responds with a shrug. Stopping at the bed on his way to the door, he puts a hand on Rebecca's shoulder. "Go with Lily. She's right. We all need a break."

She nods and mumbles an acceptance. Then Sebastian stares down at Eli for a moment. My eyes water at his anguish, apparent in his slumped shoulders and fisted hand, as he looks at his brother, powerless as the rest of us to fix the situation. My heart breaks for him as he walks out the door. He's a different man than the Sebastian I'm used to.

"You ready, Rebecca?" Lily asks quietly. It's nice of her to do this, considering she doesn't even like the woman. The opportunity for a few minutes alone with Eli means the world to me. It's a bad idea to show my feelings in front of Rebecca, and I won't be able to conceal them when I finally glimpse his face.

"Yeah." Rebecca starts to stand.

This is it. The moment she'll find out what I've been hiding from everyone. My heart is racing as she turns around.

I expected her to appear tired with bloodshot eyes rimmed with puffiness from crying or at least some sign of the pain she must be feeling, but there's nothing. No indication that she's been going through hell for the past twenty-four hours. Was she even here all night, or did she go home to sleep? My anger boils at the thought of her leaving his bedside, which wars with the fact that I don't want her here at all.

"Hey, Rebecca." I was unsure what to say, and that's the only thing to come out.

She gives me a tight-lipped smile. "Hi, Cici. Thank you for coming all this way. It means a lot to us."

"I'm here for Eli." This simple declaration could have a double-meaning since I'm still conflicted about whether I'm here to win him back or merely include him in our child's life. My mind isn't made up on the matter, but if Rebecca proves to be the woman that Lily senses she is, it'll tip the scales.

She twists her engagement ring, bringing my attention to it, and I cringe inside. However, I can't help but notice that it's nothing like the one he picked out for me.

Gah! Do not turn this into a contest, Cici.

"All right, let's go to the café so Cici can say hi to Eli," Lily says from the doorway.

"Let me grab my purse." Rebecca walks toward the table beside the sofa and gasps as she passes me. "You're pregnant?"

"I am."

"Wow. I had no idea you were with anyone. That's so great! When are you due?" she asks, sounding much happier than when she first greeted me.

At least she didn't ask who I'm with and just assumed it was someone else. Like Lily and I talked about, I decide not to correct her. "Mid-September," I answer as she reaches for her purse.

"Well, congratulations. Let's talk more later. Take care of him for me," she says as Lily starts walking out, forcing Rebecca to follow.

This time, it's me who responds with a tight-lipped smile rather than giving in to what I really want to say, which is, "Only fair since you've been taking care of him for me," but this isn't the place to be catty.

The minute the door closes and the room is empty, I heave a sigh of relief before my eyes shift to the bed. There he is. No breathing tube, no cuts or blood, just Eli. He has an oxygen mask and an IV, but other than that, he appears to be sleeping. The room is silent except for that damn beeping. Although it's annoying, I'm thankful for it since it means his heart is still beating. Taking a deep breath, I slowly move forward until my hips hit the bed.

I stand frozen, unsure what to do, and then crumple over his body and hold him as I let myself go. It's astonishing how good it feels to touch him even in his unconscious state. He's still warm, he's still Eli, and I've missed him like crazy for so many months. Oh my God, what have I done? Why did I make such terrible choices and not resolve them sooner?

After letting myself weep for a few minutes, I scoot the chair closer so I'm literally next to his face when I sit down. His hand feels so good in mine, other than being limp and lifeless. Would he hold mine back if he woke up, or would he ask for Rebecca's?

"God, I've made a mess of things," I say out loud. It's weird hearing my voice in the empty room, and it's strange to be talking to someone who's asleep, but what a perfect time to say everything I want to without worrying about the reaction. Knowing I only have so long before someone comes back, I dive in.

"Eli, I'm so sorry for hurting you. For lying to you… and to myself. I wish I could have told you the truth—that I love you so much, it hurts." The tears are pouring down my cheeks at this point, but I don't stop, already feeling relief, knowing I need to make it through the rest while I can. "It scares me how in love with you I am. It's been hell ever since I left, and I've regretted leaving you since the day I walked away. But guess what? You inspired me to get a counselor. I've been seeing her every week like you do. You're right. It's really helpful. Turns out I have this thing called gamophobia. Yeah, it's a stupid name. But it means I'm legitimately afraid of marriage and commitment. So something *was* holding me back, but it was never you. I wasn't saying no to you at all—only the commitment part."

"Are you ready for the good news?" I ask even though he can't answer. They do say you should talk to a comatose patient as you would if they were awake.

"We've been working on it in counseling, and I've come a long way. In fact, I've made so much progress that I'm finally ready to admit that there's nothing I want more than to be with you for the rest of my life. The bad news is that it took me too long to figure that out, and now it's too late." I can't help but start crying again at the truth of the matter. "Dammit, Eli. I fucked up. I'm just too late." My head hangs, shaking. "The worst part is, I didn't only screw up my life but my baby's too." I lift my head and look at him. "*Our* baby, Eli. We're having a baby. You're going to be a dad." I kiss his hand and let the tears keep streaming.

"I'm so sorry for not telling you sooner. By the time I found out, you were already dating Rebecca, and I was trying to wrap my head around it, and then I was worried it would get in the way of you moving on, and I didn't want to interfere. And then, when I decided to tell you, you were getting engaged, and I just… ugh. It was stupid. I was stupid. I should have just spit it out somehow, and then maybe you wouldn't be here. That's why you have to wake up, Eli. I need you. We both do." I start sobbing again and rest my head on his hand, letting the tears flow for who knows how long.

Suddenly, the door flies open, making me startle and jerk up to an enraged Rebecca with Lily tight on her heels.

"It's Eli's, isn't it? You're fucking pregnant with Eli's baby, aren't you?" When I stare at her, too shocked for words, she screams, "Answer me!"

"Yes!"

Sebastian and Jackson come rushing into the room, probably hearing her yell from down the hall.

"You bitch. You came back here to what… take him back?"

"No. I was already scheduled to fly home this week to break the news, and then this happened."

"Well, you're too late. He's moved on, and not only are we getting married, but I'm pregnant too." She puts her hand on her hip and juts it out pretentiously.

The shock is evident as the room goes silent, and I recoil as my stomach heaves at her declaration. I can't believe I was right.

Lily breaks the silence with the exact question ringing through my mind. "Is that how you got him to marry you? You got pregnant?"

Rebecca scoffs, "Ha. Got *him* to marry *me*? Yeah, right. He begged me to—"

"Enough," Sebastian barks.

But what was she going to say—that he begged her to marry him? So is he really in love with her and not being coerced? Dammit, I don't know what to believe.

Sebastian continues, "Now is not the time to be arguing while my brother is lying there fighting for his life." Lily goes to him, and he automatically pulls her into his side as if she were his security blanket. "Rebecca, I didn't plan to do this under current conditions, but since you've brought it up yourself, I'll have the doctor here today for an appointment. Eli told me about your conversation yesterday and the plan to have you seen. Conveniently, we're at the hospital, so we'll follow through with his wishes… since he can't." The last part sounded oddly accusatory. Does he blame Rebecca for telling Eli about being pregnant right before his race? Oh shit. Maybe I'm not the only one to bear responsibility.

Rebecca's eyes go wide. "Oh, let's not do that today—I don't want to leave him any more than I have to."

"You went home last night to sleep, so I'm sure you'll be fine for an hour. Besides, it's what Eli wanted, so we'll make it happen," Sebastian states in finality.

It's obvious she wants to argue but ends up agreeing. Sebastian isn't someone you argue with. Once that's settled, her gaze moves toward me and where I'm seated beside the bed in *her* spot, holding Eli's hand. The look she gives me is unmistakable, so with one final glance at his peaceful face, I rise, squeezing his hand before releasing it and walking over to stand next to Jackson.

Jackson suggests we drop my things off at his place, say hi to Mia, and grab lunch. Afterward, he'll bring me back to sit with Eli when Rebecca is scheduled to visit the doctor. With a plan in place, we leave the hospital, my mind buzzing with thoughts and filled with turmoil over different possible outcomes. On the way, Jackson fills me in on what he learned from Sebastian.

The head trauma Eli sustained is what put him in a coma, but there are no signs of damage to other areas of his body, and the scans they've done so far show everything else functioning properly. The doctors said they won't know for sure until he wakes up, though. They can't tell us when he'll regain consciousness and said it could be today or months from now—the body decides how much time it needs to recover. But they're hopeful it will be sooner than later due to his age, sound health, and the low amount of swelling in his brain.

Leaving was difficult, but the tension in the room was palpable, and that's bad for him. The research I did at the airport this morning about comatose patients said that even though they may appear asleep, there may be times that they're aware of what's taking place around them. It also said talking to them frequently and even listening to music can help bring them into consciousness. Nothing's a guarantee, of course, but I'll do whatever I can to help.

There's still the business of telling my parents about the baby, but I've decided that can wait. They don't even know I'm in town, which is probably better for now, so my time can be spent focusing on Eli and being there for him. I'm not sure how they'll take the news, whether they'll be disappointed in me or thrilled to be grandparents. While I hope it's the latter, it won't make or break me either way. Nothing compared to the effect of what happens with Eli will have.

Having more time without Rebecca in the room would be helpful so I could talk to him and not worry about what I'm saying, constantly watching my words. We all may have our suspicions about what the story is between them, but until he wakes up, there's no way of knowing, and if they *are* genuinely in love, I can't ruin his happiness by putting a wedge between them.

Even though I enjoyed catching up with Mia during lunch and hearing all about their wedding plans, my anxiety at being away from the hospital was evident, so we cut it short, and Jackson brought me back early. Sebastian had run to the office for a few hours, so it was only me, Rebecca, and Lily in the room, and until Rebecca left for her appointment, it was awkward at best. Lily and I kept our conversation neutral, talking about our jobs, Jackson and Mia's wedding, and the fact that she'd have to postpone her visit. It wasn't until Rebecca walked out that we could relax.

The minute the door closes, both our shoulders slump in relief, and noticing the same reaction from each other, we burst into giggles.

Lily catches her breath. "Oh my God, that was awful."

"It *so* was. Hey, now that she's gone, let's move a chair to the other side of the bed and sit with Eli. Maybe if we talk his ear off, he'll wake up just to tell us to shut up." We giggle as we work together to bring it over.

This way, I'll be near him more often and able to hold his hand. I'd planned on doing it while Rebecca was gone anyway to avoid the awkwardness of moving it while she watched.

"Anything's worth a shot, especially since Rebecca hardly talks to him."

"True, but she's probably uncomfortable with us being here and doesn't know what to say." The constant draw to defend her is weird. It could be out of guilt since I'll soon be the cause of quite a bit of drama.

It's been two of the longest weeks of my life. Eli is still in a coma, and between the crying, praying, bargaining with God, and general misery, I'm losing my mind. All of us, including Braden and Jackson, have taken turns, so there is always someone in the room with him. We play music and try to have constant conversation, whether it's talking to one another, to him, or reading aloud.

There's been no change in his condition other than removing the oxygen mask since he's breathing normal on his own. But there's still no indication when he'll wake. The doctors said it could be anytime and to keep doing everything we have been. Since the only one without a job here is me, I'm with him the most, which I'm thankful for. It makes me feel helpful, when really, there's nothing any of us can do.

There's constant tension between Rebecca and me, and I'm not sure which one of us will break first, but if Eli doesn't wake soon, there's bound to be a catfight. She never said anything about the added chair next to his bed, but the look on her face when she returned from seeing the doctor was priceless. Thank God the home test ended up being a false positive and the blood test results proved she wasn't pregnant. However, she didn't waste the opportunity to shed more tears than I've seen her cry for Eli the entire time I've been here.

And who knows? I could be completely misreading the situation. Maybe Eli was excited for the baby, and maybe they're more in love than we ever were. Am I out of my mind thinking I have any chance at salvaging something? Could it be that Lily is totally off base, and I'm just playing the role of a home-wrecker? The thought alone makes me cringe and want to run back to Bozeman. But that's what got me into this mess in the first place—running away.

So no, I need to stay the course and see it through, enduring all the awkward moments like the one I'm currently experiencing. Rebecca had been at work for the day and unexpectedly showed up on her lunch hour. She *never* does that. So when she came in and spotted me leaning over, kissing Eli's hand, it was uncomfortable at best.

"Were you hoping to get him back when you told him about the baby?" Rebecca adds to the tension with the last question I'm prepared to answer.

"I hadn't decided." Isn't honesty the best policy? But then again, am I being honest with myself?

"Well, if it *is* your intention, I won't make it easy for you."

"If it's my intention, it doesn't deserve to be easy. I've pretty much made a mess of things at this point, and for what it's worth, I'm sorry." *And this is the part where you apologize for going after my ex.*

But instead of reciprocating, she stands and walks out.

21

AN ANGEL

Eli

"**E**LI, WE'RE ALL WAITING FOR YOU TO WAKE UP. YOUR BROTHER'S going crazy with worry. Come on, Eli, open your eyes."

A voice penetrates my sleep. A beautiful one. The one I've been hearing in my dreams. The one I'd be happy hearing the rest of my life.

"You look so peaceful like this. I miss your voice, though."

There she is again—my angel. A light caress runs along my forehead from the softest hand I've ever felt. Why are my eyes so heavy? I want to open them, but I can't. I'm too tired.

"It's time to go home, Eli. You'd be so much more comfortable in *your* bed."

It's her. Damn, she's mesmerizing and always pulling me out of my sleep. But that's okay because I'll gladly go home and get comfortable with her. "Anytime, sweetheart, just let me rest a little longer first." *She's caressing my hand, squeezing it. I wish she were squeezing something else that's waking up.* "Come on, baby. I'm all yours." *If only my eyelids weren't weighted down by a ton of bricks. Fuck.*

"Eli. Please wake up. I need you…. *We* need you."

She sounds angry this time. Or wait, maybe she's sad. "No, don't cry. I want to hear your sweetness again." *My hand is squeezed hard, and then something else is on top of it… lips. She's kissing my hand, crying. I can feel the wetness from her tears. I can't let her cry.* "What's wrong, sweetheart?" *Her lips go away, and I want to reach up to bring them back, but my arms are like lead. If only my eyelids weren't glued shut, I could look at my angel and tell her it's okay.*

"I just don't know what to do anymore. I keep saying the same things over and over again. There's got to be something else. What if he doesn't wake up?"

She begins to cry. Her sadness pains me, and I don't want to be the cause of it. There must be something I can do. I use all the strength I can muster to grip her hand.

"Eli? Can you hear me? Open your eyes. Lily, text Sebastian and tell him I felt something. Eli, squeeze my hand again if you can hear me."

She sounds frantic now. I squeeze as hard as I can—anything to make her happy.

"Lily, he's responding. I just pushed the button for the nurse."

Why would I need a nurse?

"Eli, please wake up. Look at me."

She's pleading now. All I want is to make her happy, so I try to open my eyes, but it's like the lines are crossed, and the signal won't reach far enough.

"Come on, Eli. Don't go back to sleep. Lily's here, and your brother's on his way. Just wake up."

"Anything for you, cutie." *Fuck, why is this so difficult? I struggle internally for a few more seconds, and finally my eyelids peel back, only to squeeze shut immediately. Holy shit, it's bright.*

"Lily, close the blinds. It's too bright."

I'm pretty sure I didn't say that out loud. I don't think my voice will work with as long as it's taking my fricking eyes to cooperate.

I peek out of one eye, and thankfully, the room is darker, so I carefully pry both open and struggle to bring my surroundings into focus. What the fuck? When did I get an IV? I'm still in the hospital, and a nurse is fiddling with the machines. Lily is pacing with the phone to her ear, telling the person on the other end that my eyes just opened and that she'd rather *he* call her—whatever that's about. Cici is next to the bed with a death grip on my hand.

"You're about to break my hand, babe."

Ah, so my voice does work.

Cici laughs and leans in to hug me with tears streaking down her cheeks.

"Welcome back, Mr. Dubree. Your vitals are looking great. I'll tell the doctor you're awake, and he'll be in shortly," the nurse says before exiting.

Cici sits back, still crying and squeezing my hand.

I smile at her. "Whoa, what's all the fuss about? I was only resting, cutie—no need for tears. Though, why did they give me an IV. I must have been sleeping pretty hard for them to do that."

She and Lily exchange an odd look as Lily sits down on the other side of the bed. Lily hesitates before saying, "Eli… you've been unconscious for two weeks."

"What are you talking about? I just got here…. They were about to release me." They must be trying to pull one over on me.

"Eli, you've been in a coma. We've all been scared out of our minds with no clue when you'd wake up," Lily answers while Cici continues shedding tears next to me.

I laugh. "This is a joke, right? Did Sebastian put you up to it to try and scare me out of racing?"

The doctor walks in then, halting the conversation. After greeting everyone, he runs through some routine checks, then reviews a file, reciting the results of the last scans they did when I was apparently *unconscious*.

Sebastian enters hurriedly, like he ran to get here, and is more ruffled than I've seen him in ages, probably playing along with the ruse.

I smirk and address the doctor. "So these guys are trying to tell me I've been here for two weeks. Supposedly in a coma. You must be in on this too?" I chuckle.

"I wish that were the case, but sadly, they're telling you the truth. How about you tell me the last thing you remember," the doctor suggests.

Hold up. I couldn't seriously have been out cold for two weeks, could I?

"My car was clipped, spun out of control, and I was admitted for a concussion. Sebastian left while I was waiting to be released after biting my head off." I scoff at Sebastian, who stands next to the doctor at the end of the bed. "Cici was on her way to take me home. That's when I closed my eyes to rest and must have passed out." Maybe it wasn't a simple concussion after all.

"What day was it?" Sebastian asks suspiciously.

"Damn, our birthday. I guess I missed the party, huh?" Sebastian's really gonna read me the riot act now.

Instead, his eyes go wide, while Cici and Lily gasp on either side of me, looking at each other in shock. The doctor flips a few pages, seems to find what he's looking for, and is about to speak when a woman rushes into the room.

"Oh my God, Eli, you're awake," she exclaims, rushing toward me and practically shoving Lily out of the way to take her place. She leans down to hug me, and I'm too shocked to push her off. I recognize her from Cici's office and the one time at the club.

"Does someone want to tell me what the fuck is going on?" I yell, frustrated at waking to a clusterfuck and a woman who I barely know throwing herself at me.

The woman, who I remember as Rebecca, leaps back abruptly and stares at me in shock.

"I'd like everyone to leave the room but the patient and Mr. Dubree so we can discuss the prognosis," the doctor interrupts sternly.

Lily hugs Sebastian while whispering something in his ear and then comes around to the side of the bed where Cici sits. "I'm so glad you're awake, Eli. We'll be back in soon." Cici rises behind her and starts walking to the door when something catches my eye.

"Wait! Cici, turn around," I demand, causing everyone to freeze.

Time slows as she pivots, and I see the full picture of a very pregnant Cici.

"What the fuck? Someone better start speaking. I thought you said I was only out for two weeks. That doesn't happen in two weeks. What the hell is going on?"

The doctor intervenes. "Again, I'm going to ask you all to leave so I can have a moment with the Dubree brothers."

I'm closing my eyes tightly, trying to remember how the fuck Cici is having a baby, when another vision comes to mind. Not Cici but Rebecca informing me that she's pregnant. My eyes pop open, and I point to Rebecca accusingly. "Hold up. Why would I remember *you* telling me you're pregnant? None of this makes sense." I shake my head, trying to clear the fog.

"Brenda, please escort Eli's guests to the waiting room. I'll be out shortly to speak with everyone. Thank you," the doctor instructs the nurse who entered the room since he's been ignored so far.

When the door shuts, I shout, "Mind telling me what the hell is going on? If this is some kind of joke, I'm fucking over it." I'm getting angrier by the second.

"Eli, the best thing you can do is calm down. This probably feels overwhelming, but it's better for a full recovery to stay calm. You said it was your birthday the last you remember, correct?" the doctor asks.

"Yeah. So what's the deal? Have I been out for longer than two weeks?"

"No, what you're experiencing is called retrograde amnesia. Your birthday was eight months ago, and since you were admitted for a concussion that day, it makes sense that your mind went back to that moment. Memory loss varies per case, as does recovery time. Your memories could come back to you at any moment between now and months from now. They may come back all at once or in pieces. The most important thing you can do is take it easy and not overwhelm yourself with facts and details. Don't try to force it, as your memory should naturally come back on its own when your brain is ready. There are rare cases where it doesn't return, but that would be irregular with your age and overall health."

"You're telling me I'm missing everything from the last eight months of my life?"

"That's what it appears, but you seem to have remembered a conversation based on your comment earlier, so that gives me hope that you'll recover your memories sooner rather than later, although there's no way of knowing for sure." Brenda walks back into the room and starts unhooking cords from the machines while the doctor continues, "I'll have Nurse Brenda take you down for new scans so we can evaluate any recent changes and see how everything looks now that you're awake. I'll be in to discuss the findings after reviewing them. In the meantime, I'd like to limit your visitors to one person at a time until further notice."

As the nurse pushes me out the door, I hear the doctor address Sebastian. "Mr. Dubree, I'd like a word with you and the others before I go."

On our way to the other room and during testing, my mind swirls with questions and hypothetical situations. What happened between me and Rebecca, and why the fuck was she telling me she's pregnant? Did I cheat on Cici? I can't imagine that happening, not to mention why I'd ever want to. Cici is everything to me.

And what's with Cici being pregnant? No, she's not just pregnant; she's about to pop. Who the fuck is the father? Did she cheat on me, or did we break up for some reason? I mean, I knew she was always meant to go back to Bozeman, but I was devising a way to convince her to stay. Hell, in my mind, we were dating one minute, and the next, she's having a baby. Nothing makes sense, and the more I think about it, the more frustrated I get at not knowing what the hell is happening. Did I seriously forget the last eight months of my life? My mind can't fathom it.

Only Sebastian is there when I'm brought back to the room, and rather than the stern lecture I'm prepared for, he sits next to the bed and hangs his head, shaking it. "You have no idea how relieved I am that you're awake. I can't even begin to explain what these last two weeks were like, wondering when or *if* you would wake up. It was hell, man. You can't scare me like that again."

He's right, I can't imagine it because I was awake only yesterday in my mind. "So how did I end up here since it wasn't the accident on my birthday?" I was going to ask the nurse but was so caught up in my thoughts that I forgot to bring it up.

"You really need to ask?"

"Yeah, fine. I'm assuming it was racing, but how did it happen?"

"I wasn't there, but I watched the footage. No more, Eli. I mean it this time." He looks at me sharply and stays silent until I acquiesce.

My hand flies up. "All right, all right. I'll stop." Which seems to appease him for now.

"You were trying to pass a car on the inside, and one moment you were doing fine, and the next you started careening into the center of the track. You must have caught something because your car went flying. Rolled six times before landing upside down. I've never seen you drive that aggressively. It was hard to watch. Luckily, there was no fire, and they extracted you without any issues. I made it to the hospital at the same time as the ambulance and saw them wheel you in. It was the worst moment of my life."

"I'm sorry, Seb. Damn, I didn't mean for this to happen."

"No one ever does. That's where choices come in. We can discuss that more after you have a couple of days to recover." He pauses before continuing, "Dammit, I can't handle losing you, Eli. You're all the family I have left."

"I'm sorry. I really am. I'm not trying to make light of the situation, but can you please tell me what the fuck happened to my life the past eight months? Last I remember, I was dating Cici. Now she's pregnant with someone else's baby, and I supposedly knocked up Rebecca? What the fuck, man?"

For some reason, he hesitates with a pained expression. When he opens his mouth to answer, the doctor enters before he gets a word out, preventing me once again from getting the answers I'm dying for—or rather living for.

Turns out the remaining swelling is minimal, and other than the fact that I went into a coma for two weeks and lost eight months of my life, there won't be any lasting effects. They're keeping me overnight for observation, which is understandable, and they'll run one more set of scans to ensure everything is normal before I'm released. But

I should be able to go home tomorrow, thank God. The doctor said my memory could return within a few days, and if it doesn't, there are drugs or therapies I can do to help recall events, but nothing has a high success rate, so hopefully it comes back naturally.

Once the doctor leaves the room, I try again. "Start talking. What did I miss while I was unconscious, or rather what did I forget?"

He hesitates again but only for a moment before the resolve sets in. "A lot. You forgot a fuck ton, and I'm not sure how you're going to handle this all at once. The doctor said not to stress you out, but I don't see any other way than to give it to you straight."

"Then do it. Tell me what the hell happened. I can take it."

So for the next ten minutes, Sebastian details my life, beginning with the marriage condition of our trust, to asking Cici to marry me only to have her turn me down on New Year's Eve and go home the next day. He recounts my odd relationship with Rebecca, from being fuck buddies to getting engaged, and finally the last day before the accident when I texted him about Rebecca telling me she was pregnant. The scene that replayed in my mind from earlier must've happened then. He assures me she isn't pregnant, which gives me tremendous relief, but he won't tell me about Cici's pregnancy at all, insisting that it's for her and I to discuss.

According to what I told him, there was no love between Rebecca and me, and until I was forced into marriage, we'd simply been having weekly hookups for sex at various locations. It sounds like she'd never even been to my place until that fateful day. All I can think of is how Cici feels about my relationship with Rebecca and the engagement. How could I do that to her? Fuck, we weren't even together, though, were we? So maybe she didn't give a damn. But something tells me that's not the case—otherwise, why would she be here?

And that's the million-dollar question. She's the only thing I care about right now, and if my brother is correct, I never stopped caring.

"Trade places with Cici. I want to talk to her."

"Is that wise at the moment? She doesn't know your engagement is a scam. How do you plan to navigate this without telling her about the trust? That was a big sticking point for you, and I don't know that you should do something you weren't okay with before. Give your memory time to return and then talk to her when you're in your right mind." Sebastian is always the voice of reason, but reasonable is the last thing I'm feeling at the moment.

"I'm not sure how to go about it, but since you're not giving me anything to go on, I need to find out where she's at. Why she's here, whose baby she's carrying—if it's mine. Fuck. It's not helping my stress level to have unanswered questions, and if you're concerned about my recovery, the doctor said that's important. Go get her. Please, Sebastian, I need some fucking answers."

He sighs in acceptance. "All right, but if things go south, you realize it could cause lasting damage."

"Or something could trigger my memory. I'll be okay, just send her in and tell the nurses to stay out for a while."

"Fuck." He runs his hand through his hair. I can tell he's torn, but he'll do it. Sure enough, he stands and shakes his head on the way to the door.

"Hey," I call out, stopping him. "I'm glad I'm still here, and it doesn't make it right, but I am sorry I put you through this. It was selfish and unfair to you. I won't do it again."

"You better not, because next time might just give me a heart attack, and I think we both have more important things to live for now." He smirks before he walks out the door.

Wait, is he saying what I think he is?

22

FALSE REALITY

Cici

LILY AND I ARE IN THE WAITING ROOM, WHISPERING IN HUSHED tones. I called Jackson the minute we left the room, and he's on his way. I told him only one person could be in the room at a time, but he wanted to be here for everyone. We're all in shock that Eli is not only awake but has lost his memory. It's wild that in his mind, we're still dating, no one's pregnant, and no one's engaged. Hell, he doesn't even know that Jackson is back and has Mia home with him.

We filled Rebecca in on Eli's amnesia since she was still confused as hell by the time the nurse ushered us from the room. The craziest part is that she's been completely wiped from his memory. What if he never remembers those last eight months? How could he ever move on, with no recollection of the woman he's engaged to? It's insane. She definitely has more at stake than the rest of us, but it's hard to feel bad for her when her response to the news was "How convenient for you."

Thankfully, Sebastian and the doctor came out then, while Eli was taken for testing. The doctor explained Eli's condition and told us how important it is to keep him as calm as possible. The memory loss associated with short-term coma patients is usually temporary, but there's no time frame or guarantee that it will come back. Being upset and stressed hinders recovery, though—thus the limit for one visitor at a time in his room. I don't blame him after seeing what happened when we were all in there at once.

Sebastian appears around the corner after spending the last half hour in with Eli, and we all stand in anticipation. He makes his way closer, looking pensive, and whatever he's thinking about makes him uneasy, which isn't something often seen in Sebastian. He reaches us and immediately brings Lily to his side, hugging her, and kisses the top of her head.

Rebecca joins us. "Can I go see him now?"

"Actually, he's asking for Cici," Sebastian says.

I might be imagining things, but I swear Rebecca rolled her eyes right before the irritation on her face became unmistakable. To say I'm shocked is an understatement. I expected him to ask for Rebecca, his fiancée, of course. I mean, he may not remember her, but isn't he anxious to find out about their relationship?

Still, is it terrible that I'm gloating inside? Yes. Yes, it is.

Lily squeezes my arm in encouragement, and I walk toward his room. When I enter, I'm unsure whether to take the couch or sit in the chair beside his bed, so after shutting the door, I stand uneasily, staring at the orchid on the table by his bed, wondering if it looks a little droopier than usual.

"Come here, cutie." He pats the bed next to him.

I'm surprised at the use of his nickname for me. He used it when he first woke as well, but I was too in the moment to consider it. But now, assuming Sebastian has filled him in on the past eight months, he must know we're not together—that we haven't been for seven of the months he lost.

My feet feel like they're weighted with a hundred pounds each as

I slowly make my way closer. On top of being relieved that he's awake, I'm panicking inside. It was so much easier to tell him the truth when he was asleep and couldn't respond, but now I'm afraid of what his response will be.

He scoots over and pats the bed again. And as much as I want to be near him, it feels wrong. He's with Rebecca. It makes no sense why I'm here instead of her. And regardless of what he thinks he feels, there's really no way of knowing unless he regains his memory. There's no way forward until he's able to go backward.

So I take the chair instead.

His eyebrows go up mockingly. "Scared of me, are you?"

"Shouldn't Rebecca be in here?"

"Why don't you let me worry about that?"

I shake my head, exasperated. "She wasn't happy that you asked for me."

His face goes stern. "I'm not worried about Rebecca right now. What does concern me is this puzzle I'm trying to work out in my head. From what I remember, it looks a little like this: I'm seeing someone who, I've been told, I said I loved and asked her to marry me but was rejected nonetheless. Now I find out she's pregnant, and it appears as if, correct me if I'm wrong, her due date may correlate with the last days we were together. The missing pieces aren't fitting, though, and I can't figure out how we're not together or why the hell I'd be marrying someone else when she's the only woman I've ever loved, not to mention possibly having my baby. So are you ready to help me by filling in the last few pieces of the puzzle?"

The tears started falling seconds into his speech and wouldn't stop. I nod but can't seem to form any words.

"Talk to me, Cici. Tell me what's going on. Are you carrying our child?"

I nod again, and despite the smile that lights up his face, I choke on a sob. "I'm sorry."

"What are you sorry for? Did I know you were pregnant?"

I shake my head since I can't speak because I'm crying so hard.

"Shit, baby, come here." He holds his arm out.

No matter how wrong it is, I can't hold back anymore and crawl beside him as he envelops me in his arms while I cry and confess my guilt over not telling him and how it's my fault he's in here, apologizing repeatedly.

"Ssssh. Cici, it's not your fault, baby. Everything will be okay. Just talk to me, cutie. Tell me what happened and why you didn't feel you could share the greatest news in the world."

When his hand reaches my protruding belly, I'm jolted out of my despair and watch as he makes soothing circles over our baby. It's also when I realize I should not be this close to him, and I scramble to move, only to have his arm clamp around me.

"Eli, this isn't right. You're engaged."

"And if I weren't? Would you still be trying to get away? Would you still be denying your feelings for me?" We go silent for a moment. "Why are you here, Cici? I want the truth." His arm tightens.

"It's complicated."

"Uncomplicate it," he says as he resumes the slow circles on my belly.

I inhale deeply and let it out slowly before diving in. "My flight was already booked to come here and tell you about the baby. But then Lily called about the accident, and I came the next day. There's no excuse for not telling you sooner, but by the time I found out when I came back for Jackson's proposal to Mia—"

"Holy shit! Jackson's getting married? Sebastian didn't tell me that."

This is so weird.

"Yeah, he proposed in March, and they're getting married in a couple of months. I'm pretty sure you're in the wedding." He has a contemplative look, like he's trying hard to recall the details. "Anyway,

I was three months into the pregnancy, and you were seeing Rebecca. I didn't want to interfere in your relationship, so I sat on it for a while. Then the second time I planned to tell you was when you called about your engagement, and I just couldn't. It didn't seem right to come between you. Finally, Lily gave me a deadline, but I was ready to fess up anyway and let you decide what part you wanted to play. And here we are."

"I'm glad to hear Lily had my back. I'll have to thank her later. There are so many questions, but two come to the forefront. How did you get pregnant? We always used condoms, and you were on birth control."

Does he not believe he's the father?

"And before you think I'm doubting you, I'm not. I'm only trying to understand since I remember nothing."

I fill him in on our last night together, including the antibiotics I was on in addition to going sans condom.

"Damn, that's a memory I'd pay for."

"Eli, you can't say things like that." I slap his chest, and he chuckles. This feels too much like before, when nothing stood in our way. "What's your second question?" I ask to change the subject.

"What role were you hoping I'd take after telling me about our baby?"

He holds tight as I try to move again, but I don't back down. "I'm not comfortable answering that question in this position. We shouldn't be so close, not with your fiancée out there. If you want an answer, you need to let me go."

This time, he complies. "Fine, if that's the only way you'll talk."

My body feels the loss of his immediately, and I'm tempted to crawl right back, but my conscience wins out as I settle in the chair.

"Give me your hand at least." He holds his hand out, palm up, on the bed.

I don't give in. "We shouldn't be holding hands."

"I bet you had no problem doing it when I was unconscious." He smirks.

I tilt my head and roll my eyes. "That's different. You couldn't reciprocate. Plus, they said touch helps bring patients out of their coma."

"In that case, you really should have been touching something else. I might have woken up sooner." He chuckles.

"Seriously, Eli, no more. You're making me feel like the other woman, and I won't be. I can't handle this. Maybe I should trade places with Rebecca—she's probably dying to see you."

"I'm the one who almost died, and you're the one I want to see right now."

"*Why?*" My exasperation boils to the surface, and the question comes out as such.

"Because I still love you, goddammit!" he practically yells.

A gasp escapes, and my head shakes vigorously. "No. You're only saying that because you're stuck in time. You just don't remember that you love Rebecca. You're *marrying* her, for Christ's sake—you obviously love her. I can't do this. It would be one thing if you had your memory, but you're acting from a false reality."

"What if I wasn't? Tell me this: What would you do if you could go back in time? Would you have stayed? Pregnancy aside, do you regret leaving me?"

"We can't go back, so it doesn't matter."

"It matters to me. Please, Cici, just fucking be honest and tell me how you feel." His frustration is evident, and mine is ratcheting up with it. Stress isn't good for him, so we need to tone it down.

Taking a deep breath, I try to calm myself before answering. I get that he's still in the mindset from when we were seeing each other, but I'm positive his brother told him about his relationship with Rebecca. In fact.... "You can't just ignore your engagement. Just because you can't remember it, doesn't make it any less real." I release a breath of frustration. "Listen, I wouldn't be here if I didn't have feelings for you, but to ask me to declare my love now, when we're an impossibility at the moment, isn't fair to either of us."

"So you do love me." It's not a question but a statement of fact that I can't dispute. And the smile on his face to go along with it about does me in. He's right in front of me, yet I miss him so fricking much it hurts.

Ignoring his revelation, I continue from where we were earlier. "I'm not sure exactly *what* my goal was when I came to tell you about the baby, but whatever it was… feels wrong given the circumstances. I'm sorry, Eli. This isn't how I wanted things to end, but I think it's time to cut our losses and figure out a way to move forward. We'll obviously need to talk about the baby at some point, but for now I should go."

"Will you give me an honest answer to one last question before you do?"

"I'll try."

"It's a simple yes or no. If Rebecca weren't in the picture and we were sitting here in this exact moment, would you be with me if you could?"

My eyes glisten and my heart constricts as I look into his eyes and finally give him the answer he's been waiting for.

"Yes."

23

LIFE'S TOO SHORT

Eli

F I WEREN'T SURE OF MY PATH, I'D NEVER HAVE LET CICI WALK out the door moments ago, but knowing what I do now only solidifies my decision. According to Sebastian, the reason I wouldn't tell Cici about the marriage condition is that I wanted her to choose me freely. It may be a bit late, but I finally got what I needed. Now it's time to rectify the situation with my current engagement. That, and hope like hell my memories return so Cici will believe that I still love her, because even though I don't remember, there's no way a love this strong simply disappeared.

"From the look on Cici's face, I'm gathering that didn't go well," Sebastian says, entering minutes later.

"It went great. Can you get the paperwork rolling to end my sham of an engagement?"

"Well, that certainly isn't what I expected to hear walking in here. Holy shit, did your memory come back already?"

"No, but I don't need it to know what I want, and she just walked out that door."

Sebastian paces the room, his hand running through his hair. "Bro, I told you the basics of the trust condition, but you're not understanding. If you fuck this up, you'll lose everything. You don't have time to start over if this thing with Cici goes south."

"It's not a thing—that's my future wife. And it won't, I'm sure of it. Did we put any cancellation clauses in the contract with Rebecca?" I'm not ignoring his concerns—I simply don't have any, and the faster we make this happen, the faster I can move forward.

"Of course we did. This isn't our first rodeo. But you can't be sure Rebecca won't talk to the press, NDA or not. And then you have the problem of a required six-month engagement period."

"Didn't you say I proposed to Cici on New Year's? That means her ring was purchased then, and if push comes to shove, I'll contest that requirement. When it's obvious our marriage is real, there'll be no need for that baseless condition."

"And how about getting married before the end of the year?"

"I'll handle it. I've already got a plan."

Sebastian shakes his head in resignation. "Don't you think you should wait for your memories to return before you start making rash decisions? You'll probably have a completely different perspective then."

"Exactly. I'm in the perfect frame of mind to make this happen *now*. In fact, send Rebecca in. There's no better time than the present," I say, more jovial than ever.

Sebastian huffs on his way out, "Except you're not living in the present."

"Don't forget to start the paperwork!" I call out after him.

Instead of Rebecca, the nurse comes in to check my vitals, which look exceptional.

"At this rate, you'll be released tomorrow morning—you're doing amazing. Being in as good of shape as you are helped quite a bit, and even though you shouldn't have any downtime, don't go all out at the gym right away. Take it slowly. Remember, it's the tortoise that crossed the finish line."

"Good advice. I'll be sure to keep it in mind." I give her a friendly smile.

She shakes her head and laughs. "For some reason, I doubt that. I'll send your next visitor in."

Once this next hurdle is over, I can move on to more important things. With the way it sounds, things are tense between Rebecca and me, so it shouldn't be difficult. She may be upset at losing out on the full payout, but that would take two years, and this way, she'll have money in her pocket immediately. It's unfortunate I can't remember a single thing about her, but that may be in my favor at the moment.

"So you finally have time for your fiancée, huh?" she questions sarcastically, waltzing into the room.

"Come on, you and I both know this isn't real."

"Do we, though? Or is that what you're telling yourself since you can't remember?"

"Cut the crap, Rebecca. My brother and I tell each other everything, which means he holds all my memories and didn't waste time filling me in. I'm not sure the exact nature of our relationship, other than sex, but judging by the final incident and ensuing panic it caused according to the text my brother received, we weren't the happy couple we pretended to be. So I have a proposal."

"Ooh, another one? This should be good, since the last proposal you made had two million dollars attached to it."

"Don't forget about the two years that went with it. I'm offering you an out… with compensation for your time, of course."

She blows out a breath and shakes her head in disbelief. "Wow, so that's it. Poof, you wake up eight months in the past, and now I mean nothing to you."

"Did you ever mean anything to me? From what it sounds like, we merely entered into an agreement. How did we even meet? I remember you initially from Cici's office and then that time at the club when I told you she and I were dating. How did you enter the picture?" She smirks, and I backtrack before she answers. "Actually, it doesn't matter. This isn't going to work. I'm sorry for stringing you along if that's what I did. Hell, I'm sorry for making this insane arrangement in the first place. I never should have done it."

"Yeah, well, it's not like you wanted to. For what it's worth, I like you. I may not love you, but it would've gotten there. The problem is, Cici was always the one you wanted. It was apparent the night of our engagement party when you said you loved me"—my eyes widen in shock—"except Cici's name followed those words, not mine. So when I heard she was coming to town, I panicked. I mean, who wouldn't? Here's an amazing opportunity to marry the perfect guy with a ton of money and be set for life. I guess I thought if I told you I was pregnant, you'd suddenly realize you were in love with me, and we'd ride off into the sunset. Boy did that backfire. Maybe I'd have had a chance if you hadn't lost your memory." She shrugs. "Or maybe not, but either way, I'm sorry. I'm honestly sorry if I was the cause of your accident." Her eyes are tearing up, and her sincerity rings true.

With apologies out of the way, we're both ready to move on, and the path forward couldn't be clearer. "Rebecca, crazy enough, this is the best thing that could've happened, so don't feel bad. We just weren't in the cards. But I'll make it worth your while."

It didn't take long for us to come to terms. Once she left, Lily and Sebastian were allowed in together and stayed until I started drifting off to sleep. Sebastian tried to keep me awake for fear I'd fall back into a coma until the nurse assured him that I'd be okay and that they would check on me throughout the night. She also said that after the scans and my progress so far, it was unlikely to happen. Nevertheless, the relief in his eyes was palpable when they returned the following morning to bring me home.

We filled Lily in on the conditional trust issue and ensuing engagement to Rebecca. But I made her promise she wouldn't speak a word to Cici. She said that between this and knowing about the baby for so long, she's been clouded in secrets, but she'd keep this last one since she approves of my plan to win her back.

Smoothing things over between my brother and Lily for Sebastian withholding information from her went better than expected. Apparently, my insistence not to tell her and his reluctance to agree aided in her forgiveness. It also helped that she knew about the baby without telling him. I'd say they're even with the way they each held their own in the discussion—it was fascinating to watch. Few people fare so well going head-to-head with my brother. They've been married for a year, but it's only been a couple of months in my mind. Either way, it's clear they're perfect for each other. I'm happy for them, and it makes me crave that for myself.

If all goes according to plan, it should happen sooner than later. I've been home for a few days and have yet to regain my memory, but I'm hopeful. I've had snippets here and there, but nothing that makes sense without the entire picture. It's frustrating as hell, but not enough to deter me from my goal. I'm rummaging around in my nightstand, taking stock of anything different, when I stumble upon a ring box. It's not Rebecca's, since I let her keep the damn thing, so that leaves one possibility.

Pulling out the turquoise Tiffany box, I inhale deeply, anxious to look inside. Opening the lid slowly, I examine the exquisitely designed ring. It's nothing like the one Rebecca wore and rightly so, since this one means so much more. I carefully remove it, and the minute my fingers grasp it, I'm flooded with visions… memories. The night I proposed, the night I met Rebecca, the next month, and the month after—it all comes rushing back in one fell swoop, making me jolt as I fall back on my ass to the mattress and slide to the floor.

With my eyes closed, I take it all in, every detail, every moment, every emotion. Love, anger, resignation… until the only thing remaining was despair. The day of the accident comes last and the terror I felt from my life taking a nosedive in the wrong direction. The helplessness I felt at losing control. My head explodes at the powerful sensation of having all these emotions at once. It's surreal to envision your life from completely different perspectives one second to the next. Breathing deeply, the memories continue to replay, one after another, until everything makes sense and falls into place.

I open my eyes, and they instantly go to the plant on my nightstand that I brought home from the hospital. It's the orchid I gave Cici. The same one she took to Bozeman with her and must've brought back when she came while I was in a coma. She obviously felt it was time to leave it behind. But I'll take it as a sign if there ever was one, because if that thing can survive through all that, then we can too.

It's true when I said this was the best thing to happen, because if I'd stayed the course I was on, I'd never have made it out intact. Something would always be missing and out of reach. My goal of not having any regrets in life would've been smashed to pieces had I gone through with marrying Rebecca, because losing Cici would have been the biggest regret of all.

This fresh start I've been given is the miracle I needed, and the only thing left to do now is play it out. Now is not the time to look a gift horse in the mouth. With my memories intact, I'd like nothing more than to go to Cici right the fuck now and convince her that we belong together, but there's one more matter to take care of. Her family needs to approve.

With renewed determination, I contact Cici's parents and Jackson, asking them if I could come by this week, saying time was of the essence. Luck is on my side since they agreed to tonight, probably curious as to what I have to say. Hopefully, if this goes well, I'll be on the jet tomorrow. But let's not get ahead of ourselves, since I'm not sure how they feel about me knocking her up. This may be more difficult than I imagine—but there's only one way to find out.

When I pull up, Jackson's car is already in the driveway. I'm nervous, knowing this could make or break my future. The last thing I want to do is come between Cici and her parents, especially after their reconciliation. Gathering all my courage, I raise my hand and knock.

Jackson is the one who opens the door, which gives me little relief. He has no idea what I've done since I regained consciousness and isn't too happy that his baby sister left with no indication that I would be a part of our baby's life. But I've had to focus on getting shit handled before I came clean to everyone. I'm ready to set the record straight.

"This better be good," Jackson says as he steps aside for me to enter.

"You can decide for yourself, but to me, it's everything. Thanks for seeing me."

With a nod of acknowledgement, he leads me to the living room, where Mia and his parents are waiting.

Taking the easy target first, I address Jackson's fiancée. "Hi, Mia. I'm happy you're here."

We hug as she responds, "You too, Eli. I'm glad you're okay."

I chuckle. "Thank goodness someone here is."

Jackson glares, but his mom stands to hug me. "Eli, we're all happy you're okay. Come here." She embraces me, and I'm humbled. Knowing I knocked her daughter up, she still shows kindness.

"Thank you, Hazel. That means a lot. Here. These are for you." I pass the flowers I've been holding.

"That was sweet. Thank you. I'll put these in water and be right back. Would you like anything to drink?"

"I'm fine, thanks."

She goes to the kitchen, and I turn to the last and most

intimidating one in the room. I reach out to shake his hand. "Jack, I appreciate you taking the time to see me. I need to explain a few things regarding your daughter, if that's all right with you."

He shakes my hand, giving it a firm squeeze. "I think that would be appropriate given the circumstances. We're certainly interested in your intentions now that there's a child involved."

"That's why I'm here. When Hazel returns, I'll start from the beginning and fill you in on where I'm at."

"Before you start, I'm hoping your memory came back? Because a lot's happened in the last eight months," Jackson says from his seat beside Mia on the sofa.

"It did, and I understand everyone needs to be sure I'm in my right mind, but I didn't need my memories to know where I stand. It's no different today than it was back then, just a lot of bullshit in between."

"You're telling me," Jackson sourly replies.

Hazel breezes into the room and sits in one of the wingback chairs while Jack sits in the other. "All right, thanks for waiting. Go ahead, Eli. We'll give you the floor since this was your request."

Sitting on the couch across from Jackson and Mia, I dive in. "Thanks, Hazel. First of all, I'm in love with your daughter and have been for the last two years, and there's a good chance she loves me too."

I proceeded to tell them about asking her to marry me and taking full responsibility for subsequently getting her pregnant without going into the gory details. The condition of the trust was easy to explain since that wasn't the secret to begin with; it was the fake marriage that ensued because of it. They stuck with me while I told them my reasons for not telling Cici about the trust, not wanting to pressure her. It could be wishful thinking, but it looked like approval on their faces.

Explaining my engagement with Rebecca was a little more sensitive, and I'll admit that I may not have divulged how we met or exactly when that was. Nor did I fess up to the fact that we were only fuck buddies but instead portrayed our relationship as a means to an end with only a contract and business arrangement between us.

"I ended the engagement and severed ties the day I woke up. And now that my memories have returned, I'm ready to take the next step toward what I've always wanted, which is your daughter's hand in marriage. Let me assure you, this has nothing to do with the trust. If she still refuses to marry me, then I'm willing to live with the consequences of my actions, and although I'll be heartbroken, I'll survive. So, Mr. Soloman, may I have permission to marry your daughter?"

Tears gather in Hazel's eyes as she glances at her husband, who stares at me speculatively. Mia smiles next to Jackson, who has finally loosened up and looks at me like the guy he remembers, the one he respects. Fuck, having him doubt me was brutal, but there was no other choice in the matter.

"Well, that's quite the story, Eli. Had I not seen for myself the way you felt about my daughter at Christmas, I might find it all hard to believe, but I did. I've also seen the difference in Cici's happiness since then, which means she might feel something along those lines as well. If all you've said is true, then you have my blessing, but the rest is up to you."

The second he says the words, the feeling is indescribable. I'm beaming, for lack of a better word, and jump from my seat to shake his hand, but he stands to embrace me. Okay, there might be a slight glistening in my eye, but I'm not acknowledging it. Hazel is next, followed by Mia, saving Jackson for last.

"Hey, buddy, it's good to have you back." He throws his arms around me, and the feeling of… family humbles me.

"Phew." I exaggeratingly wipe my forehead, and everyone laughs. "With that settled, there is one more thing I need to ask. Jackson, you remember that favor you owe me?"

He furrows his brows suspiciously. "Yeah?" he drawls.

"Well, if it's okay with all of you, assuming she says yes, I'd like us to marry before the baby is born." I look at Jackson and Mia. "And since you happen to have a wedding already planned, I was hoping you might be okay with another bride and groom joining you."

Mia's face lights up, and she grins at Jackson, who's smirking at me. "Well, aren't you smooth thinking you can just poach our big day."

"Jackson!" Mia swats his chest. "It's your sister."

"I'll pay for the whole thing."

"Hell yeah, I guess we're having a double wedding!" Jackson says and high-fives me. Then he starts laughing. "I'm kidding. I was gonna say yes before you offered to pay, dude."

Happiness permeates the room.

"Even if you had, I was still offering. In fact, I insist."

Jack interrupts by clearing his throat. "Not to burst anyone's bubble, but Cici needs to be on board."

"I'm on a jet first thing tomorrow morning. Just needed your permission first, and yours." I address both Jack and Jackson.

"Well, you've got it. Now it's in your hands. Go get her," Jack says, patting me on the back.

"Thank you, sir. Jackson." I nod to both and make rounds to say goodbye.

As Hazel hugs me, she welcomes me to the family, which fills my heart with hope.

24

FREEING

Cici

LEAVING THE HOSPITAL TWO DAYS AGO AFTER BARING MY SOUL has been added to my list of the top ten most difficult things I've done, and yesterday morning's task was right up there with it. Jackson, Mia, and Mia's mom joined me at our parents' house for breakfast to surprise them with the news of a grandbaby before my flight out that afternoon. If you'd asked me how I felt about that, I'd have told you it was stressful enough to put me right into labor, which was why I decided to bring backup. Yeah, it may not have been the brightest idea to spring it on them with an audience, but the thought of doing it alone terrified the crap out of me.

Mia's mom came because she's become a permanent fixture in our family since (a) she lives in the same building as Jackson and Mia, (b) they've all been planning the wedding together for weeks, and (c) she's the reason our parents forced Jackson to hire Mia in the first place. Mia's mom was their housekeeper then and often talked about her amazing daughter, who needed a job at the same time his assistant was taking maternity leave. It's amazing how fate works sometimes.

Luckily, the additional guests worked out in my favor because although their initial hesitation was evident upon our arrival, they kept their shock to a minimum. By the end of breakfast, it was obvious what kind of grandparents they would be—the doting, loving, spoiling kind. In hindsight, I should have leaned on them from the beginning.

Of course, as any parent would, they worried about me being a single mother, but once we got that out of the way, they practically begged me to move back home so they could have me and their grandbaby close by. All that worry over their disappointment was for nothing.

Now here I am, back in Bozeman with an odd sense of contentment. Having everything out in the open is a relief—not only with my parents but Eli as well. And even though I left without any plan for the future, just having him know is enough for now. I'm sure we'll eventually end up at the part where we talk about how to navigate dual parenting in the future, but we have time for that. Strangely, considering how things ended, it felt like there was closure this time. No hidden feelings, lies, or secrets, and nothing either of us can do but move forward. It's freeing in a way. I've always craved control of my life, but in losing Eli, I've realized I'm not really in control of anything.

Our love for each other was beautiful, but unfortunately, it blossomed at the wrong time. But it was meant to be, because if it hadn't happened, then I may never have sought help and been able to overcome this odd phobia of mine. I'll be forever grateful that the experience pushed me to do that and also for the baby growing inside of me that I can't imagine my life without. Loving Eli is now something I can live with, and although nothing would make me happier than to be with him, I'm finally ready to be happy without him.

Which is why, even though I'm exhausted as hell, I'm excited to meet Matt and Poppy for brunch this morning. Breakfast happens to be my friend these days, since by the time dinner rolls around, I'm always too tired to function, let alone socialize. Entering the restaurant, I find them immediately with a pitcher of bottomless mimosas already on the table. I head in their direction, thinking they should really be warned about those.

Poppy spots me and jumps up from her chair to give me a squealing hug. "Aaaah, I've missed you! And you're already so much bigger."

"Thanks, that's just what every woman wants to hear when she's greeted."

"You know what I mean. I feel like I missed so much in my baby's life," she coos as she rubs my belly, doing well to redeem herself.

Matt gets up to hug me. "Hey, Cici. Glad to have you back. How are you feeling?"

We take our seats, and the waitress rushes up to ask for my order before I can answer.

"I'm feeling great," I say with a big smile that I truly feel. "In fact, I couldn't be better. Everyone knows about the baby, and I don't have to hide it anymore. My brother's getting married in less than two months, and my parents are excited to be grandparents. Life couldn't be better." *Okay, maybe a little.*

Matt and Poppy look at each other skeptically before Poppy says, "Who are you, and what have you done with Cici? She's about this tall." Her hand lifts. "Blonde hair, blue eyes with a constant chip on her shoulder and enough stress to fill a football field."

I laugh. "That Cici is not coming back." At their hesitation, I add, "I'm serious. All is right with the world." *Or close enough.*

The waitress arrives with my tea, and we give our orders before conversation continues.

Matt chimes in first. "I feel like something's missing. Why don't you tell us what happened in San Diego and how you left things."

So I do. From when Eli woke up to walking out after admitting

I'd be with him. The story of my parents will have to wait since Poppy takes over.

"That's it? You said 'yes' and just walked out?" she asks incredulously.

"There was nothing left to say. We can't be together." My tone may suggest stupidity, but she skips over it and gives a dose right back.

"How about, 'Oh hey, let's talk about this baby we're having together. What will your involvement in our child's life look like? Such as visitation, child support—you know, general parenting concerns?' That may have been a good idea before you left." She looks to Matt. "Or is that just me?" Poppy's not one to mince words when she's passionate about something.

Matt uses a little more tact. "Did you both agree you'd talk about that at a later time?"

"No," I sigh. "It seemed like the only thing he wanted out of the whole conversation was to get me to admit my feelings, and once that was done, he was satisfied." I shrug. "Besides, I don't need child support. I mean, at this point, I'm fine. Maybe when they get older and start costing more. With things like sports, cars, and college, he can pitch in, but not until then. I'm sure we'll figure something out for visitation, especially since I'll be home a lot to see my parents."

"So you basically say you love each other, and just like that, shazam, you're fine now?" Poppy's hand flies up exaggeratedly. Her tipsiness would be cuter if she weren't giving me shit.

"Just like that," I confirm. "It's almost like all I needed was to get everything off my chest. Once I did, it felt like a ton of bricks lifted off my shoulders. I'd been carrying this around for so long that I didn't even realize how much it weighed me down."

"Well, I'm happy for you. And I believe you when you say you're good, but that doesn't mean you won't have bad days. You can't simply shut off your feelings, so if you do have a bad day, you'll call one of us, right? Because we won't fault you if you slip up now and then."

Leave it to Matt to be the clearheaded one who evidently handles his alcohol better.

"Thank you, Matt. That means a lot. I couldn't have made it this far without both of you. And I'm sure I'll be leaning on you more over the next couple of months until this little one makes their appearance," I say while rubbing my stomach.

"I see someone's ready for breakfast. Hope you're all hungry," the waitress says as she sets down three heaping plates of food before us.

I get a few minutes of reprieve while we dig in until Poppy picks up where she left off.

"So let me get this straight," Poppy starts in between mouthfuls of food. "You're by his side for two weeks, he wakes up, asks to see you before his fiancée, you both profess your love, you admit to wanting to be with him, and then he just lets you go? That's fucked up. It sure doesn't sound like everything's great to me."

Matt's eyes go wide, and he's about to intervene, but I shoo him off.

"I'm choosing to focus on the positive and not dwell on the negative. The ideal scenario would be that he's not engaged to another woman he doesn't remember falling in love with. But guess what, he is, so it doesn't matter how fucked up it sounds—it is what it is, and there's nothing me, you, or anyone else can do about it. What would you expect him to do? Call off the wedding and choose me? What happens when his memory returns and he realizes he's already gotten over me and loves Rebecca? How would that feel, huh? It'd be far worse than being at peace with where we left things. So please just let it be."

Between the food she's been shoveling in and my speech, Poppy sobers right up. "Oh my God, I'm so sorry. What am I thinking? You're trying to move on, and I'm acting like a total bitch about it. Please forgive me," she says and rises to hug me.

"Of course I forgive you. It's probably my fault anyway for not warning you about bottomless mimosas. Been there, done that."

Matt's looking at us like we're from another planet. "Women. I don't think I'll ever understand you creatures."

We all laugh and stick to lighter topics for the rest of the meal, and I'm happy that my parents now fit into that category as I relay the details of our visit. We end on a good note with Poppy going home to nap. And because it's Sunday and I have the greatest excuse in the world, I do too.

The following week flies by with periodic updates from Lily about Eli's recovery. She's been somewhat vague—I'm assuming not to hurt my feelings—but it's probably for the best with my new take on the situation. It really has been quite freeing not to constantly be thinking of him and all he entails. Although it never fails that when you're basking in the calm, something always comes along to rock the boat.

Poppy saunters into my office late one morning, holding an article she must've printed. "Cici, have you been reading the gossip columns recently?"

"Nope. Because I decided whoever said 'ignorance is bliss' was right, and ever since I stopped reading them, I've been blissfully ignorant." I smile sardonically as she rolls her eyes.

"That's what I thought. Well, Ms. Ignorant, something came out today you might be interested in hearing."

"Uh-uh." My hand goes up, palm out. "Don't do it. I do *not* want to know."

"You do. You really, really do. You'd be mad at me if I knew about it and *didn't* tell you, I swear. Just hear me out." She gives me her best puppy dog eyes.

"Ugh." I look to the ceiling and breathe deeply. It's probably something I'll find out sooner or later anyway if she's this insistent. Plus, I don't think she'd be this excited if it was something bad, so I should just let her tell me and move on. Otherwise, she'll probably pester me until I relent anyway. "Fine. Spit it out."

She holds up the article and takes a dramatic breath before

reading, "The illustrious Eli Dubree of Dubree Enterprises called off his engagement after two months." She looks at me with hearts in her eyes. "Would you like to hear his statement?" I'm stunned speechless, which is fine since she doesn't give me time to answer. "While Rebecca is a wonderful person, my recent near-death experience shed light on how important life is and reminded me that it's too short to accept anything less than what one truly wants. It would not have been fair to either of us to follow through with the wedding when my heart belongs to someone else." She pauses dramatically and brings the paper to her chest for effect before continuing, "When asked about the other woman, Dubree responded that if all goes accordingly, the world will know soon enough." The smile on her face tells me she knows exactly who he's talking about, while my thumping heart happily agrees.

"That came out today?" It's the only thing I come up with.

"Yes! So now what? Have you heard from him?" she asks, beaming.

"He was on your shit list last we talked, and now you're suddenly team Eli?" I snap in defense because no, I haven't heard from him. At. All.

"I was always team Eli. I was just mad at him for forfeiting the game. But look." She holds up the article. "He's back in!"

Her enthusiasm makes me laugh. "What should I do? Do you think he meant for me to see it?"

"Of course he did. This is Eli announcing that he's coming for you. If I were you, I'd hurry home and do a full body makeover before he gets here since it's been ages since you've had to shave for anyone."

"Gee, thanks. Not bad advice, though. But he could just make a phone call."

Ironically enough, my phone rings at that exact moment. My heart jolts until I look and see that it's Lily.

"Hello?"

"Did you read the article?"

Putting it on speaker, I answer, "Yes. Poppy's here, and she just read it to me."

"He's talking about you," Lily says excitedly.

"No, I thought he was talking about another mystery woman," I say sarcastically.

"Okay, smart-ass. What are you going to do about it?"

"Nothing? What am I supposed to do?"

"I'm no rocket scientist, but you should probably be prepared for him to show up on your doorstep."

Poppy gives me a smug look. "Told you so. You better hustle home and manage that forest you've been growing."

Lily laughs. "Oh my God, that's what I was thinking."

"That's why we need to meet. We're destined to be friends," Poppy says.

"Is this seriously happening?" I'm in shock and can't wrap my head around it. "Wait! Lily, did his memory come back? What if he's making this decision without all the facts?"

"Sweetie, I love you, but I'm not getting involved. This is between you and Eli. You're both special to me, and whatever is meant to be, will be. Now get your ass home and deforest yourself."

"Hey, it's taken a long time to grow out."

Poppy makes a gagging motion. "Gross, if nothing else comes out of this, at least that will."

25

DEMANDS

Eli

'VE NEVER BEEN TO MONTANA. BUT FLYING OVER IT THIS afternoon, I understand the draw. There are mountains for miles—rivers, lakes, and bare land in every direction. I'm not exactly sure what real estate Jackson's been talking about, but there must be something somewhere. After he visited Cici last year, I planned to make a trip over, but since she ended up in San Diego again, I never needed to.

I've been chasing that woman since the night we locked eyes in the club almost three years ago. It was always her. Deep down, I felt it from our first kiss, but it took a while for my brain to catch up and the wild streak I was sporting to come to terms with it. By the time I realized she was the one, she made the move to Bozeman. I always knew how against relationships she was, and early on, that was A-okay with me, but when the idea of being more started to take shape, she certainly wasn't on board. I eventually found out she never would be.

Until now.

Nothing stands in our way at this point. Well, other than the thousand miles between us, but that's simple logistics. I'd love for her to move back to San Diego, but my home is wherever she is. I'm slightly concerned about not being honest with her about my trust, but shouldn't I get a hall pass since she didn't tell me about *our* baby? Our baby. I'm about to be a father. Holy shit. It still blows my mind every time I think about it, which is often, and never fails to make me smile.

I'm constantly looking back and thinking how different things might have been if I'd shared the condition of marriage from the beginning or if she had told me about being pregnant right when she found out, but I reach the same conclusion every time—that I wouldn't change a thing. Because it all brought me to this moment, right here, knocking on a door, waiting for the woman I love to open up and save me from a life that I can't fathom to live… without her in it.

The second it opens, I'm overwhelmed by the sight before me. It's my angel in the flesh. She's an absolute vision of beauty from top to bottom, and her pregnant belly only accentuates every detail.

When I planned this out, I knew I'd have to prove to her, without a doubt, that my memory came back. So I hold the orchid out. "You left something behind."

Tears spring to her eyes as she takes it and steps back for me to enter. Shutting the door, she goes to the living room and sets it on the coffee table, turning to me in silence.

Adding the proof she needs, I recite the words only I would know from my first proposal. "When you turned me down on New Year's Eve, you told me I deserved someone who could give me everything in return, but what you don't realize is that there's nothing anyone can give me that I want… more than I want you."

"Eli," she gasps before leaping into my arms.

Suddenly, all is right in the world. Her lips are on mine, and as I match her ferocity, it's as if we've been starving for each other our whole lives. Maybe we have, but the famine is over, and I'll never let her go again.

The only way to accomplish that is to do what I came here to do, so I reluctantly extract her from my arms. Her whimper of protest makes my heart swell and assures me I'm on the right track. Without further ado, I take a knee, pull the box from my pocket, and open it as her hands fly to her mouth in shock.

"Cici, you mean everything to me. I was enamored from the first moment I laid eyes on you and knew I had to have you. You, Cici, are truly it for me. I've been in love with you for two years and in absolute misery without you for the past eight months." I shake my head and scoff. "You've kept me waiting so damn long. Please don't make me wait any longer. I'm asking for forever, because forever is how long it will take to prove there's only one true love in life, and for me, that's always been you." She nods as tears stream down her beautiful face, and as much as I want to wrap her in my arms, there's a confession to make. "But before you say yes, there's something you need to hear."

Her brows furrow in confusion. This is it—the last piece of the puzzle, and the only one left that could ruin everything.

Taking a deep breath, I continue, "My engagement to Rebecca was a sham. It was only to satisfy a condition of our trust requiring me and my brother to marry by the age of thirty to keep our inheritance and company. I found out on my twenty-ninth birthday."

Her eyebrows scrunch as she puts the pieces together and takes a step back in retreat. *Please don't let this be the thing that breaks us.*

"Wait. That was right before you proposed last time. Is that why you asked me?"

"Yes and no. Marrying you was something I'd already wanted, but I always knew you weren't there yet—that you may never be. I was willing to wait, but because of the condition, I couldn't and was forced to ask you too soon, praying I could persuade you before you were ready. I should have known better than to try and convince my stubborn girl of anything, but nonetheless, I tried and failed."

"Why didn't you just tell me? I probably would have said yes."

"I have no doubt, but that's not the yes I wanted. The yes *I* wanted had to come from *here*." I put my hand over her heart. "I didn't want you to marry me because of an obligation and certainly not out of charity. I wanted you to marry me because you love me as much as I love you."

She's crying harder now, but there's one more box to check. "There's one more thing you'll have to agree to if you say yes," I say with a smirk.

"Now what?" She laughs through her tears.

"Well, cutie, we'll be getting married next month, because if you can't beat 'em, join 'em. And Jackson and Mia already agreed." I wink. "Oh, and your mom and dad give their blessing."

"WHAT?" Her gasp cuts her tears off while she swipes them away.

Grabbing her left hand, I hold the ring around the tip of her finger. "That's the deal. Yes or no?" I slowly begin to push it up, hearing no objection.

Her free hand goes to her jutted hip as I slide it on the rest of the way. "Are you really in a position to be making demands?" she asks in that sassy way I love so much. But what do I not love about this woman?

Keeping hold of her hand and placing my other over hers on her hip, I rise to stand. "You haven't seen anything yet, baby. I've got eight months of demands ready to unleash."

"Is that so? What kind of demands?"

"How about we start with this one? Tell me you love me."

She giggles but then goes serious before saying the words I feel like I've waited my whole life to hear. "I love you, Eli Dubree. More than I ever thought possible to love another human being."

"Now this one." I cup her cheek and stare into her eyes, showing every ounce of emotion, before I slowly make the most important demand of all. "Say. Yes."

"Yes."

Epilogue

Cici

Three months later

"Our baby better be this good. Why didn't we have one months ago?" Lily asks Sebastian, making me laugh silently as Sebastian's eyes bulge. Lily's cradling Abby and has been staring at her most of the time we've been here, except while I fed her.

"You're joking, right? I've been trying to knock you up since our wedding night. You were the one who wanted to wait," Sebastian argues.

"Well, you should have tried harder," Lily pouts.

"Trust me, sweetheart, if I'd tried any harder, you'd be broken."

"Okay, I think that's our cue to leave," Eli says next to me and lifts Ebony to the ground before helping me off the couch.

"No," Lily whines. "You can't take her from me."

I laugh. She's been like this from the moment we brought our daughter home, which was eight weeks ago now. Thank God she's due soon, or we'd have to work out a visitation plan.

"How about this?" Eli says. "You keep her for a while, and Mom and I will go take a nap."

"That's what you're calling it these days?" Sebastian quips, making Lily and me giggle.

"Just wait, buddy. Your time's coming." Eli chuckles as he leads me to the door.

We walk hand in hand down the hallway toward our home, which takes up the other half of the top floor in the downtown high-rise they own. Eli stayed in Bozeman the week after his second proposal—the one I said yes to—and helped me pack while I worked with Poppy to take over my clients. Eli got to meet Poppy and her family when we went to our weekly dinner, and of course, they fell in love with him. Poppy couldn't stop gushing over my ring, and whenever Eli's back was turned, she would fan herself, give me the thumbs-up, or smile in giddy approval.

We had dinner another night with Poppy and Matt, which Eli was eager for after I told him I'd gone on a date with Matt and that he was with me for my miscarriage scare. I was nervous at first that it might be a problem, but all Eli did was thank him for being there when he couldn't and tell him he appreciated him taking care of me. My heart grew tenfold right then and there, and when we got home that night, I made sure to show him just how much I appreciated him.

Oh, and we also did the gender reveal that week with Jackson, Mia, Lily, Sebastian, and my parents on FaceTime. I'm glad I saved that special moment for both of us, and the tears in Eli's eyes made it worth it. He doted on me like crazy, trying to make up for the time he couldn't. It felt special to be taken care of. And he hasn't stopped since. It was also nice to retire my vibrator, because *wow* was I one of those women who became a horndog during pregnancy, so Eli had a lot of making up to do. I'm happy to report that he succeeded and is still going strong, except for the six weeks he couldn't after Abby was born, which is why we take these moments when we can.

However, when Eli closes the front door, I can't hold back from asking something that's been bothering me for a while now. "Hey, so there's something I never did ask you that I'm curious about." I pause to make sure I have his attention. "Did Sebastian ask Lily to marry him because of the trust thing?" I'm afraid of the answer, but it's been on my mind ever since I found out.

"Hell no. He heard about it when I did. He's had it bad for Lily since the day they met." He pulls me to him and wraps his arms around me, kissing the tip of my nose. "Where did that come from, cutie?"

I shrug. "It was something I thought about when you told me but was too afraid to ask. Today I decided it doesn't matter because they're so happy regardless."

"You know who else is happy, Mrs. Dubree?" He kisses each corner of my mouth, then looks into my eyes.

"Let me guess. You."

"Damn right I am. I have the sexiest wife on the planet and the most perfect baby in the world. And right now? *We* have the next hour to ourselves." He nuzzles my neck, grazing my skin with his lips and tongue.

"Should we take a nap?" I try to make the question sound as serious as possible given the lustful state I'm in as of a few seconds ago. It amazes me how fast he can put me in the mood still with all the changes in our lives. I'm glad being a parent didn't alter that aspect of our relationship, since it does happen to be one of my favorite parts. It helps having Abby's aunt and uncle down the hallway.

"Definitely wasn't my plan, but if that's what you need, sweetheart, that's what you get. On the other hand, you could always nap with Abby… after I've tired you out even more. I'm willing to do whatever it takes to help you sleep." His head pops up, and he wiggles his brows.

"Hmmm. Not a bad suggestion. What do you have in mind?"

"Way too many things to list, but it starts with you naked. Why don't you go take care of that while I grab some water and meet you in the bedroom?"

I giggle, thinking of the first time he had me go wait for him. "You sure that's a good idea? I remember falling asleep one time you told me to go wait for you. These days, that's even more likely."

"Fair point. Screw the water." He hauls me up bridal style, pulling a squeal out as he carries me to our room, then sets me on my feet in front of the bed.

"Let me help you with this," he says, grabbing the hem of my shirt and lifting straight up as I raise my arms to accommodate.

Only my bra remains after Eli tosses the shirt aside, causing my nipples to immediately pebble from his ravenous gaze. It's not the sexiest number in the world since breastfeeding tends to put a damper in that department, but you'd think I was wearing the Taj Mahal of lingerie with the way Eli stares in adoration.

"How did I get so lucky?" he asks.

I snicker in disbelief. "Eli, this is the most unflattering bra I own."

"Good thing I'm not talking about your undergarments, then." He leans in to devour my neck, making me break out in glorious goose bumps as he reaches back and undoes the unflattering item in question.

He knows right where to go, to that spot right below my ear, causing me to moan and writhe as he slides my bra down. Both hands immediately claim their prize, lightly squeezing each freed breast.

"Fuck, I love these things. I need to get you pregnant so they stay like this."

"They're not going anywhere for quite a while, don't worry."

"Good, because I'm getting too used to helping myself." He kisses downward until his mouth finds my nipple, and after a few laps of his tongue, he engulfs it with his mouth and sucks.

My head goes back. Oh God. I love when he does this. There's something so sexy about him taking from me. Something so deliciously wrong and depraved. His hand reaches into my leggings, and I push into him, my body begging for more. His fingers find their target, and he lunges in without delay, giving me exactly what I want.

He pops off my breast. "Damn, baby, I can't get enough of you." Eli kisses me as he thrusts in and out, making my body clench in anticipation of its pending climax. "Need to keep you pregnant so this never goes away."

His mouth latches on to my other nipple, pulling hard as he drinks, while his fingers curl deep inside, his thumb hitting my clit and sending me over the edge.

"Oh my God, Eli! Yes! Oh God, yes… aah," I cry out in ecstasy, bucking my hips as the sensations from high and low take over.

"That's it, baby. Ride my hand." And I do like it's all I know. "You're so goddamn sexy," he says as he rises.

Exhaling the last of my climax, I slump into his shoulder, hanging on for dear life since my legs seem to have gone out on me. "Holy shit. I needed that."

"Apparently. Glad I could be of service—although I'm pretty sure I got as much out of it as you did. That's some mighty fine milk you have there."

I shake my head on his shoulder, still too weak to move. "You're terrible."

His body vibrates in a silent laugh. "I'd be happy to repay the favor if you're thirsty. You'll just work a little harder for it. You want a drink, baby?"

"I don't think I have it in me," I say honestly. Not because I'm opposed to the idea—I love Eli's dick—but I truly don't know if I can function at the moment.

"How about this? Let's get you comfortable and then see what's on the menu." He gently helps me onto the bed, laying me back against the pillows. "Lie there and relax while I help you with the rest of these unnecessary items."

My leggings and underwear are removed within seconds, and after grabbing the shirt from earlier, he heads into the closet, returning a minute later equally naked. Damn, he's hot. Would it be too much to ask for him to keep the six-pack and never end up with a dad bod? Not that I'm perfect after giving birth two months ago, but Eli is somehow attracted to the extra pregnancy weight. Though if things keep moving the way they have, it should be gone within a couple more months.

He stops at the far side of the bed and raises his brows. "If you keep looking at me like that, you're going to be sorry, tired or not."

"Did I say I was tired? Weird, I meant to say wired—it must've come out wrong."

He smirks, fisting his cock and stroking it slowly. "Hm. See something you like?"

Yes. Yes, I do.

"Spread your legs and touch yourself. Show me how needy your pussy is."

He walks to the end of the bed for a better view, staring between my legs as my hand creeps down to lightly stroke my clit.

"Like this?" I ask seductively.

"Whatever feels good, baby. Let me see you come. Get yourself all nice and slick for this, and I'll let you have it." He squeezes up and down his length, matching the pace I've set, moving faster as I increase the intensity.

"God, I love watching you do that. I'm so close."

"You and me both, baby. Bring yourself home, and I'll fuck you so hard. I'll give you what you need."

"Oh God. Eli!" My climax hits me, and my eyes close in ecstasy while the pulses take over.

The bed dips, and suddenly Eli's head is between my legs as he dives in with his tongue, drinking as if he's been stranded in the desert for days. The contact on top of my orgasm sends me further into ecstasy, bucking and pushing his head into me greedily.

Seconds later, he rises, eyes thick with lust, wiping his coated mouth with the back of his hand. "Fuck, baby, you're delicious. I could eat you for days, but my dick needs to be in you right the fuck now."

There's no warning before he flips me over and grabs my hips to pull my ass up, making me squeal in surprise. Rubbing his cock up and down my slit a couple times, he works his way in, rocking and pushing through the initial resistance while we moan and pant in pleasure. There's nothing like that first penetration, the feeling of being stretched—glorious inch by glorious inch.

When he's fully seated, he pauses, sighing in contentment. "Damn, this never gets old. I'm in love with your body. I don't think I'll ever get enough, baby."

"Good, because I feel the same way. Now where's my reward?"

"So impatient. You know what happens when you're a brat. I'm usually up for setting a new record, but we only have so much time."

"Thank God for small miracles."

"That doesn't mean I won't remember for later. You'll get your punishment, sweetheart."

"Fine. Later. Can we get to the good part now?"

Eli reaches down and grabs my hair, pulling to lift my head. "What's that, baby? I must've misheard. Did you ask me nicely to please fuck you?"

"Ugh. Yes. Eli, will you pretty please fuck me like you mean it?" I know what's coming, and the anticipation has my core clenching with need.

"That's a good girl asking so sweet. Now take it like one."

Without any more pauses, he shoves me down and pounds into me relentlessly, forcing unholy sounds from my mouth. "That's it, Cici. Let me hear how much you like my big fat cock fucking you like an animal."

"Yes, please, more." I can't seem to get enough. These moments are rare nowadays, when it's just us, Abby's next door, and we can finally unleash, satisfying our deepest cravings.

"I'm gonna fill you so full, baby. Keep you pregnant and full of milk for me. You'll take my cock as much as it takes."

"Yes!"

He holds me down and ruts into me harder and harder, like his life depends on it.

Lifting my hips slightly, he raises us both and snakes his hand under to reach my clit. "You're going to come one more time for me, Cici. Milk my cock so my seed can do its job. I want your belly to grow with another baby. And this time I'll be there to watch it."

Oh God, he knows just what to say to put me over the edge. That, and his hand working its magic. "Fuck, Eli! God, yes. Oh God, please. It feels so good."

His hips still, and he holds himself deep inside, releasing into me at the same time. "That's it, Cici. Oh fuck. You feel so good squeezing my cock. Damn, baby." He finishes, slumping into me and breathing heavy.

"God, Eli, that was… amazing."

"You're amazing." He kisses my back, then gets up.

I roll over to my back and look up at him with googly eyes. I'm so in love with this man. "I love you."

"I love you. And I'm serious about getting you pregnant." He reaches for a pillow. "Lift your hips." He places the pillow under my butt. "Stay that way while I go wash up."

I laugh as he walks away. "You know I can't get pregnant while I'm breastfeeding."

He pauses at the doorway and looks at me. "It can happen. I looked it up, so don't move until I say so."

I roll my eyes but comply, smiling to myself at his outlandishness. I'm not sure that I'm ready for another baby yet, but the thought of doing it over with Eli by my side this time is too enticing to argue or overthink.

"Hey, cutie? I think I should bring our daughter home. What do you think?" Eli yells from the bathroom. He's adorable, and I think he's more attached to her than I am, and I'm pretty darn attached.

"Yes, please. I miss her, not to mention I need her to nurse," I answer as he saunters over in his low-cut sweats that look so sexy, I'd be up for round three if I weren't ready to feed Abby this minute.

"I'm standing right here. Let me help you out with that." He lunges, taking my breast in his mouth and sucking hard.

"Eli, no! Abby needs it. You've had enough," I say, laughing.

"Those words aren't in my vocabulary, Cici."

"They will be when your daughter doesn't get enough to eat. She's probably hungry by now."

"Well then, in that case, you just stay there looking beautifully fucked, and I'll be back before you know it with a package in tow." He leans down for a panty-melting kiss.

I shove him away, laughing. "Go and hurry up."

Picking up my phone from the nightstand after he leaves, I see a text from Poppy and start giggling.

> Poppy: What the hell is Braden doing in Bozeman again? He doesn't give up! Did you know about this?
>
> Cici: Not a clue. Sorry, not sorry. Good luck!
>
> Poppy: Ugh! Seriously? I'm making it clear this time that we are NOT happening.
>
> Cici: Let me know how that goes ;) LOL

Wow! What a whirlwind the last year has been. After writing and publishing my first three books, I must say… this fourth one was a hurdle. I'm not sure whether it was timing, uncertainty, or the obscene pressure of wanting to do these characters justice, but something certainly slowed me down.

Having said that, I hope you agree that the finished product didn't disappoint, and getting through Eli and Cici's love story was amazingly sweet, yet utterly heart-wrenching. They went through a lot to reach their happily ever after, but wasn't it worth the wait to get there?

We all owe a big thanks to my daughter Cassie, who is the ultimate marketing guru, and for this book, my sounding board and co-conspirator. I couldn't have made it to the end without her. She's finally coming around to her romance era by way of audiobooks and was a massive help in crafting the finer details of Eli and Cici's story.

As for finishing the book, my husband and biggest cheerleader, John, is solely responsible for pushing me to get it done. Procrastination mode has been in full force over the last few months, and without John's encouragement, the deadline would have come and gone. I'm lucky to have him by my side. Otherwise, you'd still be waiting for this one.

While Cassie helped me set the stage for the story, my other daughter, Abby, helped me refine this beauty. She was there each step of the way: critiquing, suggesting, and downright arguing for certain things to make the pages… or not. In the end, she was *mostly* right about everything and did well championing for the ultimate love story.

I'd be remiss if I didn't thank my other two girls, Sami for her constant encouragement, and Izzy for giving up quite a bit of mom time during her final year at home. I'll make it up by visiting you in London—I promise.

Thank you, Jolene, for another beautiful cover. You are a master graphic designer and true visionary.

Michele, thank you for constantly listening to me gripe about whatever hang-up I'm going through and keeping me laughing while getting me out of my head.

And a big thank you to all my friends and family for putting up with my spotty communication and non-existence at times. You're all so important to me, and I truly appreciate your love, encouragement, friendship, and support.

Many people have provided me with valuable insights along the way and have been an outlet for banter, brainstorming, and feedback. Kaley, Tricia, Jolene, Michele, Samantha, Abby, and Cassie… thank you for answering my off-the-wall, quirky questions and being available at the drop of a hat at times. Having you all by my side is a gift.

And lastly, the book wouldn't be what it is without my team of editors and beta readers. Keely, you make me feel ten feet tall with your feedback and comments, and the finishing touches you add are always spot on. To my ARC team that devours the book within days to find any last-minute errors—you are amazing! And of course, my formatting guru, who makes everything appear beautiful on the pages.

Did you miss Sebastian and Lily's story in *Pursuit of Innocence*, book one in The Pursuit Series?

"I'm done waiting around. You're mine. No more games or pining over someone else when it's me you want. You won't remember his name after I get through with you."

Lily knows exactly what she wants in life. To graduate, land a high-paying job, and forge her own way. Nothing will distract her. Until the ultimate playboy, billionaire Sebastian Dubree, barges in. Not to be overlooked, Lily's longtime crush, Jackson, decides she's worth the fight.

Reluctant to succumb to either, she quickly becomes a challenge to conquer. Lily must decide between the familiarity of her childhood longing or the newly discovered passion ignited by the dominant CEO. But can she surrender without losing herself in the process, or will someone take matters into his own hands?

Boundaries blur between desire and resistance in this gripping coming-of-age romance, leaving readers yearning for more.

Visit bethanyrosa.com or scan below for a link to explore other books in *The Pursuit Series*

Did you miss Jackson and Mia in *Dangerous Pursuit,*
book three in *The Pursuit Series?*

Mia Nightingale Marcos is more nightmare than nightingale.

I'm handed the reins to the family business along with an
inexperienced assistant barely out of high school. Not to mention,
she's distractingly beautiful and completely off-limits. I plan to be
so unbearable she'll quit, but she's tougher than she looks. Now
she appears to be hiding something and the deeper I dig, the more
invested I become, causing my world to spin.

Just when I think I've got her figured out, she vanishes,
leaving a trail of unanswered questions, sending me on
a dangerous pursuit.

Jackson Soloman is the boss from hell.

But I can handle him. Balancing work by day and poker by
night was a breeze until Jackson stepped in. It was easier
when he was making my life hell, not trying to play hero.
Now, I can't shake him off, and with the growing attraction
between us, I'm not sure I want to.

Just when I think I've hit the jackpot, I'm forced to fold, leaving
everything behind for a chance at salvation.

Will Mia and Jackson survive the trials of deceit and danger that lie ahead? In a heart-wrenching climax that tests their love and commitment, every decision could be their last bet.

Visit bethanyrosa.com or scan below to explore book three, *Dangerous Pursuit,* in the unbelievably hot *Pursuit Series.*

Ready for a fun, holiday novella in The Pursuit Series?
Check out Lucy and Justin's story in *Holidate Pursuit.*

**Do I have a sign on my back that says, 'Love her and leave her'?
Because that's what it feels like these days.**

I thought I'd never see Justin again when he ghosted me after the best night of my life. But guess who shows up at the company Christmas party months later wanting to talk? I don't think so Mr. Burns. Burn me once, shame on you. Burn me twice, shame on me. That's sober Lucy talking. Drunk Lucy has a different idea—she asks him to stand in as my fake fiancé this Christmas. Thank God he's smart enough to say no… or is he?

One week. One bed. How could I resist?

I had my reasons for disappearing on Lucy, and I've regretted it ever since. So, when the opportunity presents itself, I can't refuse my shot at redemption. Just as it starts to feel like a second chance, the tree comes crashing down.

**Filled with humor, heart, and holiday magic, Holidate Pursuit
is a fun, steamy romance about second chances and choosing
love over all else.**

To purchase this or other books in the extremely hot Pursuit Series,
visit www.bethanyrosa.com
or simply scan the barcode below.

My dear readers and fans, you are truly what keeps me going, and I wholeheartedly thank you for your support. You are all so special and integral to this journey

If you'd like to purchase other books in the Pursuit Series or keep up with upcoming releases and learn more about author Bethany Rosa, visit www.BethanyRosa.com

Or scan below:

www.ingramcontent.com/pod-product-compliance
Lightning Source LLC
Chambersburg PA
CBHW032347310726
48973CB00007B/1899